PRAISE FOR THE NOVELS OF

Anything You Can Do... is "a good-humored look at sexual politics, intelligent and entertaining."
—Betty Webb, *Mesa Tribune*

"Roz Denny Fox is my kind of writer. First she grabs you with a page-turner, and then when you're not looking she steals your heart."
—*New York Times* bestselling author Vicki Lewis Thompson

"Roz Denny Fox is a master at satisfying readers with emotionally riveting stories containing rich and colorful characters."
—*Writers Unlimited*

Dear Reader,

Spring is on the way, and the Signature Select program offers lots of variety in the reading treats you've come to expect from some of your favorite Harlequin and Silhouette authors.

The second quarter of the year continues the excitement we began in January with a can't-miss drama from Vicki Hinze: *Her Perfect Life*. In it, a female military prisoner regains her freedom only to find that the life she left behind no longer exists. Myrna Mackenzie's *Angel Eyes* gives us the tale of a woman with an unnatural ability to find lost objects and people, and *Confessions of a Party Crasher*, by Holly Jacobs, is a humorous novel about finding happiness—even as an uninvited guest!

Our collections for April, May and June are themed around Mother's Day, matchmaking and time travel. Mothers and daughters are a focus in *From Here to Maternity*, by Tara Taylor Quinn, Karen Rose Smith and Inglath Cooper. You're in for a trio of imaginative time-travel stories by Julie Kenner, Nancy Warren and Jo Leigh in *Perfect Timing*. And a matchmaking New York cabbie is a delightful catalyst to romance in the three stories in *A Fare To Remember* by Vicki Lewis Thompson, Julie Elizabeth Leto and Kate Hoffmann.

Spring also brings three more original sagas to the Signature Select program. *Hot Chocolate on a Cold Day* tells the story of a Coast Guard worker in Michigan who finds herself intrigued by her new downstairs neighbor. Jenna Mills's *Killing Me Softly* features a heroine who returns to the scene of her own death, and *You Made Me Love You* by C.J. Carmichael explores the shattering effects of the death of a charismatic woman on the friends who adored her.

And don't forget, there is original bonus material in every single Signature Select book to give you the inside scoop on the creative process of your favorite authors! Happy reading!

Marsha Zinberg

Marsha Zinberg
Executive Editor
The Signature Select Program

Hot Chocolate on a Cold Day

ROZ Denny FOX

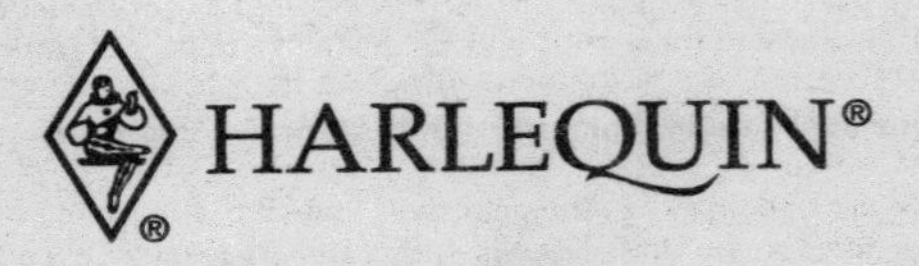

TORONTO • NEW YORK • LONDON
AMSTERDAM • PARIS • SYDNEY • HAMBURG
STOCKHOLM • ATHENS • TOKYO • MILAN • MADRID
PRAGUE • WARSAW • BUDAPEST • AUCKLAND

ISBN 0-373-83700-3

HOT CHOCOLATE ON A COLD DAY

This edition published by arrangement with Harlequin Books S.A.

www.eHarlequin.com

Printed in U.S.A.

Dear Reader,

Once I finish writing a book, my characters have always stayed in my mind the way they were in the story. Until now...

In *Hot Chocolate on a Cold Day* I've had the pleasure of bringing forward three teens from two previous books. I got to find out how they've grown, how they've turned out and I've had a chance to know them as adults.

It may sound odd, but I'm as proud of Megan Benton as I wold be if she were my own daughter. Her brother, Mark, has caused his parents a few anxious moments, however. I came to love his folks a lot in *Anything You Can Do....*

So I decided to peek in on Emily and Nolan Campbell again, to show the changes time has wrought for them and for Camp's sister, Sherry, and her husband, Garrett Lock, who were featured in the book *Having It All*.

Because I wanted to find out what their son, Keith, was doing, too, I thought it wouldn't be fair to find Megan's true love, and perhaps even a nice young woman for Mark, yet leave Keith out. Keith Lock is and always has been an animal lover bent on becoming a veterinarian, which doesn't mean he can't fall for a girl who loves animals as much as he does....

Take my word for it, this book has a lot packed into it. I hope you all enjoy catching up on the lives of these two fine families as much as I enjoyed launching them forward through time. If you haven't read *Anything You Can Do...* and *Having It All*, the stories in which these characters originally appeared, they're both available in a volume entitled *Coffee in the Morning*, also from the Signature program.

As always, I love hearing from readers. You are important to me. Write to me: Roz Denny Fox, P.O. Box 17480-101, Tucson, AZ 85731. Or e-mail me at rdfox@worldnet.att.net.

DEDICATION

I have so many people to thank for providing information for this book and for the special bonus features. First, my editor, Paula Eykelhof, for continuing to believe I'm capable of writing a variety of stories. And to editor Marsha Zinberg, for launching the Signature program, which gives Harlequin authors another avenue for our work.

Thanks to the Ninth Coast Guard District, Grand Haven, Michigan station, for all the direction they provided, including the books and brochures that I read and reread many times.

And to my sister-in-law, Linda Cofer, for sending me a great article about a woman who chose to make the Coast Guard a career, and for introducing me via e-mail to Giles Vanderhoof, Chief Warrant Officer, Retried. Thanks also to Giles, who kindly shared his thirty-year experience in the service for inclusion in my bonus feature.

I owe Eve Gaddy a big thank-you for sending me to Kathy Garbera, who called her sister, who put me in touch with William E. Bulman, Boatswain's Mate Chief, a twenty-two-year veteran of the Coast Guard currently working in California as a recruiter.

Lieutenant Brad Terrill, Community Relations in Washington, D.C., also gets my special thanks. He didn't write me off as a crank caller, and went the extra mile in finding me Jacquelyn Zettles PA1, who gave me a personal interview for the bonus feature in this book. She spent time on the phone with me, and sent e-mail messages even though I know she's fighting carpal tunnel syndrome and working on the *Coast Guard* magazine.

This book is a work of fiction, and any errors are mine. If there are situations in the story that may not quite reflect how a real Coast Guard unit or individual would operate, they are strictly my own fantasy.

There were other people who helped me along the way, but asked to remain nameless. Although I respect their wishes, I give them my heartiest thanks all the same.

CHAPTER ONE

St. Ignace, Michigan

WHERE WERE THE NEW RENTERS? Megan Benton parted heavy drapes designed to shut out the cold, and for the umpteenth time in half an hour scanned the street below her top-floor Victorian rental. The thermometer she'd set in her window box said twenty-six degrees. Practically balmy compared to the minus fifteen that had gripped Michigan's Upper Peninsula at her arrival on New Year's day. Last week, March blew in and the ice had finally begun to break up in the channel and harbor.

Steam rising from her cup of hot chocolate obscured her view of the marina at the bottom of the hill. She let the drape fall, then made her way into the bedroom to dress in her Coast Guard uniform. As she struggled into long johns and skier-weight overalls, she thought enviously of her last duty station in Mobile, Alabama. Having been born and raised in northern Missouri, she never would've guessed that her Midwest blood could have thinned so much in the few weeks she'd spent in Mobile's helicopter training school. After a scant two months in the northland—and as the only woman at this station—crew mates who were like a mob of brothers still ribbed her mercilessly about how she bundled up whenever they had to navigate the Mackinac Straits.

A knock sounded at her front door just as she downed a last swig of chocolate. Leaving off her jacket, Megan pasted on a smile to welcome the new folks her landlord had said would be moving in downstairs.

The house owner, crusty old Hank Meade, was off fishing warmer waters. He'd phoned to ask if Megan would mind if his rental agent left a key with her to make it easier for the renters to pick up. A family, Hank had indicated. With kids. Megan loved kids. Nevertheless, she had mixed feelings about acquiring neighbors. For two months she'd had Lady Vic, as she called the place, to herself. Usually she ran five miles every morning for exercise. But because it was so cold, she'd fallen into the habit of an early a.m. aerobics program in her bedroom, where she cranked hip-hop music up high to get her blood moving. Neighbors meant she'd have to use earphones, she lamented, yanking open the door.

The face staring down at her wasn't one she expected. Stunned, she gaped at Mark, her brother. Two years younger than her twenty-five, Mark had shot up and surpassed her skinny, five-three frame when they were still in high school. She wondered now if she was hallucinating.

This past Christmas, she'd spent a week at home. Mark had remained at his university in Western Missouri, determined, according to their mom and stepdad, to graduate in January with his master's in psychology. When Megan had last called home, their mom had said Mark would walk straight from school into a job at the college in Columbia, where their folks lived and worked. Yet here he stood.

"Hey, did you take a wrong turn in St. Louis, or are you just plain lost?"

Grinning, Mark blew on red-chapped, gloveless fingers. "Invite me in and I'll tell you my sad story. It's colder than a coal miner's patootie out here."

Whooping with delight, Megan launched herself into his arms and let him swing her around and around until they both stumbled inside, punching each other happily. "I can offer you a cup of something warm. And shut the door, you goof. You weren't born in a barn. Wait—do the folks know you're here?"

"Yeah, they know." Shrugging out of a Gore-Tex ski jacket, Mark Benton removed his knit cap and tossed both on his sister's flowered couch before following her into a bright yellow kitchen. Using his hands to bring order to his unruly auburn hair, he propped a hip against the counter as Megan darted from cupboard to stove, where she lit the gas burner under a well-used saucepan.

"Something in your tone tells me all isn't well in little ol' Columbia. Okay, brother, out with it. I have to leave for the station in fifteen minutes. When we talked after the holidays, you told me you were flat broke. Mom said if you finished your dissertation on time you were a shoo-in for a counseling job at Wellmont. So what's up?"

Mark wrinkled his lightly freckled nose. "Right! *Mom's* campus. Where she's head of women's studies, and our stepdad teaches history. Where Aunt Sherry's in charge of the crisis center, and Uncle Garrett's just been made vice-chancellor. On top of that, there's a whole danged wing at Wellmont named for our great-grandfather."

"Campbell Hall is a dormitory, not a wing."

"So? It's intimidating," he mumbled, watching Megan pour steaming water over mounds of cocoa she mixed with a dash of salt. Once the mixture had heated through, she added sugar and milk, and let it come to a boil, stirring absently. Then she removed the pan from the burner and dumped in a splash of vanilla, poured a crockery cup full and topped it with two fat marshmallows. Megan thrust the mug into her brother's hands with a frown.

"And…you're here because you don't want to join a place where most of the family works? Where you're guaranteed good pay and benefits? Have you seen the U.S. jobless stats for new grads, Mark?"

He fished out a gooey marshmallow and popped it into his mouth. "Now you sound like Mom and Camp," he said. Both of them had long ago begun calling their stepfather, Nolan Campbell, by his nickname. "I just… well, thought you'd understand, since Mom did her level best to steer you into education. Yet, here you are, a Coast Guard officer."

"That's different. I made up my mind to go into search and rescue the summer I fell off that cliff and Camp risked his life to save me…." She let her statement trail off. "That fall I joined ROTC. My career choice shouldn't have shocked anyone. But you, Mark, have spent the better part of six years getting a master's in child psychology. You interned for a year. And starting at Wellmont doesn't mean you have to stay there forever."

Mark stepped over to a window, staring out as he sipped his hot chocolate. "I wish I could say that counseling's what I want to do for even part of my life, Meg. If you recall, Gina Ames got me hooked on photography the same summer. Last year, at her urging, I sent one of my photos to a contest. I won! I'll be doing a one-man show in New York City."

"Gosh, a one man show sounds impressive, but—"

"It is," he hastened to say. "Yet Mom dismisses photography as a silly hobby. What I'd like," Mark said, turning and sounding eager for the first time in their discussion, "is to try my hand at freelancing. Gina has contacts. All I have to do is create a portfolio of worthwhile photos."

"Oh, wow! I see your dilemma. Mom and Camp paid for your schooling, and you're thinking of taking off in a whole different direction."

"If photography works out, I'll pay them back. For now, Gram volunteered to grubstake me until the show in New York this fall."

"Gram? As in *Mona* Gram? You took Benton money?" The Benton wealth had caused a serious rift between their mother and her former in-laws.

"Mona can spare the bucks. Did you get the news article I sent outlining her net worth after Grandpa Toby died? He left Mona a millionaire twice over."

"That's not the point. Mom will have a cat-fit if you take one red cent from her."

Mark's temper flared. "Mona's *our* blood grandmother, Megan. And she's getting on in years. It hurt her that you were home at Christmas and never drove seventy miles to visit her. Since Toby died, she rattles around in that big house."

"I only had a week at home. I bought and wrapped a cashmere sweater, signed both our names like we agreed and sent it for her Christmas." Megan tucked her thumbs under her bright orange suspenders and twisted her lips to one side. "She smothers me, Mark. Plus she makes snide comments about Mom marrying Camp. It's been eleven years. Why can't she let it go?"

"Then she'd have to admit Dad was a jerk. She'll never do that. Dad was their only child. Their pride and joy. But Megan…we're her only relatives now. I'm not like you, I can't flip a switch and erase the fact that I'm a Benton."

Megan didn't want to argue. "So, uh, how long can you stay? A week? Two? Longer?" The last sounded hopeful.

Mark's eyes grew guarded. "Is a month too long? Maybe two? I'd like to stay for a while to see if I can produce quality photos. I figure the landscapes around here should be pretty interesting."

Megan broke into a wide grin and smacked his arm. "You stay two months, buddy, you're no guest. Starting tomorrow, we split household chores. Cooking, cleaning, laundry. The works."

"Speaking of cooking, I'm starved. You got anything to eat around here?"

"Peanut butter cookies that I made this morning." She hauled out a fat pink pig-shaped cookie jar. "I probably have cheese and crackers on hand. If the cheese isn't moldy."

From his superior height Mark gazed on her with amused affection. "Some things never change. You always had terrible eating habits. Point me toward the local grocery store. After I unpack, I'll make a list and shop. If you don't object to me using Mona's money, that is."

"I'll pay," Megan said quickly. "I make a good salary. I don't want Mona's handouts. If you're willing to split chores, I'll gladly feed you, Mark."

"Okay," he said. "But I wish you wouldn't be so hard on Gram."

"Uh...come with me. I'll show you where you can bunk. Isn't this a great old house? I have more space here than we did in that dinky duplex Mom rented after Dad died. Oh, say, will you do me another favor? I'm getting downstairs neighbors." She pointed to a key lying on her kitchen table. "They were supposed to be here already, but they're late. I'd planned to leave them a note and take the key across the street to Mrs. Ralston. She's a busybody, so I'd rather leave it with you. Will you hold off going to the store until after the new family puts in an appearance?"

"Sure. They got a name?"

"Don't know what it is." She shook her head, then laughed. "But who else will come asking for a key?"

STERLING DODGE PAID the toll and eased his dirt-streaked black four-wheel drive Land Rover onto the five-mile suspension span of Mackinac Bridge, which connected Michigan's Upper and Lower Peninsulas. Below, the wind whipped angry whitecaps into a froth across a broad expanse of blue so dark that in places the water looked black.

"Je-zus. It's the ends of the earth," spat Sterling's fourteen-year-old brother-in-law, Joel Atwater. A comment seconded by Joel's older sister, Lauren, who jammed a pillow behind her head.

"Joel," Sterling snapped. "I'm not telling you again to watch your mouth. Next time it'll affect your allowance." Sterling called attention to his son, the youngest of his three passengers. Tyler was kicking rhythmically against the back of his dad's seat. At four, he mimicked the older kids, who'd lived with Sterling and his wife, Blythe, since their wedding. Now with Blythe gone, Sterling was left the sole guardian.

His wife's siblings had gotten out of hand back on Long Island, and he knew that was primarily because of Blythe's inattention. The kids had cultivated bad friendships and worse habits. That was the catalyst for Sterling's seeking this new job. He hoped it wasn't too late to turn their lives around.

The teens were angry about the control he had over them and their trust fund. He couldn't blame them, as thanks to Blythe's resistance, he'd never taken a hand in raising them before. This wasn't a situation he'd ever envisioned. At the time he married Blythe, he would never have believed life would change so drastically that he'd uproot everyone and move to a state miles away from where they'd all been born.

"Listen, I know you're sick of driving, and you're probably hungry. Me, too. But it's not my fault we hit a spot on the highway where the road washed out and we had to backtrack. I would've stopped at a restaurant if Hank Meade, the guy we're renting from, hadn't made it clear that the woman upstairs who has our key works swing shift. We have twenty minutes before she takes off."

"Big frickin' deal. Who cares?" Joel flung himself so hard against his seat he rocked the big SUV. "If we'd stayed in New York, I'd be hanging with my buds and eatin' burgers about now." He slapped on earphones and turned up his CD.

Sterling raised a black eyebrow. "That's one reason we're here, Joel," he said, raising his voice to no avail. "This is a school day. You had how many unexcused absences in the last six months?"

Lauren tossed her head. “Like you care? If Blythe hadn’t been killed during that stakeout, you would’ve already cut and run. I wish you had. Then the court would’ve put me in charge of my own life—and Joel’s.” She crossed her arms, looking mutinous.

“Enough,” Sterling said tiredly. He sensed that his son, already traumatized by recent events, had gone stock-still in his booster seat. “Lauren…” Sterling said with a sigh. “My separating from Blythe was never a done deal. Yes, I asked a lawyer friend, Jeff Gaines, to check on options. I’m sorry you had to take his return call.”

“Like I believe you? Too bad he phoned while you were at the funeral home arranging to bury our sister.”

The implication in the girl’s scathing response hit Sterling between his shoulder blades. The pain was so palpable he had to massage his neck to ease the tension. In hindsight, he regretted having called Jeff. Because now he was at a loss when it came to explaining what had led to his inquiry about possible divorce. The welfare of these kids had fallen to Sterling’s wife when Joel was in fourth grade. The elder Atwaters had been brutally murdered in a house robbery turned violent after they’d surprised the thieves. Joel had been at a sleepover, and he and Blythe were delayed at one of their wedding showers.

Mere days away from their wedding, they’d foregone a honeymoon and taken the kids in. From the outset, Blythe had told him to butt out of anything concerning the kids—particularly discipline. So, he had no earthly idea how to tell them that their sister had changed a hundred percent from the woman he’d once loved. First, she’d developed a rabid need for excitement. And without any discussion between them, she'd gone to the police academy and become a city cop. Granted, he'd never understood that choice. The kids needed her. Plus, she'd accidentally gotten pregnant. Accidentally, because she'd made it plain she didn't want a baby. Yet even with extra mouths to feed she didn't need to work, or not for financial reasons, anyway. He did fine as a ferryboat captain. They had a nice house left to him by his grandparents. At the very least, she should've taken a part-time job, he thought, and certainly something far less dangerous. Especially after Tyler was born. No, Sterling would not apologize for not liking his wife's career. And as much as they'd battled over her job, they'd had twice the arguments over her refusal to set limits on her siblings. Still, that wasn't why he'd contemplated divorce. If they only knew… But he couldn't hurt the kids the way he'd been hurt.

Sterling dug deep for patience as he left the bridge, finally entering the seaside hamlet of St. Ignace. "This is it," he exclaimed. "Our town. Temporarily."

"Whoop-de-do," Joel ground out. He ripped off his earphones and pressed his nose to the side window. "Hey, Lauren, what's there to do in this jerkwater hole?"

"Joel," Sterling chided gently. "It's only until a carpenter fixes the dry rot problem in the home I bought on Mackinac Island."

"How long?" Lauren demanded. "Joel's right, this dinky place sucks."

Sterling slowed, rechecking the directions he'd plugged into his GPS system. According to the readout, he had to be practically on top of the house. Ducking, he read gilt-edged numbers painted on a sprawling blue monstrosity. The house, which was at the end of a cul-de-sac, had four upper-story dormers. Twin porches sat on white spindles that didn't look strong enough to hold them up. Unfortunately, the house number matched the one blinking on his screen.

At least he'd skated in with minutes to spare. He made a U-turn, and hoped his trailer didn't hang over the sidewalk. A compact car and a pickup took up most of the parking area.

"According to Captain Meade, the woman upstairs has our key. You kids want to run and get it? I see stairs to the right of the car with the Missouri license plates."

"Me wanna go, too!" Tyler strained against the harness holding him fast.

Lauren and Joel both had their doors open. "Is it okay if the kid goes with?" Lauren asked Sterling.

Sterling's shoulders relaxed minutely. At least the kids loved Tyler, and in many ways Lauren was more nurturing than Blythe had been. "Thanks." Sterling released his seat belt and leaned back to rummage in a pile of coats on the seat next to his son. He pulled out Tyler's jacket. "Judging from that wind, you kids had better find your coats."

Joel curled a pierced bottom lip that held two rings. He slammed his car door so hard the whole vehicle shook.

Sterling stopped stuffing Tyler's arms into coat sleeves. Meeting Lauren's uncompromising gaze, he said gently, "Look, we're not going back, so it'll be easier if we try to make a go of this."

Lauren banged her door, as well, and lifted her young nephew up on her hip.

AFTER SHOWING MARK his room, and pointing out an adjoining half bath that would be his, Megan left her brother to unpack the duffel bags he'd hauled in from his car. Grabbing the jacket that completed her winter uniform, she paused to say goodbye. A banging on her front door interrupted any last-minute instructions she might have had.

"Mark, I'm guessing that'll be our late neighbors. Come with me and say hi. We'll get all the introductions out of the way."

She crossed the living room, detouring to get the key. Ahead of her now, Mark opened the door. A gust of wind tore it from his grasp. From her vantage point, Megan was afforded a view of a ragtag trio huddled on her porch. Mark's body blocked their view of her, and gave her time to assess them.

Having grown up a rebel, she instantly recognized the same qualities in the teenage boy who sported loops of chains hanging from baggy black pants. His multi-pierced ears, lip rings and bleached hair greased into orange spikes gave her a bit of a shock. Megan had long since shed her Goth lipstick, nail polish and flashy rings on every finger. Hiding her dismay, she turned her attention to the woman attempting to balance a suddenly shy four or five-year-old boy on a nonexistent hip. She was a classic beauty. Megan couldn't readily determine her age. Late teens to midtwenties? Wind swirled a mane of spun gold around a triangular face. Thick-lashed, chocolate-colored eyes added to the newcomer's exotic appeal. "I came for a key," she said.

Mark was acting like a dunce. It took a moment of silence for Megan to see the problem. Her brother was struck mute by the young woman's beauty. Or maybe he was plotting light angles and lens exposures to photograph her.

Ducking beneath his arm, Megan came up smiling and dangling the key. "I'm Megan Benton. This man of few words is my brother, Mark." She jabbed his ribs, and he finally breathed out the air trapped in his lungs.

"I'm about to take off for the Coast Guard Station where I work, but you all look frozen. Come in and warm up. I made extra hot chocolate. Mark can get you drinks, and you guys can get better acquainted." She gestured toward her kitchen, key still in hand.

The little boy, a darling tyke with huge gray eyes, untucked his curly head from where it was buried in the young woman's shoulder. He offered a shy, willing smile, and immediately wriggled down to tug the girl toward the open door.

Megan smiled at him, and wondered if the woman was the little charmer's mom or older sister. She and the teenage boy bore marked similarities in the shape of their faces. The younger boy had hair like hers, but the resemblance ended there. It was the older boy, however, who reached out a bare arm, tattooed to the shoulder with a snake and a skull with crossbones, and snatched the key from Megan.

"We can't come in," the woman said, bending to lift the little boy. "Sterling's waiting." She hiked a thumb toward the stairs. "We haven't had lunch yet, and he wants us moved in before dark."

Megan strained to peer over the rail. On the sidewalk, a man stood knee-deep in suitcases. Long-legged, and broad-shouldered, he seemed impervious to the wind gusting off the bay, in spite of the fact that it whipped his jet-black hair around his ears. Megan would have called out a greeting and invited him up for a hot drink, too, had he not glanced up and glowered at her.

Mark roused himself. "Megan's off to work, but I'm hanging around doing nothing. I'll give you guys a hand unloading."

The eldest boy swaggered. "We got it covered, dude. We're not gonna be in this dump long enough to get friendly." Whirling on the heel of a heavy black boot, he clattered down the wooden steps. His sister, if that was who she was, tried to follow. But the little guy dug in, crying, "I want hot chocolate!"

Dump? Megan wanted to smack the smart-assed kid. Instead, she turned to the crying youngster, who'd refused to let the woman pick him up. "Maybe another day," she said, dropping to one knee in front of him. "What's your name?" She mustered a gentle smile.

"Tyler," he said through his tears. The young woman calling the shots descended a couple of steps and scooped him up in spite of his protests. Containing him against his will, she was able to make her way downstairs. His sobs reached up to Megan and Mark, still hovering in the open doorway.

It wasn't until the man, the one the blond girl had called Sterling, threw another intimidating glare at them, that the pair upstairs quickly withdrew.

"Joy, oh joy," Megan murmured. "Aren't *they* going to be lovely neighbors?"

"Mmm."

As she shoved her arms into her jacket and tucked her mop of sable hair under the requisite blue Coast Guard baseball-style cap, Megan paused to eye her brother. He'd slightly opened the front drape in an attempt to peer over the porch.

Walking toward him, she punched his arm hard. "Listen, Mark, we'd better listen to that gangsta-teen. They're not planning to be here long enough to bother making friends."

Her brother sprang back. "Why'd you hit me?"

"Because you have that *look.* That I'm-*very*-interested look."

"Can you blame me? She's gorgeous! Did you catch her name?"

"Ma-a-rk! None of them gave us names, except for the little boy. That's what I'm saying. Do I have to spell it out? They aren't interested in being neighborly." She slid back her sleeve and glanced at her watch. "Holy smokes, I've gotta go. I'm gonna be late signing in. The crew will go out to check lighthouses without me."

"You check lighthouses?"

She nodded and jerked open the door. "My unit's responsible for maintaining the status quo of twenty-one maritime lights, thirteen of which are on buoys located offshore. We make sure they haven't broken loose from anchors, and we change burned-out lightbulbs. My shift ends at eleven. I'm home by eleven-fifteen. Don't feel you have to wait up, though. I usually fix something easy like bacon and eggs. I'll try to be quiet."

"I'll probably be up. It hasn't been that long since I stayed up nights studying for finals. Takes a while to unwind from that."

"Suit yourself. Oh, that reminds me. Here's money for groceries." She pulled a money clip out of her pants pocket and peeled off a sheaf of twenties as she gave directions to the store. Dispensing a final wave, Megan tripped lightly down the stairs. She held her key tight so the wind couldn't rip it away. The sporty red imported pickup with oversize tires, a roll bar and a full set of fog lights was hers. Mark, she saw, still drove the beater compact their stepdad had helped him refurbish in high school. She recalled envying how the two bonded over that car.

Their stepdad, Nolan Campbell, was a man's man. Even though their mom, Emily, had filed off many of his rougher edges, it seemed to Megan that her stepfather was more comfortable with Mark than with her. Although Camp stood up for her more than once—most memorably when she'd been fleecing a bunch of rowdy cowboys at pool. Her mom threw a fit, but Camp let her finish winning. Megan grinned now as the memory flooded back.

Unlocking her pickup, Megan noticed that the way their neighbor had parked his trailer had blocked her in. Already late, she'd have to waste time hunting him down.

Luckily, he emerged from his apartment. "Hey," Megan called. "I need to get out, and you have me boxed in. Would you mind pulling up a foot or so?"

He continued toward her at a languid gait Megan admired. It took a moment for her to realize he wasn't viewing her with similar regard. In fact, he studied her uniform with obvious distaste. Maybe he thought the bulky blue pants and blue-and-orange jacket made her look like a fat ladybug. They did, but they were toasty warm.

"I'm your upstairs neighbor, Megan Benton. Lieutenant Benton," she added, thrusting out a hand. "I would've brought you a thermos of cocoa and some cookies as a better welcome, but I'm late for duty." Her implication was because he'd blocked her in.

He avoided her outstretched hand and lowered indecently long eyelashes as he slid two fingers into a tight front pocket of his worn jeans. Megan held her breath, but he succeeded in retrieving a set of keys. Setting those long legs in motion, he skirted her pickup and had his SUV open before she could move.

"Hey," she called. "I didn't catch your name."

"Dodge," he growled, "Sterling Dodge." Clearly he didn't want to share even that much.

Megan blinked as his door slammed. It couldn't be plainer. He and his whole tribe had come with bad attitudes. Wasn't that going to be fun?

She climbed into her pickup, wondering what the surly man did for a living. What had motivated him to move his family here this time of year? The area was ninety percent dependant on summer tourism. It took a hardy soul to live here year-round.

Taking only seconds to warm her engine, Megan drove off without checking to see if Dodge remained in his vehicle or if he'd gone back to unloading the trailer that bore New York license plates. Since New York was known far and wide for its job opportunities, she found his timing more curious. But they didn't plan to stay long, or so Dodge's eldest son had said.

If the two older kids were his. The man had jet-black hair shot with silver. The two blond kids had brown eyes. Dodge's gray ones were as chilly as Mackinac Straits after a wintry storm. And he might be from New York, but nothing about his attire or whipcord body looked citified or soft. He wore a lumberjack shirt with the sleeves rolled midway up his tanned, muscular forearms. And well-worn blue jeans, tucked into scuffed boots. Maybe he was a logger from upstate New York. Although logging was about gone from Michigan.

Her mysterious unfriendly neighbor remained on her mind long after Megan signed in at the station. Long after she and the crew boarded their Reliance cutter, its twin diesel engines and midship helicopter deck designed to patrol a vital shipping channel emerging from the grip of winter.

Frowning, she scanned melting ice floes. Megan had only just realized that she and Mark hadn't seen any sign of a wife or mother in their new neighbor's entourage. Granted, she could've stayed in the warm SUV until the kids got back with the key. Unless the pretty blonde was a second wife. If so, she was either brave or naive. Megan shivered recalling Dodge's icy stare.

"Lieutenant, are you with us today?" Commander Donovan barked out as when Megan failed twice to respond to a question.

"Sorry, sir." She snapped to attention and hastily raised the binoculars swinging from a cord hung around her neck. "Guess my mind wandered for a minute."

"That's not like you, Benton. Everything all right?"

"Yes, sir. Well…my younger brother came to visit unexpectedly. Because of that, combined with new neighbors moving into the apartment below mine, I got to the station late. I'm still playing catch-up."

The grizzled old commander studied the choppy sea. "Hell of a time for anyone to visit or move to St. Ignace. Are they nuts? About now is when I'd shell out premium rates for a week's vacation in the Bahamas."

Everyone within hearing range laughed. Megan, too, especially since she knew how much Donovan loved the north country. "I can't speak for my neighbors, but my brother just graduated with a master's degree in psych. Hmm…maybe I'll bring him around to see if he can figure out what makes this crew tick," she teased. They were a small station and tended to operate more like a family than a larger crew might.

"Bring him on, Benton," shouted a fellow lieutenant. "Maybe he'll spill your secrets—like how you got to be a pool shark."

Megan grinned from ear to ear and hung over the ice-crusted rail to scan the waves for any sign of a boat, barge or container ship that might be in trouble. Her fleet also patrolled a section of the busiest waterway between the U.S. and neighboring Canada. Over the summer, pleasure boaters would appear in droves, tripling their workload. As well as rendering aid in boating accidents, their crew conducted boat safety education classes in local schools, kept their eyes peeled for all types of smugglers and assisted other agencies involved in Homeland Security. Megan had never enjoyed a dull existence. This career kept her hopping, and she loved it.

As if to punctuate her thoughts, midway through the evening a distress call came in. "What have we got?" she asked, rushing to the foredeck.

"A car drove off the Mackinaw City loading dock at the ferry terminal."

"Accidentally or on purpose?" Like other team members, Megan readied emergency equipment on board as she processed information. She and the crew were trained for amphibious helicopter rescue. But if a car went into the drink, that meant the even more dangerous task of sending down divers.

"An accident. Stupid kid took his mom's car for a joyride. Cops gave chase, he lost control and shot off the pier. Broke the guard chain. Good thing the ferries don't start running again for another week, or it'd be a bigger mess."

Her companions' faces were grim. They all knew the chances of anyone's surviving the icy water. The Great Lakes were always cold. Even in summer, rescue workers had from fifteen to thirty minutes to save someone. The fact that the icebreakers under Donovan's command had only recently stopped running, and darkness had descended, didn't bode well for the crazy kid now sitting in Lake Huron.

The commander stepped out onto the bridge. "A diving team from Sault Ste. Marie should be on-site by the time we get there. Our job will be to drop grapples their divers will attach to the kid's car. We'll winch up the auto while the Soo guys attempt to extract the victim."

Knowing their jobs backward and forward thanks to simulations run time and again didn't lessen the crew's heightened flow of adrenaline as the cutter's engines picked up speed. The dock was already a hub of activity, with cops and paramedics preparing for their roles. The Coast Guard vessel from Sault Ste. Marie had anchored fifty yards out. Her powerful lights bounced off the murky water.

Megan's vessel pulled bow to bow with the other ship. Her heart began to hammer as she watched the black, silent sea. But the water wasn't silent for long. Divers suited up in full wet gear went in feetfirst off the neighboring boat.

Megan's duty in this rescue was to lower a midship grapple. The minute the middle diver surfaced and gave his cue, she raised her arm and circled her hand several times. That told her assistant to begin tightening the winch. The cables groaned, went taut and Megan felt sweat slide down her cleavage.

Waiting was the most difficult. It was easier to be the one actively trying to rescue a victim. What seemed like hours later—but was only a few minutes—excited shouts from one of the divers echoed from shore. That happy shout said their collective prayers were at least partially answered. The kid had been sprung from his watery grave. Colored flares shot from the neighboring ship, indicating he was alive.

Megan wiped her brow and coiled in her grapple, relieved by the news.

The thing about search and rescue, she decided three hours later when they were back in station warming up and filing reports, was that nothing felt as good as a happy ending. Tonight, training had paid off. And luck. Megan never discounted luck. Four experienced divers made the rescue look easy, when every Coast Guard member knew there was a thin line between success and death.

Finished with her report, Megan flipped it into the out-basket and unhooked her jacket from a rack on the wall. "I'm out of here. See you all tomorrow."

"Want to hit the tavern for a celebration beer?" Lieutenant Junior Grade Jim Elkhorn called, peering over his cubicle.

Megan shook out her cap. "Rain check, Jim? My brother just got into town. He may be waiting up for me."

"Is he a pool shark, too?"

She laughed, knowing Jim complained loudest at being beaten regularly by a girl. "Mark's a mountain biker, and a fair bowler. But even you could beat him at pool," she said, tugging her cap over disheveled curls.

With a quick wave, she hurried into the frigid night. She got along well with all the guys, but still wished the station would get another woman. The last one had requested a duty station closer to her ailing parents. She'd left shortly after Megan arrived.

On the drive home, Megan found herself hoping Mark had waited up. After a rescue she found it impossible to sleep. Nerves that had been stretched tight remained jumpy. So she was happy to see that lights burned upstairs and down at Lady Vic. Squeezing between the big Land Rover and Mark's car, Megan noticed her neighbor on his porch. When she got out, she saw steam curling from a mug he held. Her mouth watered, all but tasting hot chocolate, although he was probably drinking coffee.

"Hi," she said, removing her cap as she approached. "You got all moved in?"

Half turning, the man gave a curt nod.

Megan set a foot on his lower porch step. She was near enough to see his gray eyes glitter silvery in light falling from the bridge. "I guess you're out here enjoying our Mighty Mac." She chuckled, and was only faintly aware that he didn't join in. "You probably think the *Mighty Mac* is a supersize hamburger. It's an affectionate name for our bridge—the longest in the country. One of the greatest engineering marvels in the world. Took four years to construct." Megan rattled off a stream of other statistics, expecting a response from the man in the quilted vest. Coast Guard personnel tended to sound like Upper Peninsula old-timers by the time visitor season rolled around. She was delighted she'd remembered so many facts.

Her neighbor let too much time pass for polite conversation, then muttered, "I came out here to enjoy the silence."

Megan's head snapped up. She was slower to remove her foot from his porch, although remove it she did. Holding back a terse word hovering on the tip of her tongue, she executed a perfect about-face and marched across the asphalt to stomp up the thirty-three steps that led to her apartment.

CHAPTER TWO

Benton Corners, Missouri

FORTY-FOUR-YEAR-OLD Emily Benton-Campbell parked her sporty convertible at the curb outside a home she hadn't visited in a dozen years. She collected her purse and turned down the visor to check her appearance. Her red hair remained as vibrant and hard to tame as when her ex-mother-in-law used to lecture her about the "excessive casualness" of her appearance.

Disgusted that she'd still allow something so insignificant to bother her, Emily let the visor snap back into place. But if the truth be known, the prospect of an audience with Mona Benton still had the power to leave Emily's palms damp and her nerves tingly. As well, her stomach boiled and churned like a washing machine.

Climbing from the low-slung automobile, Emily tugged the jacket of her no-nonsense navy-blue worsted wool suit down over her hips. This jacket had seemed loose the last time she'd worn it to a business meeting at the college. Today it felt snug. Obviously she'd let her daughter, Megan, and her sister-in-law, Sherry Lock, talk her into baking too many Christmas goodies while Megan was visiting over the holidays. Her son, Mark, hadn't made it home for Christmas. Recently, though, he'd spent a week with her and Camp, so of course she'd cooked his favorite meals. Now she was obviously paying for all the rich food.

Perhaps Mona would be so shocked seeing who was at her door that she wouldn't notice the extra few pounds worn by an ex-daughter-in-law she no doubt hoped never to see again. Having gained quite a bit of confidence in herself since getting out from under the thumb of her former husband's parents, Emily marched straight up to the door of the big white house on the hill. She rang the bell before she could lose her nerve.

A housekeeper with coppery skin and dark hair pulled back in a tidy bun opened the door. Emily didn't recognize her, and the same held true for the woman, who was on the verge of instantly dismissing her. "I'd like to see Mona Benton if she's available," Emily said quickly. "Tell her it's Emily calling. Emily Campbell—who used to be Emily Benton."

The name didn't seem to come as a complete surprise to the housekeeper, but neither did she ask the uninvited guest inside. "You wait, please?" the woman said in a softly accented voice. "I'll see if Mrs. Benton is receiving visitors."

The wait did nothing to quell the butterflies having a field day in Emily's stomach. She supposed her husband would scold her for her foolishness in coming here. They'd discussed this very thing in bed last night. Mark had left a note letting them know he'd gone to his sister's place—on his grandmother's money—and that he'd be staying there longer than Emily liked.

Suddenly the door swung inward again. This time, she saw the tall, fashionably thin form of Mona Benton. The two women, who had no reason and yet every reason to communicate, took each other's measure. "You're looking well," Emily murmured to break the tension. Secretly she thought she'd never seen Mona look as frail. Emily had attended the funeral of her former father-in-law, Toby, in July. Mona had been very much the grieving widow in black. Black shoes, hose, suit, gloves and hat. A veil had hidden her once-blond hair; Emily was frankly shocked to see it had turned quite gray. Not enhanced silver as she would've expected, but run-of-the-mill gray.

Mona Benton clutched a button at the throat of her maroon crepe dress. "Is everything all right with the children?" The woman's faded eyes filled with concern.

"Megan and Mark are both fine," Emily said quickly to ease any possible distress, because that was an instinctive reaction for her. "In fact, Mark phoned us last night."

"I see. Ah...well, I asked Lucia to brew a pot of coffee. If you have time," she rushed to add. "But wait, you never drank coffee. Lucia," the older woman called into the elegant interior, "please change that coffee to tea. Come in, come in, Emily. Whatever's on your mind that's brought you all the way out here can surely wait until we've taken refreshment." Moving stiffly aside, Mona invited the younger woman in with a sweep of one age-spotted hand sparkling with rings.

Seeing stones wink from almost every finger transported Emily back to a time when her own daughter had mirrored her grandmother's love of jewelry. Megan, at thirteen and fourteen, had conned her grandmother into indulging her every whim. Rings, bracelets, earrings, none cheap—Megan had resembled a walking jewelry store. What a contrast to Megan now. During her holiday visit, the twenty-five-year-old sported only neat gold studs in each earlobe, and her only ring was a signet one she earned on graduation from the Coast Guard Academy.

Taking a deep breath, fighting back the memories both good and bad associated with this woman and this house, Emily stepped into the marble-and-gilt entryway. Saying nothing, she followed Mona into the parlor, where a cheery fire burned brightly behind the closed glass doors of a stone floor-to-ceiling fireplace.

Emily sat on the edge of a cut velvet chair, two of which flanked the fire. This was where Toby sometimes sat, she recalled. The other was clearly Mona's chair. A pair of gold-wire glasses, another addition Emily hadn't known about, sat atop an open book dropped hastily into the folds of a cashmere afghan.

"I should have called in advance," Emily said, her eyes on the book.

Mona tucked a bookmark inside and set the book and glasses on a nearby table. "Nonsense. I trust you received my note thanking you for the lovely floral arrangement you sent to the funeral home?"

"Yes. Mona, I did attend the service at the church. Camp and I. We were both in the middle of teaching summer school, which is why we didn't go to the graveside."

Mona straightened the front of her dress. "I honestly didn't expect you to attend, Emily. But…it hurt that neither Mark nor Megan came. Mark explained that he had to spend every hour on his dissertation, which I understand. Megan, I read in the paper, was home at Christmastime after graduating from helicopter school." Veins popped out on the back of a hand that picked restlessly at the fringe knots of the afghan. "I assumed you had a lot to do with her sending a suitable Christmas gift—yet not bothering to drive seventy miles to see how I was getting along."

"Actually, no." Emily didn't want to feel remorse, but it washed over her all the same. "Megan only had a week between leaving Alabama and reporting in to Michigan. We were all busy with Camp's parents, and Sherry and Garrett's kids. Their daughter performed in a Christmas play. The time flew by so fast." She broke off speaking as Lucia wheeled a cart into the room. They waited in silence while the efficient woman poured water into china cups and passed around a cedar box filled with assorted teas. Emily chose Earl Grey, her favorite. Mona selected peppermint. They both ignored the shortbread cookies that were still nestled in a box.

Lucia slipped from the room, and silence again descended as the women sipped daintily from their cups. At last, almost as if the weight of the silence had become too much, Mona set her cup back in its saucer with a crack that made Emily jump.

"I hate beating around the bush, Emily. Why don't you get to the point of your visit?"

Emily gulped down a last bracing swallow of the fragrant tea, then lowered her cup and saucer to her lap. "This will be déjà vu, Mona. We often had this conversation in the past. You're interfering in the lives of my children again. Specifically Mark. I want you to stop." If she sounded harsh, so be it. With Mona one had to be direct.

Except the older woman's hands began to tremble and tears gathered in the corners of her eyes. She set her cup on the tray and fumbled to find a hankie tucked into the cuff of her long-sleeved dress. Crumpled as if she'd recently used it. Shaken, Emily glanced away and let Mona dab discreetly.

"I'm sorry, Emily. I assume then that you don't know Mark approached me for a loan?"

"A loan? To further a hobby, when he should be taking a job that promises a good future?" Emily, like most true redheads could go from zero to hot in a matter of seconds. Hostility burned in her periwinkle-blue eyes.

"He deserves a chance to see if he can make something profitable out of an opportunity that dropped in his lap."

Emily's lips thinned. "A showing, you mean? Of his photographs? Just because one picture he took won a half-baked contest? Do you have any idea, Mona, how many starving freelance photographers exist in this world? Mark has spent six long years getting a master's degree in child psychology. He can walk straight into a decent job."

Mona's jaw jutted out. "You never stood behind David, and now you're doing the same with his son."

"No! You're aiding and abetting a whim, Mona. Which is exactly what you and Toby always did with Dave." She rose abruptly and felt faint. Reeling, she walked toward the door and fresh air. Camp had been right. Coming here to try to reason with an unreasonable woman only increased her own stress.

Mona hurried after Emily. "I'll grant you that Toby went overboard when it came to indulging our son," she said in a placating voice. "From the time David was old enough to walk, he learned to get by on charm alone. Nor was I immune. I have no doubt it's thanks to you, Emily, that Mark has a good head on his shoulders. He swore to me that if nothing comes of this showing, he'll become a counselor. A field he settled on, by the way, because he felt pressured by you, his stepfather and his aunt and uncle."

"That's not true," Emily said, her voice vibrating with shock. "And I want you to butt out of my children's lives. Is that plain enough?"

Mona drew herself up, towering over her former daughter-in-law. "They are my grandchildren, Emily. By blood. They're adults now. Free to do as they choose." She sighed, finding herself talking to thin air. But she didn't close the door until Emily started her car and peeled away from the curb.

"JERK!" MEGAN MUTTERED ALOUD as she stepped through her door. She was so irked at her new neighbor she barely remembered in time that she'd told Mark she'd be quiet coming in from work. But the minute she stepped inside, she saw him sprawled on her too-short couch. The TV blared, but Mark was fast asleep. Seeing him like that, when for the past few years she'd been greeted by an empty house, Megan was catapulted back to a time when it'd just been them and their mom coming and going at various hours—after their dad died. Life had been tough when Dave Benton, having borrowed to the hilt, died suddenly and left his wife mired in debt. Debt Emily refused to let her in-laws pay. It wasn't until years later that Megan learned her mother had sheltered them from many truths about their dad. Especially that her grandparents had bailed their only son out of endless scrapes and tawdry affairs.

Selfish teenagers, she and Mark thought their lives were ruined back then. They didn't understand why their mom moved them into a small house instead of accepting money from their father's wealthy parents. And if, as Mark said this morning, Mona had subsidized his venture, she was still trying to undercut their mom's wishes.

But did *she* have a right to judge anyone? As a kid, Megan's manner of coping with anger and confusion had been to sneak out at night to play pool with friends. Looking back, she'd acted like a total brat. Along the way she'd grown up and was now—of course—gifted with twenty-twenty hindsight.

Mark's escape mechanism had always been to sleep his life away. He'd developed an ability to drop off anywhere whenever he wanted to shut everything out. He could sleep in front of a blaring TV, or with his stereo on high, or with their mom vacuuming around his inert form. Emily Benton used to scold until she ran out of words. At the time, they'd resented how she preached responsibility. And conservation. Electricity, Megan remembered, glancing around at the burning lights, was her mom's big deal. Living on her own, paying monthly bills, she could relate.

Oddly, she felt a belated guilt for giving her mother such a hard time. She wondered if Mark felt any of that. Probably not. Working with mostly guys, she'd noticed that guilt wasn't a word in their vocabularies.

Jeez, why did walking in and seeing her brother sound asleep on her couch spawn such a lengthy self-examination? As quietly as possible, she pulled off first one boot and then the other.

Maybe she was homesick, a condition brought on by Mark's visit. Or she supposed her feelings could be magnified by having a family move in downstairs. She missed her own family. One week at home over Christmas was far too brief. The hundred-year-old house Camp had been in the process of renovating when he married their mom now served as a hub for their extended family.

Their aunt Sherry and uncle Garrett had three kids together, a girl and two boys. Garrett's son from a previous marriage, Keith Lock, had been eight when Megan's aunt met and married the slow-talking Texan. The families lived in close proximity.

Megan hadn't realized how *much* she missed them all until this very minute.

In a thoughtful mood, she shed her heavy jacket. Picking up her boots, she tiptoed past her snoring brother.

He must not have been asleep long, because when she dropped a boot, he shot straight up off the couch. "Wha…? Whozzere? Megan?" Mark squinted and rubbed his eyes. "Is it eleven already?" he asked around a massive yawn.

"Eleven-thirty. Sorry I woke you. I accidentally dropped one of my work boots. Sorry," she said again.

Mark stretched out his kinks. "I intended to stay awake. I fixed dinner and left a plate of spaghetti warming in the oven for you. I'll go put on a pot of coffee if you'd like. Or I bought beer. Maybe you'd rather have that with your meal."

"Beer's good." She laughed. "I almost said, *since when did you get old enough to buy beer?* But of course you're old enough. My kid brother's all grown-up." There was a wistfulness to Megan's tone.

Unfolding himself Mark towered over her. "You sound unhappy about the fact that we're adults now."

"It's more that coming in, seeing you flaked out on

my couch, brought back memories of when we were kids. Then I started thinking about what a short visit I had with the family over the holidays. I miss Shannon, Tim and Gavin running in and out at the folks' place, squabbling like you and I used to do."

"We were angels compared to those holy terrors."

Megan shoved her boots under the end table and tossed her jacket over the back of a rocking chair. "What a thing to say about your cousins. They're cute kids."

"They have the entire Campbell family at their beck and call. Music, sports, dance. Name it, they're enrolled. I'll bet you got roped into playing chauffeur, like I did."

"True. But I was available. I didn't mind. Mom and Aunt Sherry, they're so busy."

"Don't tell Aunt Sherry, but I made her family a case study. Got an A on the paper, too. I swiped the idea from Camp. From that study he did on the wagon train reenactment. Granted, that was an artificial situation, while I wrote about everyday life. My assignment was to depict the pros and cons of a 'yours, mine and ours' family."

"What on earth did you write? They're so normal."

"Yes, but the *whole* extended family dotes on the rug rats? That's an anomaly, in my opinion."

"They don't spoil the kids with lavish gifts—like Toby and Mona did us. Nan and Ben Campbell don't try to buy their affection."

Mark slanted her a look. "Is this your way of chastising me for letting Mona finance my attempt to make it as a photographer?"

"It was merely an observation. I'm not one of your case studies, Mark Benton, so lay off. I happen to love the Lock kids. I wish I lived closer."

"They're good kids, I guess, but Keith says Tim and Gavin are always sneaking off with his laptop. They ruined one. Aunt Sherry bought him another one, just like that." Mark snapped his fingers. "So, they're different from us *how?*"

"Come to think of it, Mom does do things with Shannon she never did with me." Megan glanced back over her shoulder as she headed for the kitchen.

"Like what?"

Megan donned oven mitts, pulled the plate from the oven, then shut it off. "Crafts and things. Mom helped Shannon make angel decorations for the tree. They spent hours. And I remember at Shannon's dance recital, Mom fussed more with Shannon's costume more than Aunt Sherry did."

"When we were Shannon's age, Mom worked and went to college. Dad's hours were flexible, to say the least, so he took us fishing, hiking and to play pool. And you never liked girlie stuff like Shannon does. Maybe Mom missed doing that with you."

"Here I was thinking that after she married Camp, he *always* relegated me to girlie status. Aunt Sherry and Mom, ugh, forced me to go clothes shopping while you guys rebuilt a car and a barn and did other cool stuff, like cut logs with Camp's chain saw."

"Ah, now we have the truth. You were jealous of Keith and me. And now you're jealous of the Lock kids."

Megan set the hot plate on a pot holder and scowled at Mark. "That is *not* what I mean. I told you—I love those kids. I want a houseful of my own someday. Don't you?"

"Sure. Someday. Your point being?"

"I don't know. Say, do you ever wonder why Mom

and Camp never had kids together when Aunt Sherry and Uncle Garrett had three—bam, bam, bam?"

"Maybe Mom and Camp didn't want to be dealing with diapers and proms at the same time," Mark snorted.

"She could've had more, don't you think? She had us, so there's no worry about problems with getting pregnant."

"Hey…wait—is all this flap about kids because you've met a guy? Like…are you thinking about tying the knot?" Mark's eyes lit as he planted his elbows on the island counter.

"No! Good grief! What started me on the subject was seeing the family that moved in downstairs, and now you bringing up your paper on blended families."

Mark nodded. "The neighbors aren't really a blended family. I did go help them move in. Lauren and Joel are sister and brother. Their last name is Atwater. Their sister married the old guy, Sterling Dodge. The little kid, Tyler, is four. He belongs to Dodge."

"Ah, so there *is* a wife and mom. But Mark, I wouldn't exactly call Mr. Dodge old. Rude, maybe, but not old."

"He captains a ferryboat."

"Really? I wonder who he'll work for. Ferries begin limited service next week, and we're scheduled to do the inspections."

Mark straightened from rummaging in the fridge. He backed out, holding two beers. "I didn't finish giving you the lowdown. The…sister died eight or so months ago. They used to live on Long Island, and the older kids are pissed at Dodge for uprooting them and dragging them here to the back of beyond. You gotta admit," he said, noting Megan's sudden defensive posture, "St.

Ignace is a far cry from the access they had to New York City."

"Dodge has the two older kids? Why?" As unfriendly as the man had been, Megan envisioned him embroiled in a custody fracas. Maybe even on the lam.

"We didn't get into specifics. You may have noticed that Joel Atwater has a chip on his shoulder. A big chip. I talked mostly to Lauren. He kept interrupting us, griping about being forced to tote boxes. Lauren said Dodge is their guardian, but not for long if she has her way. She's eighteen. When she turns twenty-one, she plans to petition the court for guardianship of Joel."

"Oh, if their older sister died, that means that sweet little boy—Tyler?—lost his mother. Mark, that's so sad."

Her brother twisted the tops off the two beers. Neither agreeing nor disagreeing with her assessment, he set the bottles on the table and dropped into a chair.

"That explains why the man's so abrupt, Mark. He's grieving." Megan had barely sat down and started to uncover her plate. Frowning, she jumped up again. "I changed my mind. I'm going to take a plate of cookies to them, after all. When I came home, Dodge was on his porch just staring at the bridge. He's probably still there, drinking coffee. I feel awful for having such uncharitable thoughts about him."

Even as she talked with machine-gun rapidity, Megan heaped fresh-baked cookies on a plate, then deftly covered the mound with plastic wrap. "I'll be right back," she said, loping out the door. Not stopping to pull on boots or a jacket, Megan ran downstairs. Below, she slipped on a patch of ice and almost fell at Sterling Dodge's feet. It wasn't the most graceful arrival she'd ever made, but she managed to steady herself by grabbing the railing as she shoved the plate into the hands of the startled man.

"Here. A belated welcome. I hope no one in your family's allergic to peanuts. Those are peanut butter cookies I made this morning. My apologies for thinking you had a crappy attitude. My brother told me about your recent loss. I'm sorry," she said, touching his arm briefly and sympathetically. "Mark and I lost our dad when we were a bit younger than Lauren and Joel, so we know about dealing with grief. Oh, something else—Mark has his degree in child psychology if the kids need to…well…talk."

Through vapor produced by her chatter in the frigid air, Megan watched Dodge stiffen. She wasn't really surprised when he said tightly, "The kids are fine. Or they will be," he added, "once we get into our permanent home on the island."

Shivering, Megan decided the smart choice was to cut short her welcome speech and simply retreat. Flinging him a last, hesitant smile, she turned and ran back upstairs where, once inside, she rubbed life back into her cold arms. Hopping around on one foot, she stripped off her wet socks and exchanged them for fleecy slippers.

Framed in the kitchen door, Mark hooked his thumbs under his belt and studied her. "Feel better?"

"I do. Although I still think Sterling Dodge is a stiff-necked jerk."

DOWNSTAIRS, STERLING, WHO'D been about to go in to escape the biting cold before his motormouthed neighbor accosted him, fumbled open his door. In the glow cast by a lone lamp, he stared at the plate the odd woman had literally forced him to take. She had ruddy cheeks and a mop of nut-brown curls, he'd noticed earlier when she'd removed the baseball cap that was part of her uniform.

A Coast Guard officer. Her appearance made it difficult to imagine a grown man saluting her. First, she was short. Blythe had been quite tall. Almost his height, in fact. She'd called him six foot, but insisted she was five-twelve. Blythe was vain, a trait she'd passed on to Lauren. Blythe never would have worn a long-john top and ski pants to take cookies to a neighbor. Come to think of it, she wouldn't have taken cookies to a neighbor. His wife hadn't possessed many domestic qualities. Standing there, Sterling thought perhaps that lay at the root of her refusal to quit work after Tyler was born. Had he never really known his wife, or had she truly changed?

Catching his reflection in the window, Sterling saw he looked almost angry. No wonder the woman upstairs had accused him of having a crappy attitude. He winced guiltily.

The truth of the matter was, he had no time for making friends. A situation Sterling hoped might one day be rectified—after repairs to the island house were complete. Just now, he had his hands full. Joel and Lauren had skipped school so often, graduating in June was in jeopardy. And Joel could be held back a year. That had only recently come to light. Whisking them away from bad influences seemed the best recourse. Sterling hoped they'd eventually get over hating him. He hoped they'd understand he hadn't quit his job and relocated for his benefit, but for theirs.

The move wasn't a big hit. Except for Tyler. Sterling was still astounded that he and Blythe had managed to produce a kid with such a sweet disposition. Down deep, he believed Joel and Lauren had good hearts, too.

Their upstairs neighbor had some nerve suggesting his family needed counseling.

Gingerly, Sterling loosened a corner of the plastic wrap and sniffed the plate's contents. Yep, peanut butter. Which happened to be his favorite kind of cookie. And he hadn't tasted homemade in longer than he could recall. Were these safe to eat?

Moving slowly through a kitchen filled with unpacked boxes, he recalled vividly the outpouring of sympathy aimed at him from his neighbor's soft blue eyes. And…she'd touched him, right before she darted off, picking her way in stocking feet through patches of ice. She'd smiled, too. But her touch surprised him most. People weren't so spontaneous where he came from.

Giving in to a mounting desire to sample the treat, Sterling plucked a cookie from the plate and refilled his coffee mug. Hell, he probably wouldn't get to sleep until the wee hours anyway. Insomnia had plagued him even before he'd received the call notifying him of Blythe's death. Even though they'd grown apart, he deeply regretted her death. And he'd always been saddened that Blythe, such a free spirit, had had to grow up fast when her parents were killed.

He leaned against the counter to munch on the cookie. If his neighbor had laced them with poison, Sterling thought with a grin, she'd used good-tasting poison.

The scrape of a chair overhead made him pause in the act of reaching for a second cookie. It took him a minute to realize the noise hadn't come from one of the kids' bedrooms but from the upstairs apartment. So, the gaudy house wasn't well insulated? Great! Noise probably traveled both ways. It didn't set well with him to think that Lieutenant Cute and Perky might hear him yelling at the kids to get out of bed for school. Or worse, that she'd hear him showering or brushing his teeth.

As he washed down a second cookie with a swig of muddy brew, Sterling stopped to wonder about the surname of the woman who lived above him. She'd introduced herself when she asked him to move his trailer. That was how he knew her rank. Her name, though, had gone in one ear and out the other. The lanky, red-haired guy she shared quarters with—her brother—had said his name was Mark. Again the last name eluded Sterling.

Deciding it was time he quit ruminating about his neighbors, he dusted cookie crumbs off his hands and set to work opening boxes. He slit the tape on one he was pretty sure held their dishes. Most of their stuff sat in storage awaiting the day they could move to the island. Lauren had sorted out what they'd need temporarily. Not for more than three weeks—he hoped. Tomorrow he planned to register the kids in the island school. He needed to locate a day care for Tyler and meet with his real estate agent. Sterling had bought the island house online sight unseen. As it turned out, there hadn't been much choice. Most of the resales were small summer cottages. He'd needed at least four bedrooms. The home he bought was the only one that seemed at all suitable.

Then when the inspector advised him at the last minute that he'd found black mold and dry rot and they'd have to rent until the house could be repaired, Sterling's heart had sunk. For a while, he'd thought that he wouldn't be able to make the move. But one of his many phone calls to leasing agents in Mackinaw City and St. Ignace had netted him this ground-level apartment. It had three bedrooms and a den. He'd set up Tyler's twin bed in there. For a few weeks, he could've squeezed Tyler's bed into his room. It wasn't as if his bedroom served any purpose but sleeping. Not in a while. For over two years, he'd worked days and Blythe worked nights. It hadn't been until a few weeks before her death that he'd accidentally learned through one of her coworkers that Blythe had engineered her own schedule. Up to then, he'd believed she'd had the hours foisted on her.

After he stacked dishes in the cupboard to the right of the sink, he dumped the coffee and brewed a fresh pot. Whenever his mind began turning over the lies, turning over the wreck his marriage had become, Sterling knew sleeping was out of the question.

Eventually the long day of travel, followed by the physical effort of carrying in their belongings, won out over the effects of the caffeine. The clock said 2:00 a.m. when he set his alarm to be sure he could get Lauren and Joel to school by nine. Too exhausted to shower, he threw off his clothes and fell into bed.

CHAPTER THREE

FIVE-THIRTY, THE SOUND OF someone boxing or dancing directly overhead jarred Sterling out of a sound sleep. He needed several minutes to figure out where he was. *St. Ignace, Michigan. In temporary digs. In an apartment downstairs from Lieutenant Cheer and Jubilation.*

Bolting upright, Sterling grabbed his travel alarm and shook it. "Five-thirty! Holy hell." He turned gritty eyes toward the tall ceiling, where his light fixture swayed alarmingly.

Flinging off his covers, Sterling dragged on yesterday's cold jeans. Uncaring that his mouth tasted like day-old coffee, he grabbed the wrinkled flannel shirt from the floor where it'd fallen last night, and dashed down the hall and outside.

Not until his bare feet hit the same patch of ice his neighbor had slipped on the previous night and the shock of it ran the entire length of his body, did it dawn on Sterling that he'd come out shoeless.

Too damn bad. Grabbing the narrow stair rail, he took the steps up to her door two at a time and laid on her bell. When no one answered, he doubled a fist and banged on her door. Then he hopped up and down to bring circulation to his toes. He stopped to blow warm air on his hands and pounded again.

The door swung open with a blast of warm air.

"Do you know what *time* it is?" he shouted into the void. The next part of the lecture he was about to deliver caught in his throat as he got a good look at the woman responsible for rousting him from sleep.

She wore black tights and a neon yellow sports bra. Bright blue earphones held tousled curls away from an oval face glowing with the sweat of a vigorous workout. Beads of perspiration trickled in a valley formed by generous cleavage Sterling wouldn't have guessed at, given what she had on yesterday. Those shapeless ski overalls.

His tongue froze to the roof of his mouth. Since his gaze seemed lodged on the pulse beating at the base of her throat, he sincerely doubted his attack of frozen tongue had anything to do with the frosty morning.

He apparently wasn't the only person she'd disturbed. Mark Benton stumbled out of his bedroom, yanking up his pants, saying, "Megan...what the hell is going on? Are we having an earthquake?"

"Sorry, aerobics," she said, dropping the earphones before untying a towel at her waist. "I...didn't think you'd hear the music." She blotted her face and neck, not immediately noticing how Sterling Dodge's gray eyes followed the path of the towel. When she happened to catch him staring, he began dancing in place like a boxer, slapping at his upper arms.

"Goodness, you're freezing," she said, only then realizing the man at her door was barefoot and his shirt hung open, flapping in the wind. "I always make hot chocolate after my workout. Do come in and warm up." She reached out to draw Dodge inside, but he stepped back so fast he almost fell off the top step.

"I didn't come here to socialize, Ms.—what *is* your name?"

"Benton. Megan Benton. I thought I told you that yesterday." Tilting her head to one side, she frowned at her brother, who'd thrown on a shirt and come to stand beside her. "I said I'm sorry if my exercise routine disturbed you. Is there something else? Did your electricity go out? It does sometimes. Hank Meade installed a generator out back. Instructions for getting it going are posted inside the door panel. Each floor is independent of the other."

"I'm not here about electricity. Your aerobics shook the whole house."

"I assumed switching to earphones would be enough."

Mark raked a hand through his hair. "Sorry, sis, it did feel like the house was falling."

Dodge continued to beat his arms to ward off the chill. "My ceiling light swung like a damned trapeze."

"I'm sorry, but aerobics are supposed to be physical. They're designed to make a person sweat," Megan said.

Sterling, whose mind was propelled to other physical activities designed to make a person sweat, felt compelled to glower. "Then let me suggest joining a health club."

Grabbing both ends of her towel, Megan sent him an amused grin. "Don't look now, Dodge, but your New York attitude is showing again. The Upper Peninsula is advertised as the best outdoor recreation spot in the U.S., so no one's bothered to open a health club. They'd probably be laughed out of town. Shoveling snow tends to keep people fit around here. Sure you won't come in for hot chocolate before you beat yourself black-and-blue?"

Sterling would've liked to bathe in hot chocolate he was so damned cold. But he clearly wasn't getting through to the lieutenant. Turning, he descended two steps, then stopped. "Find some snow to shovel, Ms. Benton. Another morning like this and I'll call our mutual landlord to have him read you the fine print in the rental agreement."

"You do that," Megan said sweetly. *"Jackass,"* she added under her breath in a far different tone as she slammed the door.

Mark winced. "He probably will call your landlord. Lauren said he's a stickler for rules."

Megan yanked the towel from around her neck. She pulled on a set of baggy Coast Guard–issue sweats. "Let him phone Hank. He's off fishing in the south Atlantic for the next six to eight weeks."

"It's not like you to be so bitchy, Megs."

Twisting her hair in a knot atop her head, Megan ignored her brother's comment until she gave up and secured her hair with an elastic band, instead. "He just rubs me the wrong way," she finally muttered. She doubted Mark would understand if she listed some of the things that really bugged her about Sterling Dodge. His dark eyebrows were too straight. His gray eyes, too intense. His face, too tanned, masculine and rugged—probably from standing at the helm of a ferryboat. The irritating truth was that if Dodge and Hank Meade ever met, the two sea captains would get along famously.

She let a sigh trickle out. "Don't worry, I'll play the nice neighbor and exercise someplace else. I honestly didn't know I shook the house. I was worried about the music, though. Hence the earphones." She sighed again. "I work swing the rest of this week, then I go on days.

We're getting a couple of new guardsmen in. New crew members get the graveyard shift, then move up to swing and so on. I'm being bumped to days. I have to say I'm glad. There's always more happening during the day, especially when we hit the summer season."

"I hear you had some excitement last night. Were you in on the rescue of that kid who drove off the end of the pier?"

"Yes. Did we make the news?"

"A TV reporter interviewed your commander. He made it sound like saving a life is all in a day's work."

"It is, but last night we were lucky. A team from another station sent down divers. Sometimes it's all up to us. Since we're both up, Mark, how about if I fix scrambled eggs and biscuits? Plus some hot chocolate, of course."

"Sure, as long as you use Mom's biscuit recipe and not Camp's," Mark said with a snicker. It was a family joke. He and his sister had met Nolan Campbell, who later became their stepfather, on a wagon train expedition he'd organized to travel the old Santa Fe Trail. A history professor, Camp had intended to prove that modern women couldn't stand up to the same rigors experienced by their great-great-grandmothers. He'd never planned to drive a wagon himself, only follow in his car and collect daily reports. The women in his study banded together and shamed Campbell into joining. Mark and Megan, who'd accompanied their mom under protest, were no happier about being on the trip than the professor was. They loved drawing attention to his ineptness. His first try at making biscuits was a disaster. He'd attempted to bribe their mom's recipe out of them, until Emily took pity on the poor guy.

However much the kids had come to love their stepdad, the joke was too good to drop.

"Sis, speaking of the family, I owe you for a long-distance phone call I made after you went to work," Mark said as his sister began to gather milk, flour and other ingredients. "My cell phone needed charging, but I had some explaining to do, since I only left them a note about coming here."

Megan glanced up from the hot chocolate she was stirring. "Are they all okay? I wish you'd waited until I got home so I could've talked to Mom."

"She must've been grading papers, or else she was tired. We didn't talk long. But I know she's ticked at me. Even then, she asked the usual questions—is your sister living in a safe place? Is she taking care of herself? And the biggie, is she dating someone nice?"

"Jeez! We've covered all that. I hope you set her straight," she said, mixing the biscuit dough.

He laughed. "No. I said this place is a dump. As for food, you have a caribou stuck out back in the ice and you hack off a chunk now and then to roast in a pit. About dating—I said the only person who'd put up with your sass was a big, ugly iron miner."

Megan smacked him with a floury hand. A white mist flew between them as Mark hunched and jumped back, all the while laughing.

"You didn't," she muttered, her eyes narrowing. "On the other hand," she said, forming biscuits and dropping them on an oiled pan, "I wouldn't put it past you. Especially if it'd take some of the heat off yourself." She began to crack eggs in a second bowl sitting on the counter.

"Oh, I didn't escape unscathed. I confessed in my note that Mona grubstaked me."

She stuck the pan of biscuits in the oven. Then, filling two mugs with hot chocolate, Megan put the egg pan aside and took the chair across from Mark. "I'll bet that went over like a lead balloon."

"I think—I *know*—Mom hopes we'll both come home to teach."

"Surely you didn't indicate that was possible? I'll be really mad if you did. I've been down that road. The folks can't conceive of anyone not dying to be an educator."

"Then you understand the pressure I'm under."

Megan checked the biscuits and nodded glumly. "So, what are your plans for the day?"

"I'm going to get dressed, then eat and catch the ferry over to Mackinac Island. A brochure I picked up said they rent bikes. Marquette Park looks fairly primitive in spots, which is the kind of landscape I want. I'll take a few pictures, then come back and upload them to my laptop. If you don't mind I'd like to set up my printer and tie into your phone line so I can e-mail stuff to Gina Ames."

"I don't mind. So you shoot digital photos?" Megan returned to the eggs.

Mark's eyes slid guiltily away. "Ah…Gram bought me the whole setup for Christmas. Otherwise I'd never have been able to afford it."

Megan cradled her mug between her hands. "You're dead serious about doing this one-man show, aren't you?"

"Yes, I am," he answered solemnly.

"Then go for it. But don't get so caught up in taking pictures today that you miss the last ferry. It'd be too embarrassing if I had to ask my unit to spend taxpayer's money rescuing my dumb brother from the island."

Ten minutes later, Megan served the eggs, added biscuits and they ate in companionable silence, with Megan answering the occasional question about the area.

When Mark was finished, he drained his mug, set his plate in the sink and sprinted to the door. "The ferry I want to take leaves the dock down the street in fifteen minutes. I need to throw my gear together. Unless I freeze, you probably won't see me until you get home from work. And sis, thanks for giving me this chance."

"Go on, bozo, get your ugly mug outta here. I'll clean up the dishes."

Mark dived through the door, his freckled face split in a huge grin.

SOME TEN MINUTES LATER, he was surprised to run into their downstairs neighbors buying ferry tickets. "Hey," he said, singling out Lauren Atwater. "What brings the lot of you out so bright and early?"

She fluffed her blond hair and glared at Sterling. "Our jailer says we have to enroll in school today. Like, we couldn't wait and start at the beginning of next week."

"School?" Mark eyed Lauren. "There's a college on the island?"

She hurried onto the ferry that had just docked, and zigzagged her way to the stern. If she was surprised that Mark followed, Lauren didn't let on. "I'm a senior in high school," she admitted glumly.

"Ah, a late baby who got caught in the registration cutoff, I presume."

She shook her head. "I wasn't...good about attendance last year, and I'm repeating some subjects. Before my sister died, I never cared if I graduated. Now I need a diploma for the court to consider me a reliable guardian for Joel."

Mark's eyes tracked to the girl's brother. He'd gone to the far side of the boat, pulled out a pack of cigarettes and lit one. That action drew Sterling Dodge like a magnet. Mark could see the two having a major tussle of words. Dodge won, apparently, as the boy sneered and flung his lit cigarette into the murky water.

"It's none of my business," Mark said offhandedly, "But if you're going to support yourself and Joel, wouldn't it be better to get college out of the way first?"

As the wind had picked up, Lauren tightened her jacket under her chin. "Our folks left us a nice trust fund. The question is, has Sterling tied it up so I can't lay hands on it? Joel says if that's the case he'll run away."

"I can recognize that attitude in him. Megan and I both tried that route after our dad was killed in an accident. I should tell Joel it's rarely successful. The law always brings you back. Kids have zero leverage."

"I'll have leverage if I can get our money. We won't have any worries then."

Mark shifted his camera bag. "There's more to life than money. What's your plan if the old boy has your money locked up? Is there a career you'd like to prepare for? Besides, you won't be caring for your brother the rest of your life."

"Wow, no one's *ever* asked me what I'd like to do." She stared at Mark through long, curved lashes. "I used to fiddle around drawing clothes. I especially liked dreaming up accessories to go with fashions. But..." She shrugged again. "My friends said I was pretty good, but I pretty much quit sketching. What's the point?"

"Check out graphic design institutions with a school counselor and see what options are available. There are a lot of design schools around. If nothing else, you could maybe work in the field and attend classes part time."

"That's a thought. Thanks. New York City has tons of design institutes. We're going back there as soon as I can manage it." She gave the first genuine smile Mark had seen from her, and it was as if the sun had suddenly broken out from behind a cloud.

He smiled back. "You can e-mail for brochures. Do you have a computer? If not, I'll bring my laptop down tonight and we can do a search."

"I'd like that. Sterling has a computer, but I'd never ask to use it. We eat at six. Would you like to come for dinner?"

"Is that okay? Sure, my sister's working swing shift until next week."

Their ferry docked and the few travelers lined up to disembark. Lauren and Mark chatted amiably as they walked off the boat. Neither paid heed to the fact that Sterling watched them with some disfavor as he held a wriggling Tyler. Joel Atwater hung back. Not surprisingly, Mark noted, his lagging behind resulted in yet another admonishment from his guardian.

Wryly he murmured to Lauren, "You'd better go rescue your brother. I'm off to photograph the park. See you at six." He set out for the tourist bureau office, as Sterling guided his brood along the boardwalk.

Moments after they'd gone their separate ways, Mark began whistling happily. He looked forward to seeing Lauren again. It'd been some time since anything except photography had sparked his anticipation to this degree.

IN COLUMBIA, MISSOURI, Nolan Campbell was trying to calm his wife. "Emily, I can't believe you went to visit that woman after we discussed it. Why would you do that when you get sick to your stomach even talking about confronting Mona? And you've let her ruin your appetite." Camp set dinner on the table, although Emily had said she couldn't eat.

"Why is she interfering again, Camp? Mark has a wonderful opportunity for a good future at our college. Moreover, what's gotten into *him?* I can't believe he'd throw away everything he's worked for on...on...a half-baked hobby he could play at in his spare time."

Realizing that Emily was too worked up to eat even the light meal of soup and rolls, Camp stepped up behind her and began kneading her tense shoulders. "Honey, what if Mark is that good?"

She leaned into her husband's firm but tender hands. "That good? Have you forgotten he's the kid who got pictures of feet and table legs at our wedding reception with that cast-off camera Gina Ames gave him?"

"That was then. According to Gina, Mark's developed quite a talent. They've kept in touch, you know, ever since that summer we went on the Santa Fe Trail." Mark had driven her wagon after she broke her leg. "I saw the black-and-white photo he entered in that contest last fall, and I thought it was first-rate. He captured something exceptional in the faces of the child and the grandmother. He obviously made a real connection with them when they met in the park."

Emily batted his hands away and replaced them with her own. She turned her head from side to side and rubbed hard. "One lucky shot does not a career make,

Nolan Campbell. Gina is downright antisocial. I want a better life for Mark. And I want grandbabies nearby one day," she wailed. "Why can't Mark and Megan be content to settle down here? I know what it's like to be without the support of loving relatives. I don't understand why they won't listen to me."

The doorbell rang, and Camp escaped Emily's uncharacteristic tears to answer it. His niece, Shannon Lock, tap-danced her way inside and across the hardwood floor. She was followed by her grandparents.

"Are we interrupting?" Nan Campbell rose on tiptoe to kiss her son's furrowed cheek.

"Not really. I just made soup and sourdough rolls. Come on in and eat. Emily's not interested. I'd just as soon not let my hard work warming up soup go to waste," he said, grinning. "What brings you here tonight?"

"Garrett's at a board meeting and Sherry had a crisis at the college crisis center, of all things." Nan chuckled. "In case you can't tell, we took Shannon to pick up her new tap shoes. She begged to come and show them to Emily. Is she resting?"

"She's in the kitchen…crying, " Camp admitted, accepting a manly hug from his father. Ben was still spry and young-looking for a man who'd just celebrated his seventy-third birthday. Nan, at sixty-six, had few gray hairs, in spite of having taught elementary school for thirty-five years.

"Sherilyn said Emily was sick at school this afternoon. Is she fighting off a flu bug?" Nan asked.

"She's fretting herself sick over Mark these days. Em was a basket case when Megan left the nest. I thought at least Mark would stick around." Camp's eyebrows climbed into a lock of dark hair that fell perpetually over his forehead. "Your aunt Emily's in the kitchen, Shannon. Feel free to go tap in there on the tiles."

"I'll fix Em some camomile tea." Nan immediately started for the kitchen. "Mark's a good boy. He'll land on his feet no matter what. Emily will turn white before she's forty-six if she doesn't let him and his sister forge their own way."

"It's not the kids she's upset about tonight. It's their other grandmother. Emily went to see Mona. She financed Mark's trip. It's always about the Benton money. If Mona hadn't provided Mark with the funding to go to Michigan, Emily and I believe he would've taken the counseling job at Wellmont."

"But would he have been happy?" Ben Campbell shoved his hands in his pockets and rattled coins. "With all the years you and Emily have worked with hard-headed students, anyone would think you'd know that the more you preach, the less kids listen."

"That's not what Emily needs to hear, Dad."

"Maybe not, but it's true. As your mother says, Mark has the brains to do any number of things with his life. You think I ever understood why you were so gung ho about history? Did I discourage your sister from working with down-and-out women, even though some of their husbands were dangerous?"

Camp cast a dark, worried glance in the direction of the kitchen, where his mother and niece had disappeared. "You have a point. I saw talent in those photos of Mark's that won him the right to do an important show. On the other hand, I can't stand to see Emily making herself so sick over his going off that she vomits. I wish we could come up with some kind of compromise."

Ben shook his head morosely, then clapped his son on the shoulder. "That soup smells mighty good. We fiddled around town all afternoon waiting for Todd Holmgren to put the taps on Shannon's shoes. I'll bet if we all sit down at the table, it'll induce Em to relax and eat a bite or two."

"I hope so. Where are the boys?"

"Keith took Tim and Gavin to see the new colt he and old Doc Jackson helped deliver yesterday. Keith, now—there's another rebel. Ever since he lost his dog, Rags, to cancer, he's determined to become a vet. You know Garrett's ex-wife decided long ago that Keith should be a banker because she and her second husband are bigwigs in the field."

Camp thought about Keith Lock, a good-looking blond kid with big eyes and a bigger heart. "Anyone who knows how much Keith loves to fish, hike and in general spend his time outdoors is nuts to think he'd make a good banker."

"Ah," Ben said, hustling his son into the massive farm kitchen. "I rest my case, Nolan. Parents, no matter how well-intentioned, aren't the best judges of what careers their offspring should undertake."

They all converged on the kitchen. Camp hurried straight over and kissed his wife. He noted happily that her face wasn't as pale as it had been earlier, and she smiled and clapped for Shannon's dance performance. With love, maybe they'd get through Mark's career debacle, the same way they'd weathered the ups and downs of raising teens.

CHAPTER FOUR

Mackinac Island, Michigan

"WHY CAN'T WE TAKE A CAB to the stupid school?" Joel whined.

Sterling held Tyler's hand and a map of the island. "I thought I explained that motor vehicles have been banned from this island since the turn of the century. Except for a police jeep, an ambulance and a fire truck," Sterling added. "The Realtor said summer visitors get around by horse-drawn carriage. Locals, I gather, walk or ride bikes in good weather, and walk or use snow-mobiles during the winter."

Joel, who kicked the snow-edged walkway with his head down and his hands rammed in the pockets of his ever-present baggy pants, showed interest in Sterling's last statement. "Snowmobiles. Cool. Can we get one?"

"Maybe." Sterling dropped back to walk with the trailing boy. "But not right now. The weather forecaster predicted a warming trend. And we can't very well load a snowmobile on and off the ferry."

"But you bought a house over here. Can't we park it there?"

"I have to go see the house and find out how soon

we can move in. After I settle you kids in school. It might make sense to get your bikes out of storage."

"Bikes are for sissies," Joel groused. "A Sno-Cat is cool."

"Well, if you knuckle down and bring your grades up this semester, Joel, I'll consider buying you a snowmobile next fall."

"Forget it. Lauren will have moved by then. I'm gonna go live with her."

Sterling started to say *fat chance.* Instead, he tightened his lips and pointed out the school, a single-story structure directly ahead of them. White pillars supported an entry portico, and a turret with an old-fashioned bell rose from the center of the building. All in all, it made a charming picture.

Lauren, who'd said nothing on the jaunt from the terminal, slowed her steps to match her brother's. "This place reminds me of a little New England town Mom took Blythe and me to a long time ago on one of her antique-hunting expeditions."

"I don't remember. Where was I?" Joel demanded.

"Mom might've been pregnant with you." Lauren swept blond curls out of her eyes. "It was a long time ago. I barely remember, Joel, but I just had a flash of memory. We stopped in a small rural town that looked like a Christmas card. Like this. Quiet. Peaceful, you know?"

"Yeah." Sterling sensed what Lauren was trying to convey. "No matter what time of day or night, New York bustles," he said. "Even on Long Island people are always rushing everywhere."

Lauren smiled. "That's exactly what I mean."

Sterling had so much on his mind that until Lauren

pointed it out, he hadn't really focused on the difference. Yet he was already experiencing the calming effect that accompanied the slower pace. Maybe this move would turn out okay.

Joel latched on to his sister's arm and stopped her from crossing the street. He obviously didn't like that she'd connected with their brother-in-law on any level. "So, back there on the ferry, what did you and Red find to be so chatty about?"

"Red?" Lauren shook him loose and moved off the curb. "Mark, you mean? He's nice. Easy to talk to. And he's smart." She lifted a shoulder. "Mostly we talked about colleges I might be interested in getting information on. My graduation isn't that far off."

Sterling came to a halt on the opposite curb, not believing his ears. The fact that Lauren might consider higher education was news to him. In the last year her grades had plummeted. According to her previous school counselor, up until then she'd gotten straight As without much effort. The counselor also said she'd sent Blythe several notes asking for a meeting, but that Blythe offered one excuse after another. She'd promised to talk with both kids, but Sterling had ascertained that she never had.

On the drive to Michigan he'd asked about their absences, but Lauren accused him of trying to malign Blythe. Now he stepped more warily. "Is Mark recruiting for his old alma mater?" Sterling asked Lauren.

"Nothing of the sort. I invited him to dinner tonight." She lifted her chin in a challenging gesture. "Mark's bringing his laptop to do an Internet search on college programs for me."

Sterling saw that she expected him to object. But

why would he? Nothing up to now had jarred Lauren out of the depression she'd fallen into after Blythe's funeral.

Sterling wouldn't have said anything, except that another thought struck him. "Did your invitation include Mark's sister?" he asked, although the possibility of eating a meal with the irritating yet too-appealing woman he'd seen in revealing workout clothes caused him mild panic.

"Don't worry about not having enough dishes. Mark's sister's working swing shift until next week."

Joel smirked. "Who's cooking? If you wanna impress the dude, Lauren, you'd better order in."

"I can cook, smarty-pants. I've just chosen not to." She aimed an I-dare-you-to-contradict-that look at Sterling.

Again he decided not to react. By then, he'd reached the school. Opening the door, he directed Tyler to one of the chairs lining the wall. Students strode purposefully along the corridors and disappeared into classrooms.

A woman dressed in a bright red pants suit rose from a desk in what seemed to be a reception area. "May I help you?" She smiled as Sterling deposited two folders on the counter.

"I have two student enrollment forms." He glanced back to make sure the two in question had followed him inside. Then he winced, seeing them as the stranger probably did. Joel in wide-legged black pants, now wet around dragging bottoms, with his orange hair spiked, resembled a punk hoodlum.

At least Lauren wore less makeup today. But her very stance screamed hostility. Sterling interpreted the secretary's reaction from how quickly her smile faded. Opening both folders, he slid them across the counter.

"A twelfth grader, I see, and grade…eight?" she asked, peering over wire-rimmed half-glasses.

"Ninth," Sterling corrected, turning to Joel for confirmation. The recalcitrant teen threw himself into a chair next to Tyler and refused to say anything.

"Ninth, then." The woman extracted two cards from a drawer and transferred some information. Setting them aside, she glanced up. "What about your younger son, or is he also a stepchild, Mr…ah, Dodge?" she finished, running an eye down his forms. The warm smile she lavished on Tyler made up for her hesitation with the other kids.

"Tyler's four. He's big for his age. He attended a Montessori school in New York. That's where we're from. I start work here next week," Sterling rattled on to fill a void. "For now, we're renting a home in St. Ignace, as I noted there. It's temporary. I purchased a house on the island, but it's in the middle of repairs."

"One moment, please." She scooped up the records and went inside an inner office. The longer she was gone, the harder Sterling drummed his fingers on the counter top.

"What's the holdup?" Joel growled, cracking the knuckles of his left hand.

Lauren, who'd been examining a row of class pictures on the wall, said in a too-loud voice, "I had more kids in one class at my old school than they have in this whole frigging place." That announcement made Joel slump even lower. His comment was more direct and less circumspect than his sister's. It prompted a terse reminder from Sterling to watch his mouth.

The secretary returned in time to hear both remarks. "Follow me. We'll take Joel to his homeroom first." As they walked, she gave a list of general student expectations.

Joel snorted, which brought a swift nudge from Sterling.

After Joel had been dropped of, they walked in silence to Lauren's classroom. Sterling felt sorry for Lauren, as it was obvious she was nervous in spite of trying to put on big-city brashness.

"You kids have your cell phones and my cell number should you need anything," he murmured before she went in. "And you have money for lunch and to catch the ferry home. Later today, I'll check into weekly or month-long ferry passes."

"Daily is better." She rubbed her hand up and down her thigh.

"Lauren…you're too close to graduating to blow it. You said as much earlier." Sterling offered a reassuring smile, not at all sure how it'd be received. Tyler begged her for a hug. Sterling was grateful when Lauren willingly complied. Then she was gone.

Trekking back to the office, his guide at last turned to Sterling. "Before you leave, Mr. Dodge, our principal would like a word. To discuss the records that came from your students' previous school."

Wishing he could cover Tyler's ears, Sterling made a long story very short, condensing their family history. He asked to leave Tyler in the outer office while he visited the man in charge.

"Welcome to our island." The principal greeted Sterling with a firm handshake. "I'll come straight to the point, Mr. Dodge. Ours is a small but excellent school. I see that Lauren's and Joel's grades fell badly in the last two sessions. Their undocumented absences were excessive. I hope both improve significantly. Soon."

"So do I." Again Sterling relayed how he'd come to be their guardian. "The first hopeful sign I've seen was on the way here today. Lauren actually mentioned college. Is there someone on your staff who can fan that flame?"

"I have just the person. The boy, Joel, is he interested in sports?"

Sterling shook his head.

"Music? Wood shop? Art?" As Sterling continued to shake his head, the man eventually sighed. "Then I expect you and I will be in touch again, Mr. Dodge."

"Sterling, please. I'd like to iron out any problems this week, since I start work on Monday. I captain a ferry, so it's not easy for me to get off, even in an emergency. Joel's probably aware of that. Any help getting through to him will be greatly appreciated."

The men walked to the door. "In smaller schools students sometimes take care of the problem kids."

Sterling thought that was a long shot, but didn't say so. "My next order of business is to find a day care for my four-year-old. Can you recommend something?"

"As a matter of fact, we have provisions on-site for three- and four-year-olds."

That news was a bright spot in Sterling's day. "Great," he said, taking the form the principal handed him. "Considering that we're barely unpacked and I'm home this week, would it be all right for me to start Tyler next Monday?"

"I don't see why not. My secretary will show you his room. The teacher there will supply a list of everything he'll need."

Sterling filled out the paperwork and they toured the classroom. “Daddy,” Tyler exclaimed, “can I stay now, and play?” He smiled at the other children.

“Well…” Sterling waffled. “I thought you’d want to go with me to see our new house. You can tell Lauren and Joel all about it tonight.”

The boy nodded, raising his arms so Sterling could swing him aloft. They thanked their host and said goodbye. He and Tyler set off with the directions he’d printed off the Internet site where he’d first found the house. It was confusing that homes here didn’t have addresses. Part of the island’s charm, he’d been told, was that all mail went to the post office to be picked up by residents—an opportunity to gossip and socialize. The local postal folks made up addresses to make package delivery easier, but dray drivers delivered them based simply on knowing everyone on the island.

Sterling located his house by checking landmarks. It sat on a corner lot at the edge of the historic district. According to the Realtor, Sterling was lucky to get it, because such places were either handed down in families or snatched up before they landed on the open market. An Internet photo, taken in the summer, seemed cheerier than what he saw now. It was hard to imagine blooming flower beds under the drifts of melting snow. But the house had loads of potential.

He had expected to find the place buzzing with workmen. Instead, it sat empty and dark. He left Tyler on the walkway, cupped his hands and peered in window after window. He rattled both the front and back doors, to no avail.

“Don’tcha got a key, Daddy?” Tyler asked when his dad gave up on the last door with a disgusted sigh.

"I don't, Ty. We'll need to find the real estate agent." Sterling dug through his wallet until he uncovered the man's business card. They found the office after another short hike. It, too, was locked. A note on the door indicated the Realtor was having coffee at a waterfront café. That was fine with Sterling. Tyler complained of being cold and hungry. Perhaps they could warm up, eat and find the man who sold him the house.

Ten minutes later, after a harried waitress pointed him toward a bald man seated at the counter. Sterling introduced himself, but their conversation wasn't to his liking.

"Sorry if I didn't make it clear in my letter. Not much in the way of construction or repair goes on here in the winter, young fella. Didn't the building inspector forward a copy of everything that needs doing to the old Melville place?"

"He did. I authorized him to order supplies and engage a contractor."

"Well, now, wallboard, flooring, subflooring, plumbing supplies, as well as the plumbers, all come from Mackinaw City. That ferry won't run till next week."

"I know that. I'm captain of one of those ferries," Sterling said impatiently. "Do you mean to say there's no licensed plumber on the island?"

"Oh, sure. 'Cept he's gone south for the winter."

"That's just great! I'm stuck renting a place. For how long, do you think?"

"Don't rightly know." The man sipped his coffee. "Now, in New York I 'spect you snap your fingers and things get done A-sap. Here'bouts, you've gotta learn to kick back and relax. By and by, you'll get used to things happenin' on island time."

"Island time. I see." Sterling shut his eyes and shook his head at Tyler, who was announcing loudly that he was starved. "Mr. McGrath, could you venture an educated guess as to when work on my house will get underway?"

The man took a toothpick from his vest pocket. "Just guessin', mind you, since I don't know what other jobs they've lined up. With luck, early May."

"What?" Sterling's yelp brought the waitress running. She flipped open her pad and took out a pencil. "Sorry, folks, it's unusually busy today. What can I get for you?"

Sterling whirled around and realized Tyler had climbed up on the next stool. "Uh, Tyler, you want chicken noodle soup and a peanut butter and jelly sandwich?" Sterling asked after a hurried scan of the one-page laminated menu.

"Uh-huh. And can I have hot chocolate?" the boy added, bouncing in his seat. "Megan upstairs wanted to give me some yesterday, but Lauren said no."

Megan upstairs had offered *him* hot chocolate this morning. Sterling grimaced, wondering if the damned woman had stock in a cocoa company or something.

"Sorry, our cocoa machine quit working yesterday. I can do milk, soda or water," the waitress said.

"Milk, then." Sterling set the menu back behind the napkin dispenser. "Can you add a squirt of chocolate topping to the milk?" After noting the waitress's nod, he said, "I'll take the soup, too, but a BLT. And coffee for me, please. Black," he stated, feeling somewhat elated to have preempted Megan Benton of the endless hot chocolate.

Sterling wasn't elated at the news about his house,

though. Island time, indeed! Suddenly the lazy village lifestyle Lauren considered sounded so appealing had lost much of its charm. Not for the first time since chucking everything back home, Sterling was assailed by doubts.

The waitress set steamy bowls of soup in front of them. The Realtor, McGrath, finished his coffee and dropped money on the counter. He paused long enough to say again that he was sorry for the delay, and that Sterling could stop by for a key.

As Sterling idly watched Tyler slurp up his soup, he felt weighed down by all the concerns that needed his attention. His wife apparently hadn't paid heed to anything the kids did, including how they dressed or acted in public, and now it seemed he had to work on Tyler's table manners, as well. Fleetingly, he wished he knew someone he could talk with. That thought had Sterling recalling his upstairs neighbor's comment about getting the kids counseling.

Crushing his napkin, Sterling wiped his lips. Maybe *he* was the one in the family who needed counseling.

"Daddy, did that man who just left make you mad?"

Catching his reflection in the mirror that ran the length of the counter behind the soda glasses, Sterling noticed his scowl, which had obviously led to Tyler's query. It was a look that seemed permanently etched on his face lately. Sterling did his best to dredge up a smile. "I'm fine, little buddy. I'm just disappointed about the repairs on our house taking so long. I'd hoped to get us moved by the end of this month, and now I guess we have to stay where we are for a while."

"Oh." Tyler picked up half of the sandwich the waitress had placed in front of him, and he scooped out a glob of peanut butter and jelly. He twirled around on the stool, licking the goo off his finger. "I like where we are. I like the blue house, and I don't wanna move."

"The blue house isn't ours. Please don't spin on the stool. You'll get dizzy and fall off, Tyler. And don't scrape the filling out of your sandwich. Eat it properly." Even though his BLT was fat with filling, Sterling took a bite to demonstrate.

"I like my peanut butter on a spoon 'stead of on bread," the boy said, setting the sandwich down to return to slurping his soup.

"Dip your spoon and raise it to your mouth. Don't slurp. Who gave you peanut butter like that? Mom?"

"Joel. He used to eat it that way when he came home from skateboarding. Me and him like the kind with jelly mixed in."

"And Mom never insisted that Joel spread the peanut butter on crackers or bread?"

"She wasn't ever there, Daddy."

"I'm sure she was there sometimes. Because I never saw Joel dig a spoon in the peanut butter jar, and I was always home before Mom left for work."

"Yeah, but lotsa times if Lauren was home, Mama went to meet Rio for coffee."

Sterling's head snapped up. "Rio Amado? They worked the same shift. He and Mom were partners."

"Uh-huh. But this was before, when Mr. Rhodes was Mama's partner."

Sterling's teeth snapped a piece of crisp bacon in half, and he felt a nerve jump along the lower edge of his jaw. If Eric Rhodes had remained Blythe's partner, maybe she'd still be alive. The burly father of six, a thirty-year veteran on the force, very likely would've sensed trouble at the warehouse the night Rio and Blythe were killed. Sterling was sure that Amado was a hotshot aiming to make a name for himself and did risky things to impress Blythe. He'd convinced her they didn't need backup. A preliminary investigation proved they couldn't have outgunned all the firepower expected to come into play in that drug deal. The official plan had been for Rio and Blythe to do reconnaissance, then radio for backup. A plan that never materialized.

"Did you bite your tongue, Daddy? Does it hurt? I made mine bleed once."

"Tyler, eat your soup before it gets cold. I'd like to collect our key, check out the house and then see some of the town. We'll catch the one-fifteen ferry back to St. Ignace."

The boy dawdled. They did wander through the empty house half an hour later. In spite of their echoing footsteps, Sterling felt an affinity for the spacious rooms. The house had a solid feel. He poked around so long they ended up practically running for the ferry. On the way, they saw no open shops; most were boarded up until the advent of tourist season, anyway. As they got on the ferry, he tried to picture how the place would change over the coming months. The crossings could take fifteen minutes or up to forty, depending on whether a passenger took the newer catamaran or an older-style boat. During the summer, the ferries would triple or quadruple their runs.

Tyler had grown up loving ferry rides. They hung over the side, and were both surprised to see a row of Christmas trees poking out of ice floes along the route. Their captain explained, "Islanders make an ice bridge—a winter highway for walkers and snowmobilers until the spring thaw. They mark it with the trees. Some years it doesn't freeze hard enough to walk between the islands," he added. "Then pretty much the only way off Mackinac in January and February is by plane. Sure you want to become an islander?"

"Will we sink like those trees, Daddy?"

Sterling ruffled his son's hair. "Not a chance. We'll buy a book and I'll read up on what we need to know. We'll do just fine living here."

"We can ask the lady who lives upstairs."

They probably could. The previous night, the lieutenant had spouted facts and figures like a tour guide.

The ferry docked and the Dodge duo followed the few passengers who'd made the crossing. Tyler wanted to check out the moored boats lining the marina.

"Let's save that for another day, Ty. Your nose and cheeks are beet-red from the wind."

The boy skipped up the incline toward home. "Will the wind ever get warm enough so I can play outside like I did at home?"

"Sure. In a few months."

"Look, look!" Tyler shouted excitedly. He'd raced to the top ahead of his dad and now faced their cul-de-sac. Hopping around, he pointed at something Sterling couldn't yet see.

It turned out to be their upstairs neighbor, who had a bucket of suds and the hose on full bore. She was washing her pickup. Tangled curls whipped around her head like an angry cloud. Her cheeks and fingers were nearly as red as the gleaming bright paint she scrubbed so industriously.

Before Sterling could catch Tyler's hand, he ran pell-mell across the circle and skidded to a stop next to the woman. Sterling heard Tyler ask if he could help Megan Benton.

"Tyler, no!" Sterling puffed like a steam engine from running up the sharp incline. It reminded him that, in contrast to the woman who looked fit and trim, his body was sadly out of shape. Maybe he needed the services of a health club—although apparently they were nonexistent here.

"I wanna help wash her pickup, Daddy. At home you always let me."

Megan had run her five miles and now had excess energy to burn, which was why she'd decided to wash her pickup. What would it hurt to let the boy spray the last section of fender she'd doused with soapy water? Stymied by the irritation stamped on his dad's face, she sucked in her cheeks and hosed off her truck. "You know what, Tyler? I'm almost finished, anyway. Maybe next time you can help me, okay?"

Hating his crestfallen expression, she avoided looking at Dodge. Afraid she might say something she'd regret, Megan bent to the task of dumping her bucket of suds down the drain. She turned off the water and efficiently coiled the hose.

"Isn't it a little chilly to be washing a vehicle?" Sterling asked.

"Looks to me like the sun's out." She squinted over his shoulder. Her fingers were numb, but she had no intention of admitting that to him.

"Where's your brother?" Tyler abruptly inquired. "He rode the ferry to the island with us this morning. We walked through town but never saw Mark again."

"He's still over there taking pictures." She laughed, a low rippling sound. "I told him what time the last ferry heads home. If he misses it, he'll have to book into one of the few year-round resort hotels."

"So, there are hotels on the island open all year?"

"More and more, I understand. I haven't seen a lot of the island. I only reported for duty two months ago. Weren't some of the shops open, too?"

"A few. We enrolled Lauren and Joel in school, then went to look at the house I bought."

Tyler finished for his dad. "We ate at a café and Daddy got mad at a man, 'cause he said the plumber can't fix our house. We had soup and sandwiches. I wanted hot chocolate, but the woman didn't have none."

"Of all the nerve." Megan laughed harder. "Well, you're in luck, young man. I'm going upstairs right this minute to make a new pot. Would either of you care to join me? I also made snickerdoodles today," she said, continuing to smile at Tyler.

Sterling found himself staring at Megan's face, transformed by her laughter. A dimple popped in and out of one cheek. Purple flecks appeared simultaneously in both her eyes, unless that was a trick of the sun.

"Daddy, Daddy, can we go with her? I don't know if I like snickerdoodles. Have I ever had them?"

Shaking himself out of a tongue-tied stupor, Sterling intended to say *no, thanks* for the offer. His son's question threw him off stride. "Snickerdoodles?"

"That settles it. You two have been deprived if you've never tasted snickerdoodles."

"That's okay. It hasn't been long since we ate lunch."

Tyler burst into tears and Sterling found himself acquiescing in order to calm the boy.

Tyler grabbed Megan's hand and smiled at her through wet lashes. The two were partway up the stairs leading to her apartment before Sterling got his bearings. At that point he had no choice but to follow.

Heat surged from the warm apartment as the woman and boy entered. Stepping inside, Sterling saw Tyler make a beeline past the couch toward a table brimming with trophies.

"Tyler, be careful! Set that down. Carefully!" Lunging, Sterling righted the statue seconds before it crashed. He noted that the delicate top was a pair of crossed cue sticks and a cue ball.

Startled by his dad's sudden move, the boy again burst into tears. Sterling replaced the trophy and dropped to one knee to hug his son. "I didn't mean to yell, but I'm sure these represent many a hard-won game. Imagine how terrible Mark would feel if he came home and found one of his treasures lying in pieces on the floor."

Megan's laughter bubbled over them as she closed the door Sterling had left ajar. "Mark couldn't care less. They're my trophies. About all they're good for is collecting dust. Let Tyler play with them if he wants. I'm sorry I don't have any toys. I should invest in some in case my cousins ever come to visit."

Sterling scanned the dozen or so trophies. It wasn't that he didn't believe her, but he played pool and knew it was an exacting game. And yes, Megan Benton's name was engraved on every plaque.

"They're pretty," Tyler ventured, running his fingers over the marble base of the largest trophy.

Sterling rose. "If you've only been here two months, you didn't win these here."

"No, but some of us shoot pool Wednesday nights

at one of the local pubs. New blood is always welcome if you're interested."

"I don't expect to have all that much free time." He was pleased that denial sounded firm.

"Uh...okay." Pulling back, Megan pointed to the kitchen where she'd just snapped on a light. "I'll start the cocoa. I want Tyler to be able to take his time. It's two now," she said, checking her watch. "I have to dress soon for my three o'clock shift."

"Right. Mark told Lauren you work swing until next week."

Megan felt his looming presence fill her kitchen, which until this moment she'd considered roomy. Sterling Dodge had a way of shrinking any space he occupied. She hadn't meant to be rude about changing the subject to something other than her skill at pool. It always seemed, that her winning so consistently drove men away. Many a date had ended abruptly once the guy got a load of those trophies or saw her in action. Her mom and aunt suggested Megan store them at home. Perversity kept her dragging them along. It was probably dumb, but she'd take a second look at any man who didn't feel threatened by those hunks of marble and brass.

Tyler wandered into the kitchen. Without fear or hesitation, he climbed onto a chair and leaned on the table. "I like your part of the house better than ours, Megan. Can we paint our kitchen yellow, Daddy?"

Sterling swept the room in a glance. "This is nice," he mumbled. Truthfully, the place was so homey it made him nervous. He'd never changed a thing in the home he'd inherited from his grandparents, who were very formal people.

"When we get moved into our house on the island, I'll hire a decorator to give the place some life. We can't paint here, Tyler. Our apartment downstairs belongs to Captain Meade. I doubt he'd approve of tenants painting."

Megan set a plate of cookies on the table. The aroma of cinnamon wafting from the plate was unmistakable. "I painted my place. Hank didn't mind. He renovated the house into two living spaces to rent out after his wife died. That it was a long time ago. He can't bear to come back here where they raised six kids. He has a rental agent and he likes tenants who'll do some upkeep."

"I know that's what the rental agreement says. All the same, we're not going to live downstairs long enough to invest time or money painting."

"But Daddy." Tyler tugged Sterling's sleeve. "The man at the café said our island house won't be ready till May."

"That long?" Megan turned from the stove where she was warming milk. She'd already set out three mugs. "Is the interior worse than when you did your original walk-through?"

"I bought via a virtual online tour. The problem isn't the extent of damage so much as the fact that everyone who does repair seems to be on vacation until mid-to-late spring."

"Wow, you were brave to buy without actually seeing the place." Megan took the pan off the stove, stirred in vanilla, then poured chocolate into the mugs. Steam curled around her face, bringing a sheen to her skin. She took marshmallows from a canister and topped the drinks with whipped cream.

"Yummy," Tyler exclaimed, licking his lips and rubbing his stomach. This made his dad and Megan laugh.

"Let it cool a minute," she cautioned. "Have a seat," she invited Sterling, at the same moment he said, "What do you say to Lieutenant Benton, son?"

Tyler turned big eyes toward his father. "Who's Loo'tnant Benton?"

"I am," Megan said, tapping his pug nose. "But if it's okay with your dad, I'd rather you both called me Megan. I'm only Lieutenant when I put on my uniform."

Tyler bent over his mug and stuck out his tongue to lick off some of the whipped cream. "My mama wore a uniform to work."

"She did?" Megan stood at the end of the table and said the first thing that popped into her head. "Was your mom in the military?"

"Is that like a police person? That's what she was, huh, Daddy?"

Sterling hadn't sat down. Although he held his mug, he tensed visibly at his son's words.

Megan missed nothing as she set two cookies on a napkin in front of Tyler. He wasn't shy and picked one up, taking a huge bite. "This is yummy," he announced, breaking into a huge, sugar-flecked grin.

"Blow on your cocoa, Tyler," Sterling said. "We have to leave soon and let Lieutenant Benton… ah… Megan prepare for work."

Ignoring his father's edict, Tyler ate the first cookie and bit into the second. Brushing sugar crystals and cinnamon from his lips, he gazed adoringly at Megan. "These are the best cookies I've ever ate. Is that what you do at your job? Make cookies?" the boy asked with no small measure of hope.

"Afraid not. I'm in the Coast Guard, Tyler. I go out on a big ship every day and help keep people safe on other boats if they happen to run into trouble."

Rocking to and fro on his knees as he continued to munch the crisp cookie, Tyler bobbed his head. "So, you're like a police person on the water? Like on a TV show Joel watches? They wear swimsuits and zoom on a Jet Ski."

"Well, I don't ride a Jet Ski. The water around here is too cold. My crew and another team saved a boy's life last night. It was pretty spectacular, if I do say so."

"Dangerous," Sterling said in a chilly voice. Facing the boy, he said, "Tyler, finish your drink."

Dodge set his empty mug on the counter. Unfortunately, he pictured Megan Benton cavorting with a crew of young, muscle-bound studs. They all resembled Rio Amado, Blythe's partner.

Megan felt the sudden drop in temperature resulting from Sterling's frosty demeanor. Discussing danger obviously bothered him. She rose, slipped silently past him and took out a plastic bag she began to fill with cookies. "Tyler, I'll give you some of these to share with Joel and Lauren. Uh, if it's okay with your dad?" She darted him a hesitant glance. "Mark and I always hit the cookie jar and milk carton first thing when we came in from school."

The boy, busy slurping down his drink, left his dad to respond to Megan. "I'm sure even at seventeen and fourteen, Lauren and Joel still won't refuse a treat. It's kind of you to share your cookies with us, but it's not necessary. When the kids get home today, we're going grocery-shopping."

"Megan's cookies are way better than what you buy

in the store, Daddy." Tyler, who'd finished his cocoa, slid off the chair and reached for the plastic bag. He flashed Megan a broad grin through lips smeared with chocolate and whipped cream.

She was saved from comment of any kind when Mark breezed in. "Hey, guys! Lauren, Joel and I shared a ferry across. They said your apartment looked dark and wondered where you two were." He addressed Sterling.

"I didn't think they'd make the two o'clock ferry. They didn't leave class early, did they?"

Mark shook his head. "The ferry captain has teachers who are regulars on his run. He waits for them to come aboard."

"Tyler, we have to go now," Sterling said. "Lauren invited Mark to dinner tonight. If we don't go buy groceries, he'll have mighty slim pickings."

Megan waited until Sterling and Tyler had left to tease Mark about his dinner date. "So, you're tired of cooking already? How'd you wangle an invitation?"

"I'm taking my laptop down there. Lauren wants to check out graphic design programs. I can't believe she's still in high school. She acts much more mature," Mark muttered, sneaking two cookies from the jar.

"Again, may I warn you about getting too tight with our neighbors? Dodge made it plenty plain he'd rather not be friendly."

"And that's why you were feeding him and his kid a snack?" Mark yanked on one of Megan's stray curls.

"Tyler's sweet. He's the only reason I had them up, Mark. Well, Tyler actually invited himself. Dodge couldn't wait for an excuse to leave. Which reminds me, did Lauren mention that his wife was a cop?"

"Huh? No, they didn't say anything. Lauren and Joel

don't think too highly of Dodge. Want me to pump them about his wife—their sister?"

"Certainly not. It's none of my business, Mark. None of *our* business."

"Okay. Say, I think I shot some cool pictures today." he called as Megan hurried to her room to dress for work. "Do you have a few minutes to take a gander? Gram doesn't have a computer, so I said I'd print off a set and mail them to her."

"Oh, you talked to Mona? When?"

"I phoned her from the island. She's booked a big trip."

"No kidding? That's a first. Has she ever left Benton Corner before?"

"And..." he added, then held his breath. "She's gonna pop in here for a visit."

"What?" Megan's bedroom door flew open. "Mark, did I hear right? Mona is traveling up *here?*"

"Ma-ark!" She yelled again, this time marching right up to his bedroom door. He'd disappeared inside and she heard the faint click of the lock. It was a trick he used to pull when they were kids. He'd unload a bombshell—something he knew was guaranteed to send their mom into a tizzy—then he'd shut himself in the bathroom or his bedroom for an hour or so, until he knew their mother's temper had simmered down.

Megan frowned her watch. She didn't have an hour. She was due at the station in twenty minutes. Determined not to act as juvenile as he was by shouting at him through the door, she returned to her room and finished dressing. Why would Mona travel all this way? Ha! Megan would believe it when she saw it.

CHAPTER FIVE

ON THE SHORT DRIVE to work, Megan wondered whether Mona would actually visit. How would they all get along? There'd been a time in her life that Megan thought she wanted more than anything to live with her grandparents. Toby Benton, now dead, had built a farm-implement manufacturing company from the ground up. Over the years, he'd invested behind the scenes in almost every business in the small Missouri town where they were literally considered king and queen. Megan's mother often said the elder Bentons owned the town and everyone in it. It wasn't until she'd matured a lot that Megan understood that wasn't a good thing. Toby used debt to manipulate and control others, while Mona acted as if a life of luxury was her due. Not only was she entitled to it, in her view, so was anyone born a Benton. She dressed like a fashion plate, put on airs and had housekeepers and gardeners at her beck and call.

Lips pursed, Megan imagined three adults sharing an apartment that up to this week she'd had to herself. The three *M*s she thought with a scowl as she backed into a parking place at the station. *Megan, Mark and Mona.* Of course she'd had a hand in naming her grandchildren.

Depending on when Mona arrived—*if* she arrived—

and how long she planned to stay, maybe they could put her up at the Grand Hotel on the island. Megan's commander's wife had described the hotel as elegant, a vacation spot of presidents. At least five of them had visited there, Mrs. Donovan had said. The biggest problem was that the historic hotel was only open from May to October. But Megan couldn't imagine Mona wanting to visit until the weather warmed up. Just now a north wind sliced through Megan's down jacket as she climbed out and locked her pickup.

Seconds after she'd breezed into the station, Mona and everything else was forgotten.

"Hey, Benton, shake a leg," shouted one of her crewmates. He was zipping into a bulky set of coveralls. "We've got an ore boat on fire out in the channel. Ten to fifteen men on board. The caller said she's burning like beeswax."

Megan grabbed her gear and followed him out and down the slippery dock to their ship, which was ready to cast off. She wasn't the last to hop aboard, but close to it. Her heart revved up noticeably, the way it always did when her team faced an emergency.

She'd only ever seen iron ore flatboats in the distance as they chugged down-channel, laden with tons of metal causing them to ride low in the water. The ore, mined in the upper western peninsula, was transported by boat through the locks and down to railcars that would carry it to steel mills.

If this fire had flared in the ship's hold and men were trapped, the fumes alone could kill them.

Their commander summoned his crew. Donovan gave orders as their boat picked up speed and raced toward the scene.

They saw black smoke belching into the atmosphere even before their spotter zeroed his binoculars in on the distressed vessel. Fire on shipboard always sent a shiver of fear through the crew slated for a rescue. So much could go wrong. Metal boat parts got hot. Melting paint emitted toxic fumes. Explosions could blow them all out of the water.

Fortunately, the lake was fairly calm this afternoon. As they approached and cut their engines, Megan identified three lifeboats already bobbing in the water, drifting well away from the smoking craft. "Men in rafts starboard," she bellowed.

Lending her muscle to that of two petty officers, they roped up sailors from the first lifeboat.

"Port engine blew out," gasped a burly workman whose face was covered in soot. "Torkelson there, and McMinn, both suffered second-degree burns on their faces and arms. You got a doc on board?"

Megan sounded the signal to bring the chief health service tech running. "We're all trained in first aid," she assured the anxious man. "Dirk Richards is an EMT. Here he is now. I'll leave you in his capable hands." Coiling her grapple, she raced over to help haul up the men in the third lifeboat. Other crew members had already brought up everyone in number two.

A whistle squealed and Donovan's voice floated hollowly over the speaker. "We've got a fireboat from Alpena two minutes out. She'd been conducting routine exercises near Forty-Mile Point. She's best equipped. We'll assist."

A collective sigh went up from the crew. The fireboat was better prepared to douse the flames. But even after the fireboat came on the scene, the big ore ship burned in the early darkness that blanketed the bay. The crew was always sad to see a fellow ship destroyed.

Megan and the rest of the crew were kept busy tending burn victims, and were also assigned to keep onlookers circling the site in private motorboats at a safe distance. Often secondary accidents caused by gawkers—derisively known as "lookie-loos"—gave the Coast Guard more to do than an initial emergency. Media clogged the sky with helicopters. Anything like this drew news-hunters like flies. The *whop-whop* of their rotors made it difficult for guardsmen to exchange needed information with one another.

As quickly as possible, Donovan called for a tug to push the burned-out hulk away from the busy traffic lanes of the main channel. The cutter Megan served on escorted the tug to a less commercial dock than those at Mackinaw City.

After the ore boat was well and safely tied off, and the crew had treated and transported the last of the injured sailors to medical personnel in Mackinaw City, their cutter returned to its station.

Although her muscles ached, Megan felt they'd done a fine day's work. Commander Donovan debriefed his personnel, including what their role would've been had the fireboat not been in the area. They all counted themselves lucky to have had the fireboat handy nearby. The next time they might not be so fortunate. That knowledge had a sobering effect.

The remainder of their shift was thankfully quiet. A majority of the rescues Megan had worked on before transferring to St. Ignace were pleasure-boat accidents in the warm gulf waters off the coast of Alabama. She now knew some of the problems that arose on the more massive ships traveling the Great Lakes, and that knowledge shot her heart into her throat each time a call came in. At the end of this particular shift, she felt totally drained, and looked forward to going home to relax.

Her most persistent pool challenger, Ensign Hamish Tucker, snatched away the ball cap she'd just removed from the rack as she prepared to leave for the night. "Did you miss me this week, Lieutenant? I've been in Grand Haven training for deepwater rescue."

Megan battled the teaser for her cap, which was the expected reaction. "Now, why would I miss somebody's who's such a pain in the ass?" She was feeling cocky because she again possessed her cap. "Too bad a week in Coast Guard City didn't teach you more than obnoxious grade-school pranks, Ham." She tugged the bill of her regulation hat down low over her forehead. He wouldn't have messed with her on duty, but off duty they were like squabbling siblings.

"I didn't spend all my time at the training facility. A couple of guys I knew from a previous assignment are ace pool players. I learned enough new tricks from them to take you on. How about it, tigress, wanna give me a crack at beating you tonight? A buck a ball?" he crooned, diving in his pocket to pull out a wad of cash.

"Sorry, I can't." She was tempted to part him from his money again, but decided she'd better go home and pin Mark down as to exactly when she needed to brace for their grandmother's visit. "You weren't here when I told everyone my brother, Mark, is in town. Make it another night, Ham, and I'll have Mark meet us at the pub."

"He play as good as you?"

"No one plays as good as me." She laughed. "Although, if you're a pool shark now, maybe I'll need moral support."

The other men gathered around, hooting at the ensign for being stupid enough to take Megan on again. Elkhorn had already lost more than a day's wages to her.

"Guys, just because she hasn't been beaten since she moved here doesn't mean she can stay at the top of her game forever." Ham, grinning wickedly, blew on his fingers and scraped them across his shirt in a bragging manner.

"Tucker, you're so full of it," shouted one of the other lieutenants. "Our Megan will whip your ass—and we'll make you eat the cue ball."

They were joking, but she knew there wasn't one among them who wouldn't love to see someone topple her record. She knew, because word discreetly circulated each time there was a rotation out and someone new joined the team. Still, they were a fun group of guys. Like at her last duty station, though, there wasn't an officer among them she'd care to date. Or maybe it was more that she'd seen how dating among a crew could get awkward.

When she arrived home, Mark wasn't there. "Fine," she grumbled, tossing her jacket and boots into her bedroom. She'd forgone a few hours of recreation in town, and where was he? Still downstairs? *That must've been some dinner.*

Thinking of food made her stomach growl. She generally had a healthy appetite after a rescue. But this late she tended to toss together scrambled eggs and pancakes, or make French toast. Tonight she settled on pancakes, electing to mix enough batter to serve them the following morning, too.

She'd poured dollops onto a sizzling hot grill when she heard Mark bounding up the stairs. Sure enough, the front door flew open, sending a blast of night air all the way to the kitchen. A gust that shivered the March page on her calendar.

"I'm in the kitchen," she called, as the door slammed shut.

Mark bustled in, setting his laptop on the table, all the while whistling one of Sheryl Crow's newest tunes.

"You're sure a happy camper," Megan noted dryly.

"Ouch. You're not, I take it. Bad day chasing pirates and scallawags?"

She looked up from flipping the pancakes. One fell off the spatula, and she swore.

"Oops, maybe I'll go straight to my room and leave you be," Mark mused as his sister scraped the half-cooked pancake off the stovetop and plopped it in the sink.

"You startled me with that reference to pirates. The Coast Guard does track smugglers now and then. Not often, thank God."

"I was being cute, sis. It's what Sterling said tonight when Lauren pointed out a news article on your Coast Guard unit." Hefting his laptop, Mark started out the door.

"Oh, stay," she said, motioning him back. "You could fix us hot chocolate."

"Sterling also asked if you had stock in the chocolate company." Mark deposited his computer on the counter. Sidling around Megan, he lit the burner under a saucepan of milk.

Megan raised one eyebrow. "How did you come to be discussing my career and my chocolate habit with Dodge?"

"The career came up because Lauren showed him that news article. And Tyler apparently bugged his dad to buy cocoa at the store. Then he complained at dinner that Sterling's hot chocolate wasn't nearly as good as yours. I said you had the advantage of making that drink since we were kids."

"It is Mom's recipe. Don't you remember waking up at night and following that luscious smell to the kitchen? Back then, I didn't realize Mom couldn't sleep whenever she fretted over Dad, who was usually out carousing."

Mark stopped stirring the milk. "I'd have been happier never learning that. I loved him."

"Me, too. But that doesn't change what he was. Dad was spoiled and selfish. He wasn't a good husband to Mom. Or a very good father to us."

"I'm aware of that. But…he died. I felt guilty for not loving him more. Not loving him enough. Mom played into my guilt, because she so clearly didn't love him. Should she really have let us kids know how she felt?"

Megan felt tiny frown lines forming between her eyes. "I think so. But I also think she did love him, at first anyway. What did they teach in your child psych classes? Isn't honesty always best?"

He shrugged as Megan sat and began buttering her pancakes. "I guess I chose child psychology hoping to figure out our family. For every kind of screwup, there's a dozen schools of thought on the correct method for handling a kid's psyche. I was left wondering if there's such a thing as a normal, happy marriage that produces normal, happy kids."

"Wow. I think this is too deep a subject for me at… almost midnight," she said, tapping the face of her watch. "Instead, why don't we talk about whether or not you and Lauren found a school she likes?" Megan said, layering her scrambled eggs into a sort of sandwich between the pancakes.

Mark poured their mugs full of cocoa. He didn't bother with vanilla, marshmallows or whipped cream.

"Lauren's dead set on going back to New York, so it didn't take long to check out schools. She e-mailed for information on three she thought would accept her GPA."

"Not a good student, huh?"

"I gather she used to be get straight As. She and Joel are prime examples of kids from a dysfunctional family. Their parents were murdered after coming home from a play, when they surprised burglars. Lauren was at a friend's house, and Joel at a sleepover. They didn't have time to recover from the loss before their older sister, their guardian, married Dodge."

Megan paused with the fork partway to her lips. "And now their sister's dead, too? How sad. Anyone's grades would slip."

"That's not the half of it." Mark toyed with his cup. "Blythe, that's the sister, left Lauren in charge of Joel and Tyler a lot, because Blythe wanted to escape from a bad marriage. Lauren never saw him hit her sister or even yell at her, but Lauren sensed there was a lot wrong in the marriage. She sheltered Joel and gave him a lot of freedom. He fell in with a gang and started ditching classes. Lauren skipped class, too, trying to make sure he didn't get into real trouble. As a result, her grades tanked."

Megan scoffed. "Looking at Joel, I'd say she didn't have much influence."

"We don't know she didn't save him from a worse fate. We weren't there, Megan. Only Lauren and Joel were. Well, and Tyler. It's a wonder he's not messed up, too. Honestly, I have to question whether any marriage works."

"How can you ask that? Camp's parents have been happily married for almost fifty years. He and Mom are as deliriously in love as when they got married eleven years ago. The same goes for Aunt Sherry and Uncle Garrett."

"If they're all such shining examples, why do *you* avoid becoming involved with anyone?"

"What do you mean?" Megan studied him over the top of her mug.

"Dating. One reason Mom didn't totally throw a hissy about me coming to visit is that she's hoping I'll help you find some nice guy, and then you'll send me home where she thinks I belong. She's sure your competitive spirit scares off any good men."

"What?" Megan choked on her pancake.

"Are you going to sit there and swear your insatiable need to prove you're better at pool than a man isn't a side effect of Mom's messed-up marriage to our real dad?"

Megan sputtered again. "Tell Mom—better yet, I'll tell her the next time I phone—that *good* men wouldn't go out of their way to avoid honest competition. They wouldn't feel threatened. Anyway, she's a fine one to talk. Isn't competition what threw her together with Camp in the first place? She wanted to prove modern women could survive wagon-train travel as well as our great-great grandmothers did."

Mark rocked back in his chair. "Touché!"

"Aren't you the cynic." She vaulted from her own chair and carried her dishes to the sink, where she scrubbed them vigorously before putting them in the dishwasher. "For crying out loud," she snapped, "doesn't Mom have anything better to do than to fuss over my love life?"

"It's the lack of one she's concerned about."

"You went along with this? Why? Because it takes the spotlight off you? Maybe I'll sic her on you again. Tell her she ought to worry about her *son's* dating habits."

"I don't have any problem finding dates."

"Right! Like Lauren Atwater? Don't you imagine Mom would think you're a little old to be lusting over a seventeen-year-old girl?"

"I'm not lusting," he snorted. "Anyway, Lauren's eighteen."

Megan paused to lick chocolate off her upper lip. "No, this morning I'm sure Sterling said she was seventeen, and Joel fourteen."

"Lauren told me she was eighteen. Why would she lie?"

Megan debated whether or not to mention one obvious reason. Lauren was unhappy. Maybe she was looking for a way to return to New York. In Alabama, a Coast Guard officer Megan knew had dated and been intimate with a girl who'd told him she was of legal age. The pair were caught by her father in a motel room with beer the guardsman had bought, to say nothing of their being naked. The mess resulted in a costly mistake for the guy, in terms of his career and his future. She'd hate to see Mark trapped like that.

But for goodness' sake, her brother was twenty-three, and he had a master's degree in psychology. Surely he was too smart to get entangled in an inappropriate relationship.

"Let's move off the subject of our neighbors, Mark. How about if we talk instead about Mona's proposed visit? What's the deal?"

A wary look crossed Mark's face. "How PO'd at me are you?"

"Plenty, at first. You knew I'd eventually cool off. I started thinking how ironic it is that we seem to have reversed roles from when we were kids. The summer after Dad died, when we went on the wagon train with Mom, I championed Mona and Toby. You saw through them. Now we're on opposite sides. So, give. To my knowledge, Mona's never traveled farther away from Benton Corners than St. Louis for her spa treatments. What's with her sudden desire to see the world? Especially my part of the world?"

"I probably convinced her, Megan. At least, I prodded her to see what lies beyond Benton Corners. She's certainly not stuck there. The businesses run themselves. She's already volunteered on every charity board in the valley. Why not travel?"

Megan refilled their mugs. She sipped thoughtfully. "Okay, I'll buy that. When's she coming and how long is she staying?"

"You're gonna love this. She arrives April Fools' Day at the Chippewa County International Airport. She's staying three days. I'll drive her back to the airport. Then she flies to Chicago, meets her tour group and off she goes around the world."

"Three days I can probably handle." Megan flipped the calendar to the next month. "I should be able to take a day off to go to the airport with you."

"No need. I invited Lauren. We'll drive on into Sault Ste. Marie. She needs to write a paper for her Michigan history class. The Soo locks, which she's never seen, is one of the suggested sites. I'll take pictures while we're there."

"When did you make these plans?" Megan knew her tone spoke of hurt feelings.

"Tonight. I didn't think you'd be able to get off work. Plus, from the way you yelled at me this afternoon, I wasn't sure you'd want to ride that far with Mona."

"You might have given me the option."

"Sorry. I wanted to make Mona's visit as easy on you as possible. In fact, I'll give her my bed and crash on the couch."

"No. I already decided she can have my room with the bigger bath. Do you really want her spreading cosmetics all over your counter?"

"Good point. Well, that's settled. I'm going to upload the photos I shot today. Are you heading straight to bed?"

"I'll read for a while, so don't worry about leaving your lights on."

Mark jumped up, set his cup in the sink and disappeared from the kitchen whistling the same tune as when he'd bounded in earlier.

Trying not to be miffed at him, Megan finished her drink. It didn't pass her notice that Mark hadn't reconsidered and invited her to go to the locks, which she'd never seen, either. She wondered if Sterling approved of their jaunt. Lauren might have convinced Mark she was eighteen, but Megan knew what her legal guardian had said. She'd find a way to clear up the truth of Lauren's age the next time they met.

Or not. She wasn't Mark's keeper, for pity's sake. Yet, she was so annoyed she phoned home, expecting her mother to commiserate. But when Camp said Emily was asleep, Megan regaled him with stories about her job, instead.

The next night she joined her crew at the pub after work. Megan made a halfhearted excuse for her brother's not showing up. She hadn't invited him. Not that there'd been an opportunity. He'd worked late on his pictures, then slept until one o'clock. As she came back from a run, he shot out of the apartment carrying his camera, never telling her his destination. If that was how Mark wanted to be during his visit, fine by her.

Except that her still-stinging feelings affected her game of nine ball. She almost let Hamish beat her. *Almost.* In the nick of time, she buckled down and pulled out a win.

SPRING HAD FINALLY DECIDED to show its face in Missouri on the night Garrett Lock picked up his wife, Sherilyn, after work. They'd been running in opposite directions for months. He planned to surprise her with a romantic dinner at a new and exclusive restaurant in town.

"Don't you look spiffy," she said as he darted around to open her door. They kissed, and while she would've made it short because she had something on her mind, Garrett leaned into the car, unwilling to break the kiss.

"Hey, it's not our anniversary yet," she chided, narrowing her eyes. "You've got your brand-new suit on *and* the sexy cologne Keith gave you for Christmas. I thought you were saving it for a special occasion."

"I am, wife! We have reservations at Chez Blanc."

Sherry gaped as her husband slid back under the

steering wheel. "Oh, but I look a wreck." She drew both hands through her heavy mane of dark hair. "I worked like crazy all day. Not only that, I met Emily for lunch and she barfed all over everywhere. I'm not sure I didn't get some on my skirt."

Garrett grimaced. "Well, if that's not conversation designed to ruin an expensive meal out, I don't know what is."

"Sorry." She leaned across the console, framed his rugged cheeks with her hands and bestowed a better kiss. "You're a fantastic man for planning an evening out. Just stop at the house and I'll change into something more suitable."

"Hon, you were an hour late coming out of the Hub." That was what everyone on campus called the crisis center Sherry ran. "If we go by the house, we'll lose our table. You know Chez Blanc is so popular it takes two weeks to get a reservation. Besides, if we pop home, one or the other of the kids will snag you to help with their homework or their music or some special project."

Sinking back against the seat, Sherry gnawed her bottom lip. "The kids are all feeling overwhelmed. You act like you think I should refuse to help them."

He drummed his fingers on the wheel. "The house is never *not* bedlam anymore."

"Is that what this is about, Garrett? You want me to play the heavy and make the kids drop some of their extracurricular activities? They all love what they're doing."

He uttered a sigh. "What about *our* extracurricular activities? Or haven't you noticed we have none? How long has it been since we've indulged in a quiet dinner alone? How long since we even climbed into bed at the same time?"

Sherry picked at chipped nail polish and realized it'd been six weeks since her last manicure. She clenched her hands, then raked back her hair. "It's not my fault, Garrett. You've had one evening meeting after another since you became vice-chancellor. You missed Shannon's last recital, and Gavin's ball game."

"I see. You're still pissed that the board of regents bypassed you again when they tapped me for another promotion. I can't keep apologizing, Sherry. Most days I'd gladly give you or anyone else this damned job." A swath of his sun-streaked blond hair fell over his forehead, and Sherry noticed several new streaks of silver.

"I'm every bit as qualified as Ramon Lopez."

"You know hiring Ramon was strictly political. Wellmont's enrollment is declining, and he brings experience from a big ten school to the table, plus a track record in recruiting from Hispanic communities."

"It's not fair, Garrett. I work hard. And Emily. Even if they didn't pick me, what about her? She's put in so many hours these last weeks, she's made herself sick."

"Camp said she's feeling sick because she had a huge fight with her ex-mom-in-law."

"When did you see him?"

"At lunch yesterday." Garrett pulled off the freeway and swung into the crowded parking lot at the restaurant.

"I hope no one from the college sees me," Sherry said. "It's your fault I look grungy and less than appropriate for a representative of Wellmont College, Mr. Vice-Chancellor."

"You look gorgeous. There isn't anyone on or off campus who can hold a candle to you."

"Flattery will get you everywhere," she murmured as he turned off the engine.

"That's what I'm banking on."

She stopped with her hand on the door latch. "Okay, Garrett. What's up? This is about more than us having an intimate evening alone, isn't it?"

He waggled his eyebrows. "Sherry, it can wait until after we're seated."

"What can?" She jammed a finger in his ribs as he handed her from the car.

Garrett ran a finger around to loosen his collar. "Uh—Carla's on me again for allowing Keith to work for Doc Jackson over Easter break." Carla was Garrett's ex-wife.

"Oh, but his heart's set on it, Garrett. And it's great training for someone determined to be a veterinarian. Which you know Keith is."

"I know, but after talking to Camp, and hearing how Emily's so worked up over trying to convince Mark to return from the hinterland, I thought maybe we could send Keith to Michigan over Easter break. To see if he has any luck getting Mark to come home. Plus, it'll give his mother time to chill out."

"I'm not sure we want to get mixed up in the Benton-Campbell brouhaha."

"Why not? We're family. Families ought to stick together."

"You're so full of it, Lock. Like you'd push for this if it wasn't temporarily going get Carla off your back?"

"Just temporarily, you figure?" He made three grabs at the door only to have it opened by the maître d'.

"Keith will never give up his dream of being a vet. And Carla will always complain that it's somehow our fault he didn't choose banking."

"I'll settle for temporary if it shuts Carla up long

enough to let me get through the worst of my budget meetings. Sherry, hon, I really need your help convincing my stubborn son to go on this little jaunt. He listens to you."

"When push comes to shove, this is really all about your job. I probably don't have the insensitivity required for your old post. I'd never sacrifice my family for Wellmont. I see why you went to the trouble of arranging this evening, Garrett." She linked her arms around her purse, looking unhappy.

His wife lagged behind, but Garrett hurried her along behind the tuxedoed maître d', who'd stopped at a secluded nook where candles provided the only light.

They sat, and neither spoke while he placed snowy white napkins across their laps. He withdrew, and the sommelier appeared to take their wine order. In the lull after he left, Sherry fussed with the silverware. "You could've saved your money, Garrett. I'll talk to Keith. When haven't I supported you? And Em does want Mark to give up this photography nonsense and get back here before Ramon Lopez hires someone else for the counseling job."

Garrett cleared his throat, drawing Sherry's attention. "Last week in the middle of all the chaos at the house, I realized I don't tell you often enough how much I appreciate you, sweetheart." Smoothly, he popped the lid on a small white box. The flickers from the candle heightened the warmth of a gleaming citrine ring set in a twinkling circle of diamonds. "I hope you also know I told the selection committee you were the best candidate to take over my old job. We had a shouting match. I was outshouted." He set the box in her hand and brushed a finger over her quivering lower lip. "I love you, Sherry. Exactly as you are. Just…keep… being you."

Suddenly not caring how she was dressed, Sherry slid around the booth and delivered a kiss sure to make everyone nearby envy Wellmont's new vice-chancellor.

DURING THE NEXT FEW DAYS, MEGAN passed Sterling Dodge when one or other of them was coming or going. The opportunity to bring up the matter of Lauren's true age didn't present itself. Either the girl and her brother were with Dodge as they headed out, or he was entering his apartment and merely waved in response to Megan's greeting.

Thursday, she was shocked to glance up from doing her maintenance check of the Jayhawk helicopter to see Mark and Lauren standing on the gangway. Her brother was snapping pictures of her at work, and Megan felt very self-conscious.

"Hey, what do you think you're doing? You can't come on post property without clearance."

Mark lowered his camera. "The gate guard gave us passes, sis. He knows I'm your brother. He double-checked our identification."

Megan pulled a greasy rag from her back pocket and wiped her hands. "All right, then. But don't take pictures of me. I must look a fright." Some time ago she'd felt the wind loosen the ribbon tying back her hair. Now she attempted to recapture the wayward strands.

"Do you like taking helicopter engines apart?" Lauren asked. It was pretty plain from the way she tiptoed around the greasy equipment on the deck that Megan's job wasn't something the teenager would like doing.

Acting the gentleman, Mark took Lauren's hand and guided her through the maze of engine parts. He didn't, however, give his sister a chance to speak for herself. "Megan chose this occupation because she got all bummed in high school when our stepdad and rebuilt a car and he didn't let her help."

"That's a big fat lie," Megan exclaimed. "By then I'd already joined ROTC and you know it, Mark Benton. I chose this field because a search-and-rescue team pulled Camp from the bottom of a canyon."

He shrugged. "Is this how you really spend your days? Do you make up all the harrowing tales you scare Mom with? She phoned today after you left for work. She said you relayed quite a rescue story to Camp the other night."

"Yeah. Mom had already hit the hay. I asked him if she was sick, but he never really answered me. Do you think Mom's okay? She used to stay up half the night doing stuff."

"She sounded okay. Worried about you pulling guys off a burning boat. I said I didn't know anything about that."

"I told Camp it was a routine mission. He shouldn't have scared Mom like that. I'll call this weekend and ease her mind."

Two of Megan's team members, who were also helping with the chopper, came over to meet the visitors. They added their version of the rescue. As young men were prone to do when they wanted to dazzle an attractive female like Lauren, they built the story into something that would be the envy of a scriptwriter for an Indiana Jones film.

They succeeded in impressing Lauren. Her pretty blue eyes widened appreciatively. "What you do sounds even more dangerous than the undercover work my sister did as a New York City cop."

"Certainly as difficult," piped up Jim Elkhorn from over Megan's shoulder. He'd embellished the tale most.

Megan swatted his cap. "Elkhorn, you exaggerate so much it's a crime. Tell them the way it really was. As rescues go, ours lately have been pretty easy. During the last one, no one got wet—except for when the ore boat's life rafts dripped on us after we pulled them on deck."

"Do people pleasure-boat around here?" Mark asked. "Lauren and I are thinking of renting a boat this weekend to take a run up the coast." He paused to remove a photo card from his camera and install another.

The two men on Megan's crew were filled with advice on the best places to buy or rent motor launches. She busied herself with the Jayhawk's engine. Megan wouldn't embarrass her brother in front of the guys and a girl he so clearly liked, but she worried that someone born and raised in the Midwest didn't know squat about boating. Definitely not enough to take on the unpredictable waters of Mackinac Strait.

But she had no idea how to educate him without appearing the preachy older sibling.

Her commander provided the means when she received her assignment for the remainder of the week. Donovan gave Megan the task of teaching boating safety classes to area high schools. The Coast Guard offered them every year, but this was Megan's first time as an instructor. She'd just ask Mark to go and help her carry equipment. That way, he could pick up pointers on safe boating along with the students. She patted herself on the back for being so clever.

CHAPTER SIX

MARK GRUMBLED ABOUT HELPING Megan with her class until she said something about the first one being at the island school. Her brother did such a fast turnabout, it didn't take a genius to figure he thought it'd be a chance to show off in front of Lauren Atwater. Honestly, twenty-three-year-old guys were so transparent. Megan considered reversing the order and going to Mackinaw City schools first, then St. Ignace, and leaving the island for last. Deciding that was childish, she packed her cases with life jackets, life belts, and a doughnut preserver, and led the way onto the early afternoon ferry.

The captain greeted Mark by name. On the short sail to the island, Megan watched her brother interact with various locals. A small community of regulars. He seemed to know them all well enough to inquire about their jobs and families. But then, he'd been riding with them for two weeks now. Obviously, his sociable nature appealed to these people, and for the first time, she saw Mark not as her kid brother but as a vital, interesting young man.

The school's officials expected them. The high school students were already assembled at one end of the gym. Megan realized immediately after she began her spiel that a majority of the students had heard the lecture so often they were bored. It was easy to spot newcomers, like the Atwaters. New kids listened attentively and asked questions. And to be honest, kids who'd grown up as islanders could probably give Megan some pointers.

Her most avid listener shot up a hand when she asked for volunteers to help demonstrate the lifesaving devices. *Joel Atwater.* Megan almost didn't recognize him. Gone were his spiky bleached hair and all but one discreet earring. He wore a flannel shirt and cargo pants with lace-up hiking boots, a clone of the other boys in his class. Not only that, he hung around afterward and tucked the brochure on safety, as well as two she'd handed out on joining ROTC, into his backpack.

Megan saw that Joel had filled a page with notes, which he came prepared to add to. "I wanna buy a boat, Lieutenant Benton. What's the most reliable kind, and where's a good place to get a used one?"

Mark generously jumped in to provide the information he'd been given by Megan's crewmates. She deliberately tromped hard on her brother's foot. "Ouch!" Mark shut up and glared as he limped over to the cases and duffel bags.

"Joel, have you discussed this plan to buy a boat with your guardian?"

A thundercloud slid over the boy's face. "It's my dough. Sterling's not the boss of me or Lauren. He's got no right to say what I do with the money my folks left me."

Megan regretted having brought up their brother-in-law, as Joel instantly took off. Not only that, Mark laid into her, too.

"Sis, you've got no business meddling in the Atwaters' affairs."

"I wasn't meddling…exactly. Joel's awfully young to make a decision like buying a boat on his own."

"Have you forgotten how we felt about Camp's interference in our lives when we were Joel's age?"

"I haven't forgotten. Being bratty got us in a potload of trouble." She yanked up the largest of the cases and slung the rope handle over her shoulder. "Technically, Mark, Sterling Dodge *is* Joel's boss."

"I thought you didn't like him. Why stick up for the guy, Megan?"

"Mark, are we fighting because of our neighbors?"

He stopped at the door and passed her the second case. "We are. Because you're sticking your nose into something you know nothing about. You don't really need my help with this. I'm going to stay and catch the last ferry home with Lauren."

She chewed at her lip. "I can't bear for us to squabble over something so silly. A lieutenant on my crew said they're all gathering at the tavern tonight. Want to come? The place has darts and pool. The cook does great hot wings. We can kick back and plan how to entertain Mona. She arrives next week."

"Uh, thanks, but I promised to take Lauren, Joel and Tyler out for pizza tonight. Apparently Dodge has been going out on Friday nights."

"Oh. That's okay. Another time then."

"And don't be making a bunch of plans for Gram's visit. I've already set up some stuff. You were right about Lauren being seventeen, by the way. Her eighteenth birthday is the day after Gram gets in. I asked her if she'd help me throw a surprise party for Lauren.

You know, Lauren said no one's given her a birthday party since her mom died. With Gram's help, we're going to make Lauren's big day special."

"You do that." Megan took off then, and felt a definite crack in the bond she'd always shared with her younger brother.

Out of sorts, she decided, after returning the safety gear, not to go home. She spent some time working out in the station weight room. After showering and changing into jeans and a sweater, she met Jim Elkhorn on his way out. "You for sure gonna be at the tavern tonight, Megan?"

"Hamish just asked, and I said I'd be there. Why is everyone asking?"

"Um, maybe this'll be the night you lose your crown, queenie."

His delighted chortle gave Megan pause. "Are Ensign Tucker's pool shark buds from Grand Haven in town? Is that why you're all so anxious I go there tonight?"

Elkhorn looked secretive and smug. "Nope, what if I said we'd dug up some promising new blood right here in St. Ignace?"

"I'd say you've been drinking on the job." Megan ran a brush through curls that had kinked up in the early-spring humidity. She knew these guys. They wanted to beat her so badly they'd already searched the whole area to find players. To date, she'd trounced everyone they'd produced. Still, the jaunty way Jim whistled as he stiff-armed his way through the door made her think he had some mischief in mind.

She drove to the harbor, parked and wandered along the waterfront, watching the seagulls feed. A small but perfect carving of a shorebird caught her eye. She went into the shop, talked to the carver for a while, then bought it for Lauren Atwater's birthday. This would give the girl something to remember the area, if or when she returned to New York, as Mark insisted was her plan. The woodcarver wrapped the gift, while Megan chose a cute birthday card. Her new motto, she decided, was *know when to try harder.*

As the wind shifted and the sun dropped, Megan left the shop and passed a group of hardy *yoopers*, as native locals of the upper peninsula or U.P. were affectionately called. Out in shirtsleeves, they were taking their daily constitutional in spite of the fog beginning to roll in off the water. She felt like a wimp in a cable-knit sweater and jacket zipped tight.

When hunger pangs hit, she returned to her pickup. The brisk walk had cleared her head and buying Lauren's gift had improved her outlook.

Megan arrived at the tavern in a far better frame of mind than when she'd passed Lieutenant Elkhorn leaving the station. Spotting Jim, Hamish, Vince, Dooley and others clustered around the horseshoe curve of the bar, she eased into their midst. "Hi, guys." She slid onto a bar stool and signaled the bartender. "Hey, Walt, give me an order of hot wings, cheese fries and a Coke. No beer—I've got duty all weekend." Covering the room in a glance, she casually asked, "Where have you hidden this mythical new pool shark? In the men's room?"

"He'll be here by and by. We already anted up bets. Walt's holding the pot. Dooley, here, hasn't seen our fellow play yet. He's the only one who put his money on you tonight, Lieutenant."

She half spun toward them on the stool and lazily

took a slug from her glass. She grinned at Frank Dooley. "Very smart, Seaman."

"We'll see," crowed Second Lieutenant Vince Rigley. He clinked his glass around with the others. "Oh ho, get ready, our man just came in."

Megan's food had arrived. She bit into a spicy hot wing as she turned to follow their satisfied grins. It was dimmer by far near the entry, but the man standing there getting acclimated was none other than her downstairs neighbor. Megan's first bite stuck in her throat and she choked until Rigley pounded her on the back.

"*He's* your secret weapon?" she gasped.

"Yeah!" Lt. J. G. Elkhorn left his stool with a swagger. "We've had the pleasure of losing to him a couple of times in the last two weeks. Prepare to get whomped, Benton." Jim waltzed across the room and came back with Dodge in tow.

Megan had composed herself by then. She lifted her Coke in salute as Sterling approached their group. "Greetings, neighbor."

Jim Elkhorn and Hamish Tucker's faces fell. "You two know each other? But—"

"Ms. Benton is the buddy you've been dying to have me play?" Sterling frowned at the men before turning to take in Megan's polite smile. He pictured the rows of trophies he'd seen in her living room. Sterling was afraid he'd been had.

Jim tugged on one ear. "What's wrong? Has she cleaned your clock before?"

"No, but..."

"Maybe he can't bring himself to trounce a woman," Rigley ventured.

"Or be trounced by one," Megan put in, her blue eyes challenging Dodge.

"It's only a game," he muttered. "Rack 'em up."

The gleeful men got up from their stools and moved to the pool tables situated at the back of the tavern. Megan had a favorite cue. She snatched it from the wall and felt a weight in her stomach; probably that one hot wing she'd wolfed down was drowning in soda. As far as pool went, she always experienced a rush before playing someone new. Her nerves hummed in anticipation. She *had* been beaten. Not often.

The men he'd met, who'd befriended Sterling the first Friday he'd wandered into the tavern, expected him to win. It was written all over their faces. Of course, he'd beaten each of them handily enough. It probably should've dawned on him that their buddy might be Megan. But it didn't for two reasons. He couldn't reconcile her very feminine face with the word *buddy,* and he was also sure she played on Wednesdays. So what the hell was she doing here on a Friday?

"Having second thoughts?" she murmured, brushing past him to set her drink on the polished bar.

Someone, Sterling didn't know who, shoved a bottle of the dark ale he preferred into his hand. He took a healthy swallow, and was saved from admitting after the big deal the guys made, that he had an honest-to-God hankering to win. And why not? He was pretty damned good, if he did say so himself.

But from the minute the balls broke, his partner's expertise was evident. Sterling watched her sink yellow, green and blue balls, and he began to see the error in his thinking.

"She's great," he muttered to Jim Elkhorn.

"But you can take her down, right?"

Sterling tried his hardest. It took all his skill and concentration not to make a total ass of himself. He didn't hand her the wins, but she still took three out of three games.

Chagrined, her crewmates instructed Walt to hand over the kitty to Megan and Frank, who crowed for both of them. She immediately offered to buy drinks with her portion of the pot.

Sterling stepped up. "Where I come from, losers buy," he said. "And you won fair and square."

As they all crowded around a table, talk turned to new movies in town, another passion they all indulged in. Megan searched Dodge's face for signs of anger over his losses. He seemed to take them in sportsmanlike stride.

Quietly, one by one, the other men slipped away. Megan suddenly looked up and realized she and Sterling were the only two chatting at the table. He polished off his second beer and climbed to his feet. "If you're leaving, I'll walk you to your truck. This isn't the safest part of town."

She scrambled up. "Yeah. Normally we walk out as a group. Tonight the guys were bummed. They put all their faith in you and it didn't pan out."

"Serves them right for betting against someone who plays as well as they know you do." His laughter bubbled up as he held the door open for Megan.

They were instantly enveloped in fog.

"You're pretty good, yourself, neighbor. Our second game, I thought you had me." Megan produced her keys and stopped at her pickup. "Hey, where's your Rover? Lost in the fog?" she asked. Thick as pea soup, it'd swallowed up the tavern.

"I walked. It's not that far. I don't run or do aerobics," he said, patting his flat stomach. "Walking's one way to shed the calories I consume in a day."

"Yeah, but part of the route has no sidewalks. Bad as this fog is, walking's dangerous. Let me give you a lift. My truck's equipped with fog lights." Even as the offer rolled off her tongue, Megan expected him to decline. At least she hadn't met the man yet who, after getting whipped at pool by a woman, would then consent to let her drive him home.

She underestimated Dodge. After squinting into the fog and also wiping it from his hair, he motioned for her to open the passenger door. He climbed in, his presence filling the cab of her small truck. Megan was thankful it wasn't a long drive home. He hadn't said a word, and she scrabbled for conversation. "I've been told this fog plays havoc with the shipping channel. I hope it's fleeting. I'm on duty all weekend."

"How long does dense fog stick around in this part of the country?"

"Vince Rigley's been stationed here two years. He said it pretty much drifts in and out until all the ice melts. It's a result of the spring air currents, which are warm, colliding with the winter ones. Lauren told Mark that you operated a ferry in New York. I expect you ran into fog there, too."

"Yeah, but this is about as bad as any I've seen," he admitted, peering uneasily into the swirling sea of white. Sterling didn't add that he'd weathered a bad ferry accident caused by fog. And the boat he'd be captaining now was smaller, lighter and faster than his previous ferry. Channel currents here were more treacherous. "I hope the kids got home okay," he murmured absently.

Megan noticed he'd braced white knuckles on her dash. "Mark's a good driver," she said. "The best pizza place in town is only half as far from the house as the tavern."

The words had barely left her lips when the sound of a cell phone she wore clipped to her belt pierced the air. Sterling steadied the steering wheel with a hand as she fumbled the instrument out of its holder.

"It's the station," she told him. "Lieutenant Benton," she answered, all business. A fraction of a minute later, she cried, "Oh, no! At the north end of the bridge? Yes. Yes. It's not far from where I live, Lieutenant Bexel. I'm near there right now. It'll be faster if I meet the cutter on-site. I'm sure a harbor patrol boat will run me out."

"What is it? A problem?" Creases bracketing Sterling's lips appeared deeper in the eerie yellow glow cast by the fog-shrouded streetlights.

"It's this fog. A container ship hit a forty-foot cabin cruiser. The cruiser's pinned to the bridge abutment. They're calling in my entire crew for this rescue. The duty officer said they're afraid the cruiser sustained a lot of damage. She has three families and a full crew on board." Reaching the house, Megan squeezed her pickup between Mark's compact and Sterling's big SUV. She had her vehicle's engine shut off and had flown out the door before Sterling unfolded his long legs from the cramped interior.

The bridge loomed ghostly in the thick wet fog. Already the wreck had garnered onlookers. Cars stopped and parked on the bridge span above the water; their lights looked ragged and diffused thanks to the shifting blanket of white.

The container ship, lit up like a Christmas display,

rocked unsteadily in the fast-moving current. Megan heard the foghorn of her station's cutter bellow as she pounded across the pavement.

She and Sterling crossed the cul-de-sac stride for stride. They met Mark, Lauren, Joel and Tyler, who'd dashed out of Lady Vic. Other neighbors spilled from their homes, as well. "We heard a loud crash," Mark shouted. "Any idea what it is?"

Megan filled him in, talking in fits and spurts, then added, "Stay back, everyone. And hang on to Tyler. Don't let him go down near the water."

Sterling grabbed his son out of Lauren's arms. "Come on, tiger. This doesn't concern us. We'll all go back home where we belong."

"That would be best," Megan called over one shoulder as she slipped and slid down a grassy slope.

Mark didn't stop. "I have my camera. I'll bet I can get some great shots. Man, I can't believe this landed in our laps."

Joel zipped his jacket. "This is gonna be way cool. People are already lined up along the bridge. If we hurry, we can get a good spot to see the whole thing."

"You'll be in the way," Sterling said.

"How will we if we're on the bridge?" Lauren climbed after Mark and Joel. Local cops were already converging on the scene and were stopping people from climbing down the slope to the marina's dock.

Megan hauled out her Coast Guard ID. The others watched her gesture to three cops. One of them escorted her to a runabout. Soon they disappeared in the mushy fog.

Sterling's stomach balked. "Kids," he called. "The last thing the authorities need is gawkers impeding a disaster scene." He might as well have been talking to himself. The kids were halfway up concrete steps leading to the bridge. With great reluctance, Sterling tugged Tyler's hood up around his ears. Holding his son close to his chest, he sprinted after the younger group. He puffed from exertion by the time they all bellied up to the wet bridge rail. A sour taste rose in his throat when he saw they had a bird's eye view of the wreck and everything unfolding below. The scene was eerily familiar. A long, once-sleek cabin cruiser was jammed between a container ship and one of the concrete pillars holding up the Mighty Mac. The cruiser had a jagged hole in her hull.

"Hey, there's Megan's cutter." Joel pointed excitedly. "And isn't that some dude swinging her up on deck with a rope? Wow, that's so awesome!"

Sterling strained to see. His heart nearly lunged out of his chest. Megan looked no bigger than a wet kitten spinning on a rope in the misty fog. Just her, clinging to a slender line being hauled in hand over hand by two men dressed in jackets like the one she'd pulled on at the pickup. Sterling's stomach rolled and bucked.

ON BOARD HER CUTTER at last, Megan quickly donned a life vest one of the crew tossed to her. "What's the plan?" she asked the nearest officer, brushing wet hair out of her eyes to better assess the situation below.

"Our mission is to transfer six adults, four kids and five crew off the disabled cruiser," the deck officer said.

Megan eyed the portion of the bridge visible overhead. "No way we can launch the Jayhawk. Is the commander trying to jockey us close enough to the wreck for a hand-to-hand transfer?"

"He and the XO are discussing strategy now. We

pulled back because our backwash was swamping the cruiser."

"Why doesn't the container ship back away and let us get closer?"

"He's all that's keeping the yacht afloat, Lieutenant. The captain of the container ship says he didn't see the cruiser in the fog until he was right on top of her. He staved a hole the size of Texas in her bow. He pulls out and she sinks. It's as simple as that. 'Course, she's a goner anyway."

The commander summoned his crew and swiftly gave orders. They were to launch the two largest lifeboats. Two crew members from each lifeboat would board the cruiser. Two would stay in them to receive passengers from the crippled ship.

Donovan motioned Megan over. "Benton, I've been talking to the captain of the cruiser. He's got all hands on deck except for one little girl. A two-year-old. She's flat vanished below deck."

Megan blanched. "Washed overboard, sir?"

"They believe she's in the cabin area. But they lost electricity below. She was asleep in a bottom bunk, and mom thought dad had her and vice versa. The crew has their hands full pumping out water to try and stay afloat. Another thing—he said the main cabin door is jammed nearly shut. Short of dynamite, we're looking at a very narrow opening. I can't order you to attempt a rescue. All the same, I want you in the first lifeboat across. You're the smallest sailor I've got. For now, assess the damage—and the risk. At the rate the yacht's taking on water, her captain figures we've got max twenty minutes before she starts breaking apart. Damn, I'd like to get that kid."

The minute she heard *two-year-old girl,* Megan was on the move toward the lifeboat. Donovan tagged along, delivering particulars as they cut through the thicket of fog. Megan grabbed two flashlights and a coiled steel cable with a belt hook on one end and climbed into the craft being lowered from the cutter.

FROM THEIR POSITION ON the bridge, Mark was the first to recognize his sister as she dropped into the motorized rubber craft. She alone wore faded blue jeans instead of a water-repellent orange jumpsuit. And was also minus her official baseball cap. Her hair blew wildly about her face.

"Hey, once the lifeboat reaches the yacht," Mark complained, "we won't be able to see what's happening. You can stay here, but I'm going to try to get closer." He slung his camera strap around his neck and lifted his bag of accessories. "Depending on how effective my filters are, I may be in a position to get some fantastic shots."

"I'm following you," Lauren said, latching on to his arm although she was shivering in the damp fog. She took the leather bag from him.

"Me, too." Joel's face was pale, but his eyes were dark and eager.

Sterling couldn't let them go alone. Nor could he bring himself to tell them they had no idea how horrendous watching would be if the rescue fell apart. He'd been in a night collision between a sailboat and his ferry. It'd been foggy that night, too, and everything was chaos, the way it was now. He'd been forced to choose between saving a mother or her infant. He'd tried his level best to hang on to both but could only maintain his grasp on the screaming, flailing child. In spite of herculean efforts to get survivors from the sailboat onto his ferry, it sank within a hundred yards of port. His ferry barely limped in. Witnesses vouched for him. Scores verified that he'd done everything humanly possible to save everyone from both boats. But for months the memory had clung to him like a bad smell.

All his efforts were no comfort to the man from the sailboat who'd lost his wife. Sterling almost never spoke about the persistent nightmares that interrupted his sleep. He'd tried once to explain to Blythe how innocent lives could be snuffed out in the blink of an eye. She thought it was another jab at her being a cop, and she'd shrugged off his concern with a scornful laugh. His gut churned then, much like it did now.

On leaden feet, he stuck with Mark, Lauren and Joel as they moved closer to the action. Midway down the steps that led from the bridge, Sterling saw Megan climb aboard the yacht that lay partially on its side.

"Let me down, Daddy. I wanna see. I wanna see!" Tyler kicked his dad's thigh. Caught in a panic similar to the one that imprisoned him after his accident, Sterling just grasped his son more tightly. He wanted to take Tyler, who flung his arms and legs around, and run to the safety of their home. But as news of a trapped child circulated through the gaggle of bystanders, it seemed clear that Megan was the guardsman who'd be going below to search for the kid.

Sterling's feet remained rooted to the spot. He did his best to look for her through the fog.

Mark shot dozens of pictures during the brief span it took to move most of the victims from the cruiser into the Coast Guard lifeboats. A man and a sobbing woman begged to stay behind. Megan's partner literally dragged them, obviously the lost child's parents, into a lifeboat.

Sterling recalled another mother's terrified face. He was again catapulted into the horror he'd felt watching her slip from his hands and sink beneath the oily water of New York Harbor.

As he lost sight of Megan, his mind began playing tricks. That other time he'd called for help until he was hoarse, but help for that mom arrived too late. Afterward, he'd learned that she couldn't swim. Yet she'd thrust her baby into his arms.

Below the watchers, the yacht shuddered and slid several inches farther down the concrete pillar. The screech of wood against metal and cement was horrific, but it brought the people still on board back into Sterling's focus. There was a pronounced urgency in Megan's movements, evident in the jerky way she lashed a thin cable around her waist and tied the other end to a cleat on deck. Judging by an exchange between the two guardsmen remaining on the yacht, Sterling decided that Megan's stocky partner didn't want her to go below. Or else he wanted to accompany her. She kept gesturing to a narrow opening any fool could see the man wouldn't fit through. Then too fast for her crewmate to stop her, Megan tore off her life vest, turned sideways and wiggled into the narrow hole. Fog shrouded the black opening.

Mark stopped shooting pictures. "What's Megan doing?" Worry echoed in his voice. "What if the cabin shipped water? Without her life jacket she—" Blinking at the people around him, Mark swallowed several times, wiped his mouth and elbowed his way to the front of the crowd, the others right behind him.

Sterling's jaw was clenched too tight to respond. Joel had no such compunction. "Dude, your sister went to find the trapped kid. Do you think she can do it and get out?"

Lauren and Mark both turned a sickly green. Sterling shifted Tyler in his arms. "I know you're cold, Tyler. So am I. We'll go in a minute." Sterling didn't know how it was possible to sweat in this damp fog, but sweat plastered his shirt to his chest. Or maybe he was having a heart attack. Or maybe this tightness shutting off his breath was his past failure catching up with him.

It seemed a lifetime passed. Really, only minutes ticked by. All at once a muffled hue and cry went up along the bridge. Various people had moved in front of him, and Sterling pushed past them all. He identified a jacketed arm handing a squalling child through the narrow slit. The man who'd been guarding the cable let go of the steel and took the child. The sickening groan of metal stretched beyond its limits sent a hush over the crowd.

They drew in a collective breath as the cruiser tilted and scraped a foot farther down the concrete pillar until she lay nearly perpendicular to the lapping waves.

Sterling thought his heart had stopped beating. Nor did it resume its rapid thudding until Megan materialized like a wraith to cling to the slanted deck. A low murmur rose in volume, like the beating wings of ten thousand birds. Or maybe angel wings, Sterling thought grimly as the fog parted slightly and he saw Megan flash a cocky grin and a thumbs-up to someone hanging over the rail of the Coast Guard cutter.

Her gesture could have been aimed at any of the young jocks who'd been with them at the tavern. Virtual clones of Rio Amado. Hell, for all Sterling knew, Megan Benton reveled in the glory and excitement of danger. Just like Blythe…

Seeing Mark lift his camera again and start shooting as if his sister hadn't just risked her life, Sterling's lip curled and he finally insisted on being heard. "Show's over, kids. We're going home and that's final."

"No!" Lauren waited to refuse until after Megan, her companion and the child were safely on an idling lifeboat. "Mark thinks maybe he can sell some pictures to local papers."

Joel shouted at Sterling. "I'm staying, too. That gazillion-dollar yacht's gonna sink the minute the ship that smashed it moves away. I may be the only kid in my English class who can write an eyewitness account. Maybe it'll bring up my grade."

As if Sterling could argue with that logic. He'd read every account that had been written about his own accident.

Tyler began to cry in earnest then. Sterling didn't want to leave the others, but he recognized that he and Tyler had reached the end of their endurance. Quickly negotiating the wet slope to the road, he soothed the boy. "Everybody's going to be just fine, pal. Quit crying, please. You can have some milk and cookies when we get home."

"Hot chocolate?" the boy asked, pausing to rub his wet eyes. "Megan's hot chocolate. It's yummy, Daddy."

Irritation coursed through Sterling. As far as he knew, his son had never tasted hot chocolate until he met Megan Benton. And now it was all he wanted.

Tomorrow, he'd ask around to see if he could find a local carpenter who hadn't left for the season. The sooner he moved his family to the island, a ferry ride away from the Benton duo, the better off they'd all be. Sterling didn't need his son growing attached to another woman who thrived on danger. As well, Lauren was getting a little too friendly with Mark. To say nothing of how Joel soaked up everything associated with the sort of mayhem that seemed to surround Megan Benton.

NINETEEN-YEAR-OLD KEITH Lock faced his father and stepmother. More blond than his dad, he shared his father's stubborn jaw. "I don't *want* a vacation. I promised Doc Jackson I'd computerize his patient files over spring break. In exchange, he'll write me a recommendation for the school of veterinary medicine."

"I'm sorry, Keith. I really need you to do this." He paused. "After I get the college budget approved, I'll help you set up Doc's program. Here's your ticket. You change planes in St. Louis, then Chicago, and take a puddle jumper to Pellston Airport right outside Mackinaw City. Aunt Emily gave Sherry your cousin Megan's home and cell numbers. I want you to call her and make nice. Have her or Mark pick you up at the airport."

"Mom's behind this, isn't she? Darn it, I never thought you'd cave in to her and Crawford's demands." He was talking about his real mom and her banker husband. He wadded up the paper with his cousin's phone numbers, but didn't take the ticket.

Sherry, often the peacemaker between Keith, his father and the ex-wife, Carla, moved in now to lay a soothing hand on each man's arm. "Keith, your aunt Emily will tutor you in college chemistry for free if you do her this favor. She thinks Mark is making a mistake giving up years of study, all because he won a contest with one photo. We all agree. It's just a week out of your life, Keith. You like Mark. He'll tell you before he tells any of us if he's stonewalling because he's got cold feet at the thought of settling into a lifetime career."

"Why can't Aunt Emily call Megan? Mark's been at her house for two weeks."

Sherry grinned. "When parents ask questions like that, Keith, it's called sticking our noses in."

The kid wasn't buying his stepmom's argument. "It's still meddling when a cousin horns in. Mark will tell me to butt the hell out. Anyway, I talked to him the other day, and he's met this cute chick. Mark will *not* be happy if I show up."

"Why? Mark's met a girl?" Sherry exclaimed. "I'm positive his mom doesn't know. Is she another photographer? How serious is it?"

"Jeez, I don't know. Her name's Lauren. She's from New York. She lives downstairs from Megan. And Mark *won't* be glad to see me, 'cause you remember last year when I went to check out the vet school at his college? Mark was hot for a girl who worked as a library assistant at the college. We met her at the pub one night after she got off work. She fell all over me. Dumped Mark flat."

Garrett reared back. "You were eighteen. What the hell were you doing in a pub? And what's wrong with Mark that he took you?"

Sherry squeezed her husband's arm. "Like you never went to a pub before you were twenty-one?" she chided. "Or did they call them saloons in Texas?"

Her husband rolled his eyes, but did look sheepish. "Look, Keith, your mission isn't to break up a romance.

Just hang out with Mark for a week. Casually ask about his intentions regarding his future here at Wellmont."

"That's spying."

"I hear it's wild and woolly country in that neck of the woods. Great fishing. Camp tells me there's gold in them thar hills, too. I'd trade places with you in a minute, kid, if I wasn't deep in college budgets."

"Fishing? Gold?" Magic words to Keith Lock. The only thing he liked better than working with animals was fishing or gold-panning with his dad. In fact, Garrett had gone without him once—panning gold along the Santa Fe trail the summer he met Sherry Campbell. Keith had been forced to attend his real mom's wedding to the dweeb banker. It seemed to Keith he was always having to do stuff he didn't want.

"We could take a couple of weeks this summer after my classes end, Dad. You, me, Sherry. Megan and Sherry could go mall-crawling while we fish."

"Nice try," Sherry said. "No dice, Keith. Megan hates to shop. And Aunt Emily will be skin and bones if summer comes and Mark's still in St. Ignace. She's talked the college into not filling the counseling job at least until May."

Garrett nodded. "According to your uncle Camp, Aunt Emily can fret herself into tossing her cookies over next to nothing. It's only one lousy week, Keith."

"I know Aunt Emily's not herself. I stopped by the Hub on Tuesday, to see if you had time to go to lunch with me, Sherry. Your secretary said you'd run Aunt Em home to change clothes because she barfed all over her desk. What's wrong with her?"

Sherry straightened Keith's ever-crooked shirt collar. "Emily is a nester. She turned my brother's barn of a house into a family gathering place. More than any of us, Em loves having the extended family drop in. She's got this vision of us all living and working nearby. First Megan left, and now Mark's gone astray."

"Aunt Em does have a revolving door. Her house always smells like cookies or bread. She never fails to make room for stray dogs or cats." For Keith, that had always been a huge point in her favor. He reached out and slowly pulled away the ticket his dad still held. "You're sure she doesn't have like…cancer or anything?"

Sherry slid her arm around Garrett's waist. "Camp thinks maybe an ulcer. We love her to pieces, but Em's always been a worrier. I know you've heard of empty nest syndrome, Keith. Your aunt Emily's got it bad. Anything we can do to steer Mark toward the counseling job… Keith, you've gotta know it's a great job."

Keith looked at one parent, then the other and shrugged. "Okay, okay. I'll go. It won't have any influence on what Mark decides, but I'll go to—where the heck is St. Ignace? You said…Michigan?"

CHAPTER SEVEN

STERLING RAN A WARM BATH for Tyler, who still complained of being cold. Once he was settled in the tub with his toy boats, Sterling warmed a pan of milk for the hot chocolate his son requested. After the bath, Sterling sat and read his son a book Mark had apparently bought Tyler today. A story about a pirate ship that lay at the bottom of the sea. *Great!* A fitting topic to follow the wreck they'd just seen.

"Daddy, your ferryboat won't sink to the bottom of the ocean, will it?" Tyler asked, rubbing sleepy eyes.

Sterling took back the cup—at least Tyler had finished his hot chocolate without comparing it to Megan's—and laid the book aside. He ruffled the boy's still-damp hair. "My ferry runs on a lake, not the ocean, like where pirates sail. And I'm very careful."

The boy yawned and snuggled into his pillow. "If you do sink, Daddy, call Megan. She'll save you like she did that little girl, and..." As he often did, Tyler fell asleep while talking.

Sterling sat for a time stroking his sleeping son's hair. Kids were so trusting. So oblivious to danger. Call Megan Benton, indeed! She'd taken the ultimate risk in removing her own life vest. Was he the only one who saw that as foolish rather than brave? Closing his eyes,

Sterling figured he should probably question why he'd be attracted to not one but two women in high-risk fields. Blythe and now Megan. That ought to shock him, but it didn't. He'd known after spending the evening in the company of bright, energetic, completely captivating Lieutenant Benton that he was in trouble. He stood and bit back a swear word.

Snapping off the light, he made his way to the kitchen. Sleep would likely elude him tonight. He set Tyler's cup in the sink and reached for the coffee can. Then he saw the pan of warm chocolate on the stove. Megan Benton's drink of choice. Where was she now? Taking her bows and reveling in interviews like Blythe always did?

The front door opened as he filled his mug. Lauren stuck her head around the corner. "Since we don't have school tomorrow, Joel and I are going upstairs to wait while Mark checks his photos. We'll pop in a video or something."

"I take it the excitement at the bridge is done?"

"Yeah. The cruiser buckled, broke up and sank a few minutes after you left. Megan got that kid in the nick of time. Don't wait up. Joel and I may be late."

He pictured the sinking boat, and shuddered, remembering Megan's cocky thumbs-up. The hand raising the mug to his lips wobbled, spilling the contents on the counter. As he voiced no objection to her plan, Lauren withdrew. He was angry over feeling belated fear that Megan could have died in that mishap. Tearing off a paper towel, he swabbed up the spill as Lauren's footsteps receded and the door slammed.

One way he could make his hot chocolate different—Sterling dug out a bottle of bourbon and tipped a healthy slug into his cup. Sniffing the bourbon-laced chocolate, he stared moodily out the window above his sink. The fog was lifting. The milky mist was turning into a soft rain.

He loved the clean scent of the air after a spring rain. Taking his mug, Sterling wandered out to his porch. He left the door ajar so he could hear Tyler if he woke up. As a rule, though, that kid could sleep through anything.

If he wasn't so restless, he'd read for a while. But out here he breathed easier, felt less confined, less claustrophobic.

He was on a second cup of doctored chocolate, and the rain had gone from soft to diligent when a motor alerted him to the fact that Megan was finally rolling in. Sterling stepped back to blend with the darkness. Renewed anger coursed through him. He didn't want to feel relief. He had no right to feel sad, glad or anything as far as his upstairs neighbor was concerned. And it pissed him off that he'd spent the last hour worrying about her.

BEDRAGGLED, SOAKING WET and with aching shoulders, Megan caught a whiff of hot cocoa—and booze?—as she climbed out and stopped to lock her truck. Out of the corner of one eye, she detected movement on her neighbor's porch. For a minute she wondered if Sterling had waited up for her—to make sure she got home safe and sound. *Not likely!* Flirting with death as she had tonight, and later getting chewed out by her commander for shedding her life jacket, even to effect an otherwise impossible rescue, left her feeling shaky. Emotionally vulnerable.

"A convert I see," she called. "That drink smells wonderful." She paused at the foot of Dodge's porch steps and ignored the rain. "It'd sure hit the spot on a wet night like this."

His deep voice emerged from the shadows. "Then by all means come on up and have some. And maybe you can tell me what the hell drives a woman to take a job where she's constantly putting her life on the line. Is it for kicks? For glory? Or a need to prove—what the hell *does* it prove?"

Already experiencing the inevitable drain on her body, Megan recoiled from the disappointment caused by his scathing, erroneous judgement. Why had she thought Sterling Dodge was different from other men she'd met? Because he hadn't gone sulky when she'd beaten him at pool?

Megan turned away. She ran up the stairs, needing to nurse her hurt feelings in private. If Mark was still awake, she could count on him to support her.

Throwing open the door, Megan received a second shock. Her brother and Lauren sat hip to hip on the couch, sharing a bowl of popcorn. Joel Atwater sprawled on the floor in front of the TV. They were all glued to a video, and from their dirty looks, they resented her intrusion.

"Shh," Mark said, waving her off. "The Terminator is about to fight his final battle. At least in this episode."

Strangely on the verge of tears, Megan kicked off her wet boots, snatched them up and stalked between the watchers and their show. She slammed the door to her bedroom and stripped off her wet jacket and jeans. As the jacket landed with a thud, Megan was reminded of the carving tucked in one pocket—Lauren's birthday gift. She dug it out. The soggy wrapping matched the way she felt.

At the time of Mark's announcement, she hadn't placed a lot of importance on his decision to throw the girl a birthday bash. It was more that Megan hadn't liked the fact that he hadn't consulted her. Rethinking the scene she'd walked in on, she put the gift on her nightstand and mulled over how serious their relationship might be? And what, if anything, should she do about it? Was it even any of her business?

She grabbed sweats and headed for the shower, only to be stopped by a light blinking on her answering machine. Assuming the duty officer had tried to reach her here first, Megan pressed the button to erase the call. But cousin Keith Lock's voice had her instantly lifting her finger. "Hey, cuz, it's Keith. Don't panic. Nothing's wrong at home. Well, nothing other than the usual confusion and disorder." His ready laugh made Megan smile. And in smiling, she relaxed. "I'm calling to see if you'd like some company. You and Mark. The folks tell me he's up there messing around, and Dad said the fishing in upper Michigan is fantastic. I have a week off for spring break. If you've got a corner where I can toss a sleeping bag and fishing pole, phone me back. But…I already have plane ticket in hand." He gave the date he'd arrive in Pellston, and a time.

Megan was so excited, she forgot about the movie going on in the living room. With a happy whoop, she dived into her sweats, then flung open the bedroom door and stuck her head out. "Mark, guess what? Keith's coming for spring break. Luckily he lands the day Mona takes off. You can drop her off, then drive to the other airport to pick him up."

Her brother exploded off the couch. Popcorn flew every which way. "What do you mean Keith's coming here? The last time he and I talked, he said he'd arranged to work for Doc Jackson over the college break."

"Call him. He left a message on my machine. Maybe you misunderstood, and he meant summer vacation is when he'll be working for Dr. Jackson."

"Who's Keith?" Joel straightened. He and his sister spoke the same time.

Since Mark didn't answer, Megan said, "Keith Lock is our cousin by marriage. His dad married our aunt Sherilyn."

That explanation brought a reaction from Mark. "Sherry's our stepdad's sister. Technically Keith's not related to us. So, why's he flying up here all of a sudden?"

"What's with you, that you're not jumping for joy?" Megan, still in the bedroom doorway, barely glimpsed her brother's mutinous expression.

He said nothing, but began picking up popcorn from the couch and the floor.

Joel scrambled on his knees to shut off the video that had ended.

Lauren moved the bowl to within Mark's reach. She wore a faint frown. "We…uh, Joel and I better take off and let you guys talk this out." She plucked her jacket off the end table and threw Joel his. The two sidled toward the door.

"There's nothing to talk out," Megan said testily. She couldn't understand Mark's attitude.

"Say, does this dude screw up us renting bikes tomorrow to ride around Mackinac Island?" Joel inquired of the room at large as he finished shrugging into his jacket.

Mark tossed a last piece of popcorn into the bowl. "Keith's arriving next weekend, not tomorrow. Do you want to get the 9:00 a.m. ferry?"

"Are bike rental shops on the island already open?" Megan's gaze skipped from one to the other.

Lauren spoke up from the apartment door. "Mark wants to shoot more photos around the park. He planned to invite you to come, too. Isn't that right, Mark?"

"Yeah. Hey, wait till you see the shots I got of tonight's wreck. I hope you don't mind, sis, I e-mailed the best ones to the local paper."

"Why would I mind? And a bike ride around the island will be fun. Did you ask Sterling and Tyler, as well?" She thought of Tyler, and her irritation with the boy's father took a backseat. "Tyler probably can't ride all the way to Arch Rock, but one of the guys on my crew said they rent bikes with kid seats on the back, or side carts for kids."

Joel clouded up instantly. "Does *he* have to tag along? Bro-ther!"

"Tyler will enjoy this," Megan said. "Especially when we stop to buy fudge at the end of the ride."

Lauren combed a hand through her tangled hair. "Joel didn't mean *Tyler* would be a pain in the butt. It's more that he doesn't want Sterling ruining our day."

"I see. Well, Mark and I can attest from personal experience that life runs more smoothly in a merged family if you include everyone."

Because Mark agreed, Lauren reluctantly promised to ask their brother-in-law if he'd like to join their outing. Joel was still grumbling over that decision as they left.

Megan went out to straighten her sofa pillows. She waited for Mark to bring up Keith's visit. He didn't, nor did he make any move to phone their cousin. What he did was haul out the pictures he'd printed of the accident at the bridge. Mark sorted rapidly through the stack and handed Megan a half-dozen prints.

"These are the ones I like best. I e-mailed them to the biggest area paper. The night editor got right back to me, offering the standard fee they pay for unsolicited photographs."

"Mark, that's fantastic. Whoa! I look an absolute fright in this shot with Daryl Nunez." She peered at the photo of her handing the crying toddler off to her partner.

Mark sat down next to her. "Look at the next couple of pictures. I captured the relief on the faces of the parents hanging over the rail of your cutter. Anyone who sees those two shots will gain huge respect for what you do. I never realized the hazards of your job, sis. You make me proud," he said, his Adam's apple bobbing.

Feeling a flush rising, Megan gave the pictures back with a self-conscious shrug. "Not everyone shares your opinion. My commander chewed me out for taking off my life jacket. He called what I did *grandstanding*. And Sterling Dodge was on his porch when I got home. He accused me of being out for kicks or glory or needing to prove something. You sort of insinuated the other day that it's what Mom thinks, too."

Mark flipped through the photos. "She'll see. I e-mailed copies of these to her office at the college."

"Why on earth did you do that?"

"Selfishly I hope she'll recognize there's value in my work *and* yours."

"I'm starved. Come to the kitchen while I fix a sandwich? Tell me about this freelancing business. I thought you intended to photograph wildlife."

He planted his elbows on the counter and watched her assemble a sandwich. "Gina Ames offered me contacts of several different kinds. I figured it'd be tough to break into any kind of professional photography, but I sold these shots like that." He snapped his fingers. "The editor said they might be picked up by a national wire service. That would be great."

"Hey, good going." Her brother's new stature didn't stop her from slapping his hand when he swiped a slice of cheese.

"If Dodge treated you badly, why did you suggest Lauren invite him on our bike ride tomorrow?"

"I was thinking of Tyler. Anyhow, won't you be inviting them both to Lauren's birthday party? By the way, you never said if I was invited."

Mark accepted the glass of milk she passed him. "I wasn't sure you'd want to hang around here. You acted put out when I said I asked for Gram's help."

"You hurt my feelings, Mark. You and Mona are *my* guests."

"Yes, but I have the distinct impression you don't approve of Lauren. And the party is all about her."

Megan debated saying something else. In the end, maybe she would. "Maybe I'm afraid you two are getting too cozy, too fast. Frankly, Mark, she's closer to Keith's age than yours."

Her brother bristled, upsetting his milk glass and sending the plate with her sandwich dancing. Megan grabbed for a paper towel with one hand and kept her sandwich from a worse fate with a lightning-fast grab.

"That's the second time tonight you've reacted to Keith's name. Care to tell me what's going on?"

Mark ripped the towel out of her hand and cleaned up the mess he'd created. After tossing the soggy paper in the trash, he slumped in the chair across from her. "If you laugh, I'll kill you." A mutinous scowl settled over his freckles. "Keith stole my last girlfriend."

"In high school? He would've been in junior high, for Pete's sake."

"College," Mark muttered. "Keith came down last year to check out the vet program. I had a girlfriend I liked a lot. Keith bunked in my room, so when I went to pick her up from work for a night at the pub, I let him tag along. She couldn't see me for dirt. For weeks after he left, she bugged me to give her Keith's phone number."

Megan swallowed the bite of sandwich she'd taken. "I'm sure you don't want to hear this, but she's a total skank. You're well rid of her, Mark. What I have a harder time believing is that Keith would go after your girlfriend. Why would he do something like that?"

"He didn't have to *do* anything," Mark growled. "He only has to walk into a room with me. If there's a woman alive who'd go for my funny face and carrot top over Keith's blond Viking good looks, I sure haven't met her yet."

"Mark!" His sister thumped his wrist hard. "I hope to heaven not all women are that shallow. First off, you're every bit as nice-looking as Keith. You're articulate, talented and you have a sense of humor. I love Keith, but sometimes getting him to open up is practically impossible. And if you don't share his passion for animals, a conversation breaks down real fast."

"Cindy said most women prefer the strong, quiet type."

"Good grief! That incident really bugs you, doesn't it? I didn't realize you were jealous of Keith."

"I'm not!" he flung back.

"Sounds like it to me," Megan said, reading his sullen expression. "What do guys call it then, if not jealousy?"

Mark slumped lower. A rebellious scowl carved deep creases on either side of his downcast mouth.

Megan sighed. "Keith already bought a ticket. Would you prefer I called him and said it's not convenient for him to come right now?"

"You think I'm being an idiot, don't you?"

Megan thought of how often she let her own feelings get hurt. Like an hour ago, when she took Sterling Dodge's remarks to heart. She hooked her brother's pinky finger with hers. "We're family, Mark. All for one and one for all. Remember us making that pact?"

"My second day of first grade. The bully up the street gave me a bloody lip and stole my lunch money. You took him on, tore your new dress and got a black eye. Dad sent you to your room without dinner. After he went to bed, I brought you a dried-out hot dog." His mood lightened, and he sat up and laughed. "If that doesn't put this into perspective, I don't know what does. Bring on Keith."

"That's the spirit." Megan finished the rest of her sandwich and watched Mark gulp down a second tall glass of milk and a handful of homemade cookies. Deciding there was no time like the present, she launched her next salvo. "Out of curiosity, how serious are your feelings for Lauren Atwater?"

"I like her. She's easy to talk to, and I look forward to seeing her. She brightens my day. But serious? She has college ahead of her. And I need to see if I can make a go of photography. I'm not sure exactly what you're asking. That's where things stand."

"Okay." She didn't comment or ask further questions. "So, we have one of Mona's days planned with the party. That still leaves two."

"A carriage ride around the island?"

"If she was coming in May instead of April, we could wine and dine her on the island at the Grand Hotel. Very posh."

"Gram arrives next week, Megan. April first. Get used to it."

"I'll ask around at work. Or maybe tomorrow we'll see something open on the island."

THE NEXT MORNING, ALMOST from the get-go, Megan saw that her suggestion to include Sterling had the potential for disaster. Mark, Lauren and Joel voted to ride *round the rock,* as the eight-mile trek completely around the island was called.

"That's an overly ambitious plan if you ask me," Sterling said on the brief ferry ride.

When no one spoke, he flatly vetoed their plan. "Choose a shorter route," he said as they left the ferry to begin the walk to the bike rental shop. "Eight miles is too strenuous for a first trip."

"Just because you're old and out of shape doesn't mean we hafta do what you want," Joel said huffily. "You horning in wasn't our choice, man."

"I can ride circles around you any day of the week. You need to think of Tyler. He's too young for such a long ride. And...if it wasn't your choice for us to come along, whose was it?"

Joel rammed his hands deep into his sweatshirt pockets. "Megan laid a guilt trip on Lauren. See," he announced, nudging his sister's arm. "Maybe next time you'll listen to me." Spotting the bike shop, he ran off, leaving them to deal with the fallout of his anger.

Lauren avoided looking at her brother-in-law. Mark turned to his sister. Megan had experienced second thoughts almost from the moment the words left her mouth. In fact, she'd lain awake for hours wondering why, after the things he'd said to her, she felt compelled to stand up for Sterling. "Last night no one said you intended to ride all the way around the island," she pointed out.

Mark adjusted the backpack that held his camera and accessories. "Hey, Joel already has his bike. We need a solution here." Digging out his billfold, Mark peeled off a bill, handed it to Lauren and asked her to rent bicycles for the two of them. "Get twenty-one speeds. We'll need that many to climb the hill to Fort Holmes. It's the highest point on the island."

"Lookee, Daddy! They got bikes my size," Tyler exclaimed. He wriggled loose from his father's hand and ran to inspect a brightly colored tyke-bike. Silver streamers attached to the handle grips claimed his attention.

"Sterling, I honestly did not know they wanted to circle the island. May I suggest the two of us take Tyler as far as Fort Mackinac? It's an old British stronghold. Even that's a hefty climb, but I think Tyler will like the fort. Matt Horowitz, a petty officer in my unit, has three boys ranging from Tyler's age to nine. He said his kids love the Children's Discovery room."

"Why not all go see the fort?" Sterling said.

"I've been to Fort Mackinac, and I came to take pictures of Fort Holmes," Mark said.

"Pictures, right! I saw the ones you took of the wreck splashed all over the morning paper."

Megan, who could imagine where this line of talk was heading, interrupted. "You can ruin everyone's day, Sterling, or we can set a time to meet Mark, Lauren and Joel at one of the fudge stores." She named the first shop that came to mind and gave its location. "What about noon?"

Sterling acknowledged this with a nod, and they watched Mark take off at a fast jog.

As Sterling and Megan ambled more slowly toward the rental shop, he muttered, "I'll capitulate today, but one reason I made the move here is because Joel and Lauren have been doing exactly as they please for too many years."

In fact, Joel had ridden off without a word to his guardian. Mark waited at the corner for Lauren, who knelt next to a crying Tyler. The boy wanted to ride with the older kids. Lauren attempted to talk him into returning to his dad.

"Tyler," Sterling called. "Let Lauren go on with Mark. Megan's going to show us a fort." He scooped up his son, mustering a smile for the hesitant girl.

"I wanna ride *this* bike," the boy sobbed.

"Sure. It's just your size," Sterling said, and Tyler immediately turned off the spigot.

"We'll ride to the fort," Megan promised, "and we'll

have more fun than they will. I'll bet they'll be too tired to eat fudge after their long ride."

"What's fudge?" Tyler squinted up at Megan.

"You'll see. Fudge is good. It's a trademark export of Mackinac Island. You'll have to get your dad to bring you again between May and October. I have it on good authority that you can smell fudge cooking from a mile out. Every merchant here claims to have a secret recipe. They cook the candy in big copper kettles. There's raspberry, caramel, peanut butter, orange cappuccino. Oh, and some with liqueurs for adults."

"Okay," the boy said agreeably.

"Is that the truth?" Sterling asked. "That you can smell the fudge? By May we should be living on the island," he added as Megan chose a bike.

"Then you'll be able to verify what I said." She grinned. "That's what it says in the book I'm supposed to memorize to educate *fudgies.* And that *is* how locals refer to day-trippers. If you're going to run a ferryboat, Sterling, you should bone up. Especially if you're going to live here year-round."

His tension seemed to dissipate, and he returned her smile. Then he ruined their newfound cohesiveness by insisting on paying the rental on her bike. They nearly got into another argument until Megan backed off, but grumbled, "It's not like we're *really* together."

"What do you call it? Looks to me as if we're together." Quite relaxed now, Sterling approached the rental agent. "You see anyone else with this lady?"

The elderly man with twinkling green eyes and snow-white hair played along. "Sonny boy, I learned a long time ago never to argue with a lady. She says something jet-black is white, then I agree it's white."

"Daddy, why did that man call you sonny boy? *I'm* a boy. You're a man."

"Do you have any idea how long the *why* stage lasts?" Sterling murmured to Megan. "It started about six months ago."

Megan adjusted her pace to stay abreast. "My niece is going on five. When I was home over Christmas, she asked me *why* every two minutes."

"I'm guessing your home is in the south. I detect a slight drawl."

"Must be the time I spent at helicopter training school in Alabama. I'm a Midwest girl by birth. I used to have a distinct Midwest twang. I was teased about it incessantly in New London, Connecticut, during Coast Guard school."

"I understand I have you and the Coast Guard to thank for Joel's determination to buy a boat. I found a brochure on boating safety tips. He said you gave them out at a school assembly. Do you really think a boy his age is capable of handling a powerboat?"

"That depends. Nearly all the island kids own boats. In the winter they use snowmobiles. From what I hear, the majority are responsible kids."

"That's a relief. I've noticed a few improvements in Joel. I wish he'd make some nice friends. He used to be a loner. Then he fell in with a bad crowd." Sterling's grip on his handlebars tightened.

"A gang, right? If there's gang activity here I haven't heard of it. You know, if you had spare time to go boating with him, wouldn't that help?"

"As if he'd welcome that idea. You may have noticed

my attempts to guide or even suggest are poison to Joel. You see, my wife set his rules and Lauren's, and too late I realized they were nonexistent."

"That's rough. But as a former rebel myself, I suggest cutting him some slack. 'The tighter the rein,' my stepdad says, 'the more cantankerous the horse.'"

Sterling turned his head and ran his gaze from Megan's head to her toes and then in reverse. "Try as I might, I cannot picture you a rebel."

"Take my word for it. Picture a smart-ass Morticia Adams."

"What brought about the conversion to St. Megan?"

"Ha! Hardly a saint. But I fell over a cliff. I kid you not," she said when he looked skeptical. Then she explained about the summer she'd spent on a wagon train reenactment. "My stepdad, only he wasn't my stepdad then, risked his life to save my sorry hide. He could've died in the process. A rescue team flew into the canyon at great peril to save him and my mom, who insisted on climbing down to be with him because she loved him so much. My stepdad was my hero—and so were the rescuers That's why I joined the Coast Guard. Not for kicks, or glory, but to save other moms, dads and kids."

They'd reached a hill, and Megan got off to push her bike. Tyler and Sterling did the same. Sterling seemed to mull over what she'd said. "So, your folks divorced when you were Joel's age? Mine, too. I was raised by my grandparents," Sterling said.

"My dad died. They should have divorced. My mom's the saint here." She paused. "From a few things Lauren let slip to Mark, I gather, uh..." Megan made sure Tyler wasn't near enough to hear before she said, "that your marriage wasn't all moonlight and roses."

"What has Lauren said?" Sterling's voice dropped.

"Nothing to me. I got the story secondhand, so I shouldn't even have brought it up. Sorry."

Air slid out of his lungs. "That's okay. I'm surprised Lauren would say anything. She has my wife, her sister, on a pedestal. As a sidebar, may I ask if you've noticed something of a romantic nature developing between your brother and my sister-in-law?"

Tyler had ridden fast down the dip and now waited for them to catch up. Walking uphill again, he fell in beside Megan and slipped his hand trustingly in hers at the same moment Sterling placed a broad, warm palm on her waist as he guided her around a pothole. Megan experienced a sudden wish for something of a romantic nature to develop between her and this man, complicated though he was. But the wish was quite fleeting.

"Mark has a big heart, and he enjoys Lauren's company. He's just being neighborly, I think. Like, he's throwing a party for Lauren's eighteenth birthday because she said she hasn't had one since her mom died."

Sterling's forehead suddenly became a web of furrows. "We—Blythe and I—bought her birthday gifts. Blythe didn't do parties. Not for any of the kids. I asked about it once, because they were included in their friends' parties. But Blythe said parties left a big mess, and the money spent on supplies could go a long way toward a worthwhile gift."

"Hmm. I love the mess. Makes for warm fuzzy memories. But I guess it's all in how you grow up—what you get used to. So, you don't approve of Mark's surprise?" The notion raised Megan's hackles. It was one thing for her to take her brother on, and quite another for someone else to do it. Especially over an unselfish gesture.

"You make me sound petty, when actually it's just that I'm worried. Lauren's particularly vulnerable. And…I'm partly to blame." It was Sterling's turn to check around for his son. Seeing him several yards ahead, he muttered in a voice as scratchy as sand, "I had a friend, a lawyer, check into the legal ramifications of a divorce. Lauren took his return call the day Blythe was killed. You can't begin to know how much I regret that."

He faced forward, and Megan noted a dull red creeping up his neck. Even from her vantage point, she could see bleakness in his gray eyes. She wished she'd had some of Mark's psychology training. Then she might know the right thing to say. "Maybe if you sat down with Lauren and explained. I'm sure you had valid reasons for calling your friend, the lawyer."

He turned to her, and his eyes were even bleaker. "I thought so. I found out my wife was spending more than work hours with her partner. They were both killed that night. Even if I thought Lauren would believe I had valid reasons, which I doubt, I wouldn't be much of a man if I tore down her sister as a means of justifying my action."

"Strange," she murmured. "Mark and I had a conversation like this the other night. Our real dad was a jerk, to put it mildly." Megan climbed back on her bike and Sterling did the same. The wind felt good on her face as they rode down the next incline. "Mark and I have differing views. I think now Mom should have been honest with us from the outset. Mark said he'd prefer to hold on to a false view of Dad."

"Please, don't mention a word to your brother. I shouldn't have said anything. I've told no one, so I can't think why I unloaded this on you just now."

"It's okay. I talk a lot, and fast, I know. But I can keep secrets."

He merely nodded.

Megan climbed from her bike to walk the next hill. "Don't take this wrong," she went on, "but seeing the bigger picture explains the blustery attitude you've shown Mark and me."

"How so?"

"I can see why, after losing your wife in the way you did, you'd project an unconscious dislike on me because of my rescue work."

Sterling coughed, and cleared his throat to say Megan had it wrong. His snapping at her last night had less to do with Blythe, and more to do with his failure to save a woman's life. "You did a brave thing, Megan, going down into the cabin to locate the lost kid."

She slanted him a look of surprise. "You've changed your opinion?"

"According to the morning newspaper, no one else in the crew was skinny enough to fit through the opening, which apparently was jammed in position."

She felt her face flush. "I can only hope my commander is a fan of that paper. Donovan gave me hell last night. He told me only to assess the situation and in his mind that didn't mean taking off my life vest. It probably wasn't the smartest thing I've ever done," she admitted wryly. "I'm going to have to make it plain to impressionable kids like Joel, that it's definitely a case of do as I say and not as I do…uh…did. I won't take that kind of risk again."

Thanks to her candor, he seemed to drop his guard. After that, the two of them and Tyler had a great time taking in all the sights at the old fort.

They were in much better spirits than the three who'd ridden around the island when they all converged on a restaurant near the fudge shop for lunch. Mark, Lauren and Joel were exhausted. As they gorged on the sweet candy later and caught the ferry to St. Ignace, Megan asked if Sterling was starting a full ferry route soon.

"I'm looking forward to getting back on a schedule," he said, leaning his arms on the rail as the wind ruffled his dark hair. "The kids said your grandmother's coming for a visit. I guess that means you won't be available for a rematch at pool next week."

"Mona's only staying for three days. But if the guys from my crew talked you into this, you should tell them to take a flying leap off a short pier."

His laughter was spontaneous. Turning, he treated Megan to the full flash of brilliant white teeth and she felt her knees buckle. She was forced to grab the railing with both hands and hang on tight. Even then, she wasn't really prepared for his teasing when he said, "I planned to pick a night your crew wasn't around. What do you say? Dinner, dancing, a friendly game or two of pool?"

She quickly cast a glance around the boat to see who might have overheard him. Mark, Lauren and Joel slouched on benches looking totally wiped. Tyler had his head in Lauren's lap, his eyelids drooping.

"Uh, Dodge," Megan mumbled, no small amount of suspicion tinging her words, "you wouldn't be asking me on a date, would you?"

His eyes, caught in the sinking rays of sun, looked almost silvery. He gazed at her steadily. Then he lifted his right hand and with a curved knuckle swiped her chin in a *here's looking at you, kid* sort of casualness. "I seem to be doing just that. What do you say, Lieutenant?"

"Damn," she blurted. "Mona's leaving on Wednesday, but our cousin Keith comes in that day. Oh, maybe Mark can entertain him for one night. Is Thursday good?"

Sterling nodded, then they both spun forward and stared out to sea. Megan was glad Tyler chose to run up and wedge his sturdy little body between them. His dad swung the boy aloft, bypassing an awkward moment when she might have snatched back her too-hasty consent. What had possessed her? It'd be hard to find more mismatched people. And yet, as the ferry docked and the odd but enjoyable day wound to a close, Megan's heart skipped with renewed vitality. For reasons she hesitated to admit, even to herself…

CHAPTER EIGHT

MEGAN RUSHED THROUGH THE apartment before breakfast on Monday morning, picking up, cleaning, dusting and polishing in anticipation of their grandmother's visit.

"Sis, for cripe's sake, if you vacuum one more room, you'll have Dodge up here again yelling, thinking we've set up a bowling alley over his head."

"Sterling goes in early today. He's probably gone already. Anyway, I don't care if I wake up the world. I want to be sure Mona doesn't have any reason to find fault with my housekeeping."

"Like she cares. She doesn't vacuum or dust, she has a housekeeper."

"Point made!" Megan blew her bangs out of her eyes. After completing a circuit of the living room, she shoved the vacuum cleaner into the coat closet and capped the can of furniture polish. Then she proceeded to dash about the room, straightening the artwork hanging on the walls.

"I'll collect Gram at ten and be back here by noon. Are you still sure you want to give her your bedroom?"

"Yes. Did she say to call her Gram? Toby never allowed us to use anything except their given names."

"I tell you, she's changed. Having us call them Mona and Toby was his thing. Megan, do you think it's ironic that he died first and from a bad heart? Toby was such a fitness nut. Remember how he insisted we hike all over town? And food. Toby never really ate, he grazed. I expected him to outlive us all."

Megan put the polish rag she'd used in the trash. "Toby drank whiskey neat, and he chain-smoked cigars. Both were worse habits for his health than clogging his arteries with food." She washed and dried her hands, then critically surveyed the kitchen. "I know you stocked the fridge, but Mona may prefer to eat out tonight. If so, call me on my cell. I'll meet you at whatever restaurant she chooses."

"Uh…didn't I tell you? Lauren's helping me prepare tonight's meal. They're all coming up, sort of to welcome Gram."

"No, Mark, you failed to mention that small detail," Megan said, examining him critically. "Can Lauren cook? She seems…too perfect to dirty her hands in the kitchen."

"There you go, judging again. Lauren works hard. She does most of the housework and all the cooking. Has for a long time, I gather."

"Oh, come on. Is she feeding you a line? I thought her sister only recently died."

"Yes, but according to Lauren and Joel, too, their older sister considered anything to do with house and home a drudgery. What shocked me was that Lauren said Dodge was the one who took a parenting leave when Tyler was born. Six months. Then he hired a nanny who came in until Tyler was three and entered a Montessori program."

"Why is that so surprising? Watch Sterling interact with Tyler sometime. Nurturing seems second nature to him. I noticed it during the time we spent at the fort."

"You've sure changed your tune. I wouldn't expect you to stick up for Dodge."

"I give credit where it's due, Mark. I look at Sterling and see a man trying to make a home for three otherwise orphaned kids. Well, technically not Tyler, I guess." Stopping at the laundry room, Megan took a load of towels out of the dryer and folded them. "Will you put these in the hall linen closet, Mark? I need to go or I'll be late for duty."

He awkwardly accepted the bundle. "You won't forget to request time off on Wednesday so you can meet Keith? Even if Lauren and I didn't want to see the Soo Locks, there's no way I'd be able to drop Gram at the Chippewa airport and drive back to pick up Keith on the outskirts of Mackinaw City. Who'd have thought, both coming from Missouri, that they'd land at two different airports?"

"Not me." Megan grabbed her jacket and cap. "I'm sure I'll be able to get a few hours off or switch shifts with someone." With a hand on the doorknob, she asked, "Mark, have you talked to Mom in the last few days?"

"No. You think I'd willingly ask for a lecture? The last few have been brutal. Mom has laying on guilt down to a science. Why? Have you two talked? Did she tell you to kick me out and send me home?"

"Nothing of the sort. It's just that Mom usually calls every weekend. She hasn't phoned in the last two weeks. Keith mentioned she's been feeling sick."

"I'm sure it's nothing serious or we'd hear from Camp. You know Mom's disgustingly healthy. Look at all the colds and flu she nursed us through, and she never so much as sneezed."

"Yeah. But according to the news, spring colds are wicked this year." She wrenched open the front door. "If I worry before there's a reason to worry, I'll have become my mother. I inherited all the worry genes and you got none—" she sighed "—so I guess I'll call her myself. And depending on my schedule, I'll call you during my lunch break, just to make sure Mona got in."

"You are so like Mom. If she couldn't find something to worry about, she wondered why." He waved Megan off with a grin.

At the station, she picked up her schedule and was surprised to see that after lighthouse checks, her agenda entailed recertification checks on the ferryboats being called into full service. Ferries ran from three locations, and all were vital to transporting visitors to and from the island during peak season. One of the Coast Guard duties was visitor safety. Beginning in May, traffic reportedly quadrupled. Commander Donovan had warned all his crews to expect their shifts to get hectic. As the weather improved, boating activity increased.

Yesterday Megan had overhead Joel telling Mark he'd located and made a sizable down payment on a motorboat. Sterling must've had a change of heart.

The offshore lights were all fine. By eleven, their cutter cruised to Mackinaw City and off-loaded Megan and her day crew. Petty Officer Horowitz stepped up behind her. "The wind's ripe today. He pointed at a few custom-made sailboats. They must be looking over the course for the big race. I hear it's in June."

"Two of those boats are real beauties." Megan stopped to admire them. "There's nothing so gorgeous as a boat clipping through the channel under full sail."

"They ought to be pretty," Horowitz snorted. "Those

babies each cost over a quarter of a mil. All that money, just to prove who has the fastest boat."

"I read a bit about the yearly Chicago-to-Mackinac race. Three hundred and thirty miles. I wonder if we'll get to see any of the boats cross the finish line."

"Last year Commander Donovan asked for volunteers to patrol the night hours. He said the weather often gets dicey. Not last year, though. I volunteered, but it was boring as hell."

The sun had come out, sparkling on the waves. "You see, Horowitz, that's a big difference between men and women. You guys go out on every run hoping for some colossal accident. I pray for calm seas."

"Yeah. Well, today we have a boring mission that ought to suit you, Lieutenant. Here's the background information on the first six ferry captains." He handed her a clipboard. "Last year, we just did a cursory walk-through to make sure all the ferries were equipped with the required number of lifeboats, and that licenses were current. As ranking officer of the day, you'll advise the captains of their obligation to report suspicious activity that might be a threat to homeland security and so forth. You know, like if a visitor asks too many questions about container ships in the channel. Stuff like that."

Megan flipped through the sheets on the clipboard and listened to Horowitz with half an ear. The area on the forms noting past history was of particular interest to her. She reached Sterling Dodge's background sheet and was stunned to see that his vessel in New York had been involved in a major wreck. One that resulted in injuries. And a fatality. Her heart pounded until she read the statement indicating he'd been exonerated by the investigative task force.

Going back to the top of the form, Megan checked the date of the accident. It'd crossed her mind that Sterling might not have been honest with her about the real reason for his move. She'd wondered if his motivation had been a pilot error and the ensuing damage to his reputation, instead of removing Joel and Lauren from unsavory elements, as he'd said. But the accident report was three years old. It appeared he'd worked steadily after being cleared of any wrongdoing.

Her team reviewed several boats and captains ahead of Sterling. Provided he docked on time, they could finish his boat before lunch. If Megan expected a warm greeting, the surprise was on her. He took one look at her and frowned.

"What are you doing on the Algonquin?" he asked as she appeared in his wheelhouse.

"Routine inspection, sir," Matt Horowitz called in his most professional Coast Guard manner. The petty officer produced a second clipboard full of blank forms that were checklists denoting pass or fail. "You can go about your business, Captain. Pretend Lieutenant Benton and our crew aren't poking around. We'll be as unobtrusive as mice."

Megan couldn't resist adding, "But let's hope we don't run across any mice on this vessel, Captain Dodge. That would get your boat quarantined. Plague. Hantavirus," she put forth with a mischievous grin. Still, all they got from Sterling was a stony reaction.

"Phew," Matt said under his breath as he, Megan and Seaman Dennis Brown left the wheelhouse. "Isn't that the guy Elkhorn dug up the other night thinking he'd beat you at pool?"

"Lieutenant, junior grade Elkhorn, you mean?" Megan reminded sharply. "We are on an official mission here, Petty Officer."

"Gotcha! But isn't Captain Dodge the poor schmuck whose butt you whipped? He must be PO'd about that."

Megan didn't know what Sterling's problem happened to be today. Neither was she about to discuss the captain of this vessel with a subordinate. Her crew might joke around off duty, but never on government time. Pointedly, she changed the subject. "While Seaman Brown counts the lifeboats, I'll have a look at the other safety equipment on board. Why don't you verify that Captain Dodge's license is up-to-date?"

Matthew Horowitz got her message and immediately withdrew.

They'd boarded Dodge's run in Mackinaw City. This particular catamaran ferry took fifteen minutes to reach Mackinac Island, also known as *Mackinaw.* The story behind the two different spellings dated back to French fur traders and Native Indian dwellers, who'd first called the island Michilimackinac. That supposedly meant Great Turtle, because of the island's shape. Megan had perused the history, but decided she'd leave it to the locals to explain all those facts to visitors.

She'd heard that a rivalry existed between the different ferry-line owners, as to whose boats were fastest. With the older, heavier models there was no contest. But between cats like this one and the jet boat she was slated to inspect next, there was an ongoing and spirited competition. Maybe Sterling thought they'd interrupt his timetable or something.

"By my count, everything here rates passing scores," Megan said to her crew as Sterling docked neatly with barely a nudge. "I'll sign off on our inspection with the captain. You go on and board the *Hiawatha.* Tell the captain I'll be there in a minute."

"Aye," both of her crew said and swiftly crossed the gangway.

Sterling talked on his cell phone and at the same time trimmed the Algonquin's engines. Megan watched him for a moment. As if feeling her eyes, he spun, stared at her blankly, then deliberately turned aside. It was obvious he didn't want her listening to his conversation.

No doubt he'd been through many similar inspections. Megan knew she could set the signed form under his sunglasses. The form was self-explanatory. Something in the escalating tension of his voice had her hesitating, however.

"I can't get away to come after Joel. If the principal recalls, I did say Joel might act up after I started work." He paced from the wheel, which he'd clamped off, to the wraparound window, where he gave the high sign to a worker lashing the ferry to the dock. Certainly his frustration level was mounting. Megan heard him sigh.

Moving nearer, she said softly and urgently, "Is this something Mark can take care of for you, Sterling? He should be back from the airport with our grandmother by now. I'll be boarding the jet boat going to St. Ignace soon. If I phone Mark to meet us, he can easily make the return trip to the island. Is Joel ill?" She pressed close enough to make it impossible for Sterling to ignore her.

"Not ill, in trouble," he snapped. "No, not you," he said into the phone. "I'm talking to someone at work.

It's, uh, impossible for me to get away until my shift ends." He pulled off his captain's hat and tossed it onto the window ledge. "I'm very sure Joel's aware of that. No, I'm not excusing his actions." This time Sterling sounded firm. "Can you place him on detention or under house arrest or whatever schools call it these days? Yes, that'll do—in-house detention. Can you do that until my shift ends at three-thirty?"

From the way he pinched the bridge of his nose and shook his head, making strands of black hair fall over his grooved forehead, Megan was pretty sure the woman at the other end was filling his ear with reasons that wouldn't work.

Half glaring at Megan, he said, "My only other alternative is to send someone in my stead. A young man by the name of Mark, uh, Benton. I know he's not listed on my authorization card. We were brand-new to the area when I enrolled the kids. Mark's a neighbor." Pausing, Sterling waited to read what Megan was mouthing to him in the background.

"Tell her Mark's a certified child psychologist."

Nodding, Sterling relayed that message.

Megan assumed it satisfied the caller, as Sterling's stiff shoulders relaxed. "A three-day suspension?" The shoulders tensed again. "That's a hardship for me. It's nonnegotiable? I see. I certainly will be in touch."

A male voice called up the hollow stairwell of the now-empty ferry, asking for Megan. One of her crew. She indicated to Sterling via hand signals that she had to go. But she also needed to know what to tell Mark.

Sterling wasted no time cutting short his caller. "First, uh…thank Mark." Frowning, he rubbed the back of his neck as if accepting favors was foreign to him.

"Uh, tell Mark, please, that Joel apparently got hold of some cigars. I have no earthly idea how. I've never smoked. The upshot is, the little devil passed the stogies around to his friends at lunch. Now the school nurse has four sick boys in her office. To my way of thinking, that's punishment enough, but school rules put this offense in the category of a three-day suspension for Joel, who they claim is the instigator. If Mark sees to it that Joel makes it home in one piece, I'd appreciate him not letting the kid out of his sight until I get home. Or is that asking too much?"

Megan hovered half in, half out of the door. "I'm sorry, Sterling. As pranks go, I frankly expected worse. I'll fill Mark in. Hey, on a more cheerful note, I tucked your inspection report under your shades. You passed with flying colors, Cap'n." Megan thought the man deserved some good news.

The off-kilter smile he mustered sent her silly heart into overdrive.

"My mom had a saying she lived by when Mark and I were giving her such a hard time. *This, too, shall pass.* And look how great we turned out," she said, sending him a cheeky grin before she ducked out and disappeared down the narrow passage.

"Hey," he called after her. "Thanks, neighbor. I needed a motivational speech." He realized after she left that it was true. He'd been far more nervous his first day on the job than the work warranted. Work he could do blindfolded. And he'd been surly when Megan appeared. She added to his unrest. But being upbeat seemed such an integral part of Megan Benton's personality, she'd infused him with a positive attitude. She'd also provided him with a solution to his problem. What if she hadn't come in when she did? Sterling was a man used to being in control—except when it came to his wife's siblings. From the get-go, Blythe had let him know he had no say in their upbringing. And now that her skewed world had tumbled down around them all, he had to find a way to cope. In New York he'd compartmentalized his work, his son, his marriage, his friends.

Here, his upstairs neighbors didn't fit easily in any one compartment. They kept intruding past his boundaries. Especially Megan.

Putting on his cap, Sterling went to greet the next group of passengers. Then he returned to his perch and took out his thermos, laughing when he poured the lid full of hot chocolate. He lifted the cup in a silent toast. Lieutenant Benton had definitely gotten past his boundaries. And it wasn't a bad thing, he decided. The more he saw her, the more provocative ideas popped into his head. Ideas prone to strike a man at odd and inopportune moments. Ideas Captain Dodge had held at bay for a long while. Maybe too long. What if he'd forgotten how to maneuver his way through male-female interchanges? Or, more to the point, did he have too many responsibilities to even consider getting involved?

As Joel's latest escapade loomed front and center, Sterling drained his cup and capped the thermos. He ought to put a lid on his desires as well. He'd been damned lousy at his marriage. He'd have to be an idiot to dive headfirst into another relationship.

MEGAN FLIPPED OUT HER cell phone the minute she stepped off Sterling's boat. She punched in her home number. Mark answered on the second ring.

"Yes, I'm here," he said before his sister had even

said hello. "Yes, I got Gram. And yes, all is fine on the home front."

"Ha! That's not why I'm calling, big mouth." Speaking rapidly, Megan told him Joel Atwater's story.

The line hummed, then Mark drawled, "An April Fools' joke, right?"

Megan gathered her wits. "I forgot it was April Fools' day. Listen, Mark, this is for real. It's unfortunate you have to leave Mona. But she's probably worn-out after her flight. Maybe she can take a nap while you do this favor for Sterling."

He guffawed loudly. "You have the wrong perception of Gram. She's rip-roaring ready to see the sights. We'll meet you at the dock, and I'll take her with me to the island. We'll grab Joel and pick up a few last-minute items for tonight's dinner on the way home. Remember we're all eating up here. Outside of a detour, this won't pose a big problem. I met the school secretary the day you gave the safety class, and she's really nice, Megan."

"It's more complicated than just running down to the school to pick up Joel. First, he's sick as a dog from smoking cigars. And Sterling let them know in no uncertain terms that it'd be a hardship for him if they follow through with suspending Joel for three days. Do you suppose they might be talked into having him write an essay on the evils of smoking instead? I mean, if you explain that Sterling's new at his job, maybe they'll be more lenient. You'll have to finesse them with your psychobabble, Mark. That's why you ought to leave Mona at home."

"No, that's all the more reason I should bring her. Who can refuse a nice little old lady's request? Out of curiosity, how did Dodge happen to ask for your help instead of calling me himself? Is there something going on between you two that you're not telling me?"

"What's going on is that I officially inspected his boat. We were docking when the school phoned. And if you'd hang up, I'll board the next ferry I have to inspect. Anyway, Mark *you're* the one focused on relationships, not me." She signed off, feeling a momentary stab of guilt. Because it was true that she noticed a marked difference in her heartbeat when Sterling Dodge came into view.

Her partner, Matthew Horowitz, escorted Megan onboard the jet boat and thrust a clipboard into her hand with only twenty minutes to spare before the ferry would've left without her. Unlike the captain she'd just left, the captain of this craft turned out to be fat, bald and sixty. A salty old dog who reminded her of Hank Meade. Captain Orville Patterson entertained Megan and her crew with tales about places like Skull Cave on the island. The cave, an early burial site for the Native Americans who'd once inhabited Michilimackinac, had reportedly saved the life of more than one British merchant seaman who traded at the old fort. Apparently they took refuge in the cave, confident of the fact that Indians wouldn't pursue them into the sacred site.

As Megan did her inspection, she wondered why the natives didn't just wait outside the cave and capture the British merchants when they emerged. But she decided that would make for less exciting legends told to impress modern-day visitors.

The stories took Megan's mind off the prospect of meeting her Grandmother Benton at the dock in St. Ignace. She'd avoided Mona for most of the last six or seven years, primarily because their grandmother refused to accept their mom's second marriage. Megan expected an unpleasant reception and wondered at the effect it might have on her crewmates. The Coast Guard operated on a strict hierarchy, as subscribed to by all branches of the military. Some of the men at her all-male duty station would give a week's pay to see their pool-shark lieutenant receive a public dressing-down, especially from such a delicate-looking old lady. For that reason she wished she'd been able to convince Mark to fetch Joel Atwater alone.

She handed Captain Patterson his inspection report and realized her palms were sweating as they neared the dock. From her perch in the captain's quarters, Megan scanned the area for a first view of Mark and Mona. Mark's carrot-red hair was a beacon that stood out as the ferry hit the bumper guards extending out from the dock. The ticket terminal closed off her view of the other passengers waiting to board.

Sweaty palms or no, she shook hands with Patterson and prepared to disembark. As he had the last time, Matt Horowitz left to arrange for them to board the catamaran double-decker ferry slated to return to Mackinaw City.

Megan bumped right into Mark. She glanced around and assumed Mona must have stayed home. Had a familiar cashmere sweater not caught her eye, Megan would've walked right past her grandmother, because she was grayer and appeared far more frail than at any time in Megan's long but erratic history with her.

"Megan..." Mona hesitated slightly before she reached out and hugged her granddaughter. "Don't you look impressive in your uniform?" Pulling back, Mona blotted her eyes. "Standing here, looking at you and

Mark, I find it hard to remember you as toddlers. You make me feel every minute my age."

Trapped in Mona's arms, Megan gaped at the sensible walking shoes, frumpy slacks and nondescript car coat over the cashmere sweater. Most of all, she stared at soft wrinkles framing a shaky smile in a cosmetic-free face. "Mona?" Megan gave her head a resounding shake to clear the cobwebs of the past. A past in which this woman was draped head to toe in black Armani widow's weeds, as Megan's mother had described it. "Mona, are you….have you been ill?"

The tinkle of laughter was also uncharacteristic. Mona Benton, as far back as Megan's memory stretched, had gushed, lectured or imperiously delivered edicts. Laughter was, on the fleeting occasions it was heard, brittle and short in duration.

The fragile creature standing before Megan now scraped back her hair. Then, with a touch of the old Mona, she drawled, "I should probably resent the hell out of that question, Megan, but I'll let it go because I'm sure you didn't mean it the way it sounded. It's been a while and we've both changed. To answer you, though, I'm well, and anxious to spend time with my grandchildren. Then I'm off to embrace the challenge of a world tour. Please, will you call me Gram, like Mark has for the past couple of years? Will you do that, Megan?"

Openmouthed, Megan finally slipped free of the woman she was sure must be impersonating Mona Benton. Megan sent Mark a confounded look. He, however, was impatient to board the ferry.

"I hate to cut short this reunion," he said. "Megan,

do you have anything to add to what you said on the phone about us collecting Joel at school?"

She shook her head, and backed away. "I, uh…am going to be late for my next inspection if I don't run. But…wait," she called, as Mark, taking her at her word, handed Mona a ticket and went to hustle her onto the ferry. "If Joel's sick to his stomach from the cigar, you'll probably want to have a plastic bag handy for the ride home. There's a decided chop to the waves today. His reaction won't be pretty."

Brother and sister shared a knowing grin. Both, no doubt, recalled a time when they'd sneaked cigarettes and nearly burned down their stepdad's brand-new barn. Camp had caught them and forced them to sit and smoke every single cigarette in the pack Megan had filched. They'd ended up pea-green. To the best of Megan's knowledge neither one had ventured to smoke again. That, of course, had been Nolan Campbell's aim.

"Do you think Joel will be skipping dinner tonight?" Mark asked, tongue in cheek.

"Highly possible," his sister answered, turning to hurry off. Megan hadn't been looking forward to tonight's gathering. Now she feared it might be downright miserable. Sterling had been forced to accept a bit of good-neighboring, most likely against his will. And the woman she'd been repeatedly told to call Mona had come equipped with an alien personality.

Megan found herself desperately wanting to phone her mom. Did Emily Benton Campbell know about this transformation? Megan hoped not. She wanted to be the one to break the news.

IT SO HAPPENED EMILY Campbell was at that moment barfing into a plastic bag in her doctor's office. "I'm sorry, Dr. Gregory. This nervous stomach is partly due to my ex-mother-in-law." She turned from the sink, where the nurse had led her to rinse the horrible taste from her mouth with a cool cup of water. "I just found out she's on her way to visit my children. I'm sure she's doing it to spite me."

The doctor helped her step up to sit on the examining table. Emily gestured with the cup. "I'm here because my husband hopes you'll give me a tranquilzer or something. He's fed up with my vomiting several times a week. Not really fed up," she said, attempting a wry smile. "He's worried I've let my ex-mother-in-law give me an ulcer."

A lab technician came into the room, prepared to take samples of Emily's blood. "You need blood?" she demanded of the kindly, white-haired Dr. Gregory. Emily had visited the Campbell family doctor a scant few times. This week, however, even Sherry had added her urging to her brother's, which helped convince Emily she needed to see the doctor. She had to do *something* about the fact that she'd let Mona's meddling in the kids' lives make her ill.

The doctor stuck his stethoscope in his ears and motioned Emily to be quiet so he could listen to her heart and lungs. "Em, I wouldn't be a very good physician if I didn't rule out everything that might make a young woman like yourself vomit off and on. Hush, and let Rebecca Vampire relieve you of two or three vials of blood."

That had the desired effect. She closed her mouth

and turned to gaze warily at the perky brunette tying a fat rubber tube around Emily's upper arm. "Your last name isn't really Vampire?" she asked with some shock.

Emily actually recognized the girl as having been in one of her college classes in Women's Studies a few years ago. Rebecca smiled and shook her head. "It's Velacruz, Professor Campbell." She expertly slid a needle in her patient's vein. "You get Dr. Gregory's stand-up comedy routine without paying a cover charge."

Emily nodded, not terribly amused. The girl changed vials. She filled three before pressing a cotton swab to the puncture, then flitted out of the room.

The doctor let his stethoscope fall around his neck, and got a tongue depressor to peer down Emily's throat. He asked a million questions, or so it seemed to her as he poked and prodded and then listed her responses in a scrawl she was sure he'd never be able to decipher later.

Done prodding, he pulled up a stool and sat. "Are your monthly cycles normal?" His pen was poised over the chart.

"What cycles? Oh, my periods?" Emily adjusted the crinkly paper gown that didn't cover nearly enough of her pale, freckled skin. Tossing her head, she raked an unsteady hand through her hair. She noticed she was always unsteady after one of her vomiting sessions. "I'm forty-five, doctor." She picked at the ragged hem of the paper gown. "I've been dealing with menopause symptoms for several months. Hot flashes. Night sweats. I'm sure you've heard the complaints a lot. I react badly to so many medications, I'd like to get by without hormone therapy if possible. I bought a book on natural methods at the college bookstore."

The doctor's pen scratched for a time, then he glanced up. "Marge should have allotted time to do a complete physical, including a pelvic exam. But she didn't and I've got back-to-back appointments today. I'd like you to stop at the desk on your way out and get one on the books. Oh, and let's do a urinalysis."

Emily's features tightened. "Doctors have a tendency to blame everyone of a woman's health complaints on hormones, but I know exactly what my problem is. My meddling ex-mother-in-law left a message on my answering machine over the weekend to rub in the fact that she's gone to visit my son and daughter in Michigan. That woman has been the bane of my existence since my children were born. She's got more money than the U.S. Mint. When my husband died—my first husband, her son—I thought Mona and I had parted ways. I thought we'd settled once and for all that she and her husband could not buy my children's affection." Heat suffused Emily's face, and she began to gag so much Dr. Gregory hurriedly grabbed a basin.

"It's okay, Mrs. Campbell. I'm not making light of your differences with this woman. Perhaps a mild tranquilizer will get you through a difficult patch with her. But in all conscience I can't write a prescription until I rule out anything physical." He patted Emily's shoulder. "The tests should all be back by the end of this week. Call me for the results. Oh, I'd still like you to schedule that physical. Say sometime this week?"

Emily grimaced as she reached for her clothes. "All right. It's overdue anyway. I put them off as long as I can."

"I understand." The doctor smiled. "By the way. How old are the children your ex-mother-in-law is trying to tempt away with money? Teenagers? Kids are so materialistic and shallow at that age. Try telling yourself it's a phase they're going through."

She clutched her slacks and blouse to her chest. "Uh, Megan's twenty-five, and Mark is twenty-three." She felt a blush reach the roots of her still fire-red hair. "Don't tell me they're adults who are able to make up their own minds. Their real father was ruined by his parents' wealth. If I didn't have a job I can't leave, and if I could stop this incessant throwing up, I'd hop a plane and go fight that infuriating woman toe-to-toe, like I did when the kids were twelve and fourteen." Tears began leaking from Emily's eyes. She dashed them away. "I'm sorry. Honestly, Dr. Gregory, you must think I'm a basket case. Please believe me, as a rule I'm not. I can't think what's gotten into me. I'm usually quite rational."

The doctor snatched several tissues out of a box and stuffed them into one of his patient's hands. "On second thought, Mrs. Campbell, I'd like the results of all our tests before we chat again. Tell Marge to work you in for an exam early next week. Or better yet, I'll tell her. She'll have a time for you when you leave," he said, backing out and shutting the door.

Emily calmed down after he left. She dressed, stopped to speak with Marge and tried to talk her into delaying the exam. "Oh, all right," Emily said when the woman wouldn't budge. She tucked the appointment card in her purse and rearranged her hair with a nervous hand. "I feel so stupid having these mood swings at my age. It's probably a huge waste of time, but I'll come for the exam. My husband will nag me to death if I don't."

CHAPTER NINE

THE APARTMENT SMELLED slightly scorched. Megan sniffed the air. No one heard her come in, and it wasn't any wonder. Talk and laughter spilled from the kitchen. She identified Mark's voice, and Lauren teasing him about something.

Taking off her boots, Megan headed for the bathroom. She needed a quick shower. Being on ferries for most of the day, poking into all their musty equipment compartments, had left her feeling grimy.

She'd managed to put her grandmother's visit out of her mind until she stepped into the bathroom and was engulfed in the scent of lavender. It blotted out the pungent odors wafting from the kitchen. The smell of lavender brought back memories. Every room in the big brick house in Benton Corners carried her grandmother's signature fragrance. Sheets, pillowcases, drapes, even the flower boxes on the front porch and back patio, overflowed with the scent.

Megan touched a perfume bottle and powder box with expensive import labels. She was surprised to find the recollections weren't bad. Absently reaching in, she flipped on the shower, then quickly gathered a set of clean clothes and locked herself inside the steamy room. As a kid, she'd loved to visit her grandparents.

The cook always fixed her and Mark's favorite foods. Surprise gifts awaited them. Trips to Benton Corners were like Christmas. What kid would object?

She hadn't—until she became aware of the growing battles between her grandparents and her mother.

Megan stripped off her clothes and stepped under a hot, cleansing spray. Perhaps tension always existed between Mona, Toby and Emily. As a teenager, Megan certainly went out of her way to fan the flames, but it did no good to feel guilty about that now. Still, it wasn't hard to see the contrast between the big, easygoing Campbell clan and the two Bentons, who thought they could and should buy their grandkids' affection. Megan had learned that, whether they were aware of it or not, most kids craved boundaries set with stability and love.

Hearing Mark and Sterling talk about Lauren's and Joel's loose upbringing by their sister, and looking back on her own life, Megan saw some similarities. She wondered if Mark did, too.

As she toweled off and pulled on jeans and a T-shirt, she thought Sterling faced some tough times with those two, beyond today's debacle with Joel handing out cigars. Sterling would do well to be more open and to accept help and advice.

Gazing in the steamy mirror, Megan tried taming wet curls springing out in all directions. Yet it wasn't her hair claiming her full attention, but memories of Sterling's unyielding eyes and sometimes pugnacious jaw.

She ought to butt out of his life. Except, something about Dodge had a way of stirring to life the fantasies Megan had never shared with another soul. Everyone in her family thought she was dedicated to proving she was smarter and tougher than any man. Not so. Megan dreamed of meeting one special someone with whom she'd share her life. Just because she didn't blab her secret desires like so many girls didn't mean her fantasies didn't exist.

A misty cloud of lavender hung in the air and was now mixed with her vanilla-almond soap. The bouquet followed her as she left the bathroom. She scooped up her dirty clothes to toss in the hamper. She dropped them in and stilled as a deeper, more mature laugh floated down the hall.

Sterling had come. Megan had more than half doubted he would.

It wasn't until she passed Mark's room on her way to the kitchen that she noticed a body sprawled across her brother's bed. *Joel.* "Hey," she called softly, stepping to the door. "So you're still not feeling good? Not to worry," she remarked after hearing him groan. "Whatever they're cooking up in the kitchen smells ghastly. Even so, you probably should try to eat a little something, Joel."

The motionless blob on the bed stirred and flopped over again.

"I'll take that as a *no,*" Megan said with sympathy. Pausing, she relayed the experience she and Mark had with cigarettes. She was about to add that they'd learned a valuable lesson when a gravelly voice next to her ear announced, "I'd rather he heard stories of people who didn't live to talk about their mistakes."

She gave a start, failing to understand how anyone as large and imposing as Sterling Dodge could sneak up on her like that.

"Don't be mean. Can't you see Joel's suffering?"

"I don't doubt he is. I gave him more credit than to pull such a stunt."

"Go 'way," Joel mumbled and flung an arm over his ashen face. "Let me die, okay? I don't give a shit about anything right now."

Megan felt Sterling tense. She bit her lip to keep quiet and let him handle this. She felt sorry for both the boy and the man. Yet she couldn't resist saying, "You must've done some dumb things as a boy."

Megan's springy hair tickled his chin as Sterling glanced down into her upturned face. Her question hit him like a small fist. "No. I was raised by immigrant grandparents. They came to New York from Devon, England, when I was a toddler. My grandfather was a ship builder. A fire destroyed his shipyard, and my parents were both lost in the blaze. They worked around the clock, it seemed, to rebuild a lost fortune. I was expected to do the same. I had no heart or talent for the trade, which disappointed them. The least I could do, I felt, was never cause them trouble."

Megan gazed at him in awe. That clipped statement said a lot about him. "It must've been tough trying to be a model child. I thought all kids acted out and did stupid things to brag about to their peers."

His black brows dived together. "I don't think what Joel did today is anything to brag about. And isn't someone calling you from the kitchen?"

Wanting to give the kid a reprieve, Megan hooked an arm through Sterling's and dragged him down the hall with her. "Going to the kitchen is an excellent plan. You'll probably get along famously with Mona—uh, my grandmother. Or maybe not," she muttered, thinking his grandparents were probably very different from hers.

"Your grandmother told Lauren and Tyler to call her Gram. Why do you call her Mona?"

"It's a long story. What's everyone drinking? Can I get you a beer?" They stepped through the door, and Megan's eyes opened wide. Her normally pristine kitchen looked like a train wreck. Mona and Tyler sat at the table, pieces to a board game spread all over. They'd shoved aside place mats already set with dishes, glassware and silver. And the sink was piled high with dirty pots and pans.

Mona waved. "Hello, dear. I do believe this young man is even more bent on winning than you used to be."

Tyler yelled, "Yippee," over some accomplishment, pulling Mona's regard away from Megan. And she was still distracted by the mess. The countertops overflowed. A badly charred pan stood out. Megan wrinkled her nose, now able to identify the source of the scorched smell. Not a single one of the beautiful copper-bottomed pans she'd hung above her island counter strictly for show, remained on the hammered-metal ring. They were all blackened by gas, whose flame remained high enough to heat the room and make one pan lid dance. Mark and Lauren, who were supposedly responsible for fixing dinner, huddled together giggling near the refrigerator.

Mark noticed Megan only after Mona's effusive greeting. He waggled a can of beer. "Hi, when did you sneak in, sis? Dinner's a tad delayed, so grab a soda or a beer. Oh, wait, Gram fixed Tyler hot chocolate." Mark turned his attention back to Lauren in a manner that could only be described as adoring. "Lauren's first attempt at crab soufflé appetizer was kind of a flop."

The girl reddened. "He's being kind. My soufflé

burned black and fell. Then I tried lobster bisque soup. I mean, the stores here have such great seafood. But…at home I cooked with electricity. I guess I'm still not used to gas. I had to trash the soup."

Megan counted to ten. She could use some caffeine, but not enough to wend her way through the war zone of discarded cookware. Instead, she grabbed two beers from a carton still sweating on the counter. Afraid to think what that might say about the interior of her refrigerator, she pulled the tabs on both and passed one to Sterling. "So, what is for dinner?" she asked as casually as possible. "I skipped lunch, so I'm famished."

"Third time's the charm, we hope," Mark said, again bestowing a heartfelt smile on the cook. "We decided on mac and cheese for Tyler, and Joel if he comes out. Unfortunately, the rest of us will have to make do with make 'n' bake pizza."

"If I don't burn the crust," Lauren quipped, giving a self-conscious laugh.

"I couldn't find a pizza pan, so we used your cookie sheets."

"They're brand-new," Megan pointed out. "I hope you sprayed them well with nonstick spray."

The pair at the fridge shared guilty glances. "Spray?" they gasped in unison.

Grabbing a pot holder, Megan lowered the oven door. Smoke rolled out as she peered in. The smoke alarm above the door started to shriek.

Mark almost knocked Megan over in his haste to reach up and disconnect the alarm batteries. "'Scuse me, Sterling. This happened with the soufflé, too. Your oven must cook really hot, sis."

Megan extracted two blackened trays. Both metal

cookie sheets were beyond redemption. As she prepared to lambaste her brother, Megan chanced to see Sterling all but convulsing in the corner. His wide shoulders shook in spite of an obvious effort to hide his laughter.

Lauren leaned in to see, and started to wail. Fat tears dribbled over her sculpted cheekbones. "I wanted this to be a nice meal for you all, and for Mark's grandmother's first visit. Instead I ruined everything." The tears fell faster. Mark brushed past Megan again and wrapped the sobbing girl in his long arms.

Taking pity on someone who, from the look of things, had tried hard to please, Megan dumped the smoldering pizzas, pans and all, in an already full trash receptacle.

"I offered to take us all out," Mona said from the table. "But that poor, dear boy in the bedroom looked so under the weather. It would be wrong to leave him alone."

Again Megan thought some alien being had invaded Mona. Compassion for anyone other than her husband or her son had rarely been extended, Megan recalled.

Everyone in the room but Tyler turned eyes on Megan, as if expecting her to conjure up a solution.

No, not all of them. Sterling pulled out his wallet and fanned through a sheaf of bills. Satisfied, he pocketed the wallet. "Mark, come with me. We'll go out and bring something in. Fast food of some kind, probably."

"You always do that," Lauren accused, glaring through tears. "I just wanted this one night to go well. You think I can't do anything. You'll use this as a reason to prove I can't take care of myself and Joel."

"Lauren…I…" Sterling shut his eyes and rolled the sweating beer can across his forehead.

Megan shut off the oven and turned down the burner under the macaroni and cheese. Against her better judgment, she offered a little hug to the unhappy girl. "Lauren, we all have days like this. It so happens I have a favorite Chinese restaurant not far from here, and they deliver. Their take-out menu is in the drawer next to the sink. I only ever order chicken lo mein or pork fried rice, but the guys I work with rave about everything they make. Why don't you all take a look at the menu and choose a variety of dishes?" She lowered her voice so only Lauren could hear. "I have some floating candles I've been saving for a special occasion. See that clear glass bowl on the shelf above the door? Rinse it out and fill it half full of cool water. I'll move Tyler and Mona…uh, Gram, to the living room. You and I will set the table while the guys call in our order. Oh, and get Joel wonton soup. It'll be easy on his stomach."

If Megan had had an extra minute to herself, she'd have chuckled at how everyone scurried around to follow her instructions to the letter.

Later, after they'd coaxed a reluctant Joel to join them at the cozy kitchen table, Mark said, "In spite of a rocky start, Lauren, the evening turned out to be very nice." He lifted a cup of green tea. "Welcome, Gram." He continued to hold the cup aloft as others sat theirs back on the table. "Uh…sis, I've gotta say the Coast Guard pounded organizational skills into you. The Megan I grew up with never could've pulled this off."

She blushed, and wasn't sure whether or not to sock her brother.

The siblings were surprised when Mona spoke.

"Mark, it's long past time you stopped bedeviling your sister. I love you both, but Megan, I'm exceptionally proud of your accomplishments. Women in my day could be secretaries, teachers or nurses. Or someone's wife and mother. I met Toby in college, where my parents really didn't expect me to learn a vocation. Of course, he wouldn't hear of me working. Such a waste of the talents I always thought I possessed. I so envy girls today. You can blend a meaningful career with raising a family." She lifted her eyes and caught everyone staring. "Megan, dear, you look shocked. If I was younger, and had my life to live over, I'd do so many things differently. I'd trade places with you in a minute." Her words rang with authenticity.

Megan's eyes filled and she blinked, pretending to choke on a piece of spicy Szechuan chicken. She was astonished by Mona's words. By her seemingly genuine praise.

Lauren pinned her still-unhappy gaze on her brother-in-law. "Gram's husband and Sterling sound like peas in a pod. He didn't want my sister to work outside the house. He'd rather Blythe spent all her time doing housework and micromanaging us kids."

It was plain from his frown, that Sterling didn't like the spotlight being turned on him. "I hardly think what's in the past needs discussing here, Lauren."

Mona treated him to a stern once-over. "Men should step out of the dark ages. It's time to admit that women are really more capable of multitasking than men."

Sterling's eyes cut to the older woman. "It sounds easy to say what you'd do if you walked in someone else's shoes. But not all situations or all marriages are alike."

"Be that as it may, I've had more years to sit back and observe. I can say with certainty that it never works out if you impose one person's ideals on another."

"Save your breath," Joel muttered, pushing aside his half-finished soup. "Sterling 'spects everyone to live by his rules. Like I could tell him till I'm blue in the face that it was Merle James who brought the cigars today. Sterling would just say I lied."

Sterling whirled to face the boy. "The school secretary said it was you."

A mutinous expression settled over Joel's slightly green features.

Mark roused himself. "I believe Joel's right. When the secretary left the office for a minute, I listened to the boys talking among themselves. And later, when I sat down to discuss his suspension, I asked if any of the boys had a parent who may have cigars at home. It turns out Merle's father smokes them. But no amount of talk got the boys to break their silence in front of the principal. They're not suspended, but they all have two weeks of lunch-hour detentions."

"Joel, if the other boy was at fault, why not tell the school authorities?" Sterling's question fell on the boy's bent head.

Rearing upright, Joel sneered. "Yeah, right! Kids got their own code, man. Two weeks of missing lunch break is no big deal."

Megan understood. "Sterling, new kids are sometimes subjected to unsanctioned initiations. It's probably better to let Joel cope in his own way."

Sterling recalled that the principal had said kids often had ways of dealing with tough-guy outsiders. Because Tyler came over and crawled into his lap, Sterling let the issue drop. “Somebody’s sleepy,” he said, placing a kiss on Tyler’s blond head.

Lauren pushed back from the table. “I have a paper to write that’s due tomorrow. I’ll take the squirt downstairs and stuff him into bed. Mark, you said you’d help me pull together the facts I got at the library on zebra mussels.”

“I know about those,” Sterling said. “The little buggers ruin our freshwater ecosystem. Not just in the Great Lakes, either. They cause millions of dollars’ worth of damage to the intake water pipes of boats. That’s how mussels, native to the Caspian sea, travel from locale to locale. They stick to the bottoms of boats in large clusters, and they multiply like wildfire.”

Lauren showed interest. “I pulled up a picture. They *look* harmless. But one article I read said they deprive native species of food. And they reproduce so fast they smother smaller mussels.”

“A good topic, Lauren. Because fishing and recreational boating are so important here,” Megan said. “Just the other day my station received a directive for our teams to urge all boaters to inspect and clean their hulls regularly.”

“Clean a boat hull how?” Joel, who seemed better, aimed the question at Megan. “Tomorrow I’m picking up the runabout I bought. Do you think the boat place already cleaned my hull? It’s not a brand-new boat.”

“You bought a boat? When?” Sterling demanded. “How?”

“I used part of the cash I got from Blythe’s insurance policy,” Joel was quick to say. “All the guys in my class own runabouts. Jason, Fritz and Merle helped me find a good one.”

"These wouldn't be the same kids involved in the cigar incident?" Sterling tried to see Joel around Tyler's dangling legs as he was being lifted by Lauren.

Mona climbed abruptly to her feet. "Megan, if the youngsters have other fish to fry, shall we tackle kitchen cleanup?"

That sidetracked Sterling. "Lauren and Mark set up dinner tonight to welcome you to Michigan, Mona. You shouldn't have to wash dishes."

Lauren skidded to a halt at the door. "Dishes! He's right. Mark, I left an unholy mess in the kitchen. Oh, I'll be up all night doing that darned paper," she wailed.

Megan waved her off. "Go get cracking on your homework. Mona, you go rest, like Sterling said. One vacation day's gone already. I know you and Mark have plans for tomorrow." She didn't elaborate, as she didn't want to spoil the surprise birthday party. But when a secretive smile passed between Mark and their grandmother, Megan knew they both understood.

"All of you take off," Sterling ordered. "I'll give Megan a hand tidying up." Amid shocked expressions all around, he rose and began to stack dirty plates.

Mona lodged a feeble protest. Feeble, because she'd been yawning. She bestowed brief hugs all around, which Megan thought wasn't like her, either. Saying good-night, she departed for her borrowed bedroom.

"There's no need for you to stay," Megan told Sterling moments later when they found themselves alone in her kitchen, which needed a lot of tidying. "You have to work tomorrow."

"And you don't?" Sterling surveyed the mess and began to shift pans to give them access to the sink.

"I gathered from what Lauren said that you don't approve of women working outside the home. Guys like you are why women like me have to prove a female can do it all. Take care of a house, care for kids, plus do well at our careers."

He straightened from where he'd been hunting in the cabinet under the sink for soap. "Ask Lauren who did it all at our house for months after Tyler was born."

Megan angled her chin. "According to Mark, that would be Lauren."

"What? Well, she did a lot. But not until later, after Blythe fired our housekeeper-nanny and enrolled Tyler in a Montessori school."

"You objected to your wife putting Tyler in school?"

"No. Listen, Megan, there was a lot going on." He ran water in the sink, and for a minute it seemed he wasn't going to say any more. Then he gave a half shrug. "Blythe switched from day shift to nights. She supposedly slept days."

"Supposedly? I've worked graveyard. It's hard. Sleeping when it's light isn't easy."

"Maybe it depends on who you sleep with." There was a definite bitterness to his words.

Megan could have let it pass. "You said that day we rode bikes on the island, that your wife spent extra time with her partner—oh, wow!" Her gaze collided with Sterling's.

He briskly began scouring a pan, which he set in the dishwasher with a bang. "Look, I shouldn't have shot off my mouth. The kids have no idea Blythe and her partner were carrying on a—well, carrying on. For quite a while, it seems. I was one of the last to learn, as spouses usually are."

"You're right, the kids don't know." Megan scraped

plates and busied herself finding places in the fridge for the beer, sodas and leftover Chinese cartons. "Surely you're aware that Lauren blames you for all the trouble in your marriage?"

He loaded two more pans into the dishwasher. "How do you know I'm not at fault? Your grandmother believes I'm a chauvinistic bastard."

"She sorta floored me. But...you did sound hard-nosed."

"I *am* hard-nosed."

Megan raised an eyebrow and let the fridge door slam.

"I am."

"It's hard to take a man seriously, when he says he's hard-nosed while he's elbow-deep in suds."

That got an embarrassed laugh from Sterling. "On another topic. Do you believe Joel was telling the truth about that other kid and the cigars?"

"Yes. Maybe if you gave him the benefit of the doubt sometimes, the two of you wouldn't clash so often."

Sterling dropped a skillet and splashed sudsy water. Soap landed on his nose and stuck to his chin. He hunched his shoulders forward attempting to wipe his chin.

Megan tore a paper towel from a roll and blotted his face. Their eyes locked and both went absolutely still.

Sterling's felt her fingers touch his cheek, but he instantly felt the effect in another part of his body. He was plunged headlong into a sudden urge to take her hand and kiss each soft fingertip.

She read the change that darkened his pale gray irises and made them flare. Megan wasn't terribly experienced when it came to men. She did recognize that his response sent shockwaves down her arm and had her heart pounding at the mere implication of a promise—of what, she wasn't altogether sure. But she could guess, and a thrill shot through her.

"I shouldn't," he murmured, letting another pan slide into the sink. "*We* shouldn't." He didn't get any further than that. He wrapped wet hands around Megan's upper arms and dragged her onto her toes. His hungry mouth landed unerringly on hers. Open, hot and wet.

The paper towel floated to the floor behind him. Megan let it go in order to feather her hands through the silky dark hair curling over his collar. She tried not to think about the two of them kissing in her kitchen surrounded by dirty dishes—with her brother downstairs and her grandmother in the next room. Mercifully, the hotter the kiss, the less able she was to think. Her eyes drifted shut, and Megan lost herself in the unfamiliar desire sucking away her free will.

His legs buckling, Sterling urged open her mouth with his tongue. He reveled in the fact that Megan Benton gave as good as she got. Yes, he thought somewhere in a brain gone slack with lust, women were on an even par with men in every way. And that was an excellent thing.

As his arms wrapped her tighter and they both began to shake with need for more than kisses, something fell in the next room—something glass sounding like it'd shattered. The noise cut through the haze, jolting them.

Sterling lifted his head ever so slightly. His fingers dug restlessly into Megan's back. "What was that?"

Slower to ease the erratic jumping of her heart, Megan continued to breathe in short spurts. "What? Where?" she murmured.

He released her and pointed at the back wall. "There. Downstairs. That would be my bathroom."

"Uh-huh. Mine, too. Oh, goodness, Mona!" Taking off, she sprinted through the door and nearly flattened her grandmother who hurried toward her. "Megan, I need a dustpan and brush. I'm sorry to be so clumsy. That pretty candle in the glass holder, sitting on the side of your tub… I knocked it off and it must be in a thousand pieces."

"Were you hurt?" Sterling asked from behind Megan.

"Only my dignity. Smashing a favorite knickknack on a first visit is no way to get invited back."

"Nonsense! I'm relieved you weren't injured. That candle probably came from a dollar store." Megan turned, and her body skimmed Sterling's as she brushed by him. His very proximity sent waves of heat skittering through her abdomen. To hide the fire rising in her cheeks, and to busy her unsteady hands, she dived into the broom closet and came out with the items Mona asked for. But Megan refused to let her grandmother pry them away. "I'll clean up. You're ready for bed."

Mona fumbled to sash her robe around her waist. Her face had been scrubbed clean. She looked her advancing age, and that jarred Megan far more than the loss of a silly candle. Her grandmother had always skillfully hidden age lines. Now she looked all of her seventysomething years.

"I suppose I should get some sleep. Mark has big plans for us to bake a birthday cake tomorrow. He also wants to decorate the house. Oh, you wouldn't think that at my age I'd get too excited to sleep. I couldn't bring myself to admit I've never baked a cake before.

Toby always had David's birthday parties catered. Megan, I hope our attempts go better than Lauren's. I want to do justice to the faith Mark's placed in me." Veined and freckled hands clutched convulsively at the neck of the fleecy robe.

Tiny shivers of empathy coursed through Megan. Mona appeared earnest. And vulnerable. Megan was sufficiently moved to slip an arm around her grandmother's shoulders. "The effort is what counts. I'll be happy to make a list of things to shop for when you and Mark go out tomorrow. Candles for the cake, a can of frosting, ice cream. I know where you can get party favors."

"Oh, please. That would be so helpful, dear." Having reached the bedroom, Mona turned and patted Megan's cheek. "I wish your mother had invited me to your birthday parties. Toby wouldn't ever set foot in Emily's new husband's house, but I would've defied him. We missed so many of your special events."

Megan clamped her upper lip between her teeth. "Someday you and Mom should sit down and talk."

Her grandmother gave a sad shake of her head. "Too late for overtures, I fear."

Megan chewed her lip in distress. "We can't erase the fact that we're family, Mona." But Megan didn't know if the older woman heard as she'd gone in and closed her door.

Heart heavy, Megan withdrew and swept up the shards of broken glass and wax. She didn't return to the kitchen until she had her nerves under control. She even carried the dustpan of glass outside first, dumping in the trash.

When she returned, Sterling closed the dishwasher

and spun the dial. As the sound of gushing water filled the silence, neither he nor Megan seemed inclined to look the other in the eye. What had happened between them still hung heavy in the air.

Or *had* anything happened? Megan thought she might've dreamed that kiss.

To keep his hands occupied, Sterling shoved them in his back pockets. "I'd, uh, better take off. But before I do, can I ask a favor? Would you have any idea what I might buy Lauren for her birthday? Gifts were something Blythe handled."

"Does Lauren collect anything special?"

"Collect? You mean like CDs? I wanted to get something more…significant. Eighteen is a milestone." His lips lifted in a half smile, making Megan's heart flutter again.

"W-well," she stammered. "There's a nice jewelry store not far from the dock in Mackinaw City. Maybe a gold necklace with some kind of charm. I see girls her age wearing them. I'd say her birthstone, but I think April is a diamond. A gold initial, perhaps? Or if that's too common, a teddy bear or some other cute charm."

"Thanks." He angled toward the door. "That gives me a starting point. I tried to give Mark money toward the party, but he refused. He says it's his gift to her."

"His and Mona's. They're jazzed. It's probably best not to butt in."

"Right. So, I'll see you tomorrow? And Thursday? We're still on, right?"

Megan leaned against the door casing. "Unless you think we're seeing too much of each other, what with Mona's welcome dinner and Lauren's party, and all."

"We're not," he said so fast and with such gravity Megan couldn't suppress a nervous laugh.

"Okay, but you have two days to reconsider. I doubt our paths will cross on Wednesday."

"That's right, your grandmother's leaving."

"And our cousin Keith arrives. It's crazy. A regular traffic jam."

"Are you throwing a welcome party for Keith?"

Megan shook her head. "I think Mark's worried that Keith will ace him out with Lauren. I understand there's a bit of rivalry between those two."

"I'd just as soon they both let Lauren alone. She's finally talking about college." Sterling paused at the head of the stairs. "For the near future and beyond, she needs to focus on school. Education is lasting, romance fleeting."

Megan nodded, closing the door against a cold draft that made her shiver. Had that statement been his subtle way of warning her off, as well? He certainly didn't appear to suffer any effects from their kiss. She, on the other hand, couldn't get it out of her mind.

She played it over and over even after falling asleep. The outcome was always the same—that steamy, steamy kiss put a whole different spin on how Megan felt about her downstairs neighbor.

THE NEXT AFTERNOON AFTER WORK, Megan walked in on a flurry of activity. Happy Eighteenth signs hung everywhere from pink and lavender streamers. She knew from what the girl chose to wear that those were Lauren's favorite colors.

"Sis," Mark hollered from the kitchen. "Can you come here a minute? Mona and I can't get the cakes out of the pans. It's only an hour until everyone arrives. I want to meet Lauren at the door with a frosted cake and eighteen candles burning."

Megan tossed her jacket over a chair. The weather had taken a turn for the better. She'd needed her jacket only in the early-morning hours.

Mark and Mona gazed in consternation at the pans, all but wringing their hands.

"Four layers? Wow, you guys are ambitious." Megan felt the pans. "I think they need a little more time to cool." She touched a finger to one of the layers to make sure it was done. And it was. "I need to shower and wrap the gift I bought Lauren. I suggest you brush some of the flour off your clothes." She grinned when they hurried off to inspect their appearances in the hallway mirror.

"We would've had this done a long time ago," Mark explained, "but Joel nabbed me when he got home from school. He wanted my help bringing his boat back to the marina at the foot of the hill."

"So, he did get the boat? What do you think, Mark? Is it seaworthy? I'm pretty sure Sterling's worried."

"Worried or pissed off? Oops, sorry, Gram. That sorta slipped out."

Megan narrowed her eyes. "He's genuinely concerned, Mark. As well he should be. I gather all Joel knows about boats or boating safety is what he got from my hour-long lecture at the school. Mackinac straits are pretty unforgiving. It doesn't pay to be uninformed—or cocky."

"Then you'd better give him more facts. The kid's not going to listen to Sterling. The boat ran okay, and it's cool-looking. Red with silver racing stripes. But heck, what do I know about boats? Can we, uh…talk about this later? I need to clean up for the party and go over a last-minute checklist. What did you think when you came in? Are the decorations festive enough?"

"They're fine." Megan's mind was still on Joel's new purchase. She paused to listen to Mona.

"I know you said to buy hamburger fixings and potato salad, Megan, but Mark and I decided just to order pizza. I bought a premade green salad."

"Well, that's certainly easier. How did you keep all this a secret from Lauren?"

Mark, on his way down the hall, stopped. "That's the coolest part. She's totally bummed—thinks everyone forgot her birthday. At breakfast, no one said a word. She thought Sterling might give her a card and cash, at least. Hey, if I show you how to work my camera, will you take pictures when I meet her at the door with the cake?"

Megan headed for the bathroom. "Sure. Don't expect gallery quality. But I'm willing to give it a whirl."

"It's pretty much aim and shoot, sis."

Thereafter the apartment buzzed with activity. Following a hasty shower, Megan turned the bathroom over to Mona while she wrapped the carving. She set her gift on a small pile already on the coffee table. Megan detected Mona's handiwork in the increased numbers. She knew her grandmother tended to go overboard and privately hoped Mona hadn't upstaged Sterling. Last night he seemed to really want to buy Lauren a special present.

The layers of cake came out of their pans undamaged. And after frosting, the four layers only looked a little lopsided. Using decorating tubes turned out to be more fun than the three Bentons could recall having shared in a very long time. Their happy laughter was stifled the minute they heard footsteps on the stairs.

Megan grabbed the camera. Mona lit the eighteen candles they'd stuck in the cake. "Remember," Mark whispered, "when Gram opens the door, we'll all sing 'Happy Birthday' really loud. Okay, here goes."

Mona threw open the door and Megan aimed the camera in the direction of the flames. She followed her brother's lead when he warbled the first notes of the song. Megan was a stanza into the song when it struck her that she was the only one singing. Lowering the camera, she blinked once, then again.

It wasn't the guest of honor framed in the outside light, but their cousin Keith. A very dumbfounded cousin Keith.

Megan sputtered his name as he loped inside, grinning from ear to ear.

Beside her, Mark swore, while trying to snuff out the candles. "Aren't you a day early?" he muttered, meeting Keith's grin with a glare.

"Ah. And here I thought you were all clairvoyant. Dang, I take it the big celebration isn't for me."

CHAPTER TEN

"DAMN, OH, DAMN! Here comes Lauren," Mark hissed. "I blew out the candles. Quick, somebody, the matches!" Flustered, he was in serious danger of dropping the heavy cake.

"Where are the matches?" Megan realized the cake tilted way more now than it had earlier. But there was no time to rectify the matter. Voices drifted up from below, which meant Lauren was about to appear.

Megan grabbed Keith's arm and tried to yank him inside.

"Keith," she said, "Move it! Mark and Mona have worked hard to keep this party a surprise. Go! Sit on the couch while I find the matches." She pushed his resisting six-foot, three-inch frame toward the sofa, then detoured to the kitchen where she collided with her grandmother in the darkness. A matchbook popped out of Mona's hand and sailed over Megan's head.

By then Mark was frenzied. "They're on our porch. What's taking so long?" The cake canted more as he bent to see what the women were doing crawling at his feet.

"If you didn't tell Lauren about the party," Megan asked suddenly, patting the carpet in search of the elusive matchbook, "What excuse did you use to get her and the others here? Well, the others, I suppose, know."

"Sis!" Mark shoved the listing cake into Mona's hands. "The whole surprise is going down the toilet thanks to Keith. Why in hell are you here a day early?" Mark dived for the book of matches at the same time Megan spotted it. They butted heads.

Keith snaked a long arm between the pair, picked up the matches and struck one. "A new agent at the travel service screwed up. This place isn't exactly a high-volume traffic area," he said. "They finally found a flight headed this way. I caught a cab at the airport. There, your cake is lit. Is it 'sposed to be a replica of the Leaning Tower of Pisa?" The match burned his fingers. He yelped and shook it out.

Mark heard the remark and tried to shove the layers together. As a result, he got chocolate frosting and lavender rosebuds all over his hand.

A timid knock sounded on the partially open door. "Mark?" Lauren's hesitant voice drifted into the room. "Are you home? Why is it dark?"

Without letting her enter all the way, Mark strode forward and burst into an off-key rendition of "Happy Birthday."

Megan, still rubbing her head, joined in two or three words behind. The result was a horrid version that would make most people cringe.

Not, however, Lauren Atwater. When Mona hit the lights and everyone shouted, "Surprise!" the girl at the door burst into tears. Megan, who'd forgotten she was in charge of the camera, belatedly snapped away in spite of the fact that Lauren probably wouldn't want pictures in which she resembled a raccoon, thanks to her runny mascara.

Mark stuttered, "Lauren, I th-thought you'd be

p-pleased." He looked so helpless, this gangly young man who awkwardly clutched a burning pyre of eighteen dripping candles.

Everyone else more or less froze in place as Joel skidded in behind his sister. He scoffed at her with all the finesse of a younger brother. "You're supposed to be happy, dummy." He jabbed an elbow in Lauren's ribs.

Sterling brought up the rear guiding Tyler, who was also upset by Lauren's reaction. The little boy grabbed her around the knees and tried to console her. It was Sterling, though, who herded them all inside, and closed the door. "Mark, Joel, Tyler—Lauren *is* happy. Everybody back off and give her a minute to compose herself." He leaned over and whispered in the girl's ear, "I think Mark would like you to make a wish and blow out that forest fire before it melts the frosting off the cake."

She smudged the heels of her hands across her eyes and was finally able to pucker up and blow. Several candles wavered. Three flickered out. By now Tyler, hopping on his toes, helped her finish. Everyone laughed. The tension faded and the decibel level rose as everyone began talking at once.

Joel was first of the new arrivals to discover Keith. "Whoa! Who're you, dude?"

As the room went silent, the shy nineteen-year-old stuttered a response. Megan clapped her hands. "I apologize for not getting to the introductions quicker," she said, prying Keith out of his jacket as she ran through everyone in the room. "A change in his flight schedule gives him an extra day to visit."

"Lucky us," Mark muttered, scowling at their cousin.

Finding his stride, Keith snapped back, "Like I

wouldn't rather be spending my vacation computerizing Doc Jackson's files? But no, the family elected me to come see if you've taken leave of your senses, Mark-o. I told them this would be your reaction."

Feeling the rising testosterone, Megan placed her fingers between her lips and whistled. "Time-out, guys." She relieved Mark of the pathetic cake and passed it to Mona. "We're here to celebrate Lauren's big day. I know you ordered pizza, Mark. Did you want Lauren to open her gifts before or after we eat?"

He tore his disgruntled gaze from Keith long enough to check his watch. "Before, I guess. Or maybe we should leave that up to Lauren. Shoot, nothing's going like I planned, anyway."

Joel removed a mashed, flat package from his hip pocket. Sterling took a much neater one from inside his jacket. Their gifts, and one Sterling added with Tyler's name on it, joined the growing mound on the coffee table.

Lauren, recovered from her crying jag, floated up to Mark. "You are so *sweet.* I can't believe you did this for me. We only talked about my birthday a few days ago. But I know it had to be your idea. Sterling and Joel have never cared before."

Sterling absorbed the slight. "Lauren, Blythe bought you gifts every year. I assumed you—"

Megan broke in. "Hey, why don't we all find places to sit? Lauren, you take the middle of the couch. We'll gather around you. That'll let everyone see the gifts."

"Can I help?" Tyler fell on his knees in front of Lauren, drawn by the lure of the gaily wrapped packages.

She pulled him up. "Sit next to me, tiger. I'll untie the bows and you can tear off the paper." She patted the other cushion. "Mark, come here. I'm sure Keith won't mind moving."

It was obvious he'd like nothing better, he shot away so quickly.

"Don't you want pictures to commemorate your day, Lauren?" he asked. "No offense, but if Megan got anything but the floor in those first two frames, we'll be lucky."

Megan rolled her eyes. "Mona, you sit next to Lauren then. You worked as hard as Mark did to put this party together."

Waiting near the kitchen doorway, their grandmother seemed pleased to be singled out. "My knee's been bothering me all afternoon," she murmured. "I could use a soft place to park these old bones."

Megan had noticed Mona rubbing her knee. Now a decided limp was evident as she crossed the room. But Megan didn't want to forestall the party any longer by asking questions about Mona's health. It was bad enough to have Mark sniping at Keith, and Lauren taking potshots at Sterling. So she engineered everyone's seating before dropping cross-legged on the floor between Keith and Sterling.

"So many gifts," Lauren said, sniffling again, but this time happily. In typical girl fashion, she picked up and shook first one box, then another.

"Jeez, pick one and get on with opening it," Joel growled.

"I'm only going to be eighteen once, smarty-pants. If I choose to make the excitement last longer, that's my prerogative."

Her brother groaned. "Let her turn eighteen and suddenly she's using the big words."

Keith didn't break into a full smile at that, but Megan noticed that his lips twitched. "Give her a break, Joel," she said. "I know guys tend to rip stuff open. Women like to draw out the mystery by guessing what's under the wrapping."

"Hurry, Lauren." Tyler pressed his small body against her leg. "You haven't untied one bow. How can I tear off paper?"

"Oh, all right!" Ruffling his fine blond hair, Lauren blindly picked one. It came from Mona. A trendy T-shirt. Lauren held it up for all to see. "Mrs. Benton, thank you so much. Mark must've told you I drooled all over the store window the other night."

Mona laughed. "He may have mentioned it about a dozen times. Please, Lauren, I thought you all promised to call me Gram."

Megan felt Sterling shift. At first she thought maybe he didn't want the kids calling Mona *Gram.* But from his fixed expression, Megan realized Lauren had pulled his gift from the stack. The ribbon on the store-wrapped jewelry box was impossible to break. Megan bounced up and found a pair of scissors to help her open it. She was as relieved as he when Lauren's eyes went to her brother-in-law in excited pleasure.

"Sterling, this necklace is gorgeous! Where on earth did you find a charm of the Empire State Building in St. Ignace? The windows—are they…diamonds?"

"They'd better be. Or so the jeweler certified." Flushing, he tugged on one ear. "I, ah, know how much you miss New York."

"Well, duh!" Joel exploded. "Lauren, haven't you told him the design school you applied to online accepted you? They called today," he told Sterling defiantly. "As soon as Mark helps you find an apartment, I get to go back home for good, too," he added.

Lauren sent him a silent warning with those dark eyes. A warning that, of course, came too late.

Megan felt heat and anger emanating from the man seated to her left. "I'm sure the lawyer who processed Blythe's will made it abundantly clear to both of you that I have complete control over your living accommodations until you turn twenty-one," he said.

Heads whipped from one to the other. Breathing slowed to the point that the only noise in the room was the hiss of the gas register.

Joel clenched his fists as he leaped up. "I'll run away then. So will Lauren."

Mark, who'd knelt to take a picture of Lauren holding her necklace, reached over and gripped Joel's rigid arm. "Don't, Joel. Don't spoil Lauren's party." The tension continued as Lauren picked up the gift from her brother. A gift card from a local music store. She tore straight into the present Megan had wrapped.

"A carving of a shorebird," she exclaimed. "My first knickknack for wherever I end up living at college. I'll think of the birds that sit on the bridge. Thanks, Megan."

"You may well be on the island taking online courses," Sterling said.

Lauren snarled, "No. You'll see. I wish you'd left Blythe, then you wouldn't have any say. But it doesn't matter. I'm old enough to file a lawsuit."

Keith acted as if he'd like to be anywhere but in the room. Mona, too, shifted, then patted Lauren's hand.

Only Megan found herself siding with Sterling. Lauren and Joel had ganged up on their brother-in-law. She was angry for him and didn't know how he could resist slamming them with the facts about their dear sister. Megan let her fingers creep over Sterling's knotted fist. In the low light provided by the two lamps at either end of the couch, she didn't think anyone would notice. Especially as half the people in the room were completely self-absorbed.

Mark's gift and the one from Tyler were all that remained to be opened.

A tread on the stairs followed by a loud knock, ended the strain in the room. Mark went to the door. It was the pizza delivery boy; Mark paid him and carried in two large cartons.

The arrival of food provided the best possible break. An enticing aroma filled the room. Mona struggled up off the couch and hurried to drag out festive plates and napkins, which she stacked on the coffee table. "Megan." She motioned to matching paper cups. "There's soda in the fridge."

Tyler made them all laugh when he announced, "I bet pizza tastes good with Megan's hot chocolate."

Sterling tickled his son. "Megan created a hot chocolate monster," he said, growling in Tyler's neck. The boy's giggles were infectious. It was the very thing needed to revive the party spirit.

Joel poked Tyler. "Hey, kid, hot chocolate's for cold nights. We're coming up on picnic season. You'd better toughen up, matey, if you're gonna go fishing in my new boat."

Mark returned to shut the door.

"Brr!" Megan rubbed her arms as a blast of night air swept into the room. "I'm with Tyler. I don't know if it'll ever warm up enough in this north country for picnic weather."

Sterling's smoldering gaze remained on Joel. "Before you make plans to go fishing, we need to set ground rules. And don't be filling Tyler's head with ideas. He doesn't even have a life vest. Which brings up another question. What equipment came with the boat?"

Megan, and apparently Mona, sensed another storm brewing. They hurriedly passed around slices of pizza.

Joel doubled his. "The guy at the marina threw in fishing rods and tackle, and I counted two life vests, plus other stuff. I'm not stupid, you know," he added sullenly. "I listened when Megan gave the class on boating tips."

"That's something, I guess," Sterling said, eyes swerving toward Megan.

Keith plopped down next to Joel. "I hope to do some fishing while I'm here. What's anyone catching?"

Mark claimed a space on the couch next to Lauren. "I talked to some guys yesterday who'd caught whitefish. Joel, I know you don't want to go with Lauren and me tomorrow to drop Gram at the airport and then on to the Soo Locks. After school, why don't you and Keith test your new boat and maybe fish a little?"

The neat way he'd managed to get rid of his cousin did not escape Megan.

"Me, too, Joel. I wanna fish." Tyler bounced around nearly losing the topping off his pizza.

Feeling Sterling's muscles tighten, Megan offered what she thought was a solution to the problem. "Tyler, you said you wanted to help next time I washed my truck. It's on my agenda for tomorrow, but I don't get home until five. Is that too late for you guys to go fishing?"

Sterling cleared his throat. "Mrs. Ralston across the

street has said several times that anytime I need someone to watch Tyler, she'd be glad to. I could check in the morning. If it's okay, Joel can drop Tyler there after school, and, Megan, you can collect him when you get home."

"That's a perfect answer. How about it, Tyler? If we finish with my truck before your dad gets home, we can make a batch of peanut butter cookies."

The boy was clearly torn. Sterling settled it. "Ty, take Megan's offer. There's no way I want you going on a shakedown cruise on some tub a boat-dealer foisted off on Joel."

Joel flared. "It's a good boat! You have to go and ruin everything! At least now everybody in the room knows why I can't wait till Lauren moves to New York."

"That's not happening!"

The birthday girl flung down her pizza. "That sucks, Sterling. My folks left me money. A lot of money. Part of it's earmarked for our education."

"Lauren." Sterling sighed. "I suggest we postpone this for another day. Tonight we're here to celebrate your birthday. And you still have a couple of unopened gifts."

The girl wiped her hands on a napkin and reached for the gift obviously wrapped by Sterling, although the tag said it was from Tyler. The boy helped her tear off the wrap to expose the flat box. Then came a box within the box, which went on until she reached a plastic card.

"What do you want that dumb old thing for?" Tyler asked with a huff. "Daddy, I wanted to get Lauren something pretty."

Lauren's eyes filled. Her fingers kept stroking the card. "I've wanted my own credit card for ages. All my friends had them at fourteen. Blythe said you refused to let her give me one."

"I didn't, I swear. I don't know why Blythe would say that." He pinched the bridge of his nose. "Lauren, honest to God, Blythe never consulted me about gifts. This card has a limit," he added. "It's negotiable, so let's see how it goes."

As the silence stretched, and comprehension slowly dawned on Lauren's face, Megan said, "There's still one gift. I can tell Mark's getting anxious for you to see what he got you."

"I didn't actually buy this," Mark murmured as Lauren tucked the coveted credit card in her pocket and reached for the last present. It wasn't well disguised. They could all see it was going to be a framed photograph.

Megan expected it to be a picture Mark had taken of Lauren. She wriggled closer to have a look when Lauren unexpectedly burst into tears and clutched the eight-by-ten frame to her chest. Tyler got up, hugged her tight and patted her face. "Daddy, why is Lauren crying *again?* Birthdays should oughta be fun."

Mark, ready to take a picture, sank to his knees in front of the sobbing girl, the camera sitting idle in his hands.

Mona pried the frame loose. "Let us see. Mark overwhelmed you, I think. Oh, a collage. Megan, perhaps you can bring Lauren a tissue. Then she can share with us who these pictures are of."

Lauren began wiping her eyes on her shirt before Megan jumped up and returned with the requested tissues. "Mark, where in the world did you find baby pictures of me? Blythe said she threw out the family albums after our folks died, because she said she hated the reminder."

"Nonsense," Sterling burst out. "Blythe sent me to clean out your parents' house before we put it up for sale. The albums and other bric-a-brac have sat in storage ever since. You only had to ask, which is what Mark did. I took him to our storage unit and let him take the box I'd marked Atwater Photographs."

They all crowded around to study what Mark had done—matting ovals around a center picture that could only be of Lauren's parents at their wedding.

Surprisingly, Joel's eyes, which were normally cold or held an edge of hostility, moistened, too. He ran a forefinger lightly over the glass. Snuffling, he finally asked, "Are there any pictures of me as a little kid? Pictures of my birthday parties or anything?"

Reacting to the hoarse sound of his young brother-in-law's unsteady voice, Sterling responded gently. "There should be some pictures in that box, Joel. It's true Blythe didn't want any reminders of life in that house before the murders. I figured one day she'd regret asking me to get rid of everything. But she never did. I kept my grandparents' albums, too. And I saved an assortment of toys and baby clothes for each of you. Plus mementos of Blythe's important events. Locks of hair, school papers, her graduation cap and gown. Our house on the island is big enough to unbox it all and save or discard whatever you choose. I'd like to put some of Blythe's old photos in an album for Tyler."

Lauren shot to her feet. "Why? You're such a fraud, Sterling. Making everyone here think you loved my sister. I know better. I took that phone call from your lawyer friend."

Joel, having regained his composure, blinked. "What phone call?"

Sterling acted as if he might defend himself against Lauren's attack, but then he closed his eyes. "The cake Mark had on fire when we came in," he said in a tired voice. "Is it for eating? No birthday party's complete without cake."

Megan again came to the rescue. "Lauren, do you want to cut your cake, or shall I? You and Mark can dish up ice cream if you'd rather. I believe he bought vanilla and double chocolate fudge."

There was at once a cacophony of noisy shouts in favor of the double chocolate fudge. "I'll take vanilla," Mona said. "That cake has enough chocolate calories to last a lifetime."

"I'm terrible at cutting cake," Lauren said. "Unless you want a picture of me doing the honors, Mark, I'll gladly turn cutting it to your sister."

Megan barely waited for Mark to shrug before she sped to the kitchen. She was surprised when Sterling followed. "If you slice the cake, I'll scoop out ice cream," he said. "Oh, and your grandmother wants a small piece of cake with no ice cream."

"She changed her mind?"

He juggled the two cartons Megan pulled from the freezer. "She decided it's too chilly for ice cream. I left her clearing the coffee table to play dominoes with Tyler. He loves games. I wish I had more time to play with him."

"How's your job going, Sterling?"

"So far, fine. I suppose you consider what I do boring."

"Why would you think that?" She quickly cut several slices of cake and plopped them in plastic bowls that matched the pizza plates. "Because you didn't choose to set Lauren and Joel straight about their sister doesn't mean you can be sarcastic to me."

"Sorry. Defending my job to Blythe became a habit. She said I should take over the boat construction company—she thought it would be more exciting, and was furious with me when I sold it. But that gave me some options, including the means to take six months off when Tyler was born. Anyway, I assumed that since you opted for an exciting field, you'd agree with her."

Megan watched him dip out the chocolate fudge ice cream. "Wouldn't it be a sad world if we were all crazy about the same things? I suppose a lot of people might look at what I do and only see the danger. When we perform rescues, Sterling, I never have time to think about anything but to saving a victim. Who gets these three bowls?"

"Lauren, Mark and Joel."

She sprinted off to deliver them. He surprised her with another question the instant she returned. "Have any of your rescues been unsuccessful, Megan?"

"Yes," she said, her eyes suddenly sad. "In Alabama, my team lost two teens who hit a snag with their boat. The current was swift. We dived and dived, but misjudged how far the undertow would take them. Are you thinking about Blythe again? Surely you don't imagine you could've kept her from her shift that night?"

"No." He hesitated, holding her eyes. "A forty-foot sailing vessel lost electrical power one foggy night," he began. "She clipped my ferry hard as I made a swing toward port. It was a nightmare. Some of my passengers trampled others. Nobody listened to the instructions I tried to give with the bullhorn."

"I saw the inquest note the day we inspected the *Algonquin.* You were absolved of any blame."

"Ah. Absolution should let me sleep at night? Tell it to the family of the woman who slipped from my grasp. I thought I could save her and her child. *Should* have. Everything happened too fast. The lower deck was chaos. A wave knocked me sideways. The kid was terrified. She practically cut off my supply of air as the mother literally threw her into my arms. I managed to loosen her grip, but…the mother…was gone. She—her body, I mean, washed ashore ten days later."

Megan left him to his grief while she delivered the next batch of bowls. Capping the ice-cream cartons when she came back, she made her next statement carefully. "The motto at the Coast Guard Academy, *Scientiae cedit mare,* means The Sea Yields to Knowledge. What that says to me is that man or woman cannot win one hundred percent against the will of the sea. But we can always build on what each encounter teaches us. As for peace of mind… Maybe it's a matter of living each day to the fullest. Maybe it's holding your loved ones closer. I sleep at night by focusing on the people I save, not on the two I lost."

Sterling looked at her expressive face. Moving closer, he ran his fingers through the curls framing her eyes. Megan felt the need quivering between their skin. She thought he intended to kiss her, and held her breath, tilting her chin. But someone yelled, "Hey, what's keeping you two?" They both jumped back a couple of guilty steps.

Mark thrust his head into the kitchen. "We're waiting

until everyone has cake. Crank it up to full speed, sis! Everybody's ice cream's starting to melt."

The two in the kitchen grabbed their bowls. Their ice cream was melting, too. Inside, Megan was a tangle of nerves.

She admitted she yearned for kisses and more from this complicated man. It made no sense. She wasn't one to take risks in her private life, and the growing attachment she felt to Sterling Dodge certainly came with risks.

Megan spent the rest of the party well outside the range of his touch, accidental or otherwise. As the party wound to a close, and the various factions solidified their plans for the next day, she thought she should've found a way to cancel Thursday night's date. But she said nothing.

"I'll take the decorations down in the morning." Mark punctuated his promise with a yawn. "Keith, I see you brought a sleeping bag. You can crash on my floor."

Megan was already dumping debris in a garbage sack. "You guys are turning in? It's still early, and we haven't had a chance to catch up with Keith on what's happening at home. Oh, where's Mona—uh, Gram?"

"Sorry, Megan, she said good-night. I think she's excited but nervous about starting her round-the-world jaunt tomorrow."

"We hardly had any time together. Yeah, yeah, I know I bitched about her coming, but..." Megan didn't complete her sentence.

Keith gathered his duffel and sleeping bag. "I guess you realize your mom's upset that Mrs. B. is here. She thinks the old broad's gonna use her millions to tempt you to leave the family. The Campbell family."

"It's not a secret that there's no love lost between Mom and Mona." Megan spoke softly, casting an eye down the hall in case her grandmother appeared.

Her cousin's sunny features darkened. "Why can't grown-ups *act* grown-up, and put their differences aside?"

"Is your mom fighting with your dad again?" Megan asked.

"When *aren't* they fighting? I used to think it was Crawford's fault. He's such a stuffed shirt. But it's Mom and my dad. They're like oil and water. I'm tired of them making me the accelerant. So, what's the story on the kids from downstairs? Sounds like another screwed-up family. Will I be taking my life in my hands if I go boating with Joel tomorrow?"

Mark snatched Keith's sleeping bag out of his hands. "Come on, I'll fill you in. Hey, I'm sorry I gave you such a hard time when you showed up early."

Watching them saunter down the hall on better terms left Megan smiling. Mark could be a pain sometimes, but so could Keith. Basically they were good guys. They'd make a couple of lucky women fine husbands one day. Who and when, she had no clue, although it'd be impossible to miss the sizzling looks between Mark and Lauren.

She went to bed thinking she'd feel more favorable toward Lauren Atwater if the girl had thanked Sterling for saving the Atwater family history. A small gesture, but one that would've gone a long way toward mending their rift.

MEGAN WOKE UP WITH her neighbors still on her mind. Having slept poorly, she decided to opt out of her morning run. She met Mona bustling around in the kitchen, trying to be quiet while she fixed her morning tea. It struck Megan that she had some peace offerings of her own to extend.

"I didn't mean to wake you, dear," Mona said.

"You didn't. My alarm went off an hour ago. Do you know that you and my mom both start everyday drinking Red Zinger tea? That ought to give you something in common."

Mona laughed and carried her tea bag to the trash. "I've finally accepted that Toby and I made a mess of things with Emily. We always took Dave's part. Oh, we had such high hopes and dreams for our son. It was easier to blame his shortcomings on the woman he married than to accept that he had faults."

"I loved Daddy," Megan said. "But he needed to grow up."

Mona pulled out a chair and sat. "I've had a lot of time to think since your grandfather passed away. Toby tried to mold David in his own image. He kept thinking if he got Dave out of this scrape or that, he'd come around. It became a pattern. Which is the main reason I know parents can't choose a life course for their kids. I see it so clearly now. Your mom believes I'm meddling in Mark's future the way we did in David's. She's wrong. I gave Mark seed money for this venture for exactly the opposite reason. I saw him being smothered, trying to be the son Emily wants. You know, her son the college counselor. That's her desire, like having Dave be a top developer was Toby's."

Megan nodded. "You should tell Mom what you just told me."

"A week or so before I came here, Emily drove out

to the house. Our meeting ended in a shouting match. Sometimes there's too much bad history, child."

"I don't believe that," Megan insisted stubbornly. "And maybe Mark's like Daddy. He should've made his wishes known to Mom and Camp earlier. He went along with them, and now he's letting you do his dirty work."

"Megan, dear. That's what I meant when I said I envy you. You have more grit than all of us put together."

"I don't know about that." She dismissed the compliment. "I conveniently didn't visit you over Christmas because I didn't want to upset Mom. And I wasn't really happy when Mark said you were coming here. Now, I wish we had more time."

Mona smiled. "Time is all I have. I've sold the business, and I put the home place on the market before I left Benton Corners."

"Sell Benton House? Well, it *is* big. But that's a huge decision."

"I feel freer already. Now I'll be able to pick up and go wherever my great-grandchildren are."

"Great-grand—" Choking on tea her grandmother made for her, Megan let Mona pound her on the back.

"Yes, great-grandchildren. And I won't live forever. So, you and Mark had better get on the stick. All old ladies yearn to hear the pitter-patter of little feet again."

Mark and Keith stumbled bleary eyed into the kitchen and asked what was for breakfast. Megan prepared waffles and eggs. Then she had to dash off to shower and get ready for work. She came out just as it was time for Mark and Mona to leave. Lauren was already waiting at Mark's car, and the girl lit up when he helped his grandmother down the steep steps. His answering smile gave Megan something else to consider. She'd always assumed that, as the eldest, she'd be the first to marry. Now, she wasn't so sure.

"Megan, I'm going to spend the day bumming around the island while I wait for Joel to get out of school, if that's all right with you." Keith came up behind her.

"It's your vacation, Keith. Do whatever you want. You have my office number and my cell. I, ah…have plans for tomorrow night. Nothing big, just dinner and pool or maybe a movie."

"Are you still beating the socks off all the guys at pool?"

"Mostly. Keith—how do you think guys feel about that? Do they get bent out of shape? Would men really prefer that I acted like I can't play so well and let them win?"

"I'm not a good one to ask. I found out long ago that a pool shark I'm not. Why not ask somebody you beat all the time? Or maybe that's no good. Huh, I see your point. Guys do like girls to think they're cool at everything. Know what I mean?"

Megan didn't answer. She didn't really understand. "Hey, I've gotta go. Mark and Lauren won't be back until really late. Around midnight, I think. I thought we'd go out for hamburgers."

"Sounds good. Or if Joel and I get lucky, how about fixing whitefish?"

"Deal. You catch 'em. I'll clean 'em and cook 'em."

HAMISH TUCKER CALLED UP from the dock to Megan's cutter as it tied up that afternoon. They'd had a full day on the water. She was wind-battered and thirsty.

"What are you hollering about, Ham? I'm almost finished here. Two minutes and I'll be in the office."

"You need to phone your brother. There's been some kind of accident."

Megan's fingers froze on the rope she was coiling. "A car wreck?" She flew over the side and down the ladder, landing on the dock next to Tucker with a thump. "Injuries?" Her heart hammered wildly even though she tried to remain calm.

"Relax, Lieutenant. Not a car wreck. Your grandmother slipped going into the airport. A patch of ice. She broke a hip, and your brother has her at the hospital. I jotted a number on the message pad at your desk."

Already running to the door, Megan flipped open her phone and punched in her brother's cell number. "Mark? I just got back into port. Mona did what? How? I—yes, I saw her limping. Is the break bad? They're going to pin the bone? No...no, I'm not blaming you or Lauren. Accidents happen. How long will she be in the hospital? And where is that? I'll have to see if I can get off tomorrow. Wait. She can't ride home in your small car or my pickup. Mark, what are we going to do?"

CHAPTER ELEVEN

AFTER A BRIEF PHONE consultation with Mona's doctor, Megan hunted up Commander Donovan and arranged for two days off. The doctor had said they wanted to pin Mona's hip later in the day, once they got the swelling down. He also said the operation was fairly routine and that Mona was otherwise in good health.

Driving home, Megan felt better in one sense and worse in another. Better knowing her grandmother's health was good, worse knowing how much she'd looked forward to her world trip. Megan recognized how much courage it took for someone who'd lived in a small Missouri town her entire life to book a world tour with a group of strangers. Mona might never venture out again.

As she parked at the house, other more pressing problems became apparent. The doctor said that if everything went well, they could bring Mona home on Friday or Saturday. But how were they going to get here with her broken hip? They'd have to carry her up that steep set of stairs.

That was the short term. What about her long-term care? The doctor had said broken hips often healed slowly.

Since Megan had been out on the boat all day, her hair was stiff from sweat and wind. They'd changed burned-out lights in some of the deep-water buoys, which meant crew members had to climb around the bobbing buoys. Their afternoon was devoted to simulating rescue techniques and exercises. With boating season right around the corner, it was imperative to practice skills they might have to use.

She called out "Hello?" as she unlocked the door. She thought perhaps Keith and Joel would be tired of fishing by now. The apartment seemed almost eerily empty after the traffic over the last few days.

The boys weren't back yet, but since they could return at any moment, she gathered up everything she needed to bathe and dress, and locked the door to her bathroom while she showered away the grime and stress of the day.

She felt much better afterward. By the time she came out refreshed, she'd assembled a plan of sorts. Her whole life, her mom had been her go-to person. Bad blood or not, Mona was Emily Benton Campbell's former mom-in-law, and she was still family.

Finger-combing her hair, Megan checked the time. Columbia was an hour ahead. Depending on after-class meetings or other things on campus, it was possible her mom or stepdad or both might actually be home.

Megan punched in their home number before she could chicken out. The phone was answered so fast, Megan's blood started pumping fast in her ears. "Hello. It's Megan, Camp."

"Hi, Megan. Everything all right? You okay? Mark? Keith?" He ran down the list in his deep, cultured voice. Megan felt the reassurance of her stepdad's presence even across the miles. "We're all okay—But Camp, Mona… uh, Gram Benton fell at the airport and broke her hip."

There was a brief silence, then his voice took on a harsher tone. "What happened? The old witch fall off her broomstick?"

Megan bit her lip. She hadn't expected sarcasm from Camp. "Maybe you'd better let me speak with Mom. I'd hoped we could set old animosities aside." She took a deep breath. "My apartment is up a set of steep stairs. And with Keith here now—having come, I gather, at your and Mom's request—I don't have room for a sick bay."

"I'm sorry, honey. I understand your frustration. But visiting that woman a week or so ago put your mom's nerves in such a state she hasn't recovered yet. In fact, Emily's at the doctor's again today. Her second trip. Last week, the lab ran a battery of blood work. They're doing more tests today. I'm afraid she's worried herself into an ulcer."

"Gosh, Mom doesn't have anything like a possible heart problem or anything? Like my dad and granddad died from?" Her voice quavered.

"My mother and your aunt Sherry think it's Emily's nerves. Your mom's worked herself into a state over Mark's behavior. That said, what were you hoping Emily would do for Mona?"

Pushing out a sigh, Megan paced the room. "I hoped there was an outside chance she'd drive up here in one of the SUVs and take Gram home to recover at your house. Mark's old room and mine are vacant and on the ground floor."

"Out of the question. What's wrong with the old bat's staff?"

"She let them go. Benton House is on the market, Camp. She's already sold the business. Mona was on the first leg of an around-the-world trip."

"Good Lord!"

Megan heard Camp doing some pacing of his own.

"Maybe this is fate," he said slowly. "I've got a solution. Mark and Keith can drive Mona home in Mark's car. Having Mark under our roof again will fix your mom's nerves and sleeplessness. My parents have contacts all over town. I'll see if they can pull strings and get your grandmother into a nice, reputable, long-term care facility where your brother can look in on her."

"Don't make those plans just yet. That solution might suit you, but it's not fair to Mark. Besides, his car would barely hold him and Keith on a long drive. Where would you suggest they put Mona? Tie her on top?"

"What do you mean my plan's not fair to Mark? That kid needs to get his head on straight. He spent six years in school preparing for a career in counseling and now he's throwing his life away tramping around taking pictures of—what the hell *is* he taking pictures of up there? Bull moose in heat?"

Megan had never heard such a rant from her stepdad. She might expect an emotional overreaction from her mother, but from Camp she expected compassion and logic.

"If this is the way you and Mom carry on about Mark, no wonder she's a mess. How many times did I hear the two of you preach that education is never wasted? Aunt Sherry says so, too. If you'd quit trying to bend Mark to *your* plans for his life, and really listen when he talks about photography, you'd see the difference in him. Photography makes him light up. He comes alive, Camp. But don't worry, I'll figure out something else for Gram."

There was a knock at the door. "Someone's here. I have to go. Bye." She hung up, and wished she hadn't been so confrontational. Maybe Keith was back. But she'd given him a key. Still, shy as he was, he might not want to use it.

"Sterling?" Megan was shocked to see him at her door. "Oh, God, tell me nothing happened to Joel and Keith. I don't think I can handle another piece of bad news today."

"They're fine as far as I know. I saw them fishing off the island thirty minutes ago. I stopped in to check on you because Lauren phoned to tell me about your grandmother. I assumed you'd need to cancel out on Tyler helping wash your truck." He dragged a hand through wind-tangled hair. "I can't believe how fast they're patching Mona up. Lauren said they plan to release her on Friday. I, ah, have you thought about how you'll care for her?"

Megan leaned against door. "Come in. I need a cup of hot chocolate so I can think. I just hung up from a conversation with my stepdad. He's got no sympathy for Mona, and he doubts Mom will have any, either. Oh." She sighed heavily. "That's not really fair. I never actually spoke with Mom. I'm taking Camp's word. Is Tyler still at Mrs. Ralston's? I can go ahead with washing my pickup."

"They're playing Chutes and Ladders and eating cheese popcorn. The woman is delighted to have his company."

"That's nice. Maybe she's not as much of a busybody as Captain Meade made her sound. He claimed she's why he fixed up the house to rent out. Hank said Mrs. Ralston was always over here pestering him with food he couldn't eat and making cow eyes at him. Maybe she *wasn't* angling for him. She could've just been lonely."

Megan filled the saucepan with milk. "About my grandmother. I'm not sure, Sterling. I haven't got enough seniority at this station that I can request a lot of time off. I need a day to go get her and bring her home. But I can't install her in my place. Even if you and Mark or Keith could carry her upstairs, it'd be dangerous to leave her here alone. What if there was a fire or some other emergency?" On autopilot, she added the remaining hot chocolate ingredients.

"I could ask Joel to temporarily give her his room. Maybe he could bunk up here with the boys."

"You'd do that?" She paused in the act of setting out mugs. As she put one in front of Sterling, he crooked a finger under her chin and raised her eyes to his.

"Isn't that what you told me neighbors are for?"

Megan swallowed several times. "Guilty. I didn't think you heard me."

He released her chin and pulled her into the circle of his arms. "I'm hardheaded, but not incapable of admitting it and trying to rectify the problem." He rested his chin on the top of her head, just enjoying the feel of their casually entwined bodies. "Involvement with a neighbor—or any woman—was the last thing I wanted when I moved here. I believe you cast some spell over those peanut butter cookies you brought downstairs, Lieutenant Benton."

"Is that your way of calling me a witch?" she asked, her nose plastered against his windbreaker.

"Bewitching, maybe," he murmured, pausing a moment to nibble on her earlobe.

She instantly went still and strained toward his lips. But she stepped back and filled their mugs. "Pleasant as this interlude is, Sterling. Bad idea, I think when I need to be able to think," she said wryly. "I have to figure something out for my grandmother."

"So I affect your ability to think rationally." He smiled teasingly, taking the mug she'd poured full.

"You seem pretty happy today."

"Yeah. I got word that the workmen have started repairs on my island house."

"Oh. Then I guess that means we won't be neighbors for long." Her thoughts on this prospect were easily read.

His smile fled. "I'll miss seeing you every day." He bent to sip from his cup.

"I'll miss seeing you, too," she said with honesty. "Did I hear a decided *but* at the end of your statement, Sterling?"

He let his long stride take him to the window, where he drew aside the curtain and stared out over the street. "If you did, it's because I have my own troubles. I'm not making any headway with Joel. It's that blasted boat. I don't want him taking off in it whenever the whim strikes him."

"Won't he still have the boat after you move to the island?" Megan dunked her marshmallow in the creamy chocolate.

"I suppose. Maybe I'm counting too heavily on the cohesiveness of a smaller community to settle him down. I can't help hoping that if he feels a sense of permanence, and can build friendships with kids in the neighborhood, it'll help him over this rough patch."

"He expressed interest to me in joining the Reserve Officer Training Corps. That's a small but great group of kids at his school. You might want to encourage him to join."

"Are you kidding?" Sterling let the curtain drop. "Encourage him to be even more of a daredevil?"

"Is *that* what you think ROTC does? Not true! It teaches discipline, esprit de corps and prepares young men and women to step into leadership roles. It'd be an incentive to raise his grades and keep them up."

"I'll admit I didn't read the brochure he brought home."

"I don't want to mislead you. A lot of kids in ROTC go on to serve in the military. That's a choice he could make, anyway, though, and the program does give him options."

Sterling was torn, and it showed. "I'll read the material. You know, I didn't come up here to talk about Joel. I came to offer assistance with your grandmother."

"I'll accept." She smiled. "I was thinking…if I could borrow your bigger vehicle to bring her home, it'd be more comfortable for her. Neither my pickup nor Mark's small car will allow her to stretch out."

"I'll drive you up there when she's released from the hospital."

"Would you? It could be Friday, but the doctor told me probably over the weekend. I hope so. That'll give Mark and me time to figure out how to get her back to Missouri."

"Is there no one else in the family who could come and escort her home? I mean, if your parents won't. What about Keith's family?"

"I couldn't ask Aunt Sherry or Uncle Garrett. From

what Keith said, Uncle Garrett is dealing with budget crunch time. Plus, they're already doing battle with Keith's real mom and stepdad, who want him in finance instead of veterinary medicine. So, you see, Sterling, your family isn't the only one with problems. Last night, Keith said adults should figure out how to settle their differences, and I agree."

"That's pretty idealistic, Megan."

"So?" She drank from her cup, her eyes remaining pensive.

"Hey, we don't have any reason to fight." He paused. "I expect you'll cancel out on tomorrow night."

"You want to cancel?"

"Not me. I assumed with your grandmother's surgery today and all, you'd probably prefer to stay home."

"There's nothing I can do from here. Her surgery will be over by then. And I already extracted a promise from Mark and Keith to do a movie night at home that includes Lauren, Joel and Tyler. Although Joel told Mark he's already made plans with friends."

"Really? What friends?"

"You'll have to ask him."

Sterling rubbed his cheek. "He went out after Lauren's party last night. Joel bypasses me and checks with his sister, and I can't convince her it's dangerous for a fourteen-year-old boy to be walking around town after midnight. Her feeling is that it's so much safer here than it was in New York. At least he came home at one o'clock, which is when he told Lauren he'd be back."

"One? What was he doing? There's not much open during the week to occupy kids his age. And the ferries aren't running that late yet, so he's not hanging out with school pals. Sterling, you're his legal guardian, not Lauren. So if he ends up getting into trouble..."

"I know, but Blythe set the tone. If I get too heavy-handed, I'm afraid he'll just take off."

Megan remembered when she'd acted out as a troublesome teen. She and her mom were constantly at odds. "I'm not the best one to give advice. I resented authority at Joel's age, too. But I did grow up okay."

"That you did." He eyed her as if she were a piece of delectable island fudge.

"Stop." She blushed. "I know what you really believe—that I still tempt fate."

"And me. You tempt me, Megan. I'm very attracted to you. You make me think a lot of X-rated thoughts. Damn," he said, rolling his eyes, "why can't I ever fall for a nice, boring woman?"

"Boring as in dull? It's beyond me why you or anyone would want that. But if it's true, we should probably call off our date, Sterling."

"I guess dull isn't what I meant. Safe. Is that better?"

"Ah. You want a house in the suburb? And you'd drive off to work leaving a stay-at-home wife slaving over a hot stove? *That* kind of safe, Sterling?"

He shifted uncomfortably and couldn't meet her eyes. "With you, Megan, I can't say that I envision driving off. And the heat in the kitchen wouldn't be coming from a stove." He shook his head. "There's obviously a big gap between what I think *should* attract me and what *does* attract me." He set down his mug and slowly tugged hers away. The large hand he drew through the soft tendrils at her nape held the mark of possession.

The tips of her ears grew hot. Megan was aware that

men were often more direct than women. She'd overheard guys at work speak pretty plainly. She wasn't used to being the person at the center of the plain talk, however. But maybe it didn't matter. Because the minute Sterling's lips covered hers, any idea of carrying on further conversation flew right out the window.

She tried to tell herself they were unsuited. That notion melted in the heat rising from the fantastic things he did with his mouth and tongue. His warm lips nipped at hers. And his tongue stroked. Tracing her eyelashes, cheekbones and traveling damply down her neck to a pulse threatening to jump through her skin at the base of her throat. Could a man who kissed with so much passion think he'd ever be happy with a *safe* woman?

Megan's knees started wobbling. She'd read about couples making love on kitchen counters, or on tables and floors. Had she scoffed at that in disbelief? If so, she wasn't scoffing now. Instead she tore at the buttons of Sterling's shirt. His skin blazed red-hot against her palms. Against her lips.

Suddenly, he lifted her up on her toes and held her at arm's length. "Wait," he mumbled, his breath coming fast and furious. "Megan, we have to stop."

"Why?" The inane question slowly left her numb lips.

"Because I hear the boys. Joel and Keith. We need to pull ourselves together. Listen, they're almost at the top of the stairs."

No matter how much she wanted to deny it, the loud, boyish exuberance penetrated the fog of passion. There was nothing like a dose of reality to drop her back to earth. Her fingers fumbled with the open buttons of the cardigan sweater she'd donned after her shower.

"Stop, you're doing those up crooked." Sterling suffered no similar problem with his shirt. Now he batted her hands aside and without missing a trick, had her sweater done up to her chin.

So much for her earlier theory that Keith wouldn't use his key. She heard it rattle in the lock. Then another clatter of boots and raucous laughter.

"Megan? Come see the fish we caught! They're beauts. Wait until I call Dad. He'll be so jealous."

"In here," Megan called, hoping her voice sounded steady. "Are you guys frozen solid? Sterling and I were just having hot chocolate. Give me a second and I'll whip up some more for you guys." She moved quickly to get milk from the fridge."

They tramped into the kitchen, their muddy boots and slimy fish bringing the scent of the lake.

"Those are nice," Sterling exclaimed, examining the string of fish. "Megan, can they toss the fish right in your sink?"

"Uh, sure." She turned and faced the glassy eyes of four good-size fish.

"What are you doing up here?" Joel asked, belligerently accosting his brother-in-law.

"Not that I answer to you, but Lauren phoned to tell me Mark and Megan's grandmother fell on some ice and broke her hip. After the surgery, Mona won't be able to navigate the stairs. Megan and I were discussing the possibility of you letting Mona have your room until they can move her to Missouri. What would you say about bunking up here for a few days with Mark and Keith?"

At first Joel's eyes narrowed. By the time Sterling

finished, they could see the idea had grown on him. "Sure. For Gram. She's a nice old dame."

"Joel!" Sterling's exasperation might have taken him straight to a shouting match had Megan not shoved a mug of hot chocolate into each boy's hand. She had the preparation of her recipe down to a few minutes.

"Mona had to miss her trip?" This from a suddenly thoughtful Keith.

"Yes. Sterling will help me bring her here, but I may have to rent a van or an SUV and have you drive her back to Columbia, Keith."

"Me? I hate driving. It took me four tries to get my license. What about Mark? Your mom wants him home, by the way."

"I know. And he'll balk. But I don't have that much leave on the books yet. I'd like someone in the family to travel with her."

"Sure. I guess I can do that."

Joel eyed the older boy scornfully. "I can't wait till I'm old enough to get my license. I can't believe you've got a license but don't have wheels, man."

"My dad's forever buying cars and tinkering with them. I have my pick of wheels anytime I need to go someplace. There's no need to drive around campus. Besides, I like walking better. I like being out in the fresh air."

"I used to think I wanted to be a NASCAR driver. One of my friends said you have to get into the junior races to be considered, unless you grow up with a family in the business. That lets me out."

"Yeah?" Keith set his cup aside and ran water over their catch. "I've always known I'm gonna be a veterinarian. Megan, do you have a plastic bag for the heads and guts? Are we cooking them tonight, or do you want to wait until Mark and Lauren are here tomorrow?"

"It's up to you guys. They're your fish. Uh…I think you kids are ordering in tomorrow night. Mark mentioned a video. Something appropriate for Tyler, I hope. Sterling and I are going out for dinner, and uh—what? A movie?"

"Or pool," Sterling said with an offhanded shrug.

"You wanna go out with *him?*" Joel's mouth dropped as if to say no one in their right mind would want to go anywhere with his brother-in-law.

Seeing another potential storm brewing, Megan redirected Joel's attention. "We'll cook the fish tonight. While Keith finishes cleaning them, will you run across the street to Mrs. Ralston's and collect Tyler?"

"Let Sterling go. That woman gets you in her clutches, she never stops talking."

"I will go," Sterling said. "I need to thank her and pay her for babysitting. If we're eating here, is there anything you'd like me to pick up at our place?"

Keith dried his hands and pulled a wrinkled scrap of paper from his pocket. "We met a group of old guys day-fishing. One of them wrote out this barbecue sauce recipe. I see you have a barbecue on your porch, Megan."

"If you guys man the barbecue, I'll fix a rice dish and a green salad. I have pudding I can whip up for dessert. Although I told Tyler he could help me make peanut butter cookies…." She glanced at the recipe, then checked a cupboard and a drawer. "I have everything we'll need, Sterling. Just help me remember to cover the barbecue again after it cools. According to the National Weather Bureau, we're looking at the possibility of a storm blowing down from Canada. If I don't have to get Mona on Friday, I'll probably be out posting warnings."

Sterling pulled aside the curtain on the door that led to the upper deck. "With that red sky? What was your weatherman drinking? Red sky at night, sailor's delight. Red sky in morning, sailor take warning."

Megan peered over his shoulder. "It's red, all right. Do you believe there's truth to that old saying? I tend to trust the weathermen. And that looks like dark clouds forming over the island."

The boys crowded around. Keith whistled. "I wonder if Mark got a shot of that sky. With the right angle it'd make a fantastic postcard."

"Speaking of Mark, he and Lauren were going up to the Soo Locks, but hoped to be back at the hospital before Mona's surgery. Before I start the rice I think I'll see if I can reach him on his cell."

"See what time they plan on rolling in tonight. And tell him to drive carefully," Sterling reminded her on his way out to get his son.

"Like Mark's gotta do what *he* says," Joel spat. "All the years we lived with him and Blythe, he didn't give a shit what me and Lauren did. Now he acts like our dad or something."

"Joel, in New York your older sister was responsible for you and Lauren. How can you fault him for stepping into the role he got handed when she died?"

"He's such a phony. He doesn't care what happens to us. He only wants the bucks our trust gives him every month."

Megan frowned. She didn't know enough about their legal status to stand up for Sterling on that issue. "It'd be easier if you met him halfway," she muttered, heading off to find her phone.

"Mark and Lauren are back at the hospital," she said once they'd gathered in the kitchen again and sat down to eat. "They're going to stay until Mona's out of recovery. Mark says they should still be home by midnight. I tried to talk to him about future plans, but he didn't offer any. He's probably as confused as I am."

"Maybe your gram will have suggestions of her own," Keith said. He cut slabs of the whitefish and set a chunk on everyone's plate.

"Hmm, this looks great. I'd never have thought of barbecuing fish. I'm glad you met those fishermen. By the way, how's Joel's boat?" Her question launched a conversation that then lasted through dinner.

"When can I go in your new boat, Joel?" Tyler spoke around a mouthful of rice.

"Don't talk with food in your mouth, Tyler. And you'll be waiting until some fine Saturday when I'm home, before you take a ride in Joel's boat. I arranged with Mrs. Ralston to keep you after school on the days he goes out for a spin."

"Why? 'Cause you don't trust me with the kid?" Joel thrust out his chin, his whole body tense.

"It's you I'm thinking about," Sterling said evenly. "I know how distracting kids can be jumping around in a boat. I don't want Tyler to go until the chop is off the water, which gives you more time to get comfortable handling your boat."

The boy had no comeback, and Megan used the opportunity to clear their plates and serve bowls of chocolate pudding. Sterling teased her about loving chocolate. The others joined in, and a stressful day ended on a lighter note.

"I've decided I'll work tomorrow," she told Sterling as she took out the ingredients for cookies. "I'll save my day off for when we go get Mona. Are you sure you can take a day off work?"

"The office is still working out our permanent schedules. I'll stop in tomorrow and ask not to be put on this weekend."

Keith, Joel and Sterling watched a soccer game on TV while the cookies baked. She bagged some for Tyler to take home, and afterward leaned a shoulder against the door and watched Sterling herd his son into the night. "See you tomorrow. Six-thirty, you said?"

"That works for me. I thought we'd go to the Hunan Restaurant at Bay Plaza. One of the other ferry captains said the food's pretty spicy."

"Sounds great. I'll probably wait up for Mark to get home tonight, if you want to sack out and let me stay up to do the worrying."

"Thanks, but I've been planning to start a new thriller I bought. Seems like a good night to see what it's like."

They parted, and Joel hung around for another hour. Keith had no such compunction about waiting up for his cousin's return. He was yawning when Megan shut the door and snapped on the outside light for Joel. "I'm going to mess around in the kitchen," she said. "I'll try not to wake you."

"Once I'm out, it takes a tornado to wake me. I sleep right through sirens sometimes. And today I got my fill of fresh air while fishing."

"Since we're alone, Keith... Between us, what do you think of Joel's boat?"

"The kid got a good deal, Megan. He's a little green when it comes to docking and tying off. He'll be fine with practice."

That left Megan feeling better. She put together a couple of casseroles and was tucking the last one in the freezer when Mark and Lauren drove in. They beat Mark's estimate by half an hour. As Megan went to greet him, she noticed it had begun to spit rain.

"Gram came through surgery with two thumbs-up. I know you'd like to hash over what we're gonna do next, but I'm beat, sis. Can we wait and talk tomorrow? You have the day off, right?"

"I did ask. But I changed my mind, since I don't have to go and get Mona. I don't have leave to spare, Mark, and I thought I should wait in case Mona needs my help later."

He nodded, but still ambled off to bed. Megan turned off the lights and reclaimed her bedroom for a few more days, or until they settled on where to put Mona. Now she wasn't sure whether or not she'd be turning her room over to Keith and Joel and be sleeping on the couch.

There was no sign of the guys when she dressed for work the next morning. The storm predicted by the weather bureau had moved in with slow churning clouds that intermittently dumped heavy rain. Megan rummaged in the closet for her slicker and boots. The deck of the cutter was always slippery when it rained.

Jim Elkhorn glanced up in surprise as Megan slogged past his desk. "Hey, Loo'ten'nt," he drawled, "I thought the commander gave you today off. How's your grandmother?"

"She had hip surgery last night. They want to keep her hospitalized for a day or so. I'll need my day off to go pick her up. What's on our docket today, James?"

"More trial runs with those big expensive sailboats. These are called half trials or something. Hamish has been monitoring their progress. Ten boats left Port Hope at some ungodly hour this morning. He just said they're waist-deep in a rainstorm. Those dudes have more money than brains."

"They're all seasoned sailors. I read rundowns on all the boats in last week's paper. Pretty impressive stats."

"Yeah, but a couple of the boats are brand-spanking-new out of the boatyard. No one can predict how they'll perform."

"Huh. That must be why they're starting practice runs this early. It's smart to see how the boat's going to handle in various kinds of weather."

"Well, there are thousands of shipwrecks littering the floor of Lake Michigan."

"Thousands? Aren't you stretching the facts?"

"Nope. I visited the Shipwreck Museum. The water in these lakes is so cold, one information panel said that whenever salvagers find an old wreck, the boats are remarkably intact. I think it'd be cool to bring up one of the old three-masted schooners, don't you?"

She nodded absently. "I suppose during the summer we'll have to deal with salvagers. Especially since detection equipment's getting fancier every year."

"No doubt. The museum curator said during calm seas you can look straight down and see wrecks sitting in sixty feet or more of water. Because the lake's so cold there's none of the algae and marine life that gums up saltwater wrecks."

"Maybe while my brother and cousin are here visiting we'll take a trip to the museum. It sounds fascinating."

"Yeah. Oops, there goes a call. Time to get back to the real world. Jeez, it's a good day for ducks," he said as they shrugged into slickers and tore down the gangplank toward their cutter.

"What's the call?" Megan shouted to the others who'd beaten them on board.

"The lead boat in the trials hit a goose-downer rain as she rounded the point headed into the straits. We're clocking twenty-foot swells in that area." Their cutter was already outbound before her anchor was fully locked into place.

The storm lashed at them from all directions the minute they cleared the jetty. Reports coming in from the distressed sailboat indicated she'd snapped a mast and had shortened her sails to almost nothing. Word came down that she'd begun spinning like a top. Waves were burying first her bow, then her stern. She was at dire risk of capsizing.

Commander Donovan ordered Vince Rigley to get on the radio. "I want all ferry traffic stopped," he shouted above the squeal and crash of the waves.

One ensign signaled he'd contacted the main ferry terminal via their two-way. "Two ferries just docked. Another is midway through its run and is bucking a terrific headwind. They estimate having her in port in another ten to fifteen minutes."

Torrents of rain met deep troughs gouged in the angry swells by the relentless wind. Although the gloom setting over the water was more reminiscent of impending nightfall.

Megan had only ever seen a sky this ochre-gray and yellow once before. When traveling across the prairie, Camp's wagon train got caught between tornadoes, and they were hit head-on by what was later called a microburst. Her stomach tensed the way it had then. Megan scanned the sky for funnels, even though she'd never heard of tornadoes hitting the Mackinac Strait.

Their cutter steamed past the last ferry, now pulling up to the dock. The double-decker was swallowed in purplish fog almost before the cutter's stern slid past the undulating ferry slamming against padded docks.

ABOARD THE FERRY, CAPTAIN Dodge snapped out orders. He was glad he'd been told to stand down. *So much for the damned red sky at night.*

Snatches of a report about a sailing vessel in distress began to circulate as his passengers filed off to wait out the storm. Sterling checked all the cleat lines himself before he made his way back to the wheelhouse.

He soon discovered he had a bird's eye view of an attempted Coast Guard rescue taking place midchannel. "Look," his first mate called. "The sailboat buckled. Is she breaking up? Jeez, how stupid can they be? The Coast Guard's going to try and send up their chopper."

Sterling grabbed a pair of binoculars. He ran out on deck, only to be hit by crosswinds and knocked sideways against life preservers hanging outside his wheelhouse.

The Jayhawk had lifted off. It didn't get far when he saw it go into a full spin. He could see guardsmen on board all suited up in bright orange. They wore stark white helmets. His stomach corkscrewed as he watched the chopper. He knew this was what Megan had said she'd trained for, helicopter rescues, but he was terrified that he might bear witness to a crash. It spun a number of times, shuddered, rose, dipped and rose again briefly. It hovered above the cutter, then dropped heavily back to the landing pad. The crew tumbled out as others ran to tie down the copter. From the way one jumpsuit caressed a feminine shape, Sterling knew Megan had been aboard. He bent over the railing and proceeded to lose his lunch. *How could she?* How could she risk her life time and again for strangers?

ON THE CUTTER, MEGAN'S team didn't have an opportunity to feel grateful for being spared. They had a ship on their watch being battered to bits. There was very little time to launch a powerboat now. If they didn't collect survivors within minutes, hypothermia would claim their lives.

Megan was one of six in her team who pulled on cold-weather frog suits. They wore air packs with ten minutes of air in case heavy wave activity drove them underwater. Even with the suit, it was a shock when she went in feetfirst. She hugged her line while she forced air into her stunned lungs, and waited for the radio in her headgear to crackle to life. In swells of this size, saving anyone required the eyes of a spotter on deck.

Six crew members had gone in the water to save four people from the sailing ship. Her colleagues had three in hand, all lashed flat on open-weave body cots. The victim Megan pulled out shook horribly and was blue about the mouth. She climbed up after the shivering man and hovered over him while their medical personnel worked to stabilize him. He was the boat owner and captain, he said, once he was able to speak. His concern was for his crew, and he named them. One was missing.

Donovan was within seconds of calling off the search when Hamish Tucker yelled that he could see a life vest bobbing farther out than where they'd been looking. A team set out in a lifeboat. They grappled in a woman. She was in bad shape, and succumbed to hypothermia before they'd loaded her onto a waiting ambulance.

It was a subdued crew that made its way out to clear the channel of wreckage. Loss was always a risk, but it was this team's first. And it took a toll. No one talked much during the rest of their shift.

The storm blew out by four o'clock. A full, colorful rainbow arced over the island, as everyone on the team stared in pain and wonder.

Megan's muscles ached from being smacked around by the wind and waves. But she filed her report along with her crewmates. Frankly, she looked forward to spending the evening with Sterling.

On the drive home, she felt a hole in the pit of her stomach. Maybe he'd just hold her close for a while. Sometimes that was all a rescuer needed. To feel the steady beat of a compassionate heart.

CHAPTER TWELVE

THE APARTMENT WAS EMPTY when Megan walked in. Because hot chocolate spelled comfort, she headed straight for the kitchen.

Mark had left a note on the counter stating that he, Lauren and Keith had decided to take Tyler to a kids' movie in town. Joel, apparently, had other plans, as someone had said the night before. Mark's note also indicated that he'd checked on Mona. The nurses had gotten her up, he said.

Megan couldn't believe they'd do that a day after surgery. She phoned the hospital while her milk heated.

"Mona? It's Megan. What's this I hear about you being up and about already? I certainly hope they're not rushing you. Are you okay? Do you need anything?"

"Child, I feel so foolish for causing all this fuss and bother. One minute we were walking into the airport and the next I was lying on my back staring up at the sky."

"It's not your fault. Mark said your feet hit a patch of melting ice."

"Yes, at the terminal entrance. Their lawyers have crawled all over my room today. They've offered to settle my hospital bill. Probably so I won't sue."

"Gosh, I thought the accident happened in the parking

lot." Megan poured cocoa into her cup, stirred in vanilla and dropped in marshmallows. "You didn't sign anything, did you? Perhaps you should keep your options open. I mean, what if you have complications later?"

"I cleared them of any blame—just so they'd go away and leave me alone. Also because I think the knee that's been giving me trouble probably buckled when I stepped wrong..."

"But you could suffer long-term effects from the fall."

"It's short term that has me worried. I can't impose on you. Not even if Mark leaves for New York next week."

"What? Next week? New York? I'm sure he's not." Megan thought Mona was confused. She hoped that wasn't a sign of concussion.

"Yes, dear, he's driving out on Tuesday. He told me so twice. He and Lauren. She apparently learned she has enough credits to graduate early. And she can start at the design school April fifteenth. Don't you remember, the evening of her birthday party Joel said she'd been accepted to begin classes."

Megan felt poleaxed. *Did Sterling know?* They'd heard Joel blathering on about going to live in New York with Lauren. Megan could almost bank on all of this having flown past Sterling, though.

"Megan, are you still there? Did we get cut off?"

"I'm still here. I needed to shut off a burner on my stove. Ah, Mona, when should I fetch you from the hospital?"

"The doctor hasn't decided. But...it's not only a matter of imposing on you, dear. I simply won't be able to navigate those steps to your apartment. I should book a motel room until I can fly."

"Sterling has offered you Joel's room. He'll bunk up

here until we see how you fare—and figure out transportation to Missouri."

"Oh, thank heaven. I thought maybe I should take my house off the market. But I phoned Parker Bellwether, my broker. He has a full-price offer on the house and a full-price contingency backup offer. He strongly advised against backing out now. I'm frankly not sure how to proceed. I wasn't able to reach my lawyer to see if I'm legally bound by the seller's contract I signed. I also bought a small condominium in town from him and had my most cherished pieces of furniture moved before I left. Now I won't be able to navigate those stairs, either."

Megan could hear the worry in her grandmother's words. "I'll call Mr. Bellwether and ask him to stall the buyer for the house, shall I?"

"Thank you, dear. Please ask him to wait at least until I'm released to your care so we can make further decisions. I'd be so relieved."

"Not to worry. I'll phone him as soon as I hang up. You rest and do as your doctor says."

"All right. Goodbye, dear."

Megan detected relief in Mona's sigh. Cradling her cup of chocolate, she went through the operator to find the real estate broker. When she hung up, she realized Mona's house was as good as sold. That meant someone needed to help her find a temporary first-floor place to live. The most logical person to do that was still Megan's mother. But judging from Camp's attitude, it'd be a cold day in hell before Emily had anything more to do with Mona.

Wandering from the kitchen to the bathroom, Megan wondered how long Sterling would want Mona at his place. Maybe not at all after he got wind of Lauren's plans to take off for New York with Mark.

Family dynamics could sure get messy fast.

A steamy shower went a eased muscles drawn tight by the day's rescue. Megan dressed in a long wool skirt and sweater. Then, as the time for her date with Sterling approached and he didn't appear, she thought maybe he'd forgotten their evening out. Or perhaps he'd already found out about Mark and Lauren's plans. If he hadn't, should she be the one to tell him?

Fifteen minutes past the time they'd agreed on, she recognized his tread on the stairs. Not wanting to appear anxious or too eager, Megan let him knock twice before she answered the door.

"Hi. You didn't say what we were doing tonight beyond dinner. If I'm overdressed it'll only take me a minute to run back and throw on jeans."

Sterling's eyes cruised her from head to toe and back. "You, uh, look fine. Better than fine," he said, rocking forward and back on the balls of his feet. "Megan, I've been downstairs debating whether or not we should still go out."

Megan bit her bottom lip. "Uh, you wanna step inside a minute? I guessed you'd be unhappy with the news about Mark and Lauren. I just heard myself, when I phoned my grandmother."

Sterling crossed the threshold and stopped so abruptly, she was barely able to shut the door behind him.

"What *about* Mark and Lauren? I'm talking about the ringside seat I had for the boating accident you were called out on today. It's the second time in a matter of weeks I've stood helplessly by and watched you put your life on the line, Megan. I realize it's your job, and you like what you do. But that storm hit so fast and with such force, anyone on the lake was in danger of drowning. The thought of it being you…well…I…"

She rubbed her chilled arms through the sleeves of her cable-knit sweater. "We did lose a boater in that accident. It was awful. We tried so hard to save them all. It wasn't enough. Sometimes it's not."

Lackluster eyes and trembling lips conveyed how forlorn she was. And that touched the man standing there rattling the loose change in his pockets. Sterling didn't want to be affected but lost the battle. He walked over and enfolded Megan in his arms. She felt small-boned and fragile, and despite her bravery, it made him want to be her protector. After all, he knew how difficult it was to lose someone he'd tried to save. He'd been there and lived with the hell. Not only that, his son had lost his mother to a risky job. He didn't know…he just didn't know if he could go through that again.

His body heat seeped through the cold Megan hadn't been able to shake with hot chocolate or a steamy shower. Being held by him was all she'd thought about while driving home. Shamelessly, she soaked up the emotional strength she so desperately needed, even though she knew Sterling didn't want to give it.

Or did he?

He crushed her against his chest and she snuggled close and slid her arms about his waist. He wasn't holding her like a man who wanted her to go away anytime soon.

"I have no willpower where you're concerned," he breathed as if reading her mind. He rained kisses over her hair.

"I'm sorry. Well, not really," she murmured. She shivered as his lips trailed damp kisses down her throat. "I don't seem to have any where you're concerned, either, Sterling."

"One of us should have some."

"You're right," she said, tugging off his jacket as she stood on tiptoes, not breaking the kiss.

The jacket fell at their feet and lay there in a heap as she backed down the hall in tandem with the man, his hot, wet mouth on hers. Megan was no longer cold, because his wide hands had rucked up her sweater and were busy warming her skin.

He'd obviously forgotten she was a bad risk. And she forgot she ought to tell him about Mark and Lauren's plans to drive to New York.

Everything fell by the wayside as they each got lost in touching and trying to please the other.

Megan so rarely let her emotions override her good sense. But she liked the way that touching Sterling made his body harden against her abdomen. Plus, the thrust of his pelvis had heat pooling between her thighs. One exploration led to another until lethargy made her bones go limp. Why on earth would she object when Sterling lifted her in his strong arms and growled in her ear, "Which way to your bedroom?"

Megan almost didn't have the wherewithal to point. She didn't stop to think that her brother and cousin might come home early. She was consumed by need. Need and greed. She wanted to feel Sterling inside her and told him plainly, even adding a plaintive, "Please," at the end that sent him reeling over the edge.

He lifted his lips ever so slightly, and desire burned in his gray eyes. "How long has it been for you, sweetheart?"

"I, ah, quite a while."

"For me, too," he whispered. Then talk fell off as clothing did the same…

"Protection," he murmured in her ear seconds before a crucial moment. "I didn't expect this," he panted, "Damn, I didn't come prepared."

"Prepared?" She stroked his nipples, her voice soft and dreamy. She did her best to urge him to complete what he'd started.

Sterling lifted himself off her tempting body with muscles rigid and shaking. "Megan, think—doesn't the Coast Guard dispense packs of condoms?"

She went still and let her hands drop. "Oh, my Lord. I, uh, threw them all away."

"Then we can't." Sterling rolled to his back and yanked the sheet over the lower half of his body. He flung an arm across his eyes, his jaw flexing as he gritted his teeth.

Megan struggled to sit up. Her sluggish mind worked to grasp what had gone wrong. "Wait. In my bottom drawer. The team gave me a gag gift when I left Alabama." She jackknifed off the bed and pawed through a catchall drawer in her dresser. She came up with a sequined red heart-shaped box on which someone had stenciled in black, Emergency Survival Kit. Megan pulled off the top, and out tumbled a bawdy mix of porn toys. A feathered G-string, purple pasties, a small jar of chocolate body paint and an array of glow-in-the-dark condoms. She made a choking sound. "Dare we trust these?"

"How old are they?" Sterling dragged his arm from his eyes in time to see her fan three plastic-wrapped packages. One in day-glo orange, another iridescent pink and a third that was bright green.

"I got them in mid-December."

He rolled up onto an elbow to peer in the box and picked up the jar of body paint. "You hung on to this stuff because…?"

"I left Alabama with a week's leave and went home right before transferring here. I didn't want anyone in my family to find stuff like this in my suitcase, so I put them in the dresser I had ready to ship."

Sterling opened the jar and drizzled chocolate around her navel. She squealed and he laughed, pressed her into the pillow and lowered his head to taste his handiwork. "Um," he said, "Gives me ideas about all that cocoa you keep on hand."

She tried to wriggle away at first, but then fell back. Her fingers flexed in Sterling's thick, soft hair as he licked his way to a point that had her abdomen tightening in ripples. She dropped the packets she'd been holding and they glowed against the pastel blue of her sheets.

Finished playing with the chocolate, Sterling capped the jar. He grabbed up the orange condom and tore the packet open with his teeth.

Megan leaned forward on her elbows to watch a process she thought would be laughable. But when Sterling rolled on the colorful latex, her breath caught, and more than interest stirred in the pit of her stomach. Playtime was over. The man facing her looked serious. Hard, gorgeous and serious. Megan slid lower on the pillow and reached out with both arms. Sterling came eagerly into them.

Megan's few experiences with sex had been anything but memorable. She'd found nothing to warrant a steady diet. Until Sterling. He didn't rush. He asked what she liked and set about pleasing her. Megan wanted to savor each second, and she did until breathing became torture, and her eyes rolled back in her head.

She thought later that it was a good thing he was beside her, capturing her scream of pleasure in his mouth. Because if anyone had been in his apartment below listening, as he had the morning she did aerobics in this same room... Well, it was just too embarrassing to contemplate.

Anytime before, she couldn't wait to dress and leave, or have her partner say goodbye. Not now. They also tried out the hot pink condom and when both fell back on the bed, even then Megan didn't want the night's experience to be over. "Can we do that again?" she asked lazily, loving the feel of Sterling's warm damp skin on her cheek.

Brushing his thumb back and forth over her lips, he dredged up a smile. "The spirit's willing, but the flesh is weak, I'm afraid. Besides, I'm not sure we want to deal with the screaming neon in that green package. Next time, I promise I'll be better prepared."

"You think there'll be a next time?"

He sat upright. "Why not?"

"As I recall, you came to my door tonight ready to cancel our date."

"Did I? Funny, I can't remember why I'd do something so foolish." He twirled a strand of her hair around his index finger and pulled her toward him for a kiss.

Megan licked her lips and tasted chocolate. Smiling, she swung her feet off the bed. "I just realized I'm starved. Didn't you promise me dinner?"

"That I did."

She fastened her bra and slid her legs into lacy black panties she'd had no idea would be such a hit with Sterling when she'd first put them on under her long skirt.

He trailed a finger down the indentation of her spine to the flare of her hips. "You have a jagged scar. Did you get that on a rescue mission?" His finger followed its path.

She glanced over her shoulder as she pulled on her sweater, and the explosion of heat in his eyes spontaneously combusted in hers, as well. Blushing, she scrabbled around to locate her boots. "I fell out of an apple tree when I was eight. I crawled out on a limb to throw apples at a neighbor boy who'd called me names."

"What did he call you?" Sterling slid off the bed and stepped into his pants.

"Tomboy." Laughter welled up from her throat. "Thing is, he was dead-on. I'm still a bit of a tomboy I suppose."

Sterling mulled over her statement while he buttoned his shirt. He remembered why he'd planned to cancel their date—Megan's worrisome propensity for climbing out on limbs and dangling at the end of ropes. How did that image fit with the woman who served up hot chocolate, baked cookies from scratch and hosted her family and his in an apartment she'd painted and made a home? That Megan Benton was the soft, feminine woman he'd made love with tonight. Why wasn't the simple life enough for her? Uneasiness descended as he retrieved his jacket.

Megan felt a change in him before they left Lady Vic. Within minutes it was as if their lovely interlude had never happened. They rode downtown in Sterling's car, after agreeing to skip the Hunan restaurant and instead go for hamburgers at the tavern. Possibly also for a rematch at pool.

She attempted to talk about the accident, but he only looked grim. He didn't even want to discuss the weather, which had gone from balmy to stormy, to balmy all in one twelve-hour period. His moodiness discouraged civil conversation.

He held the door open for her at the tavern. Megan pointed to a booth near the back, and took off, not liking his attitude. She intended to find out exactly what had brought it on. What *kept* bringing it on. The empty booth, far enough away from the bar for privacy, seemed perfect for such a discussion.

They'd just sat down when raucous laughter at the entry claimed their attention.

"What the hell," Sterling said, half rising. "Isn't that Joel? And aren't those your Coast Guard pals he's with?"

Megan whirled and stretched out of the booth so she could see. Jim Elkhorn, Daryl Nunez, Hamish Tucker, Vince Rigley and two younger seamen were clowning around as they removed their jackets. Sure enough, Joel Atwater was in the middle of the men, acting as if he belonged.

Frowning, Megan was slow to follow Sterling, who'd vaulted out of his seat and headed straight for the group. She arrived in time to hear him demand, "What in hell do you all think you're doing bringing a fourteen-year-old kid into a tavern?"

Joel smirked. "Bug off. These are my friends."

Megan slipped an arm through Sterling's. She felt his muscles tense. Choosing Daryl Nunez, the most easygoing of the men, she tugged on his sleeve, as well.

"Daryl. Have you guys been drinking? Please tell me no one gave Joel any beer."

"We didn't," Daryl said quickly. "But we thought he was older, like almost seventeen. The kid's been hanging around the station talking about joining up soon. Honest, Lieutenant, we thought he was practically of age to join."

Sterling shook loose from Megan and nearly lifted Joel off his feet. "He'll be fifteen this month. Suppose you tell me what this is all about. Are these guys the friends you've been out with every night?"

The guardsmen were openly nervous. Several began to drift out of the circle where man and boy glared daggers at each another.

"I'm sorry, Megan," Sterling said abruptly, "I need to take Joel home. It's way past time he and I come to an understanding."

"Uh, Joel's obviously interested in joining the Coast Guard. If he bunks at my place while Mona's at yours, let me talk to him about the school's ROTC program."

"No!" Sterling's roar was loud enough to make Megan flinch, and the members of her crew who'd drifted off, came back, grouping protectively around her. "As long as I have a say," Sterling snapped, "he's not taking up anything that idiotic or dangerous."

Megan's eyes glittered as anger erupted in defense of her own and her friends' career. "If that's how you feel about what I do, then we're wasting our time pretending otherwise."

"Maybe you're right about that. Are you coming, or staying here with your buddies?"

Joel tried to free himself from Sterling's grasp, looking mutinous.

Megan placed her hands on her hips. "Fine, go! I'll get a ride home with one of the guys."

She watched them leave, and hid her unhappiness as Sterling made no further comment, only hustled a clearly furious Joel from the suddenly tense and quiet tavern.

THE STOOP-SHOULDERED doctor stepped into the room where Emily Campbell sat on the examining table awaiting the results of her most recent tests.

"Emily, why don't you get dressed? I'll talk with you in my office. Is Nolan in the waiting room?"

She shook her head, glancing up sharply from peeling off the latest layer of fingernail polish. It was getting ragged, anyway. "Camp had to advise a student after his last class, so I came alone. Is there some reason you asked? Did you find something in my tests?"

The doctor cleared his throat. "Well, uh, in cases such as yours, I prefer to go over the test results with husband and wife. Will you call and see if he's free? Since the office is so close to the college, I imagine he can be here by the time you get put back together."

Emily's stomach jumped nervously. She immediately supposed Dr. Gregory was going to relay terrible news. Maybe she had uterine or ovarian cancer. She couldn't imagine why else he'd want Camp present. Granted, the white-haired man had been Nan Campbell's physician for years. But weren't a patient's records and condition a private matter between her and her doctor?

Knees shaking almost too much to hold her up, Emily stepped down off the table and reached blindly for her pile of clothing. "What if I'd rather Camp didn't hear bad news about my condition, Dr. Gregory?"

"Now, now, Emily. Don't go jumping to conclusions. Just give him a jingle. If he's tied up this afternoon, I'll talk to him at your next visit." The old man backed from the room, leaving Emily even more worried, but also curious.

She fumbled out her cell phone, and as family numbers were programmed in, she had only to press one number. A good thing, since her hands were so unsteady.

"Camp? No, I'm not home yet. I'm still at the clinic. Uh...has your appointment come and gone?"

"Emily, what's wrong? You sound odd. Have you been crying? God, are you okay?"

"The doctor has my tests back and he'd like to go over them with both of us. I have no idea if I'm okay or not. But it sounds ominous, don't you think?"

In his campus office, Camp gripped the phone so tightly his knuckles turned white. "I'll be right there. My appointment just left. I'll give my secretary the notes to type up, and I can be at the clinic within minutes. Shall I bring anything? Do you want juice or a soda?"

"No, nothing!" Taking a deep breath, Emily closed her phone and only belatedly remembered she hadn't told her husband goodbye or that she loved him, which was the usual way they ended a phone call. She couldn't get her fingers to work, and after she'd forced her hands to button the white blouse that went with her blue suit, she realized she'd done it all wrong.

Camp arrived in less than five minutes. When the nurse showed him into the room, he was out of breath and looked more like a disheveled, absentminded professor than Emily had ever seen him.

He reached for her, eyes filled with love and compassion. She immediately broke down in tears.

"Em, what is it? Has the doctor said his news is bad?"

She shook her head, and damp strands of the red hair he loved so much, caught on her wet eyelashes. Camp took out his handkerchief and blotted her eyes. Gently, he did up the crosswise buttons of her blouse and helped her into her suit jacket. Next he sat Emily down and knelt to slip on the navy pumps that matched her suit and purse. A purse he handed her as he rose. "The nurse said we should come out when you were dressed and she'd take us to the doctor's office."

"If it's not terrible news, why wouldn't Dr. Gregory just tell me what my tests showed?"

Her husband shrugged. "Maybe he thinks you should have a hysterectomy. I think my dad was on hand when Dr. Gregory went over options with Mom. You've had really erratic periods lately. It's probably something like that."

"You think?" She stiffened her spine and squared her shoulders. "I love you, Nolan Campbell. You have a way of always making me feel better. Shall we get on with it? See what the fuss is about?"

He dropped a tender kiss on her lips and smoothed away the tears still clinging to her lower eyelashes. He tried to reassure her, although he was worried enough for the both of them. Emily had been his life since that day she'd walked into his office eleven years ago. He'd thought she was a student. A bad student at that, because when she'd knocked over her bulging attaché case, he'd glimpsed low scores on her remedial students' papers. In fact she'd come to join his wagon train reenactment. It'd started out as a bet with his sister, Sherry. He'd been sure the trek would demonstrate that modern women wouldn't fare half as well as their pioneer sisters, but women like Emily had proved him wrong as wrong could be. He'd been the one who wouldn't have survived on the trail without Emily's generosity. He'd fallen for her hard. And loved her so much that if the doctor's news was bad, he'd go to the ends of the earth to provide a cure for whatever ailed her.

A different nurse led them to Dr. Gregory's office. "He'll be right in," she said. "Make yourselves comfortable. He's almost finished with his last patient of the day."

Camp pulled out a chair for Emily across from the doctor's, and he dragged one over and placed it next to hers.

She scooted closer, and clasped his hand. Camp loosened her hold and instead slipped his arm around her shoulders.

Luckily they didn't have long to wait before the doctor bustled into the room. He dropped Emily's chart on the desk, sat and gazed at them over top of his wire-rimmed glasses. "Well, now. I'm glad you were able to get away, Camp. The last time I ran into you was at a New Year's open house your parents had…what was that…three years ago?"

Camp rested his foot on the opposite knee and bobbed his loafer nervously. "Are we making small talk, Doctor? My wife is convinced you asked me here because you have a report for us that isn't…good."

The doctor opened Emily's chart and withdrew a sheet he'd filled out in nearly indecipherable writing.

"I'm, ah, relying on you to tell me if the news I have to share is good or bad. Now, some couples I know would think it's not so hot." He set the page down and bounced his fingertips together several times. "Mrs. Campbell, er…Emily, you're pregnant. My best estimate is eight weeks or a little more. Of course, I'll want to do an ultrasound to obtain a more accurate timetable."

Emily, who'd leaned forward to hear better, fell back. She glanced over at her husband and broke into peals of laughter. "Dr. Gregory, pregnancy's impossible."

Camp's hand tightened on her shoulder. "She doesn't mean it's impossible, doctor. But…for eleven years we haven't, ah, used anything to avoid pregnancy. Early on we embraced the idea. You probably have lab reports concerning the fertility tests Em endured. Her previous doctor said our only hope of having a child would be through artificial insemination. By the time we got that diagnosis, we were in our late thirties, and decided against so drastic a step."

"You mean I'm pregnant for *real?*" Emily's jaw sagged open.

"I'd stake my forty-year career on it," the doctor said gently.

Tears bubbled in Emily's blue eyes. "That's *wonderful* news, not bad at all. It's wonderful, isn't it, Camp?"

He chewed on his upper lip a moment, then nodded his head vigorously. "It's a surprise," he acknowledged the moment he could force air past a lump in his throat. Grabbing both of Emily's hands, he again faced the man seated across the desk. "Emily is forty-five, and I'm forty-nine. But I'm sure you know that. Will, uh… will the baby will be all right? Healthy and all?"

The doctor removed his glasses and twirled them several times by the earpiece. "I won't sugarcoat this. I'm sure you both know it's quite rare for a woman of forty-five to have healthy eggs left in her ovaries. The rate of miscarriage is probably fifty percent. Ordinarily with older moms I recommend amniocentesis. But—"

He didn't finish his sentence before Emily said, "No. No amnio. We've had women in the crisis center who swear amniocentesis caused their miscarriages. Camp, we can't." Her freckled hands curved over her stomach. "The fact that I'm pregnant naturally is a miracle. I'm not messing with God's plan."

No one said anything for several moments. Then the doctor shuffled the papers in her chart and cleared his throat. "If that's your decision, I'll still want an alpha-fetoprotein done and ultrasound tests at intervals. I also feel it's incumbent on me to advise you that the possibility of having a Down syndrome baby is much higher for older moms and dads. Depending on the results of the alpha test, we may want to do a chorionic villi sampling."

"But…I'm already pregnant. You said the baby's been growing for two months."

The doctor nodded and pursed his lips. "There's still time to terminate if you deem it best."

Again silence reigned in the office. The wall clock ticked loudly, as if warning Camp and Emily how foolish they were to hope for a baby at their age.

Camp noticed Emily's face was white and pinched. The freckles he loved so much stood out in stark relief against her pale skin. He lifted her hands to his lips. One by one he kissed her knuckles, all the while holding her beautiful and expressive eyes with his. "It's your body, Em. I only donated a few sperm, and happily at that. Do I want a baby? Yes. At any risk to your health, no. I'll say that once here in front of the doctor." His eyes grew moist and he blinked hard, refusing to turn aside. His hands still held Emily's shaking fingers. "I feel that if we're meant to have this child, sick or well, we'll cope. Isn't that part of what we promised in our marriage vows? In sickness and in health…"

Emily rallied, and color flooded back into her face. "Exactly! Oh, Camp, my being pregnant when we all thought I had a nervous stomach or an ulcer is nothing short of miraculous. Being pregnant is the *last* thing I would've imagined. But I want to do everything humanly possible to have this baby. Please," she said shakily, turning her still-drenched eyes toward the doctor.

Dr. Gregory pushed back his leather chair and slapped a hand on his knee. "I'll do my part. There's greater risk of miscarriage in the first trimester, so I'd like you off your feet for the next month. I'll set up the blood test and first ultrasound exam ASAP."

Emily flung her arms around Camp's neck and cried into his shoulder. This time they were tears of joy. He was still too stunned by the news to do much more than massage her back slowly.

All too soon the doctor was shoving diet information at them. He wrote out a list of vitamins and barked out dos and don'ts. "If any spotting or other problems develop before my receptionist books your ultrasound, don't bother to call, come in at once. I'm sure you'll know, as you've had two full-term pregnancies in the past."

"Way in the past," Emily said, finally able to produce a semblance of a smile. "My babies are twenty-five and twenty-three. Oh, my Lord, Camp. What do you suppose Mark and Megan will say about having a brother or sister at this late date?"

"Mrs. Campbell." The doctor interrupted Emily's excited babble. "Since the risk of miscarriage is high, I frankly suggest you not jump the gun and tell people who'll only be disappointed and maybe not know how to treat you if something does go awry."

"But..." Her fingers moved convulsively on Camp's wrist.

"Honey, I'm sure Dr. Gregory knows best. Let's get through the next month. If all goes well, you can phone the kids and break the news."

"What about Sherry?"

"What about her?"

"Well, we work together. I'll need a sub and I'll have to hand off my duties at the Hub. And there's your folks. They're at the house at least once a week. I'm used to being active. They'll think I'm dying if I lie around week after week."

The doctor smiled. "I'm not saying you *can't* share your happy news, Emily. Only that you should keep the statistics in mind."

"You mean, no furnishing a nursery?"

"I wouldn't recommend it yet."

Camp stood and carefully brought Emily to her feet, too. "We understand. She's been running herself ragged recently. We all thought her problems were caused by nerves, because our son—well, *her* son decided to take a different career path from the one we both want for him."

Dr. Gregory opened his office door and led the way into the hall. "Keep worry to a minimum. I know better than to expect a woman to be totally without stress. But minimize any sources of stress that you can. Until this baby puts in an appearance, I want you to get into the habit of letting someone else deal with problems. I guess that would be you, Nolan."

"Definitely, that would be me." Camp smiled crookedly.

"Knowing your parents, I'm sure they'll be pleased as punch at the possibility of another grandchild. I've known them both for many years. They strike me as having quite cool heads. Let them worry about the young rascal you say is kicking over the traces. He's the twenty-five-year-old?"

Camp shook his head. "Mark's twenty-three. His older sister is a lieutenant in the Coast Guard. We thought Mark was heading for a fabulous counseling career at Wellmont. He's decided to go off and be a photographer. Em can't stand to see him pass up a solid job opportunity for such a long shot."

"Hmm. His career change could prove cost-effective for you, especially when it comes to baby pictures. I know how older parents do love baby photos." The doctor grinned at his own joke.

Emily didn't find it humorous. And because she didn't, Camp vowed to stick his nose in and attempt to change Mark's mind. He generally let Em handle her kids. But there wasn't anything he wouldn't do for her. If she wanted Mark in town and working at the college, he'd do his damnedest to hog-tie the kid and bring him to his senses.

He'd also have to make sure Megan didn't bother her mother about Mona Benton. Camp could imagine how upset Em would be over any dealings with her ex-mother-in-law. And what gave Megan the idea that her mother should look after the old witch? What was wrong with that girl? Camp knew Megan had a good head on her shoulders. On the other hand, Mona was her biological grandmother. He'd have to use some finesse when he was talking to Megan.

CHAPTER THIRTEEN

THE MEN WHO'D BROUGHT Joel to the tavern clustered around Megan after the door shut behind Sterling. "Honest, Megan," Jim Elkhorn said solemnly, his right hand raised, "we thought Atwater wanted to join up."

"How could you? He looks so young."

Hamish Tucker snorted inelegantly. "The kid's taller than Seaman Brown. Dennis gets carded every time he goes to buy a beer. Put those two side by side and Brown might even look younger. Instead of hammering us, Lieutenant, maybe you should ask the kid why he fed us such a pack of lies."

Jim piped up again. "Yeah, Megan. He sounded serious and asked all the right questions. Recruiting's been tough on all branches of the military lately. That's why Daryl lent him a stack of books, so Joel could bone up on signals and equipment. It makes me wonder why a kid would go to those lengths, knowing he can't join the guard until he's seventeen."

Megan hadn't pieced together all the whys and wherefores. What Jim said made sense. "The Joel Atwater who's been hanging out with you guys has changed drastically from the boy who first moved into the apartment below me." She described her initial meeting, then added some of his history. "In New York, he fell in with a gang and looked the part . Now he's doing his best to blend with you guys. Maybe he just feels desperate to belong."

Hamish Tucker urged the group still huddled near the door to their usual table. "Hey, that makes sense. Did your brother teach you about digging into somebody's head? Didn't you tell us he's a shrink?"

"Psychologist slash counselor." Megan laughed and accepted a beer Seaman Dooley shoved across the table. "But Mark's another guy determined to change his life. He wants to be a freelance photographer. Did any of you see the newspaper photos of the accident between that container ship and the yacht? Mark shot the pictures."

"We saw them," Hamish said. "Commander Donovan sent copies to the brass in Grand Haven. So your brother took those, huh? Now I see why you and Daryl Nunez were front and center in so many."

Vince Rigley held his beer aloft. "Why didn't you tell us you were bringing your own press photographer?"

Megan felt heat climb her cheeks. "Come off it, Vince. I was too busy to realize *anyone* was taking pictures. I didn't know until later that Mark e-mailed pictures to the paper. And I doubt he had any influence over the ones they chose to print."

"Doesn't matter. The old man was pretty quick to accept the glory for our station."

"Yeah, well, you couldn't prove it by me." Megan peeled the label off her bottle. "Donovan gave me hell for taking off my life vest to go after the little girl. The picture in the paper showed my vest lying at Daryl's feet. I wouldn't have thought Donovan would be that keen on showing off my insubordination to headquarters."

They all laughed at that comment. Her admission started a round of stories about other infractions the men at the table had been chastised for at this station and others they'd served with. Megan found them a dedicated, congenial group who loved what they did. It was easy to see why Joel would want to pretend he was one of them. People looked at them, at their uniforms, with respect.

"We were surprised to see you cozied up with Dodge when we came in," Jim Elkhorn noted during a lull. "I'll bet he's champing at the bit for a rematch at pool, huh?"

Caught off guard, Megan blushed wildly at the memory of how she and Sterling had spent the hours before showing up at the tavern. Pool had never been mentioned. "I told you Captain Dodge is my downstairs neighbor. His family and mine were out for the evening. We decided to get hamburgers."

Hamish uncoiled his long body from his chair. "We split a couple pizzas before we ended up here to play darts. Since you haven't eaten, Lieutenant, I could be talked into a burger. Ante up, you guys, if you want me to put in your order." He polished off his beer and scooped up bills being tossed on the table.

Megan slid her hand over her hip and remembered she had on a skirt. "I, uh, seem to have left the house without money. Can I borrow a few bucks from one of you? I'll pay you back tomorrow at work."

Vince handed her ten dollars. As she thanked him, Matt Horowitz stood. "I've gotta go pick up my wife and kids from the airport. She's been visiting her folks for two weeks. I'll sure be glad to see her. I hate going home to an empty house. All you bachelors and you, too, Lieutenant Benton—I don't envy you."

"Get outta here!" Hamish winked at two cute blondes ambling toward the dart boards. "I like variety," he said.

Megan rose and gathered the empty bottles. Turning, she set them on the bar and indicated they'd have another round.

"Wowzer, check out the lieutenant's duds!" Vince crooned. "You're all spiffy tonight. Or is that what you normally wear around the house?"

Jim Elkhorn looked her over. "Say again why you showed up with Dodge? *Sure,* you guys decided to go out for burgers on a whim. Megan had a da-ate," he singsonged.

Of course, the others were quick to poke fun. Razzing buddies was part and parcel of being in the Guard.

She took it for a while, then put her little fingers to her teeth and rent the air with whistle that made even the pool players turn to stare. "Stop! At work I might be one of the guys, but at home, you dumbos, I'm a girl. I do own skirts and dresses."

Vince pulled her up and twirled her around. "So, why have you gone out of your way not to accept dates with anybody at the station? What's Dodge got that we don't?"

"Manners for one thing." Megan aimed a kick at his shins. She tossed back his ten. "Forget about my burger, I'm going home." Ducking under Rigley's arm, she struck out for the door.

A pool player, a local Megan had beat on several occasions, intercepted her escape and pulled her closer than she liked. She could tell from his eyes that he'd had too much to drink and he slurred his words as he ogled her new attire. "Whaddya know, the pool shark has legs. Don't run off so soon. How about I buy you a beer?"

She shook her head. "No, thanks. I'm just leaving, Don."

The man, beefy from working the ore boats, pinned her in a corner by the door.

She had her cell phone out because she'd intended to call Mark to see if he'd come and take her home. Now she hesitated, not comfortable with letting Don Pickering know she was alone. Megan knew she could call on her crewmates to help her out. But pride was a factor, too. She could handle this lout.

Still, he was three sheets to the wind, and he wasn't easily cajoled into releasing her….

Daryl Nunez, a sweet kid, seemed to be the only one of her friends aware of her plight. He telegraphed concern to her in a frown. She smiled, but Don Pickering thought the smile was meant for him and took it as encouragement."

"My pals over at the pool table said you were too high and mighty to join us for a few beers." He coiled a strand of hair that fell over Megan's left ear around his forefinger. "I wouldn't like it if you made me look like a fool, Maggie."

"It's Megan," she snapped, shoving at his barrel chest. "Lieutenant Benton!"

She got loose and stepped aside, only to back into the jukebox that an even bigger guy in a flannel shirt had just fed. It pounded out a Brooks & Dunn tune.

Don tried to kiss her, and Megan wondered if she had room to knee him in the groin. But that would cause a scene. "Stop," she warned instead.

His dark eyes flashed in annoyance. "Just because you can whip us all at pool doesn't mean you're all that tough, little lady!"

She wedged an elbow against him, to buy herself some breathing room. "You're drunk, Don. Don't do something you'll regret when you sober up. This town, your company, relies on the Coast Guard to keep the waterways open and safe."

"Then why act so stuck-up?" He plucked at the middle button on her jacket. "I can show you a better time than those pansy-ass guys you hang out with."

The door opened, bringing in a gust of wind as Megan slapped Don's hand away.

"What's going on here?" a deep, masculine voice demanded. "Megan, is this jerk giving you a hard time?"

The two involved in the struggle parted in surprise. Megan most of all, as the last person she'd expected to see again, at least tonight, was Sterling. "I…we—Don was trying to talk me into a game of pool. But I was just going to call my brother to have him pick me up."

"Yes, well, Mark's not available. He and Lauren went dancing. I left your cousin with Tyler and Joel. Oh—Keith said your grandmother phoned right before I got home. The doctor's releasing her first thing in the morning."

Which still didn't explain why Sterling had showed up at the tavern.

"Excuse me." She pushed Pickering out of her way. "That means I have less time than I thought to prepare a place for Mona. And I said I'd work my regular shift tomorrow."

"Me, too." Sterling scraped a hand over a stubbly jaw. "Is Mark going to get her? If not, I doubt I can get away until midafternoon."

Jim Elkhorn, walking to the men's room, overheard the conversation and stopped. "We can let Donovan know for you, Megan."

Megan was tempted to take him up on the offer, but when it came to her career, she preferred to handle work-related matters herself.

"Thanks, Jim, but I need to pick up next week's schedule anyway." She might need extra time off in case she had to find her grandmother a doctor in town, or make other arrangements for her.

Her teammate glanced from one to the other, and saw Pickering stumble off. "Whatever suits you, then." Jim continued on his way to the men's room.

"Those so-called friends left you to deal with that big drunk? And Joel thinks they're such a noble bunch."

Turning up her collar, Megan pushed open the door with her hip. "Basically they are. They'd have come over if I'd asked for help. I *am* capable, Sterling."

Her sharp retort gave him pause. "Yeah, well, I felt guilty as hell for walking off and leaving you here to fend for yourself."

"No big deal."

Sterling slid a hand under her arm and turned her toward his vehicle. "I think it's a big deal. We had a date, Megan."

"Which you came upstairs to break," she told him, sighing as she climbed into the Land Rover after he unlocked the door.

"I didn't break it," he said gruffly. "I'd say I went whole hog in the other direction."

"Don't remind me. If I'd phoned home for a ride, I'd have had to send Keith into my wreck of a bedroom to pick up my car keys. He may be young, but he's no dummy."

He started the engine and stretched his arm over the seat behind her as he checked the rearview mirror before backing out. He hesitated, catching her studying him from under half-lowered lids. "Regrets, Megan?"

"None," she said. "You?" She stiffened her back. Then, unable to help herself, she brushed a thumb over his shadowy jaw.

Sterling pressed his lips to the soft pad of her thumb, shaking his head. "I *should* have plenty of regrets," he added. "I wanted to. But I don't. What I want is to take you to bed again."

She drew in a tight breath that burned right down to her belly. "But…you don't respect me. I mean, it's clear from the way you acted with Joel and just now with Jim Elkhorn, that you have no use for how I make my living."

He backed out of the parking lot and threw the shift in gear. "I don't like seeing you put yourself in danger at those rescues. Which apparently has no relation to how badly I want to hold you and kiss you. I need that like I need to breathe."

The warmth flowed languidly through Megan's body. What woman *didn't* like hearing she was as essential to someone as life-sustaining air?

"And I wanted to take apart the hulking bastard who had his hands all over you when I walked into the tavern. And if you think I'm a violent man, let me tell you I never felt like strangling the cop who was sleeping with Blythe."

"I haven't slept with anyone but you, Sterling. It bothers me, though, that you resent my job."

"I don't resent it. Worry for your safety isn't resentment in any way, shape or form."

"Okay, but to me it's like you're saying the guys on my team are more capable of doing the job than I am."

He massaged the back of his neck, and shook his head. How did he admit to someone he cared for a lot—maybe too much—that he was bigger, stronger and also capable, but he was haunted by the pleading eyes of a woman he hadn't been capable enough to save? "I have to work all day tomorrow, Megan. But I'll be glad to let you take the Land Rover to get Mona if you can arrange for time off." Sterling decided changing the subject was preferable at the moment.

Megan had expected an explanation, but she responded to his offer. "That's kind of you. I know Mona will be more comfortable having the extra leg room. I need to pin down Mark and Keith, and see if we can come up with a way to get her home. There's no direct flight here from Columbia. That's the closest town of any size to where Mona lives. She'll have to change planes twice. And someone needs to pick her up at the airport. Even then, it's a big mess. I spoke with the broker who's selling her house. He's got two full-price offers. She bought a condo, but it's on the second floor. I frankly don't know where she'll go once she gets home."

"I thought you phoned your mother—"

"I talked to my stepdad. He almost never yells, but he got cross and said I presumed too much trying to foist Mona off on Mom. It seems Mom and my grandmother had a big blowup over the fact that Mona financed Mark's trial run at the photography thing. Camp's family is mad at Mona for butting in. So my stepdad came up with what he sees as a solution—he thinks Mark should drive Mona home so they can nag him some more to take the counseling job."

"Well, that may be your best option. You have a job and Keith doesn't like to drive. Maybe you should insist Mark step up to the plate. Why *can't* he drive his grandmother to Missouri?"

Megan came close to bringing up what Mona had said earlier about Mark driving Lauren to New York. She wondered when Lauren intended to inform Sterling of her plan. And what about Mark? She intended to have a talk with him.

As she huddled in the leather seat next to the man her body knew intimately but of whom she knew little else, Megan felt overwhelmed by the circumstances they'd all become hopelessly entangled in. Everyone needed to stop squabbling long enough to really listen to what each person wanted.

Ha! Fat chance!

As Sterling pulled into the cul-de-sac and parked, Keith opened the door to the lower apartment. Mark and Lauren appeared at the top of the steps leading up from the boat marina. They all met on the porch as if their arrivals had been choreographed.

Megan knew it was cowardly, but she didn't have the stamina to face a major confrontation just then. "Mark, Keith," she called. "Come upstairs. We need to talk about what's going to happen when Gram gets home. Keith knows, but maybe you aren't aware yet, Mark. Her doctor is releasing her tomorrow."

The look that passed between Mark and the young woman whose hand he held didn't escape Megan. Which was why she grabbed her brother's arm and tugged him toward the stairs, motioning for Keith to follow. Before Mark was able to resist, Megan succeeded in dragging him up the first step. "Goodnight, all. See you tomorrow. Sterling, I'll run down in the morning and collect the key to the Land Rover. I'm sure Commander Donovan will let me leave early."

"Sis, there's something you need to know," Mark said urgently.

"Not now, Mark. I probably do know, but Sterling doesn't," she hissed. "Mona spilled the beans. You need to let Lauren deal with telling him about your plans. I'm reasonably sure he's going to go through the roof, so I wouldn't count on him agreeing to let Lauren go, even if she does have enough credits to graduate early."

Mark stumbled on the third step. For a minute Megan thought he might turn back. Then he heaved a big sigh and called down past Keith, "Lauren, I'll see you in the morning at the ferry terminal."

Keith brought up the rear, but he bolted past his cousins and opened the door.

Mark barely waited for them all to get inside. "If Gram blabbed our plans, I guess you know we want to leave tomorrow. The island school promised to have Lauren's diploma signed and available in the morning. She had no idea she could've graduated in December. Then she never would've had to come here."

Marching into the kitchen, Megan said nothing until she'd begun to make a pan of hot chocolate. If ever she'd needed the familiar comfort, it was now. "Promise me Lauren is going to tell Sterling."

Mark cracked his knuckles. "She wrote him a note. You know how he is. For Tyler's sake and Joel's, she doesn't want to get into a shouting match. And you know what? I checked on the Internet. Eighteen is the legal age in Michigan *and* in New York. Lauren phoned the family attorney. Once she proves she's enrolled in a college, she's eligible for a chunk of money from her trust that's earmarked specifically for education. I asked Gram to advance Lauren enough to pay her fees until the lawyer gets Sterling to release the trust."

"I can't believe Mona would involve herself!"

"Why not? She spoke with Sterling's lawyer, and he verified the money's in the trust. Uh, she did stipulate that Lauren had to let Sterling know."

Megan battled a tic in her right eye. Leaving a note was not a courageous way to deal with Sterling. She sank into a chair and cupped her hands around her hot chocolate. Megan finally thought she could see how their mom felt having Mona ready and willing to hand over money for every whim.

She watched Mark open the container of marshmallow. She didn't take any, but Keith stirred his marshmallow in with a stick of cinnamon.

"Mark, maybe it's none of my business, but since you two are traveling together, are you, uh, thinking about getting married?" Megan was afraid that would really send Sterling over the edge. And probably her mom and Camp.

"I already told you we aren't serious like that. We get along great. Maybe we're headed toward falling in love. I don't know yet. But she wants to finish the design course and get a job. And I have to prove to everyone that I have what it takes to be a photographer."

"Shouldn't you go home and honestly look at the counseling job?"

"Don't need to." He shook his head impatiently. "But here's the part you're not going to like. It doesn't make sense to rent *two* apartments in New York. Lauren says rents are outrageous. So we're going to share a place—a two-bedroom place—and split expenses."

Keith gulped down his chocolate. Megan glanced at him for help, but his expression was neutral. She lifted her cup and stared into the depths.

"So, go ahead, yell at me."

"You're a grown man, Mark. And, if I yell at anyone, it'll be Mona."

"Why? Oh, the money. You're just like Mom."

"You can't see she's meddling in Sterling's business exactly like she did with Mom? Camp told me Mom and Mona recently went around and around over her bankrolling your trip here. Don't you *care* that Mom's seeing a doctor, probably for anxiety?"

"Don't dump that on me, Megan! In case you've forgotten, Mom never let anyone block *her* from the career she wanted. Or for that matter, marrying Camp."

"Mark, I just want our family to get along. Not only don't I expect that to happen anytime soon, I now see you and Mona adding to the discord in Sterling's household."

"I'm not to blame for that, either," Mark said, slamming down his mug. "Sterling has custody of Lauren and Joel by default. He was planning to divorce their sister, remember."

"A lot you know, Mark Benton. Blythe sloughed off her responsibilities. And Sterling found out she'd been sleeping with her partner."

That salvo had Mark bumping into Keith, who'd straightened away from the door. "Whoa! Who said that? If it's true, why hasn't he ever told Lauren?"

"I shouldn't have said anything, and don't you tell her or Joel. That's between them, Mark. Sterling saw no reason to take away how they felt toward their sister."

He stubbornly refused to acknowledge her explanation.

"Mark, they need time." She got up and gave her brother a hug. "I wish you'd reconsider, and delay going. I have to work in the morning, and I'll go pick up Mona right after lunch if the commander okays it. I hope you're here when I get back. But if not, check in along the road, okay? And when you find an apartment, I want the address right away. Oh, and knock 'em dead at your showing." Because tears were streaming down her face, Megan ducked between the two men and ran to her room where she shut herself in to cry.

The first thing that she did once her tears had dried was dispense with all evidence of her hours of bliss with Sterling. Hours that most likely would never be repeated.

NOLAN CAMPBELL REFUSED to let his wife drive herself home from the clinic. "Humor me in this, Em. I want to see you get home safe and sound. I'll get Dad or Garrett or Sherilyn, and we'll come back tonight and pick up your car."

She climbed into his SUV and sank back against the seat and shut her eyes. "Pinch me, Camp." Slowly, Emily rotated her head and gazed at the man she'd loved fully and totally for eleven years. "I heard everything Dr. Gregory said, but I'm having a tough time believing any of it's true. I mean, we tried so hard to get pregnant the first three or four years. I wonder why now, just when I've heard you making noises about retiring." She pulled out the seat belt to fasten, although she kept the other arm protectively across her abdomen.

His angular features softened as he lightly cupped her hand with his larger one. "I love my job at the college, so I'm probably not a good candidate for retirement, anyway. We did want a baby so badly—maybe it's taken this long for our prayers to get through to the big guy. I know my folks will be overjoyed. Will you let me invite them over tonight? And we need to include Sherry and Garrett."

"Yes, oh, yes." The smiles she'd been holding at bay broke over her face like the sun coming out from behind a cloud. "It is real, isn't it? My heaven, what will everyone say? A lot of the people we work with are our age. They're crowing over becoming grandparents."

"Right, and I've noticed they're all turning into old fogeys. A baby will keep us young and vigorous."

Her smile turned mischievous. "We'll see if you still say that after a month of 3:00 a.m. feedings."

"I need to buy a book on parenting. I know you've gone through it twice, and I watched Garrett and Sherry from afar, but..." He sighed. "I'm afraid I'm pinning all my hopes and dreams on this surprise pregnancy going well."

"You really agreed with me when I said I wouldn't consider termination?"

"Are you kidding?" He leaned over the console and kissed her soundly. "I've always been proud of you, Emily, but never more so than when you advocated without hesitation for our child. Come what may, I believe we have love enough to handle any crisis."

They traded kisses and private words of love for a few minutes. Then Nolan drove home. He took care to avoid sudden stops or streets with potholes.

"You're driving like I'm nitroglycerin," she chided.

"Get used to being coddled, pampered and waited on for the next seven months. Dr. Gregory said we need to take extra-special care of you. I fully intend to follow his every instruction and more. If my mom or dad can't stay with you during the day, I'll hire a—"

"Babysitter? A nanny?" she broke in, laughing. "Honey, the doctor didn't say to smother me. We're going to have to set some ground rules. I'm not spending seven months under house arrest. I like to putter around. I like to cook and sew and garden."

"No, no and no. I've seen you stress needlessly over any and all of those things. I'll agree to simple projects you can do sitting on the couch or in bed."

"Oh, brother. Dr. Gregory has created a monster. I have visions of turning into a lethargic blimp." She crossed her eyes and pooched out her cheeks. "Is that the kind of wife you want?"

"If it keeps you and the baby healthy," he said, raising his jaw stubbornly.

Emily huffed and treated him to a frosty glare.

Having had eleven years to get used to her flash fires, as he called them, Camp knew that once the initial flare-up spent itself, Emily would review all the facts at hand and nine times out of ten she'd reach the same conclusion he had.

Two blocks from their lane, she began leafing through the stack of information the doctor had provided. "Chalk one up for you, Campbell," she said, sounding only a little disgruntled. "In the early stages of high-risk pregnancy, it says here, there should be no stooping, squatting or lifting. No horseback riding, running or jogging. As if I'm not smart enough to figure those last three out for myself."

He pulled the SUV into the detached garage and dashed around the vehicle to assist her out. Pilgrim, the golden retriever Camp owned before he met Emily, now an old dog of fifteen, had his nose pressed to the front window. He'd become Emily's dog soon after she and the kids moved in to help Camp renovate his farmhouse. His muzzle was nearly white and he couldn't see well, but he unerringly greeted every member of the family and anyone else who stopped by to visit.

Camp hurried to the door to let Pilgrim out. Emily held the dog's head against her thigh and massaged his ears. "Pilgrim will be good company for me."

"True." Bending, Camp briskly rubbed the dog's shaggy sides. "Good boy. You'll watch over Em while I'm at work, won't you, old man?"

The dog whined low in his throat, and his tail beat Camp's knee. "I still wish you'd agreed to us taking that stray lookalike pup Keith dragged home a couple of years back. If Pilgrim hadn't been neutered, I'd have sworn the puppy could've been his son."

"I didn't want Pilgrim to feel like we were replacing him. Besides, Shannon had dibs. She loves that dog." Emily slung her purse strap over her shoulder. "Pilgrim was slowing down. Our kids had flown the nest. We weren't really in a position to train a rambunctious pup."

Camp looped an arm loosely around Emily's waist. "You don't like change, Em. That's what it is. Mark's and Megan's rooms look exactly as they did the day they went off to college. We'll have to convert one into a nursery, you know. You should start thinking now about which room it's going to be."

Her steps slowed on the curved brick steps. "You're doing it, Camp. What Dr. Gregory said we shouldn't. You're making grandiose plans for a child we're not certain will ever be."

"He will be! Or she," he added quickly and ferociously. "This isn't like you, Emily. You're always the one preaching positive thinking."

"I'm just so scared this miracle will evaporate," she said, gripping his hand and working her fingers into the thick fur of the dog pressed to her side.

Camp turned slightly and stroked her face. "You're tired. It's been a stressful day. Why don't you go and soak in a nice warm tub while I fix something simple and nutritious for supper? My family can wait another day to hear our good news."

Emily stood aside with the dog as her husband held open the door. "An herbal bath is exactly what I need to restore my energy. I know you're practically bursting at the seams to share the news, so please invite them over. Besides, your mom and Sherry both know I had the appointment today. I predict if you don't call them soon, they'll be phoning us."

His eyes gleamed. "How shall we break the news? Sherry and Garrett had us all over for dinner. They weren't subtle at all. There was a copy of her ultrasound propped against each water glass."

Emily chuckled. "I can laugh now. Then I was devastated. Oh, that's not totally true. I was happy for them. Just sad for us. More for you than myself." She set her purse on the entry sideboard and slipped both arms around Camp's still-narrow waist. Placing her head against his chest, she listened to the reassuring thud of his heart, then murmured, "Professor Dad has a nice ring, don't you think?"

"How about Professor Pop?"

The phone jangled, and neither moved to answer it. Pilgrim hobbled over to it and glanced back to see why neither of them followed. The machine clicked on after two rings. It was Camp's mother inquiring about Emily's doctor's appointment.

They stood and grinned foolishly, and discussed who'd call Nan back to issue the invitation. "My family is so predictable." He dropped a kiss on the tip of Emily's nose. "You scoot and take that bath. I'll make the calls and fix a salad. Then I'll run down to the bakery and see if I can find a cake that'll spell out our surprise. Won't that be fun? We'll see which of them makes the connection first."

"You are so bad, Nolan Campbell. Everything between you and Sherry has to be a challenge." Emily kicked off her shoes and started to scoop them up, but Camp beat her to it.

"Tut tut, no bending, remember?"

She accepted the low-heeled pumps with a curtsy. "For the record, my money's on your mom."

"You could be right. We'll see. You and I didn't even make the connection, and the doctor all but drew us a diagram."

Emily enjoyed her bath. She dressed in a caftan, which she often wore around the house in the evenings. She heard Camp in the kitchen after he'd come back from his trip to the bakery. They ate their salads in the sunroom, and after they'd finished, Emily rose to take their plates to the kitchen. Camp jumped up and told her to sit. As he strode off with the dishes, she put her fingers in the corners of her mouth and made a goofy face at his back.

"I saw that," he called. And he had, as the hall mirror hung in just the right location. "You know we teachers have eyes in the back of our heads."

"Good. It'll come in handy when the baby starts

crawling." The moment Emily said that, they faced each other abruptly, twin expressions of awe on their faces. It took a sharp rap at the door to bring them down out of the clouds.

Sherry and Garrett pulled up behind the elder Campbells. "Hey, what's the reason for this gathering of the clan?" Garrett teased as his wife straightened from smelling a bouquet of spring flowers Nan carried into the house. "The tulips are beautiful, Mom. From your new greenhouse, right?"

"Yes. Emily, dear—will you bring me a vase?" Nan called as they all walked in. "These will look nice on your hall table."

Camp spun. "I'll get it. Everyone take a seat in the living room. The coffee's finished dripping. I'll bring the pot and cups, and I'll put the flowers in a vase. Be right back."

"Is he all right?" Nan Campbell asked Emily.

Sherry plopped down on the love seat and pulled her husband down beside her. "I'll bet you're going to tell us some big news about Mark."

"Mark?" Emily, who'd curled up at one end of the couch, tensed. "What about him? Did you hear from Keith today? Before I left campus, you said you planned to phone him."

Camp bustled into the room carrying the coffeepot, and a tray stacked with mugs and rows of cupcakes. Pink and blue frosted ones cleverly decorated with cradles. The proud professor plunked a small paper plate with one cupcake in the lap of each family member. He calmly returned to the coffee table and filled the mugs, omitting Emily, who'd asked for chamomile tea, instead.

If Pilgrim hadn't uttered a doggie groan as he flopped down next to Emily, the entire room would have been silent.

Camp's dad reached for his coffee. He peeled the paper off his cupcake and took a big bite. Nan frowned at the one on her plate. Garrett set his on the coffee table. He usually didn't eat sweets, but he accepted a mug of black coffee. Sherry's eyes flew wide open. She gaped at the cupcake, then at her brother and finally at Emily. "Ohmigod!" she burst out. "Emily! You've been barfing because you're pregnant."

The announcement had no sooner left her lips than the room erupted in babble. Camp attempted to talk over everyone else, trying to convey what they'd learned from the doctor.

Ben Campbell asked a question that had a hush falling again. "What did Mark and Megan have to say when you told them they're about to become a big brother and sister?"

Emily twisted her fingers in her lap. It was Camp who came to her rescue. "Uh, Dad, Mom, everyone. I've been trying to tell you that because of Emily's age—and mine—this pregnancy is considered risky. We're sharing the news with you because you're here in town and would notice something's up with Emily's new routine. Dr. Gregory advised us to not tell the world until…well, after we see results of the first ultrasound. We'd like your promise that you'll be careful not to let anything slip if you talk to the kids in Michigan."

"Of course, dear," Nan rushed to say. "It'll be hard enough for those of us who know… if…well, suffice it to say, we understand. We'll certainly abide by the doctor's orders."

The others were slower to nod, but nod they all did. Then excited chatter rose again.

CHAPTER FOURTEEN

MEGAN SLEPT FITFULLY, and as a result she woke up late. It wasn't usual for worry to interrupt her sleep. But she didn't like being privy to secrets sure to cause someone angst. Someone she cared about a lot.

Dressing for work, she stumbled into the kitchen and was surprised to find Keith already there with a piece of toast in his mouth and a half-made sandwich on the counter. "I started the coffee when I heard you in the shower." He bit through the toast, set it aside, and poured her a cup.

"Don't tell me you're about to spring more bad news on me, Keith."

"Me? I'm going fishing. Joel said I could borrow his boat. You think I want to be here this afternoon when the shit hits the fan downstairs?"

"I know what you mean," she agreed, reaching for the coffee. "I wish Mark and Lauren would talk to Sterling. I doubt he'd lock Lauren up."

"I dunno. People are complicated. I told Mark he's leaving you with a pack of trouble. I thought he was supposed to be the smart one. Meeting Lauren turned his brain to mush."

"It's called love, Keith—even if Mark won't admit that's what he feels. Love messes with people's minds," she said morosely, wondering if what she felt for Sterling was close enough to qualify as a reason for her mixed-up emotions.

"I'll be going home Sunday, Megan. If you can get your grandmother a seat on my flight, I'll see she gets safely to Columbia."

"Keith, I could kiss you. I haven't known what to do about Mona."

"Yeah, well, you'll still have to arrange a place for her to crash."

Megan dumped the coffee. It was weaker than she liked, but her cousin's heart was in the right place. "I'll find something," she vowed. "Camp's determined to run interference between Mom and me. I'll phone her at work today. Like it or not, she'll have to put her argument with Gram aside and help her over this bad patch."

"I don't envy you that phone call, Megan."

She screwed up her face. "I have another favor, Keith. Can I bribe you to run down and get the key to the Land Rover from Sterling? I'm not a good liar and I'm afraid he'll read guilt all over me. I'll finish making your lunch."

"Sure. I'll tell him you're running late, which is true."

Watching him dash off, Megan got out meat and cheese to make the sandwich. She added cookies and an apple to the sack. Maybe the winds, metaphorically speaking, had changed course. *Thanks to Keith, her life might improve.*

Keith came in whistling. "No sweat, Megan. Sterling has the early-morning run to Mackinaw City. I met him at the bottom of the steps. He was bringing you the key."

She took the chain he dangled under her nose and

tucked it in her shirt pocket. "Catch lots of fish. We'll ask Sterling to come for dinner. Maybe we can soothe him with a nice batch of baked fish. How much of a fit can he throw in front of my sick grandmother?"

Keith shoved a hand through his hair. He didn't respond, and Megan headed out to work feeling anything but cheerful.

When she'd explained the situation to Commander Donovan, he said, "If you're determined to put in a few hours, Benton, I'll ask you to be the duty officer, which will give me two full crews to deal with a task I've just been handed. Suspicious cargo on a Russian freighter sailing down the channel. After she passed through the locks, someone reported not all the containers she's carrying appear to have been sealed or registered at the port of entry. Our mission is to stop and examine her freight."

"Darn, I miss all the fun." Megan wore such a hangdog expression, the commander and several of her crewmates hooted. She waved them off like a good sport. Since she had the office virtually to herself, Megan decided it gave her ample opportunity to book Mona on Keith's plane. She first went online but couldn't find his flight, so resorted to phoning the airline. With Mona's condition that was best anyway. After being put on hold three times and being transferred to a new agent each time, Megan finally reached someone sympathetic to her problem.

In the end, she had to get Mona a first-class ticket and upgrade Keith. That venture maxed out Megan's credit card. But what the heck. Her grandmother tossed money around so freely, the additional expense shouldn't be a big deal.

She'd wanted to call her mother at the college.

Booking the flight had taken so long, Megan worried that she'd barely have time to dash home, change clothes and trade her pickup for Sterling's Land Rover.

Frank Dooley came in from a dental appointment. His arrival allowed Megan to leave. "Hey, Dooley, I'm glad to see you. I have to drive up to Sault Ste. Marie to spring my gram from the hospital. Everybody's out on a run." She gave Dooley a quick summary of the calls she'd taken.

Her apartment was dark and silent. She paused outside Mark's room, then swallowed hard and thrust open the door. His car wasn't parked in its usual spot and his photographic gear was missing, which confirmed that he and Lauren had taken off for New York. His laptop and printer were also gone, as was his duffel. The bed he'd used had been stripped of bedding.

A sadness crept over Megan. Who knew when she'd see her brother again?

She left the room and hurriedly switched to jeans and a sweatshirt. Collecting a windbreaker and her cell phone, Megan ran down the stairs and climbed into the Land Rover. There was a marked difference between driving it and her smaller pickup. But as she pulled onto the highway, memories surfaced of Camp teaching her to drive in his big Chevy SUV. Pilgrim always sat in the middle seat panting in her ear.

She winced, remembering what a brat she'd been back then. It'd taken a few years, but she'd transformed into a decent human being. Much of the credit went to her stepdad.

While home lay heavy on her mind, she pulled her phone out of the case. Megan guessed she understood Camp's wanting to shelter her mother against further run-ins with Mona. Both women possessed tempers, and when they landed in the same space it was a lot like throwing gasoline onto a fire.

Passing the first sign that mentioned Sault Ste. Marie, Michigan, Megan realized she'd become more comfortable handling the Land Rover. As there was almost no traffic on the road, Megan punched in her mom's office number. A strange woman answered. "Do I have the right extension for Emily Benton—uh, sorry, Emily Campbell?"

"This is Emily's number. I'm subbing for her today. Are you a student?"

"No. This is her daughter. No emergency or anything. I'll catch her later."

Megan clicked off and gnawed the inside of her mouth. She tried to recall if her mother had ever called in a sub. And didn't Camp imply that she was having some medical tests? He'd suggested she might have worried herself into an ulcer over Mark and that visit with Mona. But that seemed like a pretty extreme reaction to Megan.

She set the phone on the passenger seat. Had Mark called the folks to apprise them of his latest decision? If so, that'd send their mom into orbit. Megan could imagine that, if she followed his call with one pressing her mom to find somebody to look after Mona, that might push Emily into a nervous breakdown.

Was there a real danger of that? Megan considered her mother one of the strongest women she knew, outside of her aunt Sherry.

Picking up the phone again, Megan scrolled down her programmed numbers and found Sherry Lock's at the crisis center. She hesitated only briefly, then punched the button. Sherry's secretary, Angel, answered. Megan smiled, recalling several encounters she'd had with the fiery, outspoken woman her mom and aunt had once saved from an abusive relationship. Angel had come a long way since those days.

"Angel, this is Megan Benton. Is my aunt Sherry at the Hub?"

"Megan, what are you up to, girl? I thought you were out on some Coast Guard ship saving the world."

Megan laughed. "I'm off today. My grandmother Benton is visiting. She fell and broke her hip. The doctors put in a titanium pin, and I'm fetching her from the hospital today. I'm calling because I'm trying to get a feel for how Mom is. I need her help locating a ground-level apartment for Gram. Mona bought a second-floor condo that won't be able to live in for a while. Keith's flying home with her. The truth is, Angel, I'm hoping Mom and Camp will offer her a bedroom until she can navigate on her own."

Megan couldn't tell if she'd lost her connection or if the faint buzzing in her ear was road noise from the heavy-duty tires Sterling had on his vehicle.

"Angel?"

"I'm here. Sherry's in a meeting. And, well, you'd best not bother your mama, considering her condition and all."

"Condition?" Megan's heart clutched. "Is Mom worse? I phoned her office and got a sub."

"It's supposed to be on the q.t. if you get my drift. But nobody can keep a secret on campus. We're all excited for her, but no one expects Emily back to work till after the baby comes, if then."

"Ba-baby?" Megan jerked the wheel and almost ran off the road. She fumbled for the phone as it fell in her lap. Having drifted to the shoulder, Megan jammed on the brakes. "Angel, I'm afraid you're not making sense. Don't tell me Mom's going through a midlife crisis and had decided to adopt a baby?"

"Lord, girl, hasn't nobody called to say you're gonna be a big sister in about seven months?"

Megan's head felt ready to explode and her hands shook so hard it was a good thing she'd pulled over. Her legs wobbled as she stepped on the emergency brake. "Give me a minute," she said feebly. Taking several deep breaths, she began to issue rapid-fire questions. "How? Who said? When did this happen for Pete's sake?"

"Whoa! I think maybe I shot off my mouth when I shouldn't have said anything. Sherry knows. She said it was a secret, but I didn't think that would mean from family."

"I...don't understand. Mom's forty-four. No, she's forty-five, Angel!"

"So? You think forty-five is too old for sex, missy?"

"No. No, of course not. I, uh...isn't having a baby at that age dangerous?" Megan asked, suddenly panicked.

"Where you been, girl? In a vacuum? Not long ago, some lady gave birth at fifty-five. Between you and me, I think she had donor sperm in a petri dish. But your mama, she done it the old-fashioned way. I say good on her. Your aunt's all worried about a possible miscarriage. I tell her, listen, women in my family got a sixth sense when it come to babies. I'm bettin' your mama's will be fine"

Apprehension slithered up Megan's spine. "So, if

everything's fine, why isn't she working? Why would she need a sub until after the baby's born?"

"Precaution. Baby doctors, they don't trust Mother Nature. Now don't you worry. You go right on making the world safer for the rest of us, including that new brother or sister. I gotta go, there's another line ringing. Be good, ya hear?"

The phone went dead. But it was a long time before Megan shook herself out of her stupor and closed the lid. It took an 18-wheeler passing so close to the Land Rover that the whole vehicle rocked to bring her to her senses.

With hands that were less than steady, she sorted through her speed-dial menu again and found Mark's cell number. She punched it in, then almost gave up in frustration, thinking he wasn't going to answer. When he did, he said dryly, "Megan, we've barely come a hundred and fifty miles. Tell me you're not going to check on us *that* often."

"Did you call Mom and clue her in about what you're doing?"

"Not yet. I'd rather be in an apartment in New York before I open that can of worms."

"Well, hold on to your hat, Mark. Talk about a can of worms. I just hung up from talking to Angel. You remember Aunt Sherry's secretary?"

"Yeah. So? Listen, Megan, I'm coming to this place where the highway splits and traffic's picking up. Can you make it quick?"

"I can, but you may want to pull over. I almost wrecked Sterling's Land Rover when Angel hit me with this news."

"Megan, I swear, you can be so dramatic you should've gone into acting."

"You asked for it. Okay, here's the deal. You are about to become a big brother."

"Have you been drinking? Hel-lo!" he shouted when Megan broke into hysterical laughter.

"Remember the day you arrived in St. Ignace and I casually wondered why Mom and Camp never had kids? It must've been a premonition. They are, Mark. Going to have a kid. Mom's preggers."

"Now I *know* you've been hitting the sauce. If you think this'll make me drop everything and go home to take that counseling job at Wellmont, forget it. I'm not biting."

"It's not a joke. At least Angel sounded sure enough. If you don't believe me, call Camp. Or Aunt Sherry, or Uncle Garrett. Damn, I wish you sounded as worried as I am. There are dangers for an older mother during pregnancy. I've read articles in women's mags. They say all kinds of things can go wrong with the mother and her baby."

"You're serious. You mean...Mom could die?"

The merest suggestion of that sent fear shooting through her. "Don't talk like that, Mark!"

"First you want me to worry, and now you pounce on me when I do. You can't have it both ways."

"It's just that if there's nothing to worry about, why is Mom taking off work? And why hasn't Camp or anyone informed us?"

"Have you been home? Maybe someone left a message."

"I stopped at home to change clothes. No message."

"Look, we're using up my minutes on this call. If you're upset, call Mom directly. I'll give you a holler when we stop for the night. I hope to make Detroit."

Just like that he hung up, before Megan could ask if Lauren had talked to Sterling. She scowled at the phone.

Suddenly Megan was glad she was going to pick up her grandmother. Mona could help her decide what to do.

Mona was ready and waiting for Megan. "A hospital is not my idea of a fun place. I'll ring for the nurse. They insist I have to be taken out in a wheelchair. If that doesn't beat all. The doctor said I need to walk each day, but apparently not until I leave here."

"I borrowed Sterling's SUV. I saw a sign that says patient loading. I'll go pull into that, shall I?"

"Do, dear. On the way out I'll take care of my bill. I'm glad Toby paid our premiums through to the end of this year. You won't believe how much a few days in this place costs. I suppose I'll have to buy private insurance in December."

"Can't you ask the company's new owner to keep you on their package? They do that for retirees."

"I wonder… That's so clever of you, Megan. I'll ask my attorney."

Megan didn't feel clever. She felt frazzled. Especially as it turned out not to be very easy to hoist Mona into the higher front seat of the Land Rover.

"I need a derrick these days," Mona muttered as Megan and the nurse boosted from behind, taking care not to jar the injured hip.

"On the drive to St. Ignace we have some things to discuss," Megan said as she drove slowly away from the hospital. "Keith volunteered to fly back to Missouri with you. I was able to get you a ticket on his flight, but it's going to cost extra for first class. He leaves the day after tomorrow. You can use Joel's room until then and he'll come up and bunk with Keith. I…think so, anyway." Megan wasn't a hundred percent sure of that.

"Mercy, I hate being a pest. Nothing about this trip is going the way I hoped."

Megan patted Mona's wrinkled hand. "I'm worried about what'll happen after you land in Columbia. I hoped you could stay with Mom and Camp for a few weeks. Just until you can go up and down stairs. However…it's not looking good."

"Ah, I'm not surprised. I'm never been on the best of terms with Emily. My accident knocked a bit of sense into this old head, dear. There are some fences I've left unmended for too long. You see, we had a bride picked out for David. I blamed your mother for displacing our friend's daughter in his affections. I should apologize to her."

Mona's words shocked Megan, but she wasn't sure that mending the relationship was possible. Especially not at this late date, given everything that was unfolding. "Uh, Gram…I got some surprising news today concerning Mom. She's—" Megan hauled in a deep breath "—she's going to have a baby."

"Emily is…pregnant? At…how old?"

"Forty-five. She just had her birthday a month ago, but still…"

Mona wiped suddenly damp eyes with a tissue she'd almost shredded. "Emily and her new husband must be deliriously happy."

"Camp isn't really Mom's *new* husband, Gram. They've been married for eleven years."

"So they have. Well… I would've been delighted at any age."

"You would?" Megan tried to picture it. Her grandparents had lavished her dad with everything under the sun. "Doesn't every year over thirty-five increase the risks associated with pregnancy?"

Mona Benton dismissed Megan's concern with a careless gesture. "That was probably true in my day. They work miracles in medicine today. Why, I saw a documentary on TV a few weeks ago in which they delivered a baby who weighed fifteen ounces, and a team saved that beautiful baby. Emily is beyond lucky, Megan. You and Mark are adults and on your own. She has the opportunity to enjoy precious years with a baby, then a toddler, then a schoolchild. It's a gift."

Megan turned to face Mona, drawn by her enthusiasm.

"Next time you talk to Emily, congratulate her for me. I mean that sincerely. Or, no, I should to tell her. That fall made me see life's too short for holding grudges."

"I haven't even spoken to Mom or my stepdad yet. I heard secondhand through an employee at the college. I called Mark and no one had told him, either. We're not quite sure what to make of it. Well, we know they're mad at Mark."

"Ouch, and I'm to blame for that. No matter, if I were the one in that situation, I'd shout it from the rooftops. Perhaps they're in shock. I'm sure they'll phone you soon, Megan."

"I hope everything's okay." She was still mulling over everything she'd heard about the risk of later pregnancies.

"Speaking of Mark. Have he and Lauren gone, then?"

"Yes, and there's another thing you've done, Mona," Megan said with a sigh. "I suspect Sterling won't be pleased that you financed Lauren's enterprise."

"Mercy, Megan, it's a short-term advance. Sterling's lawyer said Lauren is guaranteed money from her parents' trust on proof of enrollment in school."

"She left without discussing any of this with Sterling."

"You mean she simply ran off? Oh, but she and Mark promised."

"Her idea of discussion was leaving him a note. I'm expecting fireworks when we get home. Mark said Lauren wanted to avoid a fight for Tyler's and Joel's sake."

"She is eighteen. Technically she's of age to make these decisions."

"Even so, I know Sterling will be disappointed. He wanted a chance to win her over. To improve their relationship."

Mona wrung her hands. "I see your point, Megan. I've stuck my big foot in another mess. I must tell Sterling I'm sorry, as well. I only meant to help."

They entered the cul-de-sac facing Lady Vic. Sterling and Tyler were on Dodge's porch. Megan didn't think it boded well when she waved as she swung wide to park and Tyler was the only one who waved back.

She couldn't have been more correct. In fact, Sterling yanked the driver's door open before she'd taken the key from the ignition. She guessed the wadded-up paper in his hand was Lauren's note.

"Tell me you didn't know what those lamebrains had planned."

"What lamebrains would that be?" Megan played for time. "Sterling, would you mind helping me lift Mona down? Can we settle her in your house before we have this knock-down drag-out?"

Sterling reared back. "You *did* know. Dammit,

Megan, you said nothing in time for me to stop their idiocy? Are you aware that Mark's the one who'll take the rap for kidnapping?"

"Kidnapping?" She'd circled the hood of the Land Rover and came to a halt with her fingers curled over Mona's door handle. "You contacted the police?"

"Did you expect I'd let them go off on their own and do nothing?"

"Sterling, stop yelling, you're scaring Tyler. He's crying. Lauren hasn't run off to join the circus. She's going to design school. I told Mark she should sit down and talk to you, but she did what she did. And they found out Lauren's legal at eighteen in both Michigan and New York."

When they saw that Mona had opened her door and was attempting to climb out, Sterling swatted Megan aside like a pesky fly and assisted the injured woman. "Does she have a cane or a walker?" he snarled.

Megan, close to tears, dashed a hand over her eyes and shook her head.

"Then I'll carry her. Mrs. Benton, I promised you a bed and I don't welch on my promises. However, I'm not sure you'll want to stay after I charge your grandson with transporting a minor over state lines."

"Oh, for crying out loud!" Megan said, hands on her hips. "I just explained that Lauren's not under age."

"No, but Joel is."

"Joel?" Megan tripped on the curb and almost buckled, although Sterling's hand shot out to keep her from falling. "Sterling, I swear I had no idea they were taking Joel. All Mark said was that Lauren has a place in a design school and Mark's planning to set things up for

his photography show. Did Lauren say in her letter that Joel was going, too?"

"No, she doesn't say that. Neither she nor Mark is that stupid."

Between Megan and Sterling, they managed to help Mona reach the porch. She shuffled over to a wicker settee where Tyler had retreated and eased down next to the boy. "Sterling." Mona sounded short of breath. "Suppose you start at the beginning."

"I got off work at two because I went in early. I collected Tyler from school, but learned that Lauren had come in at ten to pick up her diploma. And Joel never checked in to his first class. We caught the first ferry home. I found this letter on the kitchen table. Lauren's room has been cleaned out. Joel took one bag and half his clothes."

"Are you sure? Maybe Lauren needed an extra suitcase and borrowed Joel's."

"Not likely. His boat's gone. I figure they either bought or rented a trailer. No offense, Mrs. Benton, but Lauren said you gave her the money and I resent the hell out of that."

"Just a minute, young man. I didn't *give* her money. She asked for a loan to pay tuition and room and board until your attorney arranges for money from her trust. Apparently some of it's been set aside for college. I spoke with the man myself. I made it plain that she and my grandson need to pay me back for these loans. We even discussed terms."

"Mark's paying you back?" Megan straightened. "Mark never mentioned that. Camp doesn't know and I doubt Mom knows, either. She thinks you're undermining her with Benton money."

"I said I had a lot to square with Emily. Sterling, did you look upstairs to see if Joel's with Keith?"

"Hey, he's the one who has Joel's boat." Megan struck her forehead with a hand. "I packed Keith's lunch. He told me Joel let him take the boat fishing." Megan glanced at her watch. "In fact, Keith should be rolling in soon. He said he'd bring fish for supper."

Tyler tugged on his dad's sleeve several times. "Joel runned away."

Sterling frowned down at the boy. "You said that earlier, Tyler. But where would he be if not with Lauren?"

"Don't know, Daddy, but I heard 'em last night. Joel said if Lauren was going to New York, he'd go, too. Lauren said he had to wait three more years. He said no, that he'd run away first. Lauren talked and talked. She said he hadda stay in school. Joel slammed his door and said he didn't want nobody telling him what to do."

Suddenly all eyes were on Sterling's son. "So," Megan said after a lengthy silence, "I don't believe Joel went with Mark and Lauren, after all. I talked to Mark to discuss a family matter. Mark relayed our conversation to Lauren and I heard her responses. In all that time, I didn't hear Joel's voice once."

"Megan, you and Mark used to run away regularly at that age," Mona put in.

"Yes," she admitted. "We tried a few times. The most logical place for a fourteen-year-old kid to go is a friend's house."

"I can phone the school. Maybe they'll give me a list of boys Joel pals around with."

"Good. That's a start. But, uh, Sterling, maybe it wouldn't hurt to call the cops and give them a description of Joel. He's a juvenile, so maybe they won't wait the usual twenty-four hours before filing a missing persons' report."

Mona pointed down the street, and they all turned eagerly, hoping to see Joel. Keith trudged up the hill from the marina, carrying his fishing pole and a string of fish.

"I promised to cook whatever he caught," Megan said. "I wonder if anyone will feel like eating if Joel doesn't show up soon."

"I'll go find the school's number." Sterling left, not remarking on the fish.

"Fish are nutritious, and searchers need strength," Mona said. "I'm sure he'll offer us the use of his kitchen, Megan. If you help me get inside, I'll make a salad. I'll bet Tyler's big enough to set the table."

"Yep," he exclaimed, pushing up his sleeve to show his muscle. That brought smiles in spite of the fact that they were all unsure how worried they ought to be.

Sterling opened the screen as they were making their way toward the door. "The secretary knows all the boys in Joel's class and their families. She'll phone around and see what she can find out. The police said if he doesn't show up tonight I should stop by the station and file a report.

Keith drew abreast of the porch. "Hey, Mrs. B. Good to see you." He glanced around and noted the worried faces. "What's up? Was I gone too long? One spot on the inlet was sweet fishing, and I probably got carried away. But you can freeze the leftover fish, Megan."

She took the string. In a low voice she explained that Joel was missing and might have run off. Megan hoped that by speaking softly, she'd avoid causing Tyler concern. Although the boy seemed matter-of-fact about Joel's running away.

"Huh." Keith held open the screen. "The last couple of days, all Joel's talked about is joining the Coast Guard. Is that a possibility, Megan?"

Sterling heard him. "Megan, you know how mad Joel was at me for dragging him out of the tavern. All the way home he kept saying I'd ruined his life. He said your friends at the station would laugh at him now. Do you think one of them took pity on him?"

"Pity, how? None of them would vouch for him with a local recruiter if that's what you're asking, Sterling." Megan flopped the fish in the sink and turned on the cold water faucet. She found a knife and began cutting off fish heads, very glad Keith had already gutted them all.

"No, I wasn't thinking he'd try to join up. I wondered if instead of bunking with kids from school, if he'd go see the older guys."

"After the scene at the tavern, I can't see any of them—well, I don't know that for sure. Guys seem to have a different code of ethics than women do. Let me prepare the fish and pop them in to bake. Then Keith can stay here, and you and I will run to the station. I'm sure whoever's on swing will give me access to personnel files. I have to say I don't know where many of the crew live. We mostly meet at the tavern or at the married guys' homes. I'm sure none of them would harbor a runaway. I don't *think* any of them would."

Sterling registered that in the back of his mind. It told him Megan had never had a romantic relationship with any of her crew. She hadn't been without sexual experience. However, she did say it'd been a long time, and she'd been in St. Ignace a matter of months. He knew he shouldn't even be thinking about such things, but his mind wandered of its own accord.

During the drive to the station, Megan found herself trying to ease Sterling's worries. That helped her push aside Benton family issues. She'd sent Keith upstairs to find out if there were any calls from home on her machine. He returned to say there were no messages. That meant neither her mom or Camp had called to share their news.

In a way that was depressing. In another, it probably meant her mom's condition was stable. Surely *someone* in the whole Campbell family would get in touch if, say, her mom started to hemorrhage or anything equally bad.

Sterling had never seen the station where Megan worked. Pictures of prominent rescues hung on the walls and sent a stream of bile to his throat. Pieces of boats tossed about by too-high waves were not reassuring and hit too close to home. For every person they happily displayed as saved, how many were lost?

Hooking his thumbs in his back pockets to keep them still, Sterling followed Megan to a cubicle where she pulled out card after card and marched through phone calls. Each answer was the same. The last anyone saw of Joel Atwater had been when his brother-in-law forcefully removed him from the tavern.

Megan pulled Jim Elkhorn's number last. She pressed him hard. "Jim, I know you couldn't believe Joel lied about how old he was. Can you recall him saying anything, anything at all, about where he'd go if he just took off?"

She twisted the cord around her finger, turned in the swivel chair and lifted her eyes to Sterling. "So, Jim, you're saying Seaman Brown gave Joel a brochure describing all the steps it takes to enlist at the port of Grand Haven at seventeen? And you and Vince talked about some friends you have there while Joel was listening. Hey, buddy, thanks. This may be the break we need."

She hung up, her eyes aglow. "Lieutenant Elkhorn said maybe Joel lit out for Grand Haven."

"Where's Grand Haven?"

"Two hundred miles southwest of here."

"Joel's not seventeen. Surely no one would let him enlist when he won't even be fifteen for a couple of weeks."

"Sterling, determined kids can find ways of getting phony birth certificates and a driver's license. Joel strikes me as resourceful."

"I suppose he learned a lot—too much—hanging with that gang in New York. Or from Blythe and her partner. They were always talking about the illegal rings they broke up. So, yeah, if Joel set his mind to it, I suppose he might go to those lengths."

"It takes money. How much do you suppose he has?"

"The kid squirrels away his allowance. He and Lauren both get a monthly stipend from Blythe's insurance. Lauren blew hers on makeup and such. I wouldn't have thought Joel could save enough to buy a boat, but he did. I've never tried to decrease the stipend. It's their money." He paced back and forth and seemed to fill the small space with his intensity. "What do I do now, drive to Grand Haven tonight?"

"You could. But I suggest you go home and get a couple of the best and latest pictures you can find of Joel. While you're gone, I'll type up a letter to fax our recruiters along with his photo. Then I think we should visit the cops. If they see we're not only concerned but have some possible leads, maybe they'll put out an APB tonight."

Sterling bent over Megan and trapped her in her chair by grabbing hold of the curved arms. From his earnest expression, she could tell he had something he wanted to say.

She touched a button on his shirt. "It's okay, Sterling. Time is of the essence here. We have no idea when he left. I'm guessing he hitched a ride. That's scary enough, even if he's a good-size kid who looks like he can take care of himself."

He let his thumb stroke Megan's cheek for just a moment. "I had no right to jump all over you the minute you drove in. I'm sorry. I was beside myself. I want you to know I wouldn't have charged Mark with kidnapping. I'd have worked with you to get him to bring Joel back."

"I figured that. Tough as you act, Sterling, you have a marshmallow heart where the kids are concerned."

A weak smile played over his dark features. "If I do, it's thanks to all that hot chocolate you and Tyler poured into me recently. Listen, don't go anywhere. I'll dash home, see how Keith, Tyler and Mona are doing. Mark took some really good pictures of the kids in the park the day we went cycling. I'll be back in a flash."

"I'll keep my fingers crossed that this works. It seems the most promising possibility we have. But Sterling..." She tucked her upper lip between her teeth. "If this pans out and we find Joel and get him back, I'd like to make a deal with you. I think he's got what it takes to be good in ROTC. Even if he outgrows the notion of joining the Coast Guard, the years of ROTC training teach discipline. And he'd have to keep his grades up to stay with his group."

"How can I say no? If a kid goes to this length to join the service, I won't stand in his way—with the proviso of course that he stays in school."

"That's a must. Also, if he wants me to, I'm willing to develop and oversee his program."

"Is it any wonder I care about you, Megan Benton? And I do. A lot."

CHAPTER FIFTEEN

STERLING MADE A FAST TRIP home and back to the station, where Megan had arranged for him to pass the guard at the gate. She'd just printed the inquiry she wanted to send to Grand Haven when he ran in, out of breath. "Oh, these are good pictures of Joel," she said when Sterling spread out three on her desk.

"Mark is clever with a camera," he said, smiling fondly at the image of a laughing boy in one photo. Joel rarely laughed, Sterling realized. "Your grandmother had Mark on the phone when I walked in. I was glad of the opportunity to have a word with him. They were surprised when I wished them well, but I do, you know. I want Lauren to succeed and be happy. Only now they're worried about Joel. Lauren hadn't believed he'd actually leave his boat and the comforts of home for the unknown. She apologized about a hundred times for her part and begged me to call the minute we get news."

"I'm happy you squared things with Lauren. Everyone flies the coop, so to speak, but even under the best circumstances it's hard to give up everything that's familiar. I'm sure it helped Lauren to have your blessing."

"I should've done battle with Blythe when I saw the kids going astray. However, I could see our marriage was on the rocks, and quite frankly I threw myself into work and taking care of Tyler." He slumped in the chair next to her and clasped his hands between his knees. "I haven't handled Blythe's siblings well."

"Hindsight is always twenty-twenty, Sterling. Read this letter, okay? I think I've covered what we talked about. I'll fax it off with Joel's picture. We'll still have the originals to give the police."

"We'll make a quick trip to the police station. By the way, the fish you put in the oven is almost done. Your grandmother had Keith check it and turn down the heat. She's got everything else ready. I hope she's not overtaxing herself. She said the doctor told her to walk every half hour or so, but her face is showing the strain. She's blaming herself for not making sure Lauren cleared her plans with me. What a mess, all the way around."

"What's done is done. This will only take a minute. I've included your phone and cell, my phone and cell, and the station number. We're putting a lot of faith in Tyler's being right about what he heard, yet he is just a kid."

Sterling followed Megan to the fax machine. "Tyler's astute for his age. He walked early, talked early and mimics the older two a lot. I wasn't aware how much he acts four going on fourteen until we came here. I learned things about all the kids I wish I'd known before."

"I imagine Tyler feels the loss of Blythe more than the others do."

Sterling looked thoughtful as he pocketed the photos Megan handed him. She cornered Seaman Brown and instructed him to phone if he got any word at all from Grand Haven.

After they left the station and were buckled in Sterling's Land Rover, he returned to Megan's earlier comment. "I'm afraid Tyler will feel loss of Lauren more than he misses Blythe. I recently discovered that my son spent more time with Lauren than with his mother. Blythe had me fooled for years."

"Yeah, people tend to see what they expect to see and they wear blinders to avoid what they want to block out. It'll probably help if Tyler can talk to Lauren on the phone once or twice a week so he doesn't feel abandoned."

"Phone calls are a cold substitute for the little womanly touches. Those are important, don't you think?"

"There, Sterling, a parking place in front of the police station."

He parked and she picked up the detailed description they'd faxed to the Grand Haven Coast Guard. "I have an idea, Sterling. This involves Tyler. Mrs. Ralston is lonely, and Tyler likes her. Why not have her watch him over the school break? That way Joel has more freedom. If I can't interest him in ROTC, there's summer Sea Scouts. We work closely with them and their leaders. It's a great venue for kids who love to boat, or own a boat."

"For pulling this stunt I ought to make Joel sell his boat until he can prove he's more responsible."

"Sterling, you're angry and worried now," Megan said, hesitating at the door he'd opened.

"Running away doesn't merit some consequences?" Sterling motioned her to go on in. He shut the door behind them and glanced about to get his bearings. "The cop behind that center desk looks like a place to start."

"Running away is wrong and dangerous. I know from

experience that a teen has to be pretty unhappy at home to take that step. It's up to you, of course, but if it were me, I'd try to find ways to improve my relationship with Joel."

"May I help you?" The sergeant at the desk stood as they approached. Megan was in the lead, but she stepped aside and passed the material to Sterling. He made a bad job of trying to explain his family situation. So much so, the sergeant turned to Megan.

"I'm Megan Benton, the upstairs neighbor," she finally explained. "And a friend. My brother and our runaway's sister are traveling to New York together. Joel was upset when they insisted he stay behind with his guardian." In a few words, she spelled out her role in visiting Joel's school and sparking his initial interest in the Coast Guard.

"You think this kid will go that far to join up? Isn't it more logical he'd try to follow his sister?"

Megan shrugged. "Maybe, but Joel was awfully mad at Lauren at the time."

"He'd been hanging around Megan's crew for a week or more. We learned they supplied Joel with information on how to join, because he lied about his age. He'll be fifteen in a couple of weeks, not seventeen."

"He needs a parent's or guardian's signature at seventeen," Megan added. "But we're talking about a kid who forged school notes for a couple of years."

"I can't authorize a full APB until morning. I can, however, notify the departments between here and Grand Haven. If he's hitching his way there, maybe we'll pick up his trail. Explain again how you're the kid's guardian, Mr. Dodge."

Sterling didn't stumble over the second rundown.

The sergeant stared at the smiling boy in the picture. "Why do so many kids from mixed-up families have a tendency to think the grass is greener in somebody else's yard? You'll be lucky if he doesn't hook up with kids who are aimless drifters. A lot of them travel from town to town, living on handouts. The cities are full of 'em. If he turns up, you'll do well to settle your differences, Mr. Dodge, otherwise he'll take off again. I can't tell you how many grieving parents we see."

Megan felt shock run through the man at her side. Moving closer, she linked her hand with his. "We'll find Joel and get him back," she said with conviction.

They left the police station after Sterling had filled out a set of forms. He assisted Megan into the passenger seat, then slid beneath the steering wheel. "Blythe and I screwed up big-time," he muttered.

"You gave orphaned kids a home, food and clothing. And as you said, until recently your wife was their guardian. Not you."

"Excuses. I accepted Lauren and Joel as part of the package when I married their sister. Blythe and I grew up in the same neighborhood, but I'm starting to doubt that we ever really knew each other. We brought our individual expectations into the marriage, and they turned out to be way off base."

"Considering the divorce rate in this country, I'd say that's more common than not."

Brooding again, Sterling turned down their street. With Mark's car gone he had more room to park his Land Rover. He pocketed the keys and climbed out, then started around to assist Megan. The front door flew open and Tyler, followed by Keith, emerged from the house.

Sterling swung Tyler up into his arms. Keith waited

at the foot of the porch steps. "I took a message a minute ago from a cop," he said excitedly. " He wants Sterling to phone him back right away. Uh, is...this about Joel?"

Sterling turned a look of surprise on Megan. "We just left the station. Maybe I forgot to fill in a line on their missing persons' form."

"Supper's ready," Tyler announced. He framed his father's face with his small hands. "I'm hungry as a big ol' bear. I wanna eat before you call that policeman, 'cause Gram already hadda go lay down. Where've you and Megan been? And Lauren. I don't *want* her to go to New York. I want her home." His eyes filled with tears, and Sterling gently stroked his shuddering back.

"You get the food on the table, guys. I'll quickly phone the sergeant. Is Mrs. Benton just resting? I mean, her hip's not giving her trouble, is it?"

Keith shook his head. "I'm amazed at how well she's getting around. But she insisted on bending down to check the fish once too often. She's not out of surgery all that long. We keep injured animals in the vet hospital longer than they kept her."

"Mona said she had a new procedure developed in Austria. I hope she hasn't overdone things," Megan said. "Let's go. I'm sort of famished, too."

"Megan, do you have cookies at your house?" Tyler shifted in his father's arms and scanned her hopefully. "Keith made hot chocolate. It's not good like yours. It tasted yucky."

"I never claimed to be a cook. Megan, you didn't complain this morning when I made coffee."

"I gave you points for effort, Keith. But the real truth? It was pretty yucky, too."

Her teasing broke the tension that gripped everyone. Tyler squirmed to get down, and as Megan did have cookies upstairs, she sent Keith to fetch them. "Oh, check my answering machine, will you? I, ah, am expecting a call from Mom or Camp."

"What's up, Megan? That's the second time you've had me check. Is your mom still sick?"

"Mom's not sick, exactly."

"Did you hear from Emily yet?" Mona stood with an arm braced against the door frame.

"Keith's going to see if I have any messages when he goes up to grab some cookies. How are you?" Megan asked.

"Okay. Maybe you should call Emily. She's always had such a strong sense of duty toward family. It's strange that you haven't heard a word."

"Mmm-hmm," Megan muttered in noncommital fashion. She was concerned, but for now tried to put it out of her mind. She went into the kitchen where the table was set; it seemed there was nothing left to do but round up people to eat.

The aroma of the herbs she'd sprinkled on the fish filled the air as she lifted the lid off the pan she took from the oven. That brought Mona and Tyler to the table. Sterling strode in soon after.

Megan discovered Mona had prepared hot bread to go with the fish and salad. She placed it on the table before asking Sterling about his call.

"It was nothing. I'd neglected to list what Joel was wearing. I can only surmise he had on the clothes he wore to school."

"I figured it was too soon for any news. Sit, and we'll dish this up."

Sterling pulled out his usual chair. "Isn't Keith eating?"

"Megan has cookies upstairs, Daddy. Keith's getting them. We're having cookies and hot chocolate for dessert."

"Peanut butter cookies?" Sterling sounded hopeful.

Megan laughed. "Sorry, oatmeal with apple and raisins. Very nutritious."

Keith returned and set the cookie jar on the counter. "Only a call from someone trying to sell you storm windows."

"Now, who's anxious? Were you hoping for a response to your fax?" Sterling said, taking a slice of the steaming bread and passing the pan around.

Mona slid a piece of fish onto her plate. "Megan had her fingers crossed that her mom would have phoned. She found out quite by accident today that her mother's going to have a baby."

Keith, who'd sat and picked up his glass of milk, choked and spewed milk over his plate. "Wow, where did you hear that?"

"From Sherry's secretary. I called Mom's office and found out she had a substitute taking her classes. When I phoned the Hub, Angel spilled the beans."

Sterling swallowed a bite of fish. "This is really good. Tyler, try it or no cookies."

The phone rang in another part of the house as Tyler balked and his father got firm. "Excuse me again." Sterling rose. "I'd better take every call."

While he was gone, Megan cajoled Tyler into eating half the fish his dad had put on his plate. "See, now? That didn't kill you. Eat your bread and a few bites of the salad. Then your dad will probably let you have dessert."

"Joel never had to eat stuff he didn't like."

Megan didn't know how to respond to that. Her grandmother solved the problem. "Tyler, clean your plate and you'll have more muscles than Joel by the time you get to be his age. Weren't you telling me Joel said that when you got bigger you could drive his boat? The sure way to grow bigger is to eat all the good food on your plate."

"Okay." To everyone's surprise the boy dug in and polished everything off.

"A bit of news," Sterling announced after resuming his seat. "One of the cops the sergeant contacted talked to a trucker who recalled giving a boy answering Joel's description a lift. He dropped the kid off just south of Lake George. He said his passenger asked a lot of questions about the distance to Grand Haven. The trucker told the boy he needed to get over to state highway 131, and that's where they parted company."

"Lake George. Do you have an atlas?" Megan asked.

"Somewhere. I'll hunt it up after we finish eating. The police believe they're on the right track. The sergeant said he'd be phoning later."

Tyler held out his clean plate. "Look, Daddy. I ate everything on my plate. Pretty soon I'll be big enough to drive Joel's boat."

Sterling studied the plate, then his eyes cut to his son. "Joel's boat is off-limits, Tyler, unless I'm there. I haven't decided yet if it's going to be off-limits to Joel."

The boy began to cry. He dropped his plate, which might have broken had Megan been less agile. She caught the plate before it fell all the way to the floor.

"Gram Benton said if I cleaned my plate I'd get big 'nuff to ride in Joel's boat."

"Tyler," Megan said evenly. "She said that *if* you eat all your food, *when* you get to be Joel's age you'll have more muscles than he has now."

"But I don't wanna wait." He flexed his arm and drew attention to the small bulge. "I've got muscles now. See!"

Megan's phone rang. She tore it off the belt clip and glanced at the readout, disappointed to see her brother's number. However, hearing from him must mean he and Lauren had stopped for the night. That, at least, was one less worry. "Mark, hi. Ah, you're in Saginaw. I thought aiming for Detroit was a bit ambitious. No…nothing on Joel yet. But if Lauren's handy, I have a little boy here who'd love to talk to her. Tyler," she said, smiling at the teary-eyed child.

"Here." She passed him the phone. "Don't close the phone and don't poke any buttons. Mark's giving his to Lauren. Won't it be fun to ask about her trip?"

Tyler nodded vigorously, and soon he forgot all about the fit he'd thrown over the boat.

Efficiently, Megan cleared the table. She put cookies on a plate and set them out. "Tyler wants hot chocolate. Sterling, where have you hidden the ingredients?"

He got up and went to find what Megan needed. "Will you stay awhile after dinner?" he said, too low for anyone else to hear. "I'd like to keep Tyler on his routine, and I'm sure your grandmother will need to retire early. Myself, I can't even imagine sleeping."

"Me, neither. But I wouldn't feel right sending Keith home alone. I haven't even asked how his fishing trip went today—other than that we enjoyed the results."

"I think it's obvious it went well."

"You know what I mean." She sighed. "I'll miss him. He's going home Sunday. Oh, by the way." She turned from the stove. "Keith, I was able to get Mona a ticket on your flight. And Mona, you owe me for a first-class seat and an upgrade for Keith so you two can sit together."

"Wonderful. How much? I'll write a check now before I forget."

They completed their transaction, and by then Sterling had rummaged in the cupboard and found marshmallows.

"I liked when you put in cinnamon stir sticks," Keith said. "Maybe I'll go up and bring a few down, if you don't mind."

"Take the cookie jar back, too, please. Oh, and would you check the answering machine again?"

It only took Megan a few minutes to have mugs filled with the thick cocoa they'd all come to associate with her.

"I wish you lived here, Megan," Tyler said, smacking his lips. He'd finished his conversation with Lauren and given Megan back her phone. "Daddy, if Lauren's going to New York to school for a long time, can Megan sleep in her room?"

Sterling and Megan simultaneously choked on their cookies. He recovered first, but rather than answer, he gazed at Megan's face.

"Tyler, I just live upstairs," she said. "Until you guys move to the island, that is. Uh, how are they coming on your house, Sterling?"

"F-f-fine," he stammered. "I went by there yesterday. The contractor said work was progressing better than expected. He said we should be moved in before the official start of the tourist season. Which I gather will be nice. It sounds as if everything on the island swings into high gear then. I thought Lauren would want a summer job, so I grabbed applications for her at some of the fudge stores. Little did I know," he said, his weariness becoming apparent.

Megan's heart went out to him. Sterling had turned his life upside down for a couple of kids who obviously didn't appreciate anything he'd done. She wondered if they'd eventually see how much worse off their lives would've been had he not married their sister at all.

The house phone that had rung twice earlier did so again. The adults all went still, even their cups sat idle as Sterling hurried to answer it.

"Another sighting," he said, spending less time on this call. "In Ludington. Which proves your theory, Megan. That's less than two hours from Grand Haven."

"The recruiter's office will be closed when he arrives," she said, glancing at her watch. "Do you think he has money for a motel?"

Sterling shrugged. "Tyler, your eyes are droopy. Thank Megan and Mrs. Benton for the meal and dessert. Time to tuck you into bed."

Mona climbed to her feet with no small amount of difficulty. "Time for me to turn in, too. I can't lie down for long, so don't be concerned, Sterling, if you hear me scampering about during the night."

Picturing her scampering when she moved like a snail now made them all smile. "The sergeant promised to phone with news, no matter what time it is. If you can't sleep, Mona, come on out. My hot chocolate isn't half as good as Megan's, but together we might muddle through making another couple of drinks."

Tyler spoke from his dad's shoulder in a sleepy voice. "Nobody makes hot chocolate as good as Megan. I wish we could keep her, Daddy."

Once more Sterling's eyes zeroed in on her. His son's suggestion left Megan blushing.

But from what she saw on his face, it was plain Sterling would like to keep her, too. Plainly the man had reasons other than hot chocolate on his mind.

Megan circled the table and dropped a kiss on her grandmother's lavender-scented cheek. "Do you need help getting ready for bed, Gram? How about, uh... with other nightly duties?"

Mona patted her granddaughter's smooth face. "That's thoughtful, dear. But the nurses make sure parts work before they let you out of the hospital. I am a bit concerned about using on the plane washroom. Maybe if I'm careful not to drink anything before we go, I'll be fine on the trip."

"I wish this hadn't happened, or else I wish someone in the family could come and drive you home." Megan's fingers strayed to the phone at her belt.

"Don't bother your mother, dear. It's dinnertime there, and Emily needs to eat for two, remember."

The thought had never been far from Megan's mind. There seemed to be so much to worry about all at the same time. She felt as if she'd split up her concentration on the various problems: a fourth for her mom, a fourth for Joel, a fourth for Mona and the rest for Mark and Lauren. It dawned on her then that she needed to drive Keith and Mona to catch their flight out of Pellston on Sunday. If there was no word on Joel by then, she couldn't ask to take Sterling's vehicle. If he and Tyler had to drive to Grand Haven to get Joel, her pickup with its single front seat wouldn't work.

Keith helped clear the dishes and clean up the kitchen. "Cards, anyone?" he said just as the dishwasher started and Sterling came back.

"Ah, you can't sleep, either?" Sterling studied the gangly young man.

"Too much going on," Keith answered, cracking his knuckles. He looked sheepish. "That's a habit I picked up from Mark. If you were my mom or Crawford, you'd chew my butt for it."

Sterling extended his tanned hands. "I cracked my knuckles as a kid. Big knuckles can result from doing that. Maybe even arthritis, so you'll want to take it easy. Aren't you going into veterinary medicine? Might make it tough to hold a scalpel."

"For Mom and Crawford, that's an even worse prospect. They're sure I'll go into banking. Why do adults always think they know what's best for their kids?"

"Coffee anyone?" Sterling carried the pot to the sink and filled it with water.

Megan and Keith both declined. "I'm already too hyper," Megan said.

"Me, too, but it gives me something to do. Keith, as recently as yesterday, I would've sided with your folks. Now I'm not so sure." Sterling measured out coffee and flipped the switch. Staring at the steam beginning to bead inside the pot, he muttered, "Kids probably have to walk their own path." He turned to Megan again. "On Monday, I'll phone and make sure my lawyer releases Lauren's school funds."

"She'll be delighted. And," Megan added, while he

was clearly mellowing, "will you also approve Joel's exploring ROTC?"

He swung a kitchen chair around and straddled it, linking his arms across the back. "Tell me more about the Coast Guard. Give me some specifics."

"You already know we conduct search-and-rescue operations. We also process seamen's licenses, and conduct maritime security boardings. We educate boaters. And when planes go down in the ocean, we're Johnny-on-the-spot. We board vessels suspected of smuggling and we seize contraband—drugs or illegal immigrants, for example. Around here our biggest task this summer will be covering distress calls from recreational boaters. We perform valuable services along every coastline, twelve months a year."

Megan's phone vibrated. She'd shut off the ringer after Tyler and Mona had gone to bed, and now scrabbled to remove it from its pouch.

"What is it?" Sterling asked. "Do you—"

She strained to hear and held up a hand to request silence. "You're telling me Joel Atwater showed up on the doorstep of a friend of Hamish Tucker's half an hour ago? His friend didn't send the boy away, did he?" She sucked in a breath.

The lieutenant on night duty assured Megan that hadn't happened. "The guy, Red Crenshaw, tried calling Hamish at home. When he didn't answer, Crenshaw phoned here. Of course, all of us have the information you faxed Grand Haven."

"Where's Hamish? I need him to call his friend."

"Guess you haven't heard. We've got two cutters sent out to clean up a massive oil spill. A tanker split apart off Beaver Island."

"I hadn't heard. We've been waiting for word on Joel. I feel better knowing he's landed with someone friendly. Do you have Crenshaw's number? I'd like him to hang on to the kid and not spook him into taking off. Hey, isn't Vince Rigley scheduled to do his quals in Grand Haven next week?

Megan vaulted out of her chair. "Right, right, Lieutenant. That's what I thought. Get me Commander Donovan's cell number. If he approves Vince going to Grand Haven a few days early, I can officially fly him there and bring Joel home."

The man on the phone cautioned her not to get her hopes up.

"Yeah, yeah, I know the kid's a civilian. He *wants* to join the guard. That's why he ran off. If Donovan says okay and Joel's guardian allows it," she said, turning to Sterling, "my plan is to sign Joel up for ROTC and salvage a future seaman." She scribbled numbers on a sack she found on Sterling's counter.

"What are quals?" Keith asked the minute she clicked off.

"Qualifying tests to keep us current in areas of certification. We all have to prove at intervals that we've maintained certain skills." Sitting again, Megan scooted her chair as close to Sterling's as it would go. "You heard my half of the conversation. With your permission and Commander Donovan's, I can be in Grand Haven by daylight and home again with Joel by, say, twoish tomorrow."

"What if Joel isn't interested?"

She punched his arm lightly and grinned. "Come on, I'm pretty persuasive."

She was, without a doubt. And if Keith hadn't been

sitting across from them taking everything in, Sterling would've had no qualms about dragging her onto his lap to prove he possessed methods of persuasion, as well. "Make your calls," he said gruffly, clamping his hands over the chair rungs to keep from running them through her enticing hair, or worse, anchoring her down long enough for a kiss.

Megan tried to read the myriad intense passions streaking through his eyes. "You aren't agreeing, then thinking you'll renege once I get him home?"

He looked hurt. "What would that say about me, Megan? Didn't I just tell Keith I've come to believe that kids need to choose their own paths?"

"Yes, but..." She curtailed what that *but* might've included and shoved back her chair. She tore off the portion of the sack with the numbers. "I'll go into the living room to make these calls."

The men sat in the kitchen and twiddled their thumbs for what felt to Sterling like hours. Then Megan reappeared and he sat forward, studying her face.

"It's set. I'm meeting Lieutenant Rigley at the station at seven o'clock this evening. We're authorized to take the Sikorsky. I'll haul back some equipment the Commander wants from Grand Haven, as well. I need to go up and change into my flight jumpsuit."

"You're going tonight? Won't it be pitch-dark soon?"

"We fly helicopters at night," she said with the ghost of a smile.

"But...it's far more dangerous." He backed off at the look that came over her and held up both hands, palms out. "Forget I brought it up. You're competent and well-trained. I have to stop getting jumpy and imagining disaster whenever you head out on a mission."

"Yes, or you'll be old and gray before your time," she teased. "But I can't say that having someone a bit anxious for my return is all bad. Of course, I know you're worried mainly about Joel."

Not giving a damn if her cousin was sitting there watching, Sterling hauled Megan onto the tips of her toes and gave her a lengthy kiss.

"Wh-what was that for?" She was definitely rattled when he released her and stepped back to inspect her appearance with unmistakable satisfaction.

"You have a long flight to think about it, Megan. I'm sure you'll figure out the answer before you get back."

Keith rose, topping Sterling by a few inches. Megan heard the gangly boy's snicker. "I'll walk you up, Megan. This vacation has been enlightening, to say the least. I may jot down some notes tonight and auction them off to the highest bidder when I get home. Your mom's under the mistaken impression that Mark is footloose and fancy-free—and that you're destined to remain a bachelorette forever."

She turned and glared at Sterling. "Ruin my image, will you?" Hooking Keith's skinny arm, she literally dragged him from the house and up the steep stairs.

"He did that on purpose to shake me up and to give you a sideshow, Keith. You heard Sterling. They'll be moving to the island in a month. Our paths won't cross too often after that."

"Aren't you protesting too much?" he said as she stomped down the hall to her room. "Why can't you just admit you like the guy?"

Megan peered back along the shadowy hall. "That's an excellent question, Keith. Why can't I? Maybe because my family keeps saying I only want to prove I'm better than any man at sports and work. And maybe I'm scared that Sterling believes it, too."

She shut her door, turned on a lamp and dug out her flight gear. She realized Sterling had said some things today that showed he might be more accepting of her career. What if *she* was the one setting up roadblocks? Keeping him at arm's length?

Because her life and his were in turmoil right now, she didn't have answers. Megan was glad Keith hadn't waited to have a second go at her. A light shone from beneath his bedroom door, and she called goodbye, then scurried out.

IT WAS A BEAUTIFUL NIGHT for flying. After ten hours of backbreaking labor at the oil spill, Vince was content to snore away in the copilot's seat, leaving Megan to try and sort through her muddled emotions.

She felt left out, on the fringes of her family. Mom and Camp hadn't bothered to include her in their joyous event. Mark had made plans for his future without confiding in her. She'd developed strong feelings for Sterling.

Megan was loath to call it love, even though the mere thought of him set her heart pounding. She'd been depressed to hear how soon he'd be moving.

Maybe she was rushing through life. She ought to slow down and cope with one crisis at a time. The first happened to be surprising Joel Atwater. The second—convincing the kid to pack it in and return home.

She'd bragged to Sterling about her powers of persuasion.

Bragging got people into big trouble. What if she was all talk? That would be embarrassing; she'd feel mortified in front of her colleagues—and Sterling.

Therein lay a problem she'd battled her whole life. Megan could never stand the idea of being made a laughingstock if she didn't succeed at whatever she tried to do. If she didn't come out on top.

Sometimes people failed. Sterling admitted he'd lost a passenger he'd done his level best to save. He also took responsibility for the failure of his marriage.

But what if Joel flat-out told her to buzz off?

She landed on the helipad, shut down the rotors and had to wake Vince Rigley. "What? We're here already?" he grumbled.

Megan chuckled. "Good luck on your quals, Lieutenant."

"You plan on turning this baby around tonight?"

"Red Crenshaw, Petty Officer Tucker's friend, said if we landed by nine-thirty, to come on over to his house. If I can convince Joel to give up this futile quest and return to St. Ignace with me, I'll fly out at first light."

Vince whistled. "You think the kid may resent you and take off again?"

"I hope not." Megan finished her end-of-flight check, signed the clipboard to hand in at the office and unfastened her shoulder harness.

"I remember running away when I was twelve," he murmured.

"Don't we all?"

"Ha! You? All the guys at the station think you've been perfect your whole life."

"Far from it. I was a bratty kid and an incorrigible teen."

"Whaddya know?" He grinned and high-fived her. "Good luck."

"Thanks." She left her flight log, and caught a cab to the Crenshaw home.

Joel was sitting on the couch with a boy and girl a little younger than he. They were engrossed in a video when the kid's father answered the door and escorted Megan into the room. Then he took his children out to give her privacy.

Joel looked as if he'd bolt, but he flopped back against the cushions and flung an arm over his eyes in a move touchingly reminiscent of his brother-in-law. "How did you find me? Is Sterling waiting outside?"

"No. I came alone. But he's at home on pins and needles. Hitchhiking here was dangerous, Joel. You gave everyone who knows and cares for you a fright. Sterling, Lauren, Tyler. My grandmother, me, Mark and Keith."

"Like Lauren gives a f—! Sorry," he added, hunching one shoulder. "She lied, always saying she'd fight Sterling to be my guardian. She's singing a new tune now."

"The bottom line is, you're underage. For one thing, that means you can't join the Coast Guard until you're seventeen, and then only if Sterling signs. You and I discussed ROTC. It's your best option, Joel."

"My grades suck."

"You're bright enough to bring them up between now and the end of term. With my help and recommendation, you can join as a sophomore. After three years, you can either apply to the academy or go in as enlisted with a halfway decent rank."

"Why would you stick your neck out for me?"

"Someone believed in me once." The minute she said it, a warm feeling suffused her. Camp and her mom had stuck by her, and in her heart she knew they were still a family.

"Yeah, well, Sterling'll never sign. He threw out the forms."

"He said he would, Joel. You're both unbelievably stubborn. You need to cut each other some slack."

"Why did he send you?"

"He didn't. I flew down for parts," she fibbed. "I'll be taking off at ten tomorrow after they load the engine parts for one of our out-of-commission cutters. Captain Crenshaw said you can bunk in his son's room, and he'll give you a ride to the helipad in the morning."

"You flew a helicopter here? And I get to fly back with you?"

She nodded at the end of each question and relaxed marginally when he broke into a giant grin.

"Boy, oh, boy. Oh, man! I'm sure I can bring up my grades, Megan. So, we've got a deal?"

"Deal," she exclaimed, offering him a high five like the one she'd exchanged with Vince Rigley. The knot that had taken up residence in her stomach began to unfurl.

CHAPTER SIXTEEN

EMILY CAMPBELL AWOKE to the sound of a phone ringing and birds chirping outside her bedroom window. She stretched and sat up slowly. Camp had let her sleep in, bless his heart. She smiled sleepily as the man himself stepped to the door.

"Honey, the clinic ultrasound technician is on the phone. Dr. Gregory left her a note saying he'd like her to work you in. It so happens she has a cancellation at ten-fifteen. We can make it, right?"

Emily dropped her arms from a stretch and wrapped them around her midsection. "Oh, Camp, so soon? They do those tests on Saturdays?"

He covered the cordless phone with one hand and hurried in to sit beside her on the bed. He drew the fingers of his free hand through red curls tipped gold by a shaft of sunlight peeking through their linen curtains. "Afraid the nurses at the clinic will whisper about your bed head?"

"You know what I'm afraid of—that they'll discover something wrong with our baby." She touched her stomach protectively.

He brushed a curl out of her anxious eyes and bent to kiss her. "On the other hand, maybe they'll find everything's fine, and ease our worrying. After all, your blood test was normal."

She nodded and gripped his forearms. "You're right. Don't keep the poor tech waiting. I'll pull myself together. Tell her okay."

"Uh, she said you need to come with a full bladder. Sorry," he mouthed, backing out of the room as he firmed up the appointment.

The second Camp set down the phone, it immediately rang again. He supposed the technician had forgotten something. He was unprepared to hear his stepson's voice.

"Camp, it's Mark. A friend and I are driving to New York. We're passing through Toledo, and uh...if I drop down on highway seventy-one it'd only mean taking an extra two days to swing by and visit you and Mom."

"Unless you're coming to take the counseling job at the college, the last thing your mom needs right now is to be upset again," Camp said coldly.

"I'd rather talk directly to my mother, thank you very much," Mark responded with equal coldness.

"No. Anyway, she just stepped into the shower."

"I hope you're going to be home later. Lauren and I *are* backtracking. I know about the baby, Camp. Why is it a big secret? Lauren thinks it's cool, too. The upshot is, I need to make peace, amends or whatever with mom. And I want you to meet Lauren. She's...someone important to me."

The man on the other end of the phone heard most of what Mark said and some of what his hesitation implied. What shocked Camp through and through was Mark's mention of the baby. "Did Sherry or Garrett tell Keith about your mom being pregnant?"

"I heard from Megan. She phoned to talk to Mom at the college, but got a sub. So, she called Aunt Sherry and ended up talking to Angel."

"Say no more. That woman is the campus information directory."

"Megan and I can't figure out why no one called us."

"For one, Mark, your mom and I only just found out. And the doctor said we probably shouldn't make a huge announcement and get everyone's hopes up."

"What do you mean? Is something wrong with Mom?"

"No, no, I didn't mean that. There are perils. Our ages," he said, sounding strained. "Stress plays a part, and thanks to you and your grandmother Benton, Emily's been plenty stressed lately."

"I'm sorry. Gram's been hurt, and she's undergone a change of heart in the last little while. I've been lectured by Megan and Lauren about clearing the air. So, we're coming home and that's final. We've been stressed, too. Lauren's brother ran off, but Megan found Joel last night. She just phoned to tell Lauren she's flying him home today. Camp, you may not approve, but this is something I've gotta do. We gain an hour coming your way. Expect us between five and six."

Camp stared at the buzzing phone. That brazen kid had cut him off. "Damn," he muttered, almost dropping the receiver. Now he had to find a way to prepare Emily for… For what? First they had to get through the ultrasound.

Emily talked a blue streak on the drive to the clinic. Camp parked in a lot surprisingly full for a Saturday. He'd had no idea the doctors held a half day of office hours on Saturday until he read the sign on the door. Right before they went in, he stopped and gathered Emily close enough to steady her fast-beating heart. "Dr. Gregory said you need to stay calm, sweetheart."

"Easy for him to say. He's neither pregnant nor the one who's going to have ice-cold jelly rubbed over his stomach this morning. Camp, you'll stay with me during the test?"

"Is that allowed?" At her nod, he wholeheartedly agreed.

They entered the office on the dot of ten-fifteen and were surprised to be ushered straight to a lab. "Why today of all days are they on time?" Emily whispered.

"Just stay calm," Camp reminded her, although once they were in the room where the table was ready and the technician bustling about, his own pulse shot up a few points.

Emily had worn sweats. "It's a bit chilly in here," the young tech said. "We'll just slide the bottom half down to your hips. But you probably know the routine, Mrs. Campbell. I see this isn't your first pregnancy."

"It's been a long time." Emily stepped up to sit on the table. Sliding down the bottom half of her sweats wasn't easy when she held tight to Camp's hand.

"The real-time scanners we use now show a continuous, high-resolution picture, and that may be something new and different for you. But the rest hasn't changed."

Camp helped with the process of sliding down her pants, exposing his wife's smooth, milk-white skin dotted with freckles in secret places. An everlasting pleasure in Emily's body was what had landed them here. Yet it was the overriding fear in her eyes that sobered him.

The tech sat on a stool after applying the gel that did have Emily catching her breath. Smiling sympathetically, the woman picked up an instrument emitting high-frequency sound waves at regular intervals.

"You'll want to watch the monitor as I run this transducer lightly over your abdomen.

Camp, still holding Emily's hand, edged forward. All he could detect was a black screen and pulsing snow flurries.

"You're eight plus weeks, according to Dr. Gregory," the tech said, moving the instrument over Emily's belly. "Oh, look! There, near the top of the screen, I see a head—or a rump. Development's right on for two months I'd say." She kept moving the scanner over Emily's entire stomach.

Camp and Emily both stared at the screen. "I—the top of the screen, you said?" Emily rested her head on one arm. She rolled over to frown at the tech.

The woman clicked a button a few times. "Here, I'll print a copy for the doctor and a copy for you. Looks like we'll have three good views."

While the printer whirred, she handed Emily a packet of wet wipes to remove the worst of the gel. The tech walked away, but soon returned. Camp helped Emily sit up and all three heads bent over the black film cloudy with white whorls and numbers up the side and across the top. "See?" the woman said. "I've marked baby A right here. And down here, a little fainter, is baby B."

She'd passed Emily the three prints, which she'd fanned out like a deck of cards. Emily's red hair mingled with Camp's silver-streaked curls as they studied the unclear pictures.

"Look's like Mark's early attempts at photography," Emily mumbled.

Camp extracted the middle print, and brought it closer to his eyes. "I don't understand," he said. "Explain again about this A and B marked at the top and bottom."

The tech, who'd stapled the same prints on a page she slipped into Emily's chart, raised her head sharply. "Goodness, didn't Dr. Gregory tell you that you're carrying twins?"

Emily dropped the photos into her lap. Camp's arm came up and around her shoulders, and he held her tightly against his chest. "Tw-twins?" he gasped.

The technician reached out and clasped Emily's wrist. "Oops, I can see this may surprise Dr. Gregory, too. Just a moment, I'll run and find him. I'm sure he'll want a few words with you both before you leave."

MEGAN ROUNDED THE SIKORSKY, checking every detail as she waited for Red Crenshaw to show up with Joel. Her stomach was a veritable mess until they pulled in and she watched them pass security. She took that opportunity to phone Sterling. The relief she felt reminded her she'd skipped breakfast. She'd spent the night in spare quarters at the Grand Haven station, and despite her exhaustion, hadn't slept well. "I'll try to phone you fifteen minutes before we land so you and Tyler can come and meet us," she told Sterling. "Have you seen Keith this morning?"

"Nary a sign," Sterling said. "Do you need me to relay a message? I'll go up now and roust him out. You know how young guys can sleep in."

"I just wondered if there's been a call from my folks. You'll never believe this, but Mark phoned a little while ago. He and Lauren have decided to detour and visit Mom and Camp. Lauren wants to meet them, plus she insisted Mark make an effort to straighten out his differences with Mom."

"Funny how Lauren's changed. Last night after you called her with the news that you'd found Joel, she phoned me. She and I talked for an hour. During their drive yesterday, Lauren was blaming herself for Joel's taking off. Well, at some point Mark slipped and told her about Blythe and her partner. You were right, Megan. I should've had a talk with her earlier. She wasn't all that surprised, it turns out. But she assumed I'd done something to cause Blythe to be unfaithful."

"She believes you now, though?"

"I had to talk fast, but yes. We compared notes, and too much didn't add up for her. It was an eye-opener, and she cried. Our relationship is stronger, I believe. I wish she wasn't going to New York."

"Did she admit to you that she and Mark are planning to share a place?"

"Yes. She's eighteen. What can I say? They swear they're going to have separate bedrooms, and that she'll attend school while he tries to freelance his photos. I hope that's the truth."

"You don't sound convinced. Lauren could do worse than hooking up with my brother. He's smart, caring and a hard worker," she added defensively.

"Hey, I didn't say I don't like Mark. It's more that they're so young."

"Yeah, but moving in together is what kids do. Listen, Sterling, Crenshaw's pulling up with Joel as we speak. I have to go. We'll be taking right off."

"Megan, before you go—how can I ever repay you?"

She said around a chuckle, "Buy me a big, fat cheeseburger as soon as we touch down in St. Ignace. I haven't had a bite since last night's dinner."

"Hey, I hear your gram stirring. Do you have time for a word with her?"

"No, but can you fill her in on Mark's change of plans? Since he'll be laying over in Columbia for a couple of days, maybe he can find a ground-level apartment for her to rent. In fact, he can arrange for someone to pick her and Keith up at the airport."

"Okay." He paused. "Megan, do people ever say 'fly carefully'?"

"I know you think I take chances, Sterling. But I happen to love life. Remember that the next time I'm called out on a rescue. I promise I take every precaution to be safe, and to save the victim. Remind me one day to show you a report I saw recently on Coast Guard statistics. We conduct thousands of missions each year, and the number of our on-the-job injuries is very low. Hey, gotta dash. See you later."

"Bye," he said in return.

Red Crenshaw and Joel Atwater crawled out of Crenshaw's Jeep. "Thanks for giving him a lift over here," Megan said, extending her hand. "And for taking care of him."

"No problem. I'm on duty within the hour. I wish I'd known last night that you were Hamish Tucker's friend the pool shark. I have a table in my family room. I play pretty well and I would've loved a game with you. Tucker claims you've never been beaten."

Megan shrugged. "It's bound to happen sometime."

Joel's eyes got saucer-huge just looking at the bright orange bird anchored to the helipad. "Megan's got rows and rows of trophies," he said. "The guys I met from her station said she beat my brother-in-law. And I know he's plenty good."

"I like the game and seem to have a knack for it. If ever you mosey up our way, Captain Crenshaw, I'll be sure to save time for a friendly game."

He brushed a hand over his short red crewcut. "As a matter of fact, I told Joel I may take the family to spend a week on Mackinac Island this summer."

"Hey, don't forget—we'll be living on the island by then. Tell Jason and Maddy I know a lot of cool things we can do."

Megan surmised that Jason and Maddy were the kids she'd seen watching the video last night. She wasn't about to tell him that Sterling had made noises about taking away his boat. She actually hoped he'd reconsider. "Well, my freight's been loaded. What do you say we take off?"

"Cool. Thanks, Captain, for not turning me away. And thank your wife for feeding me supper and breakfast."

Crenshaw and Joel went through a ritual Megan had seen before between the guardsmen. Kind of a foot-shuffle shadowboxing, because most men had difficulty accepting compliments and thank-yous, so they bumped fists in what they saw as a more manly routine.

She left them to it and climbed in to start the preflight check of her instruments. Reaching across, she shoved open the passenger door. She donned her helmet, then leaned over, twirling a finger to indicate that she intended to fire up the Sikorsky's rotors. Red boosted Joel into the second seat and backed away with a final wave.

She handed Joel a helmet with built-in earphones and showed him how to attach the shoulder harness and lap belt. "This is so cool," he shouted three times.

Megan tapped a finger to her lips and spoke softly

into her boom mike. Joel's eyes got big again as he heard her clear as a bell.

He was relaxed until the rotors got enough speed for the guys outside to release the tie-downs and the helicopter rattled and shook as it lifted off the pad. She grinned at the white-faced boy, thinking this might be a lesson in itself, especially if she encountered some of the crosswinds going home that she'd flown through last night. Joel might not be so eager to dash off and join the Coast Guard.

It rained on them and even hailed some as they passed over Cadillac. Adjusting her course a bit, Megan skirted the northernmost point of Manistee National Forest. Last night the stars had been out and she'd had a great view of a ski resort. Today with the clouds socked in, nothing was visible below the chopper. Inclement weather slowed them down all the way to St. Ignace. A good forty-five minutes beyond the estimated arrival time she'd given Sterling, Megan sank down on the helipad. She flipped open her cell phone and turned it on.

"Where in hell are you?" That was Sterling's greeting.

"I don't know what it's been like on the ground, but the weather above has been messy," she said pleasantly.

"It's messy here, too. I've been sitting with Tyler outside the station for almost an hour, expecting your call."

"I thought we agreed you wouldn't leave the house until I rang you. Aren't I lucky I tried your cell phone first?"

"I've been worried half-sick. What do you expect?"

"I expect you to trust me to bring this million-dollar piece of equipment home safely. Hang up, Sterling. I've got things to do before I check out." She let the phone snap closed and noticed Joel, who'd burrowed into the seat and had barely made any comment for the past hour. He glanced at her with a pinched face.

"We're down, Joel. Sterling and Tyler are waiting. I hope they're planning to take us out for a late lunch, or we can call it an early dinner."

Joel grabbed his stomach. "I'm not feeling so good, Megan. I don't think I can eat."

The poor kid. He hadn't said anything about being nauseous, or she would've given him a strip to put behind his ear that would have given him some relief. She removed her helmet, but her hair was damp.

Joel's hands were clammy, and he had difficulty unfastening his harness.

Releasing hers first, Megan reached over to assist him. "You okay?"

"I thought flying home would be fun, but I'm glad to be on the ground again, Megan."

She nodded sagely. "Be careful when you jump down. It's not uncommon to wobble a bit."

A much subdued boy, very different from the cocky kid Sterling had hauled out of the tavern, made his way off the helipad literally dragging his duffel. Megan was thankful none of the guys he knew ribbed him as they entered the station.

"If you'd like to go ahead while I file my flight report, Sterling's at the gate waiting in the Land Rover. Tell him I'll be about five minutes."

Joel hesitated. He hung his head and spoke to his shoes. "Can I wait for you? Sterling's gonna take a hunk outta my hide for what I did. Maybe he'll go easier if you're there."

"Joel, he has a right to be angry. I happen to think he'll

be happier to see you than you're giving him credit for. If you really want my help, I recommend you start with an apology. Real men aren't afraid to say 'I'm sorry.'"

He slung his duffel over a shoulder and trudged out, standing a little taller.

Jim Elkhorn stood up and leaned over Megan's cubicle. "You believe that bullshit?" he snorted, watching the door bang shut as Joel departed.

Megan flipped through the pages on her clipboard and scratched her signature at the bottom of three. "Why am I not surprised by that question, Elkhorn? In my estimation the world would be a better place if more mothers taught their sons some old-fashioned manners." Clipping her sheets together, she tossed them into a common basket, hung her flight helmet on a peg and strode out without a backward glance. Jim Elkhorn was good at his job. He was good-looking and a sharp dresser. She hoped someday he'd meet and fall ass-over-teakettle for a nice woman who'd grab him by the ears and show him he didn't need to be so cocky.

At the gate, she shortened her stride. Joel had climbed into the backseat with Tyler, but judging by their body language, he and Sterling were having an argument.

The rain she'd encountered up in the clouds had begun splattering on the asphalt. Megan didn't intend to stand out in it while man and boy traded insults, if that was what they were doing. It appeared her remarks hadn't had any more effect on Joel than they did on Lieutenant Elkhorn. Sighing, she passed the seaman pulling security duty and sprinted for the Land Rover.

"Hi," Sterling said as Megan slid in. Tyler bounced against his booster seat. "Megan! We saw you land that orange helichopter. I told Daddy it looked like you fell right out of the sky. Joel said you didn't fall. Did you, huh?"

She laughed softly and shook her head. "I'm sure from here it looked like we fell because we dropped out of sight behind the building. But no, to answer your question, we landed according to plan."

"Will you take me for a ride in the helichopter some day?"

"Heli*cop*ter, squirt," Joel growled, then slumped in his seat.

Sterling turned the key and started the engine with a roar. "When you came out, Joel and I were discussing where to eat. I promised you a cheeseburger, but he claims the thought of eating is enough to make him puke."

"Gee, that's a visual I could have done without."

"Can't you drop me off at home?" Joel asked.

"I left Megan's grandmother napping in your room."

"Why mine? Why didn't you give her Lauren's?"

"Good question. At the time, we talked about you bunking upstairs with Keith and Mark. I had no idea your sister and Mark were going to take a powder."

"What powder did they take?" Tyler asked, kicking Sterling's seat back. "They didn't take our cocoa powder, did they? If they did, can we buy more?"

Joel managed a scowl. "What a little dork."

"Come on, Joel. Try to remember you were four years old once."

Megan's heart expanded when she saw Joel reach out and hug Tyler. "Sorry, squirt. You and me are buddies, aren't we?"

"Yep. Joel, will you let me drive your boat?"

Megan felt Sterling tense up, even though he was in the process of turning the car toward home.

Again Joel came through. "When you're bigger. I've only got two life jackets. Both of 'em are too big for you. Remember I told you Megan taught about boating safety at school? The first thing she said was everybody who goes out in a boat needs a life vest that fits."

"Oh, 'kay, Joel. I'll be five on my next birthday. I'll be way bigger then. I'll ask the birthday fairy for my very own life jacket."

Sterling swung into the cul-de-sac.

"There's Keith," Tyler exclaimed, slapping his window.

He was right, Keith Lock stared out Megan's front window at the intensifying rain.

"This morning Keith teached me how to play 'nopoly. Daddy, if Joel's going upstairs, can I go, too, and maybe we can all play?"

"Joel?" Sterling glanced at the boy in the rearview mirror. "It's your call."

"Wow, you mean—you're *asking* me, not saying I gotta take him?"

Sterling braked and swung around, hooking an arm over the seat. "Joel, I've never demanded that either you or your sister watch Tyler. Lauren was prone to volunteer, but I never required her to babysit."

"Yeah, well, Blythe did. She made me take the squirt. She said you were too cheap to pay a sitter."

"That's a lie! Oh—never mind. Lauren and I had an enlightening chat last night. She filled me in on a few things that happened in New York. After Mona goes home tomorrow, maybe you and I should sit down and get some facts straight."

"All right. But I don't mind if Tyler comes upstairs. I didn't sleep much last night. I may flake out on the couch if Keith wants to play Monopoly."

"Megan and I won't be long. I promised to feed her, and we can't have her starving on our watch."

Keith had obviously seen them drive up. He ran down the steps, shrugging into a jacket he held over his head to ward off the rain. He approached the Land Rover on Megan's side, so she cracked open a window. "Yo, Keith, I'm starved. Sterling's taking me out for a burger. Did you find enough to eat? Do you want to come with us? Or we can bring you back something."

"Mona and I had soup and sandwiches. I wanted to tell you that I phoned my dad an hour ago. He and Sherry were on their way to see your folks. Since he was driving, he handed the phone off to Sherry. She said your mom and Camp were all in a fluster, but when I asked about what, she said *never mind, we'll talk later.*"

Megan might have laughed at Keith's apt rendition of her aunt Sherry, except that she was worried. "Did you tell her we know about the baby. What the heck's going on? Oh, the whole Campbell family always gets in on the act. It's probably because Mark phoned Camp and said he and Lauren plan a detour to Columbia. I'll bet that's it. The clan will gather at our house to hash and rehash who'll say what first when the poor unsuspecting kids show up."

"Mark and Lauren are taking time to go to Missouri? Why?"

"Lauren convinced Mark he should grovel and get back in Mom's good graces. I'm glad. It takes guts to beard the lions in their den. But I'm thinking it's wise. I mean, can you see the family disowning Mark or anything?"

"I guess not. I hope it's blown over by the time our plane lands tomorrow. I asked Dad to pick me up. I neglected to add that Mrs. Benton's gonna be a passenger."

"Poor Keith. I apologize for roping you into the Benton-Campbell squabble."

"Aren't I already in, since Sherry is married to Dad?" he said, pulling his jacket around his shoulders as Joel came around and Tyler launched his sturdy body at beanpole Keith. "Wait till my mom and Crawford hear I'm really going to be a veterinarian and not some stodgy old banker."

Sterling held his tongue until the boys had pounded up the stairs. "Is every family dysfunctional?"

"According to my brother, the former child psychologist, yes. Keith's stepmother and his dad have a great family. But his real mom is a piece of work." Megan sank deeper into the car's leather seat. "When Mark first came here to visit, would you believe he and I wondered why Mom and Camp never had more kids. Mark said they probably didn't want to deal with diapers and proms at the same time. Now, all these years later, they will be doing diapers. I wonder if they planned this pregnancy or if it just happened?"

"I suppose the only way you'll know is to ask. Are you going to set aside your hurt feelings and call to let them know their big secret isn't so secret?"

"Who said I have hurt feelings?"

"Megan, it's written all over your face."

"So? If Mark called to tell them—but not me—that he's showing up, you bet I'm miffed over being totally left out."

Sterling picked up her hand and kissed it. "Hurt isn't quite the same as miffed."

"Ah, you read me so well. How is that?"

"I think because I'm growing attached. Very attached, Megan. I missed you like crazy while you were chasing Joel down. What if I said…it's because I'm falling in love with you?"

She snatched back her hand so fast and hard, she cracked it on the window. "Ouch," Megan rubbed her stinging knuckles. "Damn, Sterling."

"Well, that's plain enough. The falling's all one-sided, huh?"

"No, ah, maybe not." She plastered her chin against her chest and let her hair hide the flush she felt streaking up her face. "Love is such a…a…" She spread her hands in helpless supplication.

"Such a definitive word," he said with a smile.

"I thought love hit like a tornado and left destruction in its wake," she said slowly.

"Or it creeps into a person's heart, and fills the soul with happiness when the loved one walks into the room. It's a joy that leaves emptiness when the person you love is no longer there."

Megan's lips moved, but no words came out.

"I know there's a gap in our ages. And hell, I'd bring a lot more than me into a relationship. But I've seen you with Tyler, who dotes on you. Lauren likes you and Joel respects you. Hey, all you bargained for when you came with me today is the promise of a cheeseburger. Why don't we erase everything that went before? The guys at work say this place makes an old-fashioned burger and good fries."

He angled into a parking place, and when he reached over to shut off the motor, Megan clasped his wrist. A thick wrist her fingers couldn't fully span. "It's the love thing, Sterling. You may be surprised to hear that on the flight to Grand Haven, I considered how much I'd miss you and the boys when you move to the island. I...you...evoke strong feelings in me." She caught her lip between her teeth for second, then let go. "But I concluded that I don't know what love is. I see couples, some married, some in partnerships, who declare they're madly in love. My point is, they all seem to know that what they feel *is* love. I...can't be that definite." The last word came out on a sob.

Sterling patted her. Awkwardly because she hadn't released his hand. Seat belts and a wide console also got in the way. "Sweetheart, don't obsess over this. I'm not the world's greatest at coming up with a definition of love. What I do know is that it shouldn't cause you pain. My feelings aren't going to change. Now," he said abruptly, "you're probably tired after a long flight. I know you're hungry. Let's save this conversation for another day."

"Please," she said, quickly wiping her cheeks.

Megan didn't really expect him to let the subject drop. But he did. Maybe that, too, set Sterling Dodge apart from other men she'd known—a willingness to keep his word. To bide his time. He ordered his food and let her choose hers. As if the subject of love had never come up between them, he talked about many things over the course of the meal. By the time the hole in her stomach had been filled, Megan began to wonder if she'd fantasized the earlier exchange.

He ordered pie and coffee for dessert. She asked for hot chocolate. "If you don't mind, I think I'll try phoning home while we're waiting for the waitress."

"By all means. I admit to being as curious as Keith as to what's going on." He grinned. "And except through you all, I don't even know the parties involved."

She punched in the programmed number for her folks. Her mother answered. Megan heard a lot of chatter in the background. "Hi, Mom. It's Megan. Are you having a party without me?"

"Ah, no, dear. You haven't called in so long I was starting to feel neglected."

Megan held the phone away from her ear a minute and crossed her eyes in disfavor. "Excuse me, aren't you the one with the big news? It seems you ought to be phoning *me*."

"Big news?" Megan heard a catch in her mother's voice.

"Honestly, Mom, I don't know why you're attempting to hide the truth from Mark and me. We both know you're going to have a baby. Didn't Mark tell you that when he phoned this morning to say he's stopping by?"

"Mark's...coming home?"

Now Megan wondered if she'd dialed into the twilight zone. But then she heard Camp swear succinctly. In fact, he grabbed the phone. "Megan, damn, I talked to Mark. I didn't say anything to your mom about his visit. It's, ah, been a zoo here, and dammit to hell, I've tried to shelter her from more mental anguish."

"I'm her daughter," Megan said coolly. "Mark's her son. Pray tell how we'd cause her greater mental upset than you or anyone else in the family."

"Honey, you don't know her condition."

"I do know. Angel told me Mom's pregnant. I don't understand why I had to find out through Aunt Sherry's secretary."

"I didn't mean you weren't aware of her pregnancy. Mark explained you'd spoken with our college crier. Wait, Emily's trying to rip the phone out of my hand. And she looks pretty mad, no doubt at me for not telling her about Mark and what's-her-name's visit."

"Lauren. Her name is Lauren. And you'd better treat her right. She's the one who convinced Mark to smooth things over with Mom."

From the silence at the other end, Megan felt satisfied that she'd finally scored a point. Then she heard Camp and her mother hissing at each other. "Stop," she cried. "Mark can speak for himself. Please, somebody talk to me!"

Hearing her almost panicky voice, and seeing tears clumping her long eyelashes, Sterling grabbed the phone out of her hand. "I don't know who's on the other end of this line. I'm Sterling Dodge. Lauren Atwater is my sister-in-law. And for folks who've raised two people as nice as Megan and Mark, you are all acting very strange. Hello? Is anyone there?"

"Mr. Dodge, this is Nolan Campbell."

"And this is Emily Benton Campbell," breathed a tiny voice some distance away. "We'd like to speak with Megan, please."

Sterling wasn't at all sure he wanted to hand over the phone; nevertheless, he did so. But not before getting up out of his side of the booth and crowding in next to Megan.

"Dear, our day has been an endless round of surprises. This morning, we uh, found out I'm pregnant with…twins. Camp just admitted your brother phoned before we went to the ultrasound. Everyone seems to think I'm either a basket case or else I'm made of glass, judging by the way they're all trying to shelter me. I'm neither, and I'm so very happy, Megan."

"Twins?" Megan's heart tripped and thundered in her ears. "Oh, Mom." A thousand questions rose to the tip of her tongue. But thinking better of heaping concern on concern, she clamped down on them.

"That news was more overwhelming than learning about the pregnancy in the first place. I thought I'd reached menopause. Camp thought I had an ulcer. We love you so very much, honey. If you'll bear with us, I'll call back and we'll have a good long chat. Just give me a couple of days."

"A couple of *days?* Oh, but Mark and Lauren will have come and gone. And Keith and Gram Benton will arrive home before then."

"Keith and Gram…Benton?" Her mother's voice sounded so faint, Megan slapped her forehead and almost upended the tray the waitress carried.

She was relieved when Camp rescued the phone again. "Maybe you'd better elaborate on that last remark, Megan."

"I tried to tell you the other day. Mona fell, broke her hip and the doctor pinned it. She sold the Benton Corners house and bought a top-floor condo. Keith's escorting her home. I need Mark or someone to locate a ground-floor place she can rent temporarily. In Columbia," she added almost as an afterthought. "Near you guys. I hoped Mom would look in on her. But…that's probably not going to happen, huh? Twins, you say?"

Megan could almost see her stepdad dragging a hand

over his face. She'd caused him to do that a lot in the past. But she could tell by his huge sigh that he was weakening.

"Why am I feeling double-teamed by you and Mark again, and this time long-distance? It's obvious somebody's going to have to keep tabs on that woman."

"Maybe Grandmother Nan," Megan suggested, at the same time flashing Sterling a thumbs-up. "Your parents are on boards of clinics and assisted living facilities. Camp, you probably won't believe it, but Mona's changed. Losing Toby, selling the business and the house, and then this fall made her realize how a person can't control everything. She said she wished she'd had a career like mine. And she swore she envies Mom having a baby—or two, as it now seems. If you want my take, Gram's regretting a lot in her life."

"Your mom caught bits of what you said, since she keeps sticking her head in between me and the receiver. I need to tell her all this before I forget. Oh, and she wants to know more about this guy, Sterling…Dodge, is it? Who is he and what are you doing with him?"

"You know…I'm on my cell, and I'm getting a signal that the battery's low. Tell Mom I'll hold her to that promise to phone in a day or two. Yikes, the battery's fading." She held the phone at arm's length and murmured a throaty, "G'bye."

Closing the phone, she calmly stirred her hot chocolate.

CHAPTER SEVENTEEN

SUNDAY, STERLING DIDN'T HAVE to work. He insisted on driving to the Pellston Airport. As he fit luggage in the back, Mona engineered seating. She adjusted the seat next to Tyler for herself, and sent Keith and Joel into the very back, leaving Megan up front with Sterling. His insistence surprised Megan, who'd assumed she'd simply borrow the Land Rover as she'd done to bring Mona home from the hospital.

Keith kept exclaiming rapturously over the many lakes on the drive out of Mackinaw City. "It was dark when I flew in. This state is so awesome! If you stay here, Megan, I've gotta get Dad to come back with me so we can spend more time fishing."

Sterling slanted a strange look at Megan. "Are you thinking of leaving Michigan?"

"Only if I'm transferred."

"I never considered that possibility, but I suppose it's common." His brow creased noticeably.

"If I requested to stay, I probably could. Long, harsh winters and the frequency of spring and summer storms make ours a revolving duty station. Plus, a lot of our members start here, but later choose to work on ice-breakers based in Cheboygan."

Joel sat forward. "Matt Horowitz wants to serve on

an icebreaker. He told me all about them. I hear you can tour them. Can we do that one day, Sterling?"

"Sure. Sounds interesting. And Cheboygan has an old opera house where Annie Oakley and Mary Pickford performed."

"Now that's an unlikely duet." Mona laughed. "Not that you kids know anything about either of those women, I'm sure. They were wa-a-ay before your time."

Joel surprised them. "My history class in New York went to see a musical about Annie Oakley. She was cool. A crack shot. Never heard of the other lady."

"I tried many times to interest Toby in taking a trip to New York. I so wanted to see some Broadway plays. He repeatedly put me off and then it was too late. Kids," Mona said urgently, "go. Do. See all you can. It doesn't pay to put things off until tomorrow."

Megan reached back and clasped her grandmother's hand. "With Mark and Lauren living in New York, what's to stop you from visiting once your hip heals? I'll bet they'd love to see a round of plays, and it might be a while before they can afford it."

"I may stick close to Columbia for now. After you told me last night that Emily's pregnant with twins, I got to thinking how she's bound to need help. Twins are a handful, even for young mothers. I could sit and rock babies if she'll let me."

Privately, Megan hoped her mom would accept help from Mona, and that Camp wouldn't create barriers. "Even so, Gram, the beauty of being retired is that you're free to go and do and see."

Mona beamed. "You're right, dear. But on my next trip I'll watch out for patches of ice."

That sparked a lively debate on travel. Megan never expected to be sad to see her grandmother leave, but gloom settled over her all the same.

MARK AND LAUREN ARRIVED in Columbia, Missouri, to a house filled with Mark's relatives. Lauren's head spun trying to remember all their names. At first she stuck to Mark like a shadow. But she soon found herself in the kitchen with Emily, Nan Campbell and Sherry Lock, while the men filed out to the barn to see an old car Nolan Campbell was restoring.

Nan manipulated things so that Emily and Lauren sat at the table drinking herbal tea while Sherry and her mother prepared dinner for the crowd.

Enjoying the camaraderie of women, Lauren saw how lacking her life had been. She loved being included, something Blythe had rarely done. The Campbell group were all nice. Mark's mom especially was a jewel. But filled with endless questions…

"Last night when Megan phoned, she was with Sterling. I gather he's your brother-in-law. Are he and Megan…close?"

"We, uh, all lived in one big Victorian house. Well, upper and lower apartments," Lauren hastened to say. "Sterling's son—my nephew, Tyler—loves Megan. He's crazy about her homemade cookies and hot chocolate." Lauren sipped her tea steadily, yet the women managed to pry out most of her family history.

The next afternoon, she and Mark took one of Camp's SUVs to the airport to collect Keith Lock and Mona Benton. Garrett had planned to go, but something came up at the college at the last minute.

Mona greeted them with hugs. "I'm exhausted, "

she said, sinking immediately into her seat. "I hope you found a furnished apartment, Mark. I feel like I could sleep for a week."

"Actually," he said, exchanging a guilty glance with Lauren. "I don't know how this happened, but at dinner last night, Grandma and Grandpa Campbell, uh—Nan and Ben, they— Shoot, what I'm doing a bad job of saying is they're putting you up in their guest house for the time being."

Tears brimmed in the older woman's eyes. "Why would they do that for a stranger?"

"They're wonderful people," Lauren said simply.

Sprawled in the back, Keith Lock hooted. "Why don't you admit you got steamrollered? I'm not implying they aren't nice. But I'm sure they have an agenda."

Lauren glared, and Mark pinned his cousin in the rearview mirror. "The only agenda I saw is how they've all banded together to take care of my mom."

"As well they should," Mona said, shaking a finger. "The babies, are they okay?"

Mark adjusted his side mirrors. "Who can tell from those weird snowy pictures? The way everyone oohed and ahed over the ultrasound, you'd think they were the work of a famous photographer like Ansel Adams. I don't know how you could tell they were even babies."

Lauren piped up. "One day you'll be as famous as Adams."

"Are we going to my house first?" Keith pressed his nose to the window.

"I forgot, Aunt Sherry's fixing pot roast for everyone tonight. Lauren and I plan to take off for New York right after dinner. Grandma and Grandpa Campbell will give you a lift, Mona. They have a new Caddy SUV. But get set for a grilling about Michigan and Megan. Lauren landed on the hot seat last night."

"What about?"

"Mom's decided there's a romance brewing between Megan and Sterling. She won't take our word that they're just neighbors."

Mona smiled. "Mothers have a sixth sense when it comes to their children's love interests. Haven't you kids been paying attention?"

"Not Megan and Sterling," Lauren and Mark yelped in unison. "Oh, but my folks can make stuff happen," Mark admitted. "They made us promise we'd both come in November when Mom and Camp plan to christen the babies." Mark ran a hand over Lauren's hair and smiled. "I said it'd depend on Lauren's class schedule and my work. But Megan? I can see her telling them *no way.* She won't let them meddle in her life."

ONE NIGHT TOWARD THE end of May, the phone rang as Megan juggled a spatula and a pan of hot snickerdoodles she'd just removed from the oven. Oven mitt and all, she shifted the spatula and awkwardly held the phone to her ear.

"Mom? Hey, I forgot this is the night for our weekly phone call. It so happens I'm taking cookies out of the oven. Why don't I unload this tray, pop in another, then phone you back while they're baking?"

Megan wedged the receiver between her chin and shoulder, hurriedly scooping off the cookies to put them on cooling racks before they stuck to the pan. "Am I baking Sterling's favorite kind?" She gulped. "As a matter of fact, no, these aren't peanut butter. Why do you ask?"

She listened to her mother's explanation that Lauren had gone on and on about Megan's cookies and her hot chocolate.

"When they were visiting, did Mark tell you that I stole your recipes? No, Mother, I'm not getting fat from eating cookies all the time. I still run every morning, and the Coast Guard keeps me trim. But enough about me. How are *you?* Is everything going okay with your…uh…pregnancy?"

"Megan," her mother said abruptly. "Do you resent the fact that I'm pregnant?"

"No! In fact, when Mark came to visit, he and I wondered why you and Camp hadn't had kids." Megan gave a self-conscious laugh, and lifted the phone cord off the pan she was attempting to fill. "I wondered if your age was a factor. How silly of me."

"Well, I was thirty-four then, and both of us wanted more kids. We had every fertility test known at the time. We even considered artificial insemination. Megan, I'm already getting a bulging tummy. Pregnancy's an experience like no other."

"Yeah? Well, maybe I should have my eggs harvested and frozen."

"At twenty-five? Oh, I understand, the man you're seriously dating is six or seven years older, right? Is that why you're concerned? Or does Sterling have some kind of problem? Camp and I will be disappointed not to have a dozen grandchildren to spoil."

Megan felt the warmth creep up her neck. She almost dropped the phone. "Mother! Did Mark say I was dating seriously, the big mouth? Sterling and I have gone out to eat a few times, that's all. Even as we speak, he and Tyler and Joel are packing to move to a house he bought on Mackinac Island."

Those words barely cleared Megan's lips when she conjured up the recent excursion she'd made with Sterling to see his home. They'd ended up making love on the luxurious carpet he'd had installed in the master bedroom. He'd been pretty vocal about wanting her there again, but next time in his bed.

The heat rising up her neck grew hotter. Megan blamed it on the next pan of cookies she took from the oven.

"Mom, stop picking on me. I've said I'd come for the christening."

"Oh, But Megan, have you thought how easy it would be to combine the christening and a wedding? I've already booked the Methodist church where Camp and I were married. Where Aunt Sherry and Uncle Garrett had their wedding."

Megan remembered both weddings with fondness. She'd helped decorate the beautiful chapel. She and Grandmother Nan had sewed tons of net pillows they'd filled with rice. Suddenly, she was overcome by nostalgia.

"Honey, this morning your grandmothers and I were having tea and talking. I can't recall who brought it up, but someone said it'd be simple and fabulous for Camp and I, Garrett and Sherry, and Ben and Nan to repeat our vows, either before or after our new pastor christens the twins. Including you in the ceremony would be the crowning touch, don't you think?"

Megan strangled on her nostalgia. "It's obvious you three have too much time on your hands. Keith's right there. I don't see you hounding him."

"Keith will make a handsome groomsman, with Mark as best man. Unless Sterling would rather have Joel. Oh, and for your information, Aunt Sherry said yesterday that our Keith has had three dates recently. With the same girl! A veterinary assistant. His real mother is livid. I wish she'd chill out. Well…if I can reconcile with Mona, anything's possible. Now, about you and Sterling…"

"Oops, there's the buzzer for my cookies. Take care, Mom. We'll talk again next week."

"Wait! Promise you'll think about what I've suggested. Talk to your young man. Oh, and send pictures. I can't believe Mark brought photos of everyone but your Sterling. You might include his measurements. For a tux."

"He's not *my* Sterling. A tux? Mother!" *Darn!* Megan had intended to hang up, but Emily beat her to it. Only, of course, after she'd had her say.

Later, Megan took still-warm cookies downstairs. Joel and Tyler had retired. Sterling came to the door in bare feet. He'd shoved the sleeves of a knit pullover midway up sweaty arms. Sniffing the plate, he leaned across it and kissed Megan. "How did you know I needed a coffee break? I swear, as fast as I get boxes packed, one of the kids can't locate something they desperately need, and we're slicing them open again."

"Mmm. You taste like malt. But beer doesn't go well with snickerdoodles."

"There's iced coffee in the fridge. It's too humid for hot drinks tonight."

Megan wedged the cookies into a bare spot on the counter piled with things from his cupboards. "When do you plan to move your first load?"

"I hope tomorrow, but maybe the next day."

"Hmm. As I left work, we got word of a nasty storm blowing our way. It's sweeping down out of Manitoba. There were reports of significant damage along Lake Superior. I suppose it could peter out before it gets here—or it could turn worse."

"Hard to believe. The weather's been great. Joel and I finished the workbook exercises for his after-school lifesaving drills. He's a changed kid, and I have to thank you for setting up that program to help him apply to ROTC. I got calls from his teachers. His grades have improved dramatically. They hinted that if he keeps it up, he'll make the honor roll before school's out next week. Oh, and guess what? He's got a summer job wrapping fudge."

"Sterling, that's fantastic!" When a gust of wind rattled the window above the sink, they both stopped to look up. Megan walked to the bigger window in the breakfast nook, but jumped back as lightning struck the ground, its bolt far too close for comfort. "Zowie!" She dropped the curtain and rubbed her arms. "I guess we're not going to escape its fury. I should probably go back upstairs in case the station calls. Bolt lightning can create havoc out in the straits."

"Will you let me know if you get called out? I know, I know," he said, sliding his thumbs along her cheekbones. "You've told me over and over not to sit at home worrying. On the other hand, you admitted it's not so bad having someone care whether you make it home or not."

"I don't mind." Megan briefly leaned against his broad chest. "What'll I do after you move to the island, Sterling?"

He went stock-still for a minute, then tugged her head up with a few soft yanks on her thick hair. "The offer to move in with us is still on the table, Megan. I know you've avoided giving me an answer, but…"

She sighed, letting her troubled gaze take in his rugged features. Tonight he hadn't shaved, and the dark stubble gave him a too-tempting rough-and-tumble look. "You won't be getting rid of me totally. In July I'll pick Joel up every day for summer Sea Scouts. And Tyler heard me talking with my aunt Sherry about iced chocolate. He made me promise to make some when it gets to be swimsuit weather."

The wind gusted again, and lightning flashed, followed by rolling thunder. "Hmm, I'll take your word for it that this neck of the woods *does* get swimsuit weather. You be careful going upstairs with this lightning. How long is the storm predicted to hang around? I'm wondering about rough ferry crossings."

"A week, perhaps. Commander Donovan was bitching about it. He wants this weather out of here before the big sailboat race. It's the one those expensive boats have been practicing for. Their race marks the official start of summer here."

Sterling grimaced as he walked her to the door and stood on the porch to watch black clouds racing across a rising moon. "Summer? I'll believe it when I see it. Off with you before the next lightning strike."

Megan dashed away. She didn't get called out during the night, but the storm kept her awake. Air-conditioning was unheard of in the old houses in this part of the country, and the approaching storm boosted humidity to stifling proportions.

The next morning as she headed to work, she met Sterling fighting the wind as he took out trash he'd collected while finishing his packing. "Hey, you'll be happy to know that according to the morning newscast, this storm will blow out by noon."

She hunched against the patter of rain. "Don't expect any complaints from me. All the same, I'm taking my foul-weather gear to the station."

"I'm debating picking up a rental van today. I phoned and asked the guy if I could wait and see how the weather pans out. If it clears, I'll move one load after the kids get home from school. Otherwise I'll wait until tomorrow."

"Mrs. Ralston's going to be sad. She's loved watching Tyler after school on the days Joel takes out his boat."

"Tyler likes her. Confidentially, though, he says her cookies don't compare to yours, Megan. The little rascal got up before me this morning and ate half the snickerdoodles you brought down last night." Sterling shook his head.

Grinning, Megan threw her slicker pants on the passenger seat and waved as she drove off.

The weather cleared by eleven. Megan shed her raincoat on a run to check buoy lights reportedly battered by the wind. One that had been hit by lightning needed extensive repair. It took several hours. None of the team were happy to see black clouds boil again as they turned the cutter around to head in.

Seaman Dooley bellied up to the bow rail beside Megan. "Brr, this crud promises to dump worse weather than it whipped up last night.

Megan, who'd grown up in the Midwest, had frequently been on the lookout for what they called tornado skies. She eyed the angry-looking horizon with trepidation. "Ever have tornadoes this far north, Seaman?"

"Not that I know of. I grew up in Traverse City, not far from here. Never heard of any tornadoes. Why?"

"That sky looks mean."

It looked no better when they docked. Donovan met the crew as they filed off the boat.

"All hands, listen up. I want the whole crew to stay near phones. Munuscong Lake's getting hammered with hail the size of golf balls. Those of you who're heading home, grab some rest. I sent a team over to Mackinaw City. They'll cruise up the strait. This short reprieve we enjoyed was just enough time to lull pleasure boaters out for an afternoon of fun. I'll be surprised if we aren't running our butts off all afternoon and into the evening."

"Maybe we should all stick around the station," Megan suggested, as she tried to keep her hair from whipping her cheeks in the rising wind. She finally secured it with a rubber band.

The craggy commander tugged on his drooping mustache. "My bones tell me we're in for a major blow. Probably best if you go tie down anything at home that's in danger of ending up down the street. Like lawn furniture, et cetera." He shook his hand, muttering, "I don't know why Mother Nature teases us with a couple of weeks of sunshine, then snatches it away."

Megan drove home noting that her boss's predictions were already coming to pass. People had brought out their summer tables and sun umbrellas. Several neighbors along the street before her cul-de-sac were chasing their stuff down in neighbors' yards.

Megan noted that Sterling's Land Rover wasn't there, although she'd expected him to be home by now. The wind tore her pickup door out of her hand. Puffing, she had a tough time wrestling it shut. Hearing her name over the wind's whistle, she looked first toward Lady Vic, thinking it was Joel calling. The house was dark upstairs and down.

The call came again, and Megan realized it was Mrs. Ralston.

"Do you need some help?" Megan jogged to where the woman huddled on her porch wrapped in a shawl.

"I've been on the lookout for Mr. Dodge. This morning I came down with the flu. I was supposed to watch Tyler, but I didn't want the little guy catching my bug. I know Joel was disappointed when I turned them away after school. He has an important paper due on Friday and needed to go to a library print shop, where his teacher said he'd find the research material he needed. Joel's had quite a time choosing a subject," she said with a wry smile. "He wanted to write about the wreck of the *Edmund Fitzgerald.* Yesterday, Sterling was too late to drive him up to the shipwreck museum. Today I gather Joel settled on the history of Beaver Island, instead."

"I'm not familiar with the library print shop."

"Well, that's what I'm saying. It's on Beaver Island. He headed off there in his boat maybe an hour ago, Megan. And now the weather's turned dreadful."

"He went in his boat—with Tyler?" Icy fear sucked air from Megan's lungs. But the woman kept nodding repeatedly.

"Oh, no! I saw Sterling pack Joel's life vests."

"He had some. I know that. I saw the boys leave their house carrying backpacks, life jackets and probably snacks. Something in a brown bag."

"Do you know when Sterling is due home from his last ferry run?"

"I thought it'd be before now. Soon I should think. Megan, I'm sorry, but I have to go back in and lie down. I'm feeling ill again."

"You take care, Mrs. Ralston. I'll contact Sterling. He or I will find the boys. And I'll look in on you later. If you get too sick, call 911."

Jane Ralston clutched her wrap and weaved shakily back inside. Megan reached for her cell phone as she ran to her pickup, punching in Sterling's number.

"Cap'n Dodge." He answered on the second ring.

"Sterling, it's Megan. Where are you?"

"In line to leave Mackinac. My last crossing was a bitch. I hear we have phase two of the storm howling down the straits. They're shutting down the line after this run. I hate to rush you, but I'm scheduled to pilot the last ferry back to St. Ignace."

"Oh, Sterling, I have potentially bad news. The boys, Joel and Tyler, took off for Beaver Island in Joel's boat about an hour ago."

He sputtered in anger and disbelief, as Megan quickly summarized everything Mrs. Ralston had said. "I'm going straight to the station," she told him. "With the magnitude of this storm, I'm sure the officer of the day will order out the cutter for this."

"Tyler," Sterling said in a shaky voice. "I packed his new life vest. And Joel's. Why would the kid do this, Megan? He can spout safety rules right and left."

"Mrs. Ralston said his mind was on a school project. You know he's trying to keep his grades up. She said he left your house with two life jackets. Once you dock, see how fast you can get to our station. I'll ask the commander to let you come aboard. Times like this, we can use extra eyes."

"Don't leave without me."

"Hurry, okay? I may not have a choice."

Vince Rigley was suiting up when Megan tore into the station. "We have one cutter out and we're refueling the second," he said. "We've got sailboats capsized all up and down the coast."

Megan rummaged at her desk. "Any reports of a motorboat in distress between here and Beaver Island?"

"Not that I know of. I have this watch. Do we need to take a run in that direction?"

Describing the situation, she was more pointed with her coworker than she'd been with Sterling. "Vince," she finished, "if Tyler's dad can get here, will you authorize him to come along? He's a licensed ferryboat captain."

"Um, I guess. But the way this baby's blowing, we should leave as soon as the cutter's fueled. Otherwise we'll all get caught in an old-fashioned Nor'easter."

Preparing for the worst, Megan zipped into an orange wet suit. She assembled everything she'd need for a hand-to-hand rescue at sea. The cutter's engines fired, and a seaman released their mooring lines. Standing at the stern, Megan saw the Land Rover drive up to the chain-link fence. She yelled at the security guard to let Sterling pass. He pounded down the dock running full tilt.

Megan and Ensign Vail tossed out a rope ladder. Sterling leaped from the dock and hung in midair for a second. Megan let out her breath as his feet found purchase on the lowest rung, and he pulled himself up hand over hand, landing on the deck out of breath. His windbreaker and pants were soaked through by gusting rain.

"I phoned Beaver Island information," he said.

"There's a ferry run between Charlevoix on the mainland and St. James at the far end of the island. A ferry captain said if Joel had a map, he'll know that the lodge dock comes first. Usually they only see hunters and fishermen. A man I spoke with at the lodge promised he'd be on the lookout for the boys. He swears no motorboat landed there today."

She passed Sterling high-powered binoculars. Megan and several of the men scanned the water with their own field glasses. Megan knew the futility of trying to spot a small boat in whitecaps already swelling high.

Thunder rumbled overhead. That, too, worried her. If they needed to launch the Jayhawk, there was no sending it aloft in lightning.

They chugged up the coastline at the maximum knots the weather would allow. Sterling thought Joel would hug the shore as long as possible.

"Depending on what time the boys left, it's conceivable they're already out in the open span off Waugoshance Point."

Rounding Waugoshance, their point man spotted a good-size sail boat in trouble. Pulling alongside, everyone worked to bring the crew onboard. Vince ordered the sailboat lashed to the cutter's stern, knowing full well that if the storm worsened, as it might, the expensive pleasure boat could still capsize. Her captain was apologetic, and said he'd been caught unawares.

"Did you see a fifteen-foot motorboat on the lake? It's a bright, sparkly red."

A woman wrapped in a blanket nodded. "I may have seen it as we left Sturgeon Bay. A couple of kids? They weren't far out, so I assumed they must be headed home."

Neither Megan nor Sterling said just how far from home the kids were. The cutter turned into the wind and the storm bore down. Megan's heart had sunk to its lowest level yet. All at once, the lookout in the crow's nest signaled that he'd picked up a flare. He called coordinates, and the cutter swerved.

"Would Joel have flares?" Sterling asked, his face lined with grief.

Megan raised crossed fingers. "He would if the marina where he bought the boat supplied the required emergency kit."

Not three minutes later, the crew hanging off the starboard side caught glimpses of a bobbing red boat. Sterling shouted in Megan's ear. "I see two orange life jackets."

Frank Dooley dashed up. "That craft isn't under its own steam. Either the motor's swamped and quit, or they ran out of gas. She's at the mercy of the waves."

Erratic cross-currents driven by ever-changing winds presented one of the most difficult rescue scenarios possible. Vince Rigley, the lieutenant in charge of the deck, summoned Megan to the wheelhouse. She was afraid to hear what he had to say.

"I can't risk taking the cutter close enough to grapple the boat. You know they're foundering. We could fishtail on top of them, or we could slam that little motorboat into our steel hull and turn her into toothpicks."

"Hamish is an ace chopper pilot. He's got the ability to hover above them long enough for me to ride a basket down to their level."

"Are you too close to the family to go on this rescue, Lieutenant? What if the rescue starts going bad?"

"It won't," Megan swore through gritted teeth. "I *am*

the best person for the job, Vince. The little guy's dad had a ferry crack up in fog off New York Harbor. He knows how bad things can get. I need someone with a vested interest to lower me on the line. Will you allow Sterling to be that guide, Lieutenant?"

Rigley vacillated. But with the thunder and lightning moving nearer, he gave in with the proviso that if anything, anything at all, went wrong it'd go on Megan's record.

She finished suiting up with helmet, gloves, safety belt, goggles and snorkel, in case she landed in the drink, and told herself a little fear was healthy.

Relaying the plan to Sterling, she saw the color leach from his face, but his eyes held the steel she'd counted on. He donned the flight coveralls she handed him and fit a helmet over his wind-raked hair. It was understood that he would stay in the Jayhawk.

Seconds before they boarded the chopper, Sterling grasped Megan's shoulders. "It goes without saying that I love Tyler and Joel more than life itself. You need to know you have my whole heart, as well. I know this is about as bad as it gets. I've blamed myself for losing that mom in the harbor, but I promise, Megan, if anything goes wrong here, I won't blame you or myself."

His kiss warmed her cold lips. Inside she was a mess. Outwardly, she presented calm. She felt the rotors being pummeled by unpredictable winds as the heavy Jayhawk rose above the cutter. Megan shut her eyes and refused to think about dangling from the end of the rescue line.

The hope and trust in Sterling's eyes, as the pilot signaled it was time for her to hook up, released the knot in Megan's stomach.

An initial pass overshot the tossing boat. In a spin herself, Megan gazed down and realized that the runabout whirled counterclockwise in the water. Dropping another three feet placed her near enough to see a plea for help etched on Joel's face. She couldn't help being proud of him for having the presence of mind to set a flare and to lash himself and Tyler to the tiller. What it meant, though, was that she'd have to land squarely in the boat.

For an instant the wind slackened. Megan used the opportunity to call for more line. She almost didn't believe her luck when her feet hit hard inside the boat, although she felt it wobble. Working as fast as her gloves allowed, she slipped the first empty harness over Tyler and made sure he was buckled in tight. A crosswind caught them and sent the trio into a wild spin reminiscent of a carnival cup-and-saucer ride.

Megan judged that there wasn't time to send Tyler up and call the line back for Joel. She did what rescuers should never do—shed her harness—and as quickly as she could with fingers fumbling from cold, yanked it over Joel's head and shoulders. Giving three hard tugs on the line, she felt her heart pound as the boys swung aloft.

She didn't draw a free breath until both boys disappeared into the yawning belly of the chopper. Looping an arm around the tiller, Megan waited for the line and harness to drop again. But the storm had other plans.

Thunder and lightning descended with all the ferocity of a pack of mad dogs. The Jayhawk, of necessity, began its return to the cutter. Megan was left adrift in a craft that could disintegrate at any minute. *Her choice.* She'd do it again if it meant saving someone she loved. And she did love those kids. *And Sterling.* She didn't kid herself; she'd taken the risk for him.

Crawling through six inches of water to the back of the motorboat, she yanked repeatedly on the rope under the motor cover. The engine sputtered once and died. Obviously it wasn't going to turn over.

Keeping the cutter in sight, she counted her blessings when the thunderstorm moved on. However, it was far from done. A huge wave crashed over the runabout, followed by a hurling one that lifted the boat and slammed it down in a deep trough. Megan went soaring through air. She landed moments later in icy water that drove the breath from her lungs.

Startled, she refused to count the seconds until her blood began to thicken and turn sluggish. Instinct and her many hours of training was all that kept her from having the wind-tossed boat crash against her skull.

She attempted to paddle toward the cutter, but was swept up and thrown some twenty feet in the opposite direction. And by then, her arms wouldn't work right.

Thoughts crowded in and she couldn't keep them out. Thoughts of people who'd miss her. Of people she ought to have told she loved. *Sterling*. His face flashed before her eyes.

Hope was a fragile thing, she thought, and Megan felt it slipping away. Would she never see her mother's babies? Never hold her own children? Arms like lead weights, Megan fought a roaring in her ears. Flailing, she lost sight of the cutter.

All at once a pair of brown boots dangled in front of her. Oh, God, she was hallucinating. People said that happened. Turning her face directly into the slicing rain, she felt her heart galloping madly. She imagined it was Sterling swaying directly above her. Come to save her. Helpless laughter welled up, threatening to choke her.

But he *was* hanging there, larger than life. Though their faces were masked by wet goggles, Megan was sure those gray eyes willed her to reach up, to hang on.

Sterling's muscular form fell another foot, and the harness struck her helmet with a thunk, and then another thunk.

But she barely had the strength to wiggle into the network of black straps. It took three tries to clasp the buckle with his help. Then, suddenly, from somewhere, she was imbued with a fierce will to live—to follow up on Sterling's earlier declaration of love.

A sureness flowed through her blood and gave Megan the wherewithal to clasp the line.

Her teeth chattered. Her feet and hands went totally numb before, at last, her frosty cheek touched the throbbing floor of the Jayhawk. Then she blacked out.

There was no time for questions, or recriminations, or much of anything else. A woozy Megan came to in time to hear the crew send up a raucous cheer as the helicopter set down with a bump and a thump on the heaving deck of the cutter.

Vince hustled all his victims to port.

"I don't like being on the victim's end of a rescue," Megan told the ambulance attendant. She hated even more being poked and prodded by the emergency room doctor.

Every two minutes she asked about Joel and Tyler. She couldn't understand why Sterling didn't at least stick his head in to see how she'd fared.

Even though she was trussed up like a Thanksgiving turkey, there was no more welcome sight than

Sterling's haggard face when he finally slipped into her room.

He sat on the bed and stroked her face over and over, as if fearing she'd break apart. "You're crazy. And you're the bravest woman I know. Do you have any idea how much I owe you, Megan?"

She tried to clasp his hand, and tears flooded her eyes.

"I've been trying to talk Lieutenant Rigley out of putting you on report. He says he has to, Megan. You broke the rules, and so did I."

"The boys," she croaked. "Are they okay?"

"They're only shaken and cold, thanks to your bravery."

She laughed and cried at the same time. "You're a fine one to talk. How on earth did you convince Vince to send the Jayhawk up a second time?"

"I may go to jail for threatening to toss a Coast Guard Lieutenant overboard."

"I'll bake you cookies with a file in them, Captain. But…only if you promise you won't come down hard on Joel."

"Are you kidding? He's my hero for setting off that first flare."

"I probably shouldn't say this, but…technically you outrank Vince. And me. So…please, captain, kiss me? I want to feel alive. I want to tell you that I've learned what it feels like to fall in love."

He kissed her then. Repeatedly.

The doctor who came in to monitor her progress declared that her temperature was coming up nicely.

Sterling had a few things of his own to say after the doctor left. "I want you to know what I learned today.

After my accident I suppressed my fear. I never told Blythe the truth about that night—I thought I could compartmentalize my life, separate success from failure. I know now life doesn't work like that. Love can't thrive under those conditions. Fear can erode a man's self-esteem. And a woman with your guts deserves more from a partner than a man who fears the worst each time you go out on a mission. I want you to know I'll do my best to change. To be everything you admire in a husband."

She wriggled her hand free of the confining blankets and traced a finger over his eyebrows, nose, cheekbones and finally his lips. "We'll do fine, Sterling. I have to confess something to you. I had the first inkling we belonged together when you acted so blasé the night I beat you at pool. My family will tell you it's always taken a knock on the head to get anything through my thick skull. But once I see the light, I see it clearly. We're good together, Sterling. What would you say to getting married in November? At the church where my folks had their wedding?"

"I'd prefer sooner than that. Saying our vows at the foot of the Mighty Mac, since that's where I fell in love with you. But I'd like to meet your family. I suppose I could be persuaded."

The kisses that followed his admission brought Megan's temperature fully up to normal and then some. The last physician to check on her backed out of the room, and hung a Do Not Disturb sign on the door.

CHAPTER EIGHTEEN

MEGAN WALKED IN ONE late-October day after handling distress calls from reckless boaters winding down a season. A season too short according to many, although the signs of fall—leaves turning color and dropping—were all around, and the wind had gotten brisk again. She'd talked her way out of a reprimand the previous May, mostly, she thought, because Donovan had a hard time getting guardsmen to stay in the north country. And it was evident that Megan wanted to make her home on the island.

In another month, she mused, heading for her kitchen, she'd be leaving Lady Vic. First, to go home to Missouri to get married. Home to see a newborn brother and sister. Home to introduce Sterling, Tyler and Joel to her family. Then to return a bride to Sterling's house on Mackinac Island.

She stopped at her answering machine, where a blinking light beckoned. She smiled, expecting it to be Sterling calling to say he loved her. That had become their after-work routine. If it was up to him, she would've moved to his home and bed months ago, ring on her finger or not. Hardly a day passed that Megan didn't wonder why she held out. She laid the blame at the door of her conservative Midwest upbringing. But in her own mind it solidified who she was, and Sterling accepted that, leaving the decision to her.

After touching the button, she was surprised to hear her stepdad's shaky voice. "Megan, Dr. Gregory has scheduled your mom for an emergency cesarean section this afternoon. You remember the pictures we e-mailed a couple of weeks ago? When Emily couldn't see her fuzzy slippers and her ankles looked like tree trunks? It's because she's retaining water. Her blood pressure's risen significantly. Preeclampsia the doctor called her condition."

And that was it. Camp said he'd call back after the surgery.

Megan's hands shook as she punched in Sterling's number. They'd been through so much together. This was another of those moments. She almost couldn't talk by the time he answered.

"What is it, sweetheart?" He instantly recognized panic in her voice.

"Oh, Sterling, it's Mom. Camp left a message. She's going in for a C-section. Today. That's almost a month early."

"Pack, call Commander Donovan and ask for leave. I'll get us reservations."

"So, you think I should go?"

"We'll all go. My schedule's been cut back in preparation for winter. I'm sure another captain will gladly cover my runs to beef up his take-home pay. I'll call the school and arrange for Joel's homework, then collect the boys. I assume someone's notified Mark?"

"I imagine so. I'm so rattled I can't think. I'll get in touch with him after I arrange leave. While I pack."

Counting her months in Alabama, she had just

enough time on the books to warrant thirty days off. Relieved, she made a call to New York and discovered that Mark had also received a voice message from Camp.

"Gram's been here all week, Megan, and she says she should've stayed in Columbia instead of coming here to take Lauren and me to the theater. She's sure Mom's done too much getting ready for the christening and your wedding."

"Tell Mona to quit blaming herself for taking a well-deserved trip. They've always said this was a high risk pregnancy. Sterling's booking us flights. Can you and Lauren get away?"

"Gram thinks we should all go home. I'm not sure. I was about to call you for an opinion."

"Oh, Mark, Sterling and I need to cancel our wedding plans. Who'd be in a festive mood if anything goes wrong?"

"Gram asked whether any of us can afford the time or money to travel there now, and turn around and go again in a month. It'd be a hardship for us, even though I'm beginning to bring in some money."

"I definitely won't qualify for a second leave. And... we will all be there. Shall we play it by ear? Who even knows if we could get the church sooner? And who's to say Mom will feel like attending a wedding, even though they all plan to rededicate their vows. Will the twins even be ready for a christening?"

"I'll grant you that's a lot of *ifs*. Lauren kept Gram from spending a mint on a wedding dress she wanted to buy for you, Megan."

"What? I told her we want to wear our uniforms."

"Ah, that'll make for interesting pictures. Which, by the way, I'll be taking and charging you a pretty penny for."

"Well, you are the official family photographer. *And* a rising star."

"In case I neglected to tell you, thanks for the humongous bouquet you and Sterling sent to my showing. Bird of Paradise in bamboo looked sophisticated and classy when people walked in. I nearly sold out. I've found, though, that here in New York there's a lot of money to be made photographing people's new babies in their homes. It's fluid, and should more than pay the bills until Lauren graduates and finds a job."

"You're okay then to forge ahead with our plans?"

His laughter was rich and full. "Sis, are you becoming our mother? Quit worrying. Like I said, let's play it by ear."

At that, she said she loved him, and hung up, promising to see him soon. She hardly had time to drag out her suitcase when the phone rang again.

"I found someone to take my runs, and I got us tickets," Sterling said. "Not the best route. We'll go from Pellston to Chicago, to St. Louis, to Columbia."

"Anything's fine. Sterling, I love you so much. I don't say that often enough."

"It shows in everything you do for me and the kids. Megan, don't worry, I'm sure your mom's in excellent hands. Be positive. Isn't that what you tell Joel and me?"

It was, but this was her mom, after all. They set a time to leave. "Sterling, Mark thinks we should still plan to get married. That means we need to pack our dress uniforms."

"I couldn't be happier. But I do hear doubt in your voice?"

"No. No, you don't. This is me being positive, Sterling."

They phoned Missouri after touching down in Chicago. Megan reached Garrett Lock. "Hey, kid-all-grown-up," he teased. "I'm just this minute walking into the hospital. I see my wife. Let me find out if I can get you an update."

"Megan, Sherry here. Relax, hon. Dr. Gregory has administered hydralazine intravenously to your mom. Camp told me a minute ago that her blood pressure's dropped. That's fantastic. If it stays down, they'll prep her for surgery within the hour."

"Wait, Aunt Sherry. They're boarding our plane. I'll phone again if I can from St. Louis. We don't have much leeway, so if you don't hear from me, I'll try again when we land in Columbia."

"What time, Megan? Keith will be there picking up Mark and entourage. He'll be driving my van. Depending on how much luggage you have, he ought to be able to squeeze you all in."

"Maybe not. Sterling, his son and brother-in-law are with me. Mark thinks we should plan on still having our wedding."

"Oh, that'll be a boost for Emily. Does Camp know? He said that was on Em's mind."

"No, I couldn't reach him. I assumed he'd shut off his cell in the hospital, or else forgot to take it."

"Oh, Megan, this is going to be the grandest Campbell reunion ever!"

IT WAS TYPICAL BLUSTERY, late-October weather for the Midwest. The flight was bumpy all the way to St. Louis. And on into Columbia. Megan had no time in St. Louis to make a call. Anxious, she turned on her cell and had it to her ear as they entered the Jetway in Columbia.

"Any news, Aunt Sherry?" Megan held Sterling's hand and sent up a prayer.

"Yes, but I should probably leave the good stuff for your mom—as if I could keep still. Half an hour ago, she made you a big sister twice over. Drew Campbell put in the first appearance at four pounds, four ounces. Zoe followed two minutes later. She's four pounds, one ounce."

"Gosh, that's tiny. Is she okay? And how's Mom?"

"Zoe's a bit depressed. They have both babies in isolettes in neonatal ICU. Not uncommon for twins born early, we're told. Emily's in recovery. Camp's pacing the hall right outside her unit, as you might guess. Ah, Megan, just so you know, Em has to remain hospitalized for several days. Apparently the worst concern attached to eclampsia is risk of seizures. They'll keep her to monitor her blood pressure."

"Has she had a seizure? No? Thank God! Wait, someone's calling me. Aunt Sherry, it's Grandpa Ben. You never said he was coming for us. I'll see you real soon. Bye." Clicking off, Megan ran straight into the arms of the stocky, gray-haired man who'd impatiently tried to get her attention. Tears streamed down her cheeks. But he didn't seem to mind her soaking his jacket.

Megan collected herself enough to introduce her husband-to-be and the others. The two men sized each other up and shook hands. When Tyler got all shy and buried his head in his dad's pant leg, Joel pried him away and swung him up on a skinny hip. "Come on, Ty, after your dad marries Megan, this dude Ben's gonna be your grandpapa."

Ben saw right through the brash boy. "Son," he said, "everyone calls me Grandpa Ben. Same goes for you, if you'd like. I understand you're hankering to be a Coast Guard officer like our Megan."

"I don't know about an officer," Joel admitted with a modest dip of his head. "Megan thinks I have what it takes, but I sneaked a peek at her books from the academy. They look awfully hard."

"Well, it's nothing you'll have to decide for a while. I'll tell you a secret about this family. They make a lot of noise about planning the future. Me, I believe it's better to aim for a job that offers good health and life insurance. A man keeps his eye on that ball, everything else falls into place. In my opinion, the Coast Guard fits the bill."

Megan, walking between Ben and Sterling, laughed for the first time that day. "Spoken like a former insurance broker. Joel, he's teasing."

"True," Ben said, directing them to put their bags in the back of a new Cadillac Escalade. "But I only tease folks I like."

That set the tone for relaxed chatter on the drive to the hospital. "I passed Keith on the road. He has the other weary travelers in tow," Ben said. "My last instructions from Nan are to bring you straight to the waiting room. She's the real boss," he admitted with a wink at the boys.

"Have you seen the twins?" Megan asked.

"Nope, but Nan tells me they've got the Campbell iron jaw, combined with carrot-red frizz on their heads. Fitting for Clan Campbell I'd say."

Time passed swiftly, and finding parking was no problem. Megan wasn't surprised to see that the entire waiting room had been usurped by their family. The Lock kids were jumbled in a corner playing cards. Tim, Gavin and Shannon, good kids all, welcomed Joel and

Tyler like long-lost relatives. Once they were occupied, Megan and Sterling were able to trek down the hall to the nursery to have a look at the babies. Mark, Lauren and Mona had already had a turn.

Megan cried, they were so tiny, perfect and gorgeous in their knitted caps. Sterling held her for the longest time and dropped kisses on her head. "I can barely remember Tyler being that size. I'm looking forward to another baby. A daughter, I hope," he murmured, sharing an extremely private moment with Megan.

They only took their eyes off the isolettes when the door opened and someone clomped down the hall.

"Camp!" Megan dragged Sterling toward the rumpled man.

"I'm sure there ought to be some fatherly demands I should make of you, Sterling. For the life of me, I can't think of anything to say, except that if you choose a mate wisely, happiness surely follows. Megan, the doctor won't let anyone but me see Emily until tomorrow. But she'll rest a whole lot easier once I report that I've hugged you, met your intended, and you're both safe and sound. I can't begin to tell you how much it means to have you drop everything to come and visit. My mom and Sherry are in charge of finding everyone beds. I know that having you here will speed your mom's recovery."

And he was right. Dr. Gregory released Emily and baby Drew at the end of three days. Zoe had to stay in as her weight had fallen below four pounds. The pediatrician said she was a fighter, though, and he encouraged Camp and Emily to visit often, which of course they and the whole family did. Zoe undoubtedly felt their love and started to thrive.

Megan hugged her mom gently when she went to visit her at the house, a few hours after Emily's return home. "Mom, you're gorgeous. The twins are beautiful," she said, peeking in on Drew, gurgling in his bassinet. "I trust Camp told you we're sticking around until Zoe comes home before we take off for Michigan?"

"Nonsense, you'll stay your full thirty days. Gram Benton talked with me this morning about juggling plans at the church. The pastor has verified that the sanctuary is free the night before Halloween. That gives us a week to get Zoey home and prepare for a wedding and several rededications. Did you know Halloween is Scottish in origin? Could there be a more appropriate time to christen a pair of brand-new Campbells? Two little Campbells who, I predict, will be every bit the mischief-makers their older siblings were."

"Won't all the added hustle and bustle overtax you?" Megan asked worriedly.

"You and Mark have turned into such thoughtful adults. He offered to rent me a wheelchair. But the doctor wants me to walk. The more I can manage, the better. You appear happier than I've ever seen you, Megan. I haven't had much time to get to know your future husband, but I like what I see. I've glimpsed the boys in the distance, playing out in the yard with Sherry's three."

Megan sank to her knees and laid her head on Emily's lap, the way she had when she was young, although she was careful of her mother's recent surgery. "Mom, thanks to my hardheaded attitude, I almost lost Sterling. It would've been the biggest mistake of my life. I want what you've found with Camp. I believe with all my heart that somebody who knew exactly what I needed arranged for Sterling to move in downstairs."

"I wouldn't be one to dispute the role of fate. I've tried manipulating lives. You'll be pleased to hear I'm not so much of a Missouri mule that I can't admit to being wrong when it came to trying to choose Mark's career. Maybe I can attribute my actions to off-kilter hormones. He does have talent, and seems to have found his niche. And he and Lauren get along well. We'll see what they do in the future. I'll feel truly blessed if you both find happiness."

Megan held those thoughts close throughout the flurry of activity over the ensuing week. Angel, the Hub's longtime secretary, popped in one day in the middle of utter chaos. "I know a good wedding planner," she said as she waded through the clutter to lay a friend's business card in the middle of a kitchen table piled high with net, rice, satin ribbons and various sundries.

To get to the stove where Megan brewed hot chocolate, Nan steeped herbal tea and Sherry prepared gourmet coffee, Angel trekked through ankle-deep silk flowers. The house pulsed with laughter and love.

The true miracle, they all agreed at a wedding pulled together by Angel's friend, was that a day so many people had been involved in was such a complete success.

Lauren looked radiant as Megan's maid of honor. Sherry's daughter, Shannon, dropped rose petals on a white runner. Mark snapped photos, happy to let Joel serve as Sterling's best man.

Tyler, in his first suit, wandered down the aisle, twice dropping the pillow that held his dad's and Megan's rings.

Keith Lock, dressed in a dark suit that emphasized his height and blond good looks, probably had the hearts of several young ladies in the audience tripping. He had eyes for only one petite black-haired girl who shared his deep love of animals.

If people whispered when Megan appeared in the sanctuary door on Camp's arm, wearing her crisp white uniform, it was merely to note how handsome her soon-to-be husband was with his captain's epaulets on naval blue and plenty of shiny brass buttons.

Zoe and Drew, tucked in a fancy double carriage, slept throughout the ceremony under lavish blankets crocheted by Mona Benton and Nan Campbell. Not one among the Campbell-Lock-Benton-Dodge-Atwater group objected to the fact that the babies stole the show. Everyone knew they were the real stars of a private family reception, especially when Mark passed around a series of pictures he'd snapped of otherwise sane people crowding around the infants, cooing and clucking like happy idiots.

"Maybe we all set out with different agendas," Megan murmured, smiling at the photographs before stepping back into the waiting arms of her new husband. "All I see is one diverse and very contented family."

Camp stood and toasted his wife, their babies and the extended family with a steaming mug of Emily's Hot Chocolate, lovingly prepared by Megan. "To this circle of love," he said in a choked voice. "I propose that we make this a yearly gathering. Same time, same place one year from now."

"Hear, hear," they all responded. Megan Benton-

Dodge, new wife, new stepmom, new sister-in-law and new sister twice over, felt peace descend.

"We'll make mistakes with our kids in the years to come, I'm sure," she said, smiling at Sterling. "But everything here tonight is what family's all about."

"I owe it all to Tyler's clamoring for your hot chocolate," Sterling said, kissing her through steam rising from delicate mugs that were a special wedding gift from Gram Benton. A family heirloom. There was no question they'd be put to good use.

Maybe at future weddings…

Everything you love about romance...
and more!

Please turn the page for Signature Select™ Bonus Features.

Hot Chocolate on a Cold Day

BONUS FEATURES INSIDE

4 Recipes:

Emily's Hot Chocolate

Megan's Peanut Butter Cookies

Snickerdoodles

7 Travel Tale by Roz Denny Fox

13 A Coast Guard Career

32 Sneak Peek: *Angels of the Big Sky* by Roz Denny Fox

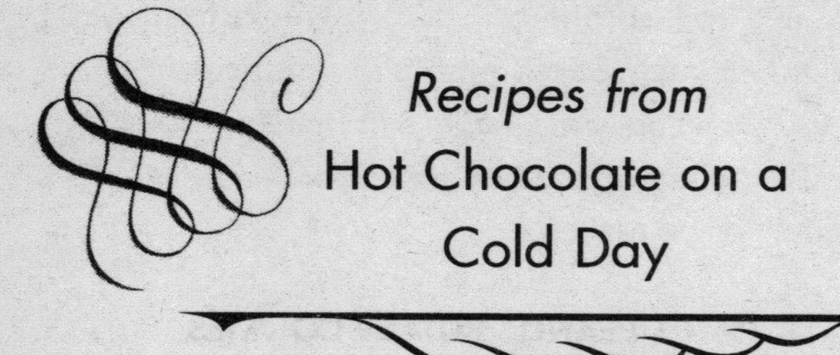

Recipes from Hot Chocolate on a Cold Day

Enjoy these recipes from Hot Chocolate on a Cold Day.

Emily's Hot Chocolate is a particular favorite of her daughter's, Megan Benton. Megan's two cookie recipes are popular with everyone—especially kids!

EMILY'S HOT CHOCOLATE

2 tbsp unsweetened cocoa
1/4 tsp salt
1 cup water
3 cups milk
8 tsp sugar
1 tsp vanilla

Combine cocoa and salt in small saucepan. Add water and warm over low heat or in top of double boiler. Boil gently, stirring constantly, approximately 2 minutes. Add milk and sugar (may use sugar substitute such as Splenda).

Bring to a boil, stirring constantly; remove from heat immediately. Stir in vanilla. Pour into 4 cups and top each cup with 2 large, soft marshmallows. May use cinnamon stick or peppermint stick as swizzle. Recipe makes 4 cups.

MEGAN'S PEANUT BUTTER COOKIES

Mix thoroughly:

1/2 cup soft shortening
1/2 cup butter
1/2 cup peanut butter (creamy)
1/2 cup sugar
1/2 cup packed brown sugar

Sift together and stir in:

1 1/4 cup sifted flour
1/2 tsp baking powder
3/4 tsp soda
1/4 tsp salt

Chill dough two or three hours (cover bowl). Roll in balls the size of a large walnut. Place 3 inches apart on ungreased cookie sheet. Flatten with fork tines dipped in flour (crisscross). Bake at 375°F for 10–12 minutes—until set, but not hard. Makes 3 dozen 2-1/2 inch cookies.

SNICKERDOODLES

Mix thoroughly:

1/2 cup soft shortening
1/2 cup butter
1 1/2 cups sugar
2 large eggs

Sift together and stir in:

2 3/4 cups sifted flour
2 tsp cream of tartar
1 tsp soda
1/4 tsp salt

Roll into walnut-sized balls.
Roll balls in mixture of:

2 tsp sugar
2 tsp cinnamon

Place 2 inches apart on ungreased cookie sheet. Bake at 400°F for 8–10 minutes—until lightly brown, but still soft. (Cookies will puff up, then flatten out.) Makes 5 dozen 2 inch cookies.

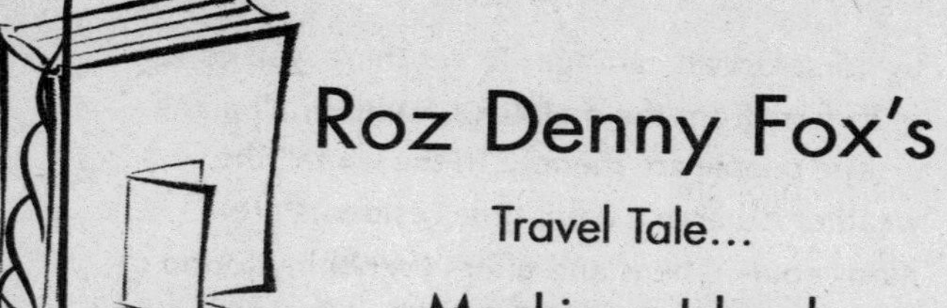

Roz Denny Fox's

Travel Tale...

Mackinac Island and Michigan's Upper Peninsula

If you've never visited Mackinac Island situated off the Michigan coast, you need to go. Be warned that if you're one who craves marathon shopping, touristy glamour or nightclub entertainment, you won't find it there. The island is peaceful, quaint and cooler than a lot of places during the heat of summer.

Set in Lake Huron, the turtle-shaped island is a woodsy setting plunked in the middle of blue sky and bluer water. It used to be *the* summering spot for the upper crust seeking refuge from the sizzling concrete parkways of Chicago and Detroit. The island's tourist season once ran from July 4 to Labor Day. Now nature seekers, romantics and others have discovered this hideaway and are stretching the season.

It's actually difficult to describe what life is like on the island. You feel as though you're stepping back in time, since the only travel is by horse-drawn carriage. To get there, you come in by ferry from the mainland, or by small plane.

The people are friendly. In the winter, the weather is harsh, so full-time residents are hardy souls. The island offers everything found in any town or city, but during winter life slows down. Winter transportation is either on foot or snowmobile. There's a wonderful school for children of full-time residents.

Fudge is Mackinac Island's main export. Yes, the gooey, yummy candy. In more flavors than you can imagine. And since you can smell it cooking from miles out if the wind is right, I'd be willing to say it's impossible to spend even a day on the island without sampling a variety.

You'll want to pack for all kinds of weather. Mackinac is near the Upper Peninsula of Michigan—the so-called north country. As I've mentioned, nights are cool even in the summer. And hot, humid days in the lower part of the state can shroud the island in thick, white fog.

You'll find parks with trails for hiking or biking, or horseback riding. Keep in mind that a circle trip of the island isn't for sissies. There are hills and woods—and year-round residents sometimes walk across the water on an ice bridge.

Depending on the time of year you go, you may see a yacht race, a horse show or the Lilac Festival.

Have I already mentioned it's peaceful? I'm sure I have. But that's one of the biggest attractions for city-weary vacationers. If you love looking at old historic homes, the island boasts a number. Many with spectacular waterfront views. The Grand Hotel is...well, grand. It gives you a sense of how the landed gentry were pampered and treated.

You might not expect to find forts and battlefields on so small an island. But it once served as a fur-trading village. Fort Michilimackinac is where the island got its name. Be prepared to hear reveille at 9:00 a.m.

History afficionados will enjoy digging into the rich military, Native American and fur-trading lore that's such a big part of the texture of island life.

There are two lighthouses visible from the island. One is the original built in 1895, and has a light-keeper's apartment. If I recall correctly, the lighthouse was manned for something like fifty-two years. I love lighthouses. When we travel, if there's one listed in the travel guide, I always want to visit it. It's fascinating to think that people worked, slept and ate in those structures, so often in virtual isolation. The many lighthouses in the Great Lakes indicate the grave danger of these waterways.

If you're a movie buff, you'll be interested to know that *Somewhere in Time,* starring the late Christopher Reeve and Jane Seymour, was filmed on Mackinac Island. An earlier movie was shot there, as well, a 1947 picture starring Esther Williams and Jimmy Durante.

I feel I've barely hit the highlights, but I don't want to give away everything the island has to offer vacationers and would-be explorers. The state of Michigan, bordered by Lakes Erie, Huron, Michigan and Superior, is divided into upper and lower peninsulas, which are separated by the Straits of Mackinac. The strait is spanned by the world's longest suspension bridge. When you're driving from the lower peninsula to the upper peninsula, the island of Mackinac, which sits between the two, is just one of the interesting, beautiful and relaxing places to visit. I guarantee if you go there, you'll see why I was moved to make it the home for my characters.

The two parts of Michigan differ in geography. The Upper Peninsula is more hilly, rugged and more forested. It's less populated than the lower peninsula, which has marshlands and gently rolling hills that are more conducive to farming and industry.

Because of its beautiful waterways and abundance of natural resources, Michigan has an abundance of recreational opportunities. The state is very attractive to vacationers, from bird-watchers, to golfers, to boaters and sport fishermen.

If you happen to be driving to the northern beaches, I can recommend a few side trips worth your time. Grand Haven, Grand Rapids and Holland are midsized cities with a lot of interesting features. For instance, Grand Haven has a two-and-a-half-mile boardwalk that follows a picturesque waterfront. There's a busy marina, and shops and eateries along the way, as well as scenic parks.

There's also a waterfront stadium with seating for approximately 2500 people. It was built for viewing the "World's Largest Musical Fountain," which can be seen nightly during the summer.

Grand Haven is home to a large Coast Guard station. Escanaba Park is named after the Coast Guard cutter that sank during World War II. The vessel's mast is a focal point for the park.

During summer months, you can also book boat tours and/or a sunset dinner cruise aboard a schooner. You'd be hard-pressed to visit at a time this city *doesn't* have something going on, be it a kite festival, a sailboat race, Big Band dances, the Coast Guard Festival, featuring five- and ten-kilometer runs, or harbor tours. It's a great vacation spot for families.

Holland was settled, as you might guess, by Dutch immigrants. The millions of blooming tulips during the spring season transform this town. There are self-guided tours through the Dutch Village with its winding canals, gardens, windmills and shops where you can see authentic crafts. If you've ever wondered how wooden shoes are made, or delftware, this is the place to see demonstrations up close. If you can't afford a trip to Europe, this will certainly give you a flavor of what you might see in some places in the Netherlands.

Grand Rapids, Michigan, was also settled by Dutch immigrants. A must-see is the 125-acre Frederik Meijer Gardens and sculpture park on land donated by the Meijer family. You'll need to allow plenty of time to explore the seasonal displays and the more than 100 bronze sculptures dotted about the enchanting park. As well as permanent exhibits, there are special traveling art exhibits. The entire park is a restful oasis, and if you're staying more than a day in the area, be sure to check out special events that may be held in the park.

In case you can't tell, Michigan—and especially Mackinac Island—is definitely on my agenda for a return visit.

A Coast Guard Career

A question I'm often asked by readers is "How did you decide you wanted to write books?" I'm not sure there's ever one single thing that launches a career. I know I've always loved to read. I enjoyed English classes in school. Originally I thought I'd like to be a reporter. Instead, I married a Marine and put my career paths on hold to raise a family. During the early years I had some interested jobs as we moved about the country. I saw great places and met interesting people.

The truth is, I began writing because characters showed up in my dreams. They interfered with my sleep and constantly said, "Do something with me. Tell my story."

I began to wonder if I *could* tell a story anyone would want to read. I found I liked researching characters, settings and careers. And it allowed me to indulge my passion for wandering about the U.S. I now have a legitimate purpose—to find the perfect situation for my story people. And I definitely prefer to scatter facts throughout my fiction.

It's exciting when the pieces all fall neatly together and a story begins to unfold bit by bit as it did with *Hot Chocolate on a Cold Day.* The heroine of this book came from a previous story I wrote. In that book, Megan Benton was a rebellious teen. Now she's all grown up. At fourteen she underwent a life-altering experience. On a summer outing with her mother, brother and several others, Megan fell over a cliff. Her ordeal in the first book resulted in a daring rescue by the man who later became her stepfather. Nolan Campbell saved Megan's life, but in doing so he fell farther into the canyon, which necessitated calling in a professional search-and-rescue team. (Find her story in the March 2006 Signature Miniseries, *Coffee in the Morning.*)

I thought Megan's experience was significant enough to change her life and set her on a course toward becoming a rescuer herself.

I discovered that the majority of sea and mountain rescues are the responsibility of the U.S. Coast Guard. So that's the career I chose for Megan.

Silly me! I live in the Southwest desert. Fortunately, I have family in Michigan. Someone happened to mention that Grand Haven, Michigan, has the distinction of being known as

Coast Guard City, U.S.A. That sounded promising—and intriguing. So, I left home armed with a scant few facts about the Coast Guard that I'd pulled from the Internet.

Although their group is the smallest of our nation's five armed services, the Coast Guard is extremely diverse and multi-missioned, while standing ready to guard America's interests at land, at sea or in the air.

The trip to Grand Haven netted me plenty of material about the *guardians of the eighth sea.* They're the men and women who patrol, and keep safe, our Great Lakes region. They have an immense responsibility. The Ninth Coast Guard District often encompasses approximately 5,400 miles of shoreline of often frigid water, where rescue and other important work is done.

I came home with a small suitcase filled with books and pamphlets. My head reeled as I attempted to absorb as much information as I could about our sea guardians, plus retain facts on interesting local lore.

The guardsmen at the station office went out of their way to be helpful. These men and women possess astounding facts and figures, which the rattled off without apparent research. Things like...in an average year the Coast Guard keeps three billion dollars worth of drugs off the U.S. streets. They undertake more than sixty-five thousand search-and-rescue missions a year.

Drowning is the second leading cause of injury-related death among children, so every spring, when a family's thoughts turn to camping, boating or fishing, the Coast Guard is on hand to distribute safety literature—and to pull accident victims from rivers and oceans. Another service they provide is addressing school students and hosting youth water-safety classes.

One and all, Coast Guard members are stewards for our environment. They work closely with local authorities to contain hazardous chemical spills and enforce regulations of fisheries. They rescue victims, both human and animal, of natural disasters such as floods and hurricanes. At critical times, they're called upon to deliver food, water and medicine to those in need.

The men and women housed at substations along the Upper Peninsula are well versed in specifics pertaining to the rigors of working in the cold waters of the upper Great Lakes region. Icebreakers keep shipping lanes open during the coldest (subzero) winters. In one shipping season, they may assist with as many as 100 shipwrecks in the various Great Lakes. Storms can blow up in this region at any time throughout the year; the severity of the storms isn't determined by season, either. These outposts are not duty stations for anyone who is less than adventurous. After my visit to Grand Haven, I came away happy with the life I gave Megan

Benton. She is a tough, feisty young woman who loves her job.

I also came away with great admiration for the work done by the brave men and women responsible for keeping our waterways safe.

For the bonus feature in this book, my editor asked if I could include and interview with a person or persons who served in the Coast Guard. Since everyone in Grand Haven had been so helpful, I didn't expect the assignment to be difficult.

As I began making calls to request interviews, it became clear that while they love their jobs, they're also a modest bunch. But I'm nothing if not persistent. I made a lot of phone calls and sent follow-up e-mails, and asked everyone I met if they knew anyone in the Coast Guard. The sister of a fellow writer gave me the number of Bill Bulman. I explained what I hoped to do and touched briefly on my story. For the interviews, I'd compiled a list of questions, some pertaining to general Coast Guard duty, and some regarding life in the Coast Guard Academy. Bill laughed and said, off the record, that officers always get all the glory, and the enlisted guys and gals do all the work. However, he kindly agreed to e-mail me a paragraph or two on how he became interested in the Coast Guard. As well, I asked if he had any advice for readers who might be looking for a new career.

Chief Boatswain's Mate, William E. Bulman is currently stationed in California and is a recruiter. The following are his comments and not the official opinions of the U.S. Coast Guard. Nor is he endorsing my book.

"From the age of ten or twelve, I watched the TV program *Emergency* and thought it was a cool job because it was exciting and they helped people. The show starred two Los Angeles fire department paramedics. I thought that had to be the ultimate job and was sure that's what I wanted to do.

"One day when I was at Jones Beach in New York with my family, a Coast Guard helicopter flew over. My dad told me they had paramedics on board Coast Guard helicopters.

"I'd been sure I knew the ultimate job, but now I'd found something even better. My father went to a recruiting office shortly after that and picked up brochures, which I read and reread.

"The years went by. At eighteen I joined the local volunteer fire department and went to emergency medical technician school through them. I took a job working on private ambulances, and I attended community colleges.

"One day, I found myself talking to an older neighbor about my future. I mentioned that I wasn't thrilled with my current situation. He asked me what careers did I think about when I was growing up, and for the first time in years I talked again about the Coast Guard. As we talked, I became more and more excited. Shortly thereafter, I visited a recruiter and have not looked back for twenty-two years. I'm happy to stay as long as the Coast Guard lets me. And hopefully it will be for a good long time.

"Reasons I can come up with for urging others to join the Coast Guard are varied, as people are different. Some might be looking for excitement, such as law enforcement (drug interdiction, enforcing fishing laws and preventing illegal immigration). The Coast Guard does those things. Another exciting category is Search and Rescue (SAR). There is just no better feeling than saving a human life. I am still proud of some rescues that occurred twenty years ago." (Bill modestly admitted to having received commendations for some of those rescues. But I had the distinct impression that commendations aren't what he is about—it's the job and the saving of lives.)

"A more practical reason to think of the Coast Guard as a career is that it's a good, solid job. For a young person, a recent high school graduate or maybe someone newly married, it's a steady job. And one that will teach new skills while offering some of the best benefits available in the current job market. Benefits include medical and dental for you and your family. Thirty days vacation the first year and every year thereafter, money for continuing education, and among other benefits, a pension that you do not pay into."

As Chief Boatswain's Mate Bulman said, the jobs and people in the Coast Guard are many and varied.

When I spoke with PA1 Jacquelyn Zettles, she was helping to publish the *Coast Guard* magazine from her office in Washington, D.C. She was charming to talk to, and the information she e-mailed me about her history in the Coast Guard left me envious of all her travel. It also left me wishing I'd met her before I wrote the book. I must add a disclaimer here: my story is fiction and no part came about as a result of any interviews in this section. Jacquelyn's story is as follows:

"When I joined the Coast Guard eight years ago, there was no way for me to anticipate the places I would go, the things I would experience, and the best friends I would make along the way. All I knew at a naïve twenty years old was that I wanted a bigger life than what I would find in Norristown, Pennsylvania.

"After boot camp, I was stationed in Sturgeon Bay, Wisconsin, on the Coast Guard cutter *Mobile Bay*—an icebeaking buoy tender. I spent the summer months renovating lighthouses in the Great Lakes and training as a helmsman, shipboard fire fighter and deckhand. Shipboard life was difficult, but the long hours of standing watch and training gave way to peaceful nights steaming across the Great Lakes. My tour there was cut short, however, after my dad died from cancer. I was transferred to Philadelphia where I worked on the Delaware River as a small-boat crewman doing search and rescue.

"As a young woman, this is the place where I experienced the greatest growing pains. I trained and qualified as a crewman, learning the skills needed for search and rescue. I learned how to navigate the river, drive the rescue boats, retrieve victims from the water and perform basic lifesaving skills. And over time, my coworkers came to be like my brothers. I have learned there is a unique bond that develops when people train so intensely together and become dependent on one another. To this day I remain closely bonded with a number of my former crew.

"After a year and a half in Philadelphia, I was sent to public affairs school. My first unit as a Coast Guard PA was at the district office in Honolulu, Hawaii. I had the privilege of covering stories on a few of the islands in the Hawaiian chain, including Molokai. This is the location of one of the few remaining leper colonies in the world. The Coast Guard maintains a lighthouse on the Molokai peninsula, which can only be reached by air or boat. The lamp inside the lighthouse needed to be replaced and I was going to write a story about the aids-to-navigation team that performed the maintenance. I flew to the peninsula on a Coast Guard helicopter and followed the ATON team to the top of the lighthouse, learning about their jobs, and photographing them in action. We were given a tour of the peninsula and learned about the tragic history of those still living with leprosy on the island. So few people, yet we were afforded such an intimate look at Molokai, and I realized when I was there that I was living the dream I had of wanting a bigger life.

"I left Hawaii for my current unit at the Coast Guard Headquarters in Washington, D.C., which has been just as rewarding as each of my past units. Here, I participated in historic events like the 2005 presidential inauguration and President Reagan's funeral. I also shot a photo during Coast Guard Missions Day, which later appeared in an issue of *National Geographic.*

Both personally and professionally, the Coast Guard has afforded me opportunities that I would have never otherwise been given had I stayed in Norristown all those years ago. I'm grateful to the mentors and friends who have supported me through the journey and made each adventure possible."

(Jacquelyn told me she's soon headed toward yet another dream. She's embarking on a quest to complete her master's in theology, and may become a Coast Guard chaplain. A rewarding occupation indeed).

Another of my contacts retired from the Coast Guard some fifteen years ago. Off the record, he provided this information. When he served in the U.S. Coast Guard, they operated under the Department of Treasury and Department of Transportation, not the Department of Homeland Security as they currently do. He said duties remain the same now as then. "The Guard has always had the responsibility of protecting our maritime ports. In fact, they're the premier protector and were even before we had need of a Department of Homeland Security."

According to his wife, when it came to my number-one question of what drew him to the Coast Guard, his reason for joining was the humanitarian aspects of this branch of the military. The saving of lives and property at sea was and still is appealing to this retiree, who is currently a commercial fisherman. She said he feels the Coast Guard plays a key role in supporting humanitarian efforts in American and international waters.

I'd asked a general question about whether or not he considered the job dangerous. He said the Coast Guard prepares for wartime missions under the Navy and when directed by the president. The mission of *saving* lives is paramount. He added that the Coast Guard is the *only* military service with law-enforcement responsibilities.

Because my main character is female and an officer, I asked whether training or expectations for women differ from those of men. Again, off the record, he said all branches of military are regimentally organized to recognize and respect authority in its enlisted ranks, as well as officer corps. Men and women operate under the same guidelines in all branches of the services.

As a former officer, he filled me in on a bit of the Coast Guard history. On August 4, 1790, President Washington signed the act authorizing ten revenue cutters. The Lighthouse Service was established on August 7, 1789. A greater emphasis was placed on Coast Guard Search and Rescue in 1912 with the sinking of the *Titanic.* It was in 1915 that the above-mentioned units merged to become what is today known as the U.S. Coast Guard. At that time, the government established ocean stations manned by cutters. They mostly provided weather reports and performed emergency rescues when required by ships and aircraft.

He recalled that it was in 1940 during World War II that the Coast Guard first allowed women to serve as SPARS, basically limited to medical and administrative duties.

I did some digging and learned the female members of the Coast Guard were organized by a captain in the WAVES. The captain chose SPARS, an acronym for the service slogan Semper

Paratus (always ready), to identify Coast Guard woman. In the early 1960s, women began to serve without restrictions on specialties. At that time, a limited number of women were assigned sea duty billets or units that could accommodate their privacy needs. Now there are no distinctions between men and women serving in the U.S. Coast Guard. The criteria for acceptance into the Coast Guard Academy in New London, Connecticut, is exactly the same for both.

In a casual conversation with Jacquelyn Zettles PA1, in which we spoke specifically about women in the Coast Guard, she mentioned that in rescues involving women or children, or even men who suffer extreme duress, it's not uncommon for the victims to gravitate toward a female rescuer, perhaps because women are perceived as nurturers.

It's my personal opinion that it would be a great career for anyone. For someone between the ages of seventeen and twenty-seven (which are the basic age requirements, although at seventeen, entry requires parental consent), this career seems very appealing. It certainly would have appealed to me.

The Coast Guard offers a steady income, a chance for advancement, paid vacation, life insurance and medical care, plus specialized training, and above all, adventure. Approximately 35,000 active duty members and around 8,000 reservists obviously feel that way. On an average day, they may board and check ninety large vessels for safety. Or process 120 seaman's documents. Seize hundreds of pounds of marijuana or cocaine, worth millions. Conduct more than a hundred law-enforcement boardings. Investigate around twenty marine accidents. Inspect sixty or so commercial vessels. Every day, they assist over 300 people in distress. Their teams save millions in property, and interdict in numerous illegal attempts at entry. Most of these areas are vital to the security of the United States.

The U.S. Coast Guard employs doctors, lawyers, dentists, engineers and accountants, as well as seamen and pilots. They serve proudly and with distinction. While the Coast Guard Academy is the only federal service academy that does not require a political nomination or appointment, standards are very high and training is demanding, both physical and academically.

I'm glad they strive for such a high degree of excellence. These are the people who help keep the rest of us safe.

I feel fortunate to have found a second retired guardsman, who first said he'd been out of the Coast Guard too long to answer questions. Ultimately I wore him down. Chief Warrant Officer (CWO4) Giles M. Vanderhoof, USCG (retired), began by answering my last question: If offered the opportunity to give an overview of his experience in the Coast Guard, what would he tell anyone considering the Coast Guard as a career?

"I enlisted in the U.S. Coast Guard in September 1949 as a seaman recruit and served continuously for thirty years, the first fifteen as enlisted boatswain's mate and the second as a chief warrant officer. I served on various lifeboat stations on both the East and West Coasts, buoy tenders in Oregon and Hawaii, an icebreaker in Alaska and the relieve lightship out of Staten Island, New York. I married and we raised three wonderful children, sons Mark and Steven, and daughter Jani. During my thirty-year career I never had an assignment I didn't like!"

I then inquired as to whether or not he was instrumental in saving lives of anyone who otherwise would not be alive today.

He modestly admits to a rescue of the *Lady Fran* and crew consisting of the father, two sons in their early twenties and a hired deckhand, who later joined the Coast Guard. "The *Lady Fran* was a newer all-aluminum ninety-foot crab-fishing boat, which succumbed to the rigors of a screaming southwest storm."

I asked if any of his children had followed in his footsteps. His reply: "None of my children chose the Coast Guard as a career, but my one and only granddaughter was accepted to attend the Coast Guard Academy. She chose to continue with her college training in the medical field.

Several of my nephews did join the Coast Guard and one is now a SW04 electrician and will reach his thirty-year service in one year."

Giles very kindly sent me a packet of information encapsulating his career and copies of his commendations.

He enjoyed fifteen years of command experience consisting of operation, administration, financial and personnel management.

For twenty-three of the thirty years, Giles served on four oceangoing buoy tenders, where duties covered complete maintenance of ship's hull, interior compartments, all buoy hoisting and handling gear, including forty-ton boom cranes.

In 1968 he was overseer for construction of the Coast Guard's Motor Lifeboat Training School. There he set up the curriculum and was in charge of the school for its first year of operation. The school provided in-depth cross-training for boat coxswains, boatswain's mates and others. Its goal is to decrease loss of life and property along both U.S. coastlines. For his contribution he was awarded the Coast Guard Achievement Medal. The school is still in operation and still uses the curriculum that he established.

For his assignment in charge of Gray's Harbor Station in Westport, Washington, he was awarded the U.S. Navy League's Captain David H. Jarvis Award for Inspirational Leadership and Professional Competence. In 1963 he received a letter of commendation for outstanding performance of duty. And in 1979 he received the Coast Guard Meritorious Unit Commendation.

During his last assignment with Group Astoria in Oregon, he assisted in coordinating the efforts of 325 people in search-and-rescue operations, enforcement of laws and treaties, pollution control of marine environment and the training of some 165 persons assigned to our coastal lifesaving stations.

Over his last twenty years of service he held security clearance up to and including top secret. He was trained in federal law enforcement that covered mainly, but was not limited to, federal boat safety regulations, smuggling and narcotic enforcement, and enforcement of the 200-mile fish-management regulations. And he's licensed to operate or navigate passenger-carrying vessels.

In May 1979 he was instrumental in helping raise Coast Guard utility boat *41332* via a submarine salvage vessel, USS *Pigeon*. The utility boat had sunk in the middle of Oregon's Columbia River eighteen months before while on a navigational exercise. The *Pigeon*'s crew conducted an underwater search using a diving bell, and side-scan sonar. The salvage and recovery took ten days in very stormy conditions with high winds and large swells. At one point they thought they may have to abort the mission. (This is an abbreviated version of an historic incident in Coast Guard events.)

I want to thank Giles Vanderhoof for his willingness to provide so much of his personal information. Like previous interviewees he has not read my book.

I have to say that after completing all of my research, I wonder why we hear more about the other branches of the military (Army, Navy, Air Force and Marines). I was certainly impressed with everything I learned, and by the professionalism of all the people, both active duty and retired, with whom I had even minimal contact.

In addition to the active duty and reservists, approximately 35,000 field jobs are held by Coast Guard auxiliarists—volunteers. They receive specific training and provide support to the Coast Guard on inland waterways. They may also provide education in safety, and give assistance to millions of boat owners in more than 2000 cities across the nation.

Reservists spend an average of one weekend a month plus two weeks a year staying abreast of the most up-to-date training by working alongside active personnel. Reservists may be assigned to port security, or monitor cargo operations, or inspect vessels for safety violations or contraband. They will probably rescue distressed boaters, fight pollution or execute a host of other duties needed to keep navigational aids functioning properly.

Something else many may not be aware of is that the Coast Guard also employs civilians—

more than 6,000, who serve in about 200 different positions. Whether they attend the academy, or are enlisted, reservists or in the auxiliary or retired, these men and women of the U.S. Coast Guard share a deep and lasting esprit de corps.

To all my readers, I hope you enjoyed Megan's story, and have found this bonus feature informative. And the next time you see men or women wearing the Coast Guard uniform, wave, smile and thank them for the good work they do in protecting our coastline and waterways, and keeping them safe.

Angels of the Big Sky

by

Roz Denny Fox

Enjoy this dramatic and emotional story, the first book in Roz Denny Fox's new series,* CLOUD CHASERS. *It's available from Harlequin Superromance in September 2006.

CHAPTER 1

MARLEE STEIN TOPPED a ridge, leaving behind Whitepine, Montana, the town closest to where she'd been born and raised. She rolled down the driver's window, breathing in the autumn scent of the piney wilderness, and felt herself relax. Until then, she hadn't been aware of how tense she'd gotten on the long drive from San Diego.

Who was she kidding? She'd been riddled with tension for the past five years.

But now, on this lonely stretch of highway with nothing but fall sunlight sprinkling pine-needle patterns across her windshield, she began to shed the stress that had become so crushing.

She realized that the sense of heaviness and regret might always be with her. It was barely a year since she'd lost Cole to the ravages of lymphatic cancer. Too young. His life snuffed out at thirty-six. There was so much they hadn't done. One of the many things they'd talked about but never got around to was visiting this beautiful country Marlee loved.

They'd been introduced by mutual friends. Had dated for a whirlwind thirty days, married on base in a fever pitch driven by the demands of their jobs—she, a navy helicopter pilot on the verge of shipping out; he, an officer with an eye to one day commanding his own ship. It seemed a lifetime ago, those scant six years they'd shared. Or not shared, since much of it had been spent apart. But…so many dreams, all left in tatters. Widowed at thirty-four, Marlee was running home to hide.

No, to rebuild a shattered life—according to her twin brother, anyway.

Mick Callen, her twin, knew about rebuilding a life. A pilot, too, he'd been shot down over Afghanistan—what was it—four years ago? Mick had come home to Whitepine and forged a new life. On almost weekly basis during the past awful year, he'd insisted that Marlee could do the same. She wanted to believe him.

Averting her eyes from the ribbon of highway, she glanced in the rearview mirror of her packed-to-the-ceiling Ford Excursion. Jo Beth slept on. Without doubt their daughter was the most precious part of her too-brief marriage.

Maybe their lives could get back on track. Mick thought so, or he wouldn't have badgered his twin to join the family airfreight business, Cloud Chasers, originally started by their grandfather, Jack Callen.

Everybody called him Pappy. He'd taught her and Mick to fly anything with wings, and they'd developed a love affair with flying.

It seemed unreal that they'd both come full circle. Fate, maybe? In the days immediately following Cole's death, Marlee had thought about the circle of life, but Whitepine was the last place she'd envisioned herself ending up. Big plans, she'd discovered, were best left to starry-eyed innocents. Reality made its own claims. And to think she and Cole worried that her naval career presented a greater risk of death. She, who'd done two tours in the Gulf.

Releasing a sigh, she wiped a sweaty palm on her jeans. Really baggy jeans, she noticed, and grimaced. She'd lost weight—was down to 105 pounds. Skeletal, her lieutenant commander growled when he signed her discharge papers.

Mick would probably be shocked. Or not. He'd suffered through his own months of hell in military hospitals after he took a leg full of shrapnel and debris from his F/A-18, when a handheld surface-to-air missile blasted him out of the sky.

The Callen twins, who'd left Whitepine for the naval academy with grandiose ideas, had come full circle, all right.

A mile to go. Nervous, Marlee wasn't altogether sure what to expect. Three years ago, Mick had said he'd found Cloud Chasers in sad shape. Pappy Jack apparently suffered from arteriosclerotic heart disease, which caused bouts of dementia. It must be true, otherwise he'd never have let the business decline.

Through hard work, Mick said he'd enticed old customers back and added new accounts. He regularly groused about needing an extra pair of hands. Marlee hoped so. Because it was crucial to end her former mother-in-law's influence on Jo Beth. Rose Stein spoiled her and undermined Marlee's control. It had taken an unpleasant court skirmish to defeat her attempt at custody.

Dipping into the last valley, Marlee was finally home. The family holdings, house, business—the whole panorama was a welcome sight. The main log house and three smaller cabins added over the fifty years Pappy built Cloud Chasers.

Marlee battled tears as she saw the runway, still with that tacky windsock at the end. Home looked refreshingly the same. As did the metal hangar with its add-on maintenance bay and cubbyhole office—so small an area their mom used to complain about it daily when she answered phones and kept the books. Before Shane and Eve Callen were killed coming home one foggy night. At an unmarked train crossing out of Whitepine. Two more senseless deaths.

Marlee blinked rapidly and swung onto the gravel drive. Memories of the parents they'd lost when she and Mick were starting junior high threatened to overwhelm her; instead, she busied herself counting his planes. A single-engine Piper Arrow, and a newer turbo prop Piper Seneca, a sliver gleam in the last bay. The battered, refurbished Huey army helicopter she loved sat in the clearing between the smaller two cabins.

Marlee could fly every machine there. But she'd told Mick she wouldn't fly. As Jo Beth's sole guardian, she owed it to her daughter not to take any more risks. Her brother had expressed disappointment, but in the end he'd agreed that if she reduced his overflowing paperwork and helped ride herd on Pappy, who sometimes tended to wander, it'd be enough. A godsend, in fact. So here she was.

Her thoughts of Mick and Pappy Jack must have made them materialize—there they were, looking solid, and welcoming and, well—beautiful.

She jammed on the brakes and the Ford's tires skidded. Uncaring, Marlee jumped out, flinging her arms wide. She damned her tears, even as she felt them rain all over Mick's blue cotton shirt. Still tall and blond and muscular, her twin squeezed her hard. And when he let go, Pappy Jack did the same. At eighty-five, he was thinner than she remembered. His full head of hair was nearly white where it'd been nut-brown. Still the same, though, were his aquamarine eyes, a trait borne by all Callens. And his and hers shimmered with unshed tears.

All three began talking at once. They were abruptly stopped by a bellowing wail from inside the Excursion. Spinning, Marlee dashed to the open door. She tried unsuccessfully to quiet the sobs and coax five-year-old Jo Beth Stein out to meet her uncle and great-grandpa. "Hey, tiddly wink, I'm right here. It's okay, I haven't left you. Jo Beth, this is our new home. Come say hi to Uncle Mick, and to Pappy Jack. Remember I showed you pictures of them before we packed my albums?"

A little girl with a mop of brown curls and weepy hazel eyes hugged a soft-bodied doll in one arm as if her life depended on it. She scrubbed her cheeks with her free hand but didn't venture out of the SUV.

Marlee turned to the men. In an undertone she said, "Maybe if you went back inside to wait… I explained about her crying jags and temper tantrums, didn't I? They started after Cole died, and escalated throughout my tug-of-war with Rose. I'm hoping…" Marlee raked a hand through her tawny gold hair as her eyes begged her brother's understanding.

"No problem, sis. We'll take your luggage. Mrs. Gibson swabbed out the largest of the cabins for you. Or if you'd rather sleep in the main house until your furniture arrives, your old room's made up. It has twin beds if you want Jo Beth to share."

Marlee waved a hand toward the Ford. "What you see is our life in a nutshell."

Pappy peered in the windows of the SUV. "That old broad stole your house, furniture and everything?"

She corrected his misimpression. "Cole and I rented a furnished condo because we were rarely home. As soon as I got pregnant, we decided to buy a house." Marlee looked pained. "Pappy, it was during house-hunting that I noticed Cole seemed tired. Draggy. Finally, after weeks of tests, he was diagnosed."

She would have let it go, but her grandfather said, "So, where did Cole's mother get off trying to take your kid away from you?"

"Didn't Mick tell you? Right after Jo Beth was born and I went off desk duty, I got orders to ship out. That's when we let the apartment go and moved in with Rose. At the time we didn't know how else to manage, what with a new baby and Cole undergoing treatments. We…just, uh, counted on the treatments working." She sighed and fiddled with Jo Beth's cap of curls.

"Don't sweat it," Mick said, ruffling his shorter, sun-lightened hair on end. "The cabin has the basics. We can fill in as you figure out what's missing. If you open up the back, Pappy and I can haul in suitcases at least."

Nodding, Marlee retrieved her keys. “Maybe we’ll sleep in the house until Jo Beth gets more comfortable. Set the two small bags in my old room, okay? Everything else can go to the cabin.” She couldn’t help noticing Mick’s prominent limp even before he picked up two suitcases. That gave Marlee pause. He’d told her he was fine now.

It took the better part of forty minutes to convince Jo Beth that she needed to go inside.

“Sis, I have freight to pick up in Kalispell for an early-morning delivery,” Mick announced. “And I’ve got an appointment. I’ll be gone for a couple of hours. Settle in, or unpack. If you feel up to it after dinner, I’ll show you around the office. You can take over where I left off billing. I’m warning you, though, I haven’t filed in months.”

“Filing’s time-consuming nonsense,” Pappy snorted. “All you need to keep them IRS guys happy is a record of income versus out-go. Most years, the latter tops the former,” he said, sounding more savvy than her brother had led Marlee to believe.

“Frankly, Mick, I’m anxious to start. I want to earn my keep. I hope you don’t object to Jo Beth playing in the office while I work.”

“Why would I? Mom raised us out there until we were old enough to tag after Pappy.”

A smile blossomed, the first genuine smile she’d felt in weeks. But then she watched Mick walk toward the Piper Arrow. She wasn't wrong; he favored his left leg. Maybe his old injury was affected by weather. The ground here looked as if it'd rained not very long ago.

She took Jo Beth by the hand. "Pappy, while Mick's gone, I'll unpack a few boxes and suitcases and find storage spots in the cabin. I need to dig out Jo Beth's toys so she'll feel at home. Want to tag along?"

"Nope. I let myself get involved in one of those silly afternoon soaps. You and the little squeak just come on back to the house whenever the spirit moves you."

Marlee laughed. Pappy used to call her *little squeak*, too. Being here felt good. Natural. As though she hadn't grown up and been left to deal with grown-up matters. If anybody deserved to kick back in the afternoon and watch TV, it was Pappy. He'd worked from dawn to dusk for most of his life.

Already in a better frame of mind, Marlee struck out for the cabin. She'd forgotten the rustic charm of the knotty pine walls and cedar plank floors. Mick hadn't been kidding. The cabin was basic, all right, boasting only the bare essentials. But to tell the truth, she didn't want a lot of memories hanging around. It was better to leave the memories with Rose, who'd turned one room of her home into a shrine for her husband, and another for Cole.

Time passed as she unpacked. Before she knew it, two hours had disappeared. Now the cabin had a few touches making it hers and Jo Beth's. Collecting toys for her daughter, Marlee put them in a tote. Together, she and Jo Beth wandered back to the main house.

Pappy appeared to be engrossed in another program, so Marlee set Jo Beth up near the couch. She emptied the tote onto a worn braided rug.

"Do they have a dining room, Mama? I'm hungry," Jo Beth said suddenly.

"Me, too," growled Pappy Jack. "I hope you can cook, girl." Shutting off the TV, he leveled a hopeful glance at Marlee.

Since they'd come in, he'd been rocking contentedly in a scarred rocker Marlee knew had belonged to his dad. She remembered every square inch of this house, while Jo Beth had only ever lived in Rose Stein's decorator-designed show-home. What a contrast. "Pappy, I wish I could say I was a great cook. I picked up bits from my mother-in-law. Whenever I was at the house, it…just seemed easier to let her cook. It was her place. She knew where everything was."

"Maybe you shoulda brought her along. Mick says I put food on to cook, then go off and let everything burn. Hell, he's a fine one to talk. Half the time he gets to tinkering with engines and doesn't remember to eat."

Jo Beth looked up from arranging her of Polly Pocket hairdresser and fashion model sets. "Mama, that man said a bad word."

Marlee had Rose Stein to thank for Jo Beth's prissy attitude, too. The woman had been married to an admiral, but even before his passing she'd insisted the profanity prevalent among military personnel not invade her home. Cole rarely slipped up. Marlee often did and got taken to task by Rose. By Jo Beth, too, from the time she could talk.

Rather than take issue now, Marlee redirected the conversation to what she should fix for supper. Another difference for her daughter—in Rose's home they *dined.*

But she needed to shut off her mind. Preparing a meal seemed a good outlet. She found steak thawing in the refrigerator and fresh corn in the vegetable keeper. There were baking potatoes in a bin that had always been in the pantry. Just as she patted herself on the back for remembering, the wall phone rang.

"That's the business line," Pappy said, glancing up. "Mick says taking orders is gonna be your job. You might as well answer it and get your feet wet, twin."

Marlee reached for the receiver and smiled. Another thing Pappy used to do was call one of them by their given name, and the other *twin.* Sometimes he called them *boy* or *girl.* "Hello," she said, her voice reflecting the remnant of her smile. The caller mumbled that he must have dialed a wrong number.

"Wait—you've reached Cloud Chasers." She grabbed a pen and hunted for a pad. "Your name is Wylie Ames?" she repeated. Marlee's eyes sought Pappy's, but he was watching TV again. "I'm sorry to have to ask if you're an old account of Mick's or a new customer. Where is he? Oh, Mick's gone into Kalispell. I expect him back anytime. Who am I? His sister." She stopped short of adding *if it's any of your business.* Not a good idea to annoy a customer her first day on the job, but the man was curt to the point of rudeness.

Her smile turned to a frown when it became apparent the guy didn't trust her to deliver a message to Mick. Tersely, the caller said, "I have a generator on the fritz. The parts house in Kalispell promises to have my order ready for Mick by the middle of next week. Yes," he snapped, sounding even more ill-tempered when she asked if Mick knew where to deliver the goods. He clicked off without saying goodbye. Glaring at the receiver, Marlee banged it back into its cradle.

"Disagreeable jerk," she muttered just as her brother walked into the house, his limp more pronounced. There were fatigue lines around his mouth Marlee didn't recall seeing earlier.

"Who's disagreeable?" Mick asked, shrugging out

of a battered brown flyer's jacket. Marlee remembered fondly when he'd saved up money to buy it, or one just like it. "A customer by the name of Wylie Ames is disagreeable." She rattled off the reason for the man's call.

Mick took the message she'd scribbled on the corner of a brown grocery bag. "Wylie's a good guy. He's a forest ranger who lives year-round at a remote station in the Glacier Park perimeter. He's the only official presence in thirty square miles."

His twin made a wry face. "He could do with some manners." Turning, she slid the potatoes into the oven and began to shuck corn with an economy of motion.

Pappy had stirred when Mick entered. Stifling a yawn, he said, "You wanna steer clear of Ames, girl. Old-timers up-region say his wife of short duration vanished in the dead of night. Just like that." Pappy tried to snap gnarled fingers.

Looking up from peeling corn silk, Marlee's mouth sagged. "You mean people think he's—" She broke off and cast a worried frown toward her daughter.

Mick hobbled to the couch, sat and picked up one of Jo Beth's plastic dolls, turning it in his big hands. "Don't pay Pappy any mind," he said. "Those are crazy rumors, sis. You know how folks in the back country love to gossip. With each repeat, their bear stories get fiercer, and fish tales bigger. Wylie's a good man raising a son alone. Dean Ames is a couple of years older than Jo Beth. You said Wylie expects his stuff when? Next week?"

Her mind shifted from Pappy's warning. "Yes. Wednesday, he thinks, or Thursday. He said you could call the parts house if you don't hear from him by Thursday morning." She found the griddle for cooking steaks and plugged it in.

Pappy shifted until he faced Mick. "What did the doc have to say about your hip?"

Marlee's ears perked right up.

"Same old, same old, Pappy. Hey, isn't it good to see Marlee fixing us some decent food for a change?"

Pappy spiked a bushy brow. "Same old, how? You mean the bone doc still wants you in ASAP to replace that socket?"

"Mick? You need more surgery?" Alarmed, Marlee straightened and twisted the top button on her blouse.

Her brother pursed his lips. He took his sweet time arranging Jo Beth's doll in a tiny chair. He even clamped a bonnet hair dryer from the toy set over the doll's head.

"You mean the boy didn't tell you he's put off havin' that hip socket replaced nigh on four months now? When Rusty Meyer called to say he couldn't fill in and fly your freight runs, Mick, I thought you told him that was okay, 'cause Marlee was due in this week and she'd handle the route."

Mick's head shot up. He sent his grandfather a killer scowl. "Pappy, why do you forget what the hell day it is, and whether or not you took your blood-pressure medicine, yet you remember every frigging detail of my private business?"

Even as Jo Beth pointed out her uncle's bad word, Marlee presented him with her back while she slapped steaks on a grill beginning to glow red. "Mick…I…"

He broke in. "I know, you made it clear you didn't come here to fly. Josh Manley at the flying school in Kalispell has a student close to qualifying for solo. Unless the weather turns bad, he thinks the kid could manage our day runs. Of course, I'd have to notify Angel Fleet to take my name off the roster for mercy missions."

"They still operate here? Why don't people just use 911?"

"Oh, you city girl. Out here we volunteers for Angel Fleet *are* 911."

"I didn't know you flew sick, injured or dying people around, Mick. What else have you neglected to tell me?" Marlee spun suddenly, hands on hips.

"Cloud Chasers is the charter service best situated to lift needy folks out of the remote wilderness. Besides, most flights are tax-deductible."

"Doesn't Glacier Park keep search-and-rescue climbers on hand during the summers?

"Yes. They use small choppers. But since I've come home, I've noticed an increase in accidents. They mostly occur in fairly inaccessible bed-and-breakfast places, or fishing and hunting lodges. Tourists have discovered our area, Marlee."

"I know you said one outfit cleared trees and put in a vineyard. And another planted huge apple orchards. I suppose their workers might get hurt," she said unhappily. "I'm just not sure about all this growth…."

"Growth is good for Cloud Chasers. More lodges laying in food, liquor and such. Plus, I fly their customers in and out. I didn't think it'd be right to make money off tourists and not fly them to hospitals if they get hurt out there."

"I suppose not. Besides, you know firsthand how a quick rescue can spell the difference between life and death. Which brings us back to the surgery Pappy said you need." Marlee flipped the steaks. When Mick remained silent, she asked him again.

"Things aren't desperate yet," he said, heaving a sigh.

When Marlee glared at him, she noticed him rubbing his weary face with both hands. "Dammit, Mick, let's have the truth," she demanded, totally ignoring her daughter's hissy fit over her mom's swearing.

"The local sawbones says if I don't get the socket in my left hip replaced soon, it's gonna wear away the ball joint. Today I got a second opinion. Same report."

"Pain?" She didn't let up.

"Yeah. More all the time. I can't take anything except industrial strength, over-the-counter, anti-inflammatory meds and still fly. But it's my problem, twin, not yours. I've got my fingers crossed that Manley will pass that student. Our routes are straight up flying. As a rule," he added.

"I've seen some of those rinky-dink landing strips," she said dryly, dumping corn into boiling water. "Do you feel like setting the table?" she asked, changing the subject.

He climbed slowly to his feet. Marlee saw what it cost him to try and do that with panache. She said nothing else until they were all seated at the table, and Jo Beth had offered a simple prayer. Pappy alone dug into his meal.

"Out of curiosity, Mick, what timetable does the doctor give you for getting back in the saddle?"

"Eight to ten weeks. But I heal fast. I figure I can take the controls again in time to handle the heavy schedule heading into winter. Between more lodges, and rangers stocking up before the snow socks 'em in, I get busy. After November, calls are sporadic until spring thaw, except for an occasional emergency. And your military emergency training qualifies you to take any of those."

Marlee nibbled at a slice of steak. Jo Beth loved baked potatoes. She was making a healthy dent in the one Marlee had cut and buttered for her. Pappy devoured his food, tuning out their talk. In fact, Marlee heard him humming. It wasn't until he'd wolfed down everything on his plate, shoved it back and went outside without a word, that she revisited a previous topic. "Mick, I want to help. With a little refresher on fixed wing planes, I can fly your route. Even into the winter, if need be. For God's sake, I landed choppers on carriers in all kinds of weather. But two things. It's imperative that you agree to let me name you as Jo Beth's guardian should anything happen to me. It'll probably take a codicil on my current will. And after surgery, how do you propose to manage here if I'm on a flight? You'll be on painkillers at first. Jo Beth can't be allowed the freedom you apparently give Pappy."

"What would you say to taking her along? I mean, we flew with Pappy and Dad from the time we could crawl into the cockpit. Mrs. Gibson—Stella, a widow down the road—handles housekeeping for us. She can look in on me and Pappy. She often prepares us meals to pop in the oven."

"Taking Jo Beth wasn't something I'd considered. I'll have to think about that." Standing, she started stacking plates. Jo Beth had excused herself to play with her dolls. Marlee wondered if her daughter would like flying. Until Cole got really ill, on weekends Marlee would rent a light plane and fly him out over the ocean he loved.

They'd told Jo Beth what her mother did for the navy—fly. Marlee had planned to ask for discharge at the end of her first Gulf tour. But while she was on active duty, Cole had better medical coverage as a spouse than he did once he took a medical discharge. Marlee had caved, letting Rose talk her into signing on for another two years. She'd never dreamed they'd promptly deploy her again. She'd already missed too many of Jo Beth's formative years. Missed being on hand when Cole's condition worsened. Hey, maybe a flight now and then would be good for her daughter. Except for her new tantrums, Jo Beth seemed far too serious.

Shaking off her sudden blues, Marlee carried her load to the sink. "I see you had a dishwasher installed. That's a four-star improvement."

"Yeah, but it doesn't extend to the cabins, sis." With a hint of the old Mick, he teased, "Guess that means you'll have to fix your meals at the main house. You don't want to end up with dishpan hands."

"I can afford a dishwasher, brother dear. Fighting Rose in court didn't go through my entire savings, even if my lawyer did his best to see I didn't end up too well off."

"Ouch…life's a real bitch sometimes," he said, lowering his voice.

"All God's chilluns got trouble," Marlee quipped back. "Hey, let me stuff these dishes in to wash, then why don't we go take a gander at your office?"

"I guarantee my plane engines are in better shape. While you tackle clean-up, I'd better see where Pappy got to."

"You said he runs off?"

"Wanders away. He's usually messing around the workshop. It's important to lock the doors on the planes. Can't trust him not to get it into his head to fly. That's why I let him ride along, especially if I'm going to the fishing lodges. He loves gossiping with his old cronies."

"I hate to see him going downhill, Mick. Is his health okay other than the arteriosclerosis? Isn't that what they used to call hardening of the arteries?"

"Uh-huh. He's got the usual health issues of a man his age. His cholesterol's sky-high. The doc said to limit red meat and dairy. Bad as I am in the kitchen, I tried. First time I told him no more steak, he walked all the way into Whitepine and ordered rib eye at Sue Jensen's restaurant. I went nuts when I couldn't find him anywhere on the property. I called the sheriff. Pappy gave us both what for. So call me negligent, but I let him eat steak or roast a couple of times a week."

"I'd never call you negligent, Mick. Cole bucked his doctor's orders, too. He loved the beach. One time, Rose summoned me home from the Gulf when things looked grim. Cole rallied, and begged me to drive him and Jo Beth to the beach. She was almost four. He wanted to build sand castles with her. But… he was too weak. He asked me to build them for him. We dug in the damp sand while he watched. Cole kept urging us to build more." She bit her lip. "Jo Beth was having fun, and I didn't realize the sun had dropped. It's always windy at the beach, but Cole got really chilled. He had no defenses to fight off infection. Rose accuses me of hastening his death. I don't know," Marlee said slowly, almost absently. "He laughed that day, Mick. I saw his old sparkle." Her throat worked and her voice had grown raspy.

"Leave the dishes for now. When we return, I'll help. Pappy heard us talking about the office, and I'll bet he decided to straighten up."

Grabbing the chance to shake off her thoughts of Cole's last days, Marlee rounded up Jo Beth and found them both sweaters. They kicked through fall leaves, saying little until Marlee noticed Mick rubbing his hip and leaning into his left leg.

"When did your doctor think he could schedule surgery?"

"Next week if I give the word. If I called tomorrow, he'd probably have me under the knife on Tuesday."

"That doesn't give us much time to draw up an addendum to my will, or for me to check out the fixed-wing planes. But...do it, Mick. I can't bear to watch you suffer like this."

"Are you sure? I've got a run tomorrow. Nothing again until Wednesday—supplies going to Finn Glenroe's lodge. You remember him and his wife, Mary?" As Mick opened the office door, Pappy turned, feather duster in hand. Mick hadn't exaggerated; the place needed cleaning. The desk held an ancient, dusty computer almost hidden by stacks of invoices.

"What about Finn?" Pappy flipped his duster, and they all choked. "Oops," he said, "should've stepped outside."

"I was telling Marlee what jobs are firm. The Glenroe order can go any day. Oh, I almost forgot Wylie's generator parts. That'll have to be whenever Don Morrison gets 'em in."

"You tell Marlee that Wylie Ames is part Blackfoot?"

Mick stared at him. "He's Chinook Native. But what's that got to do with anything?"

"He's tight-lipped, and I've heard the boy's got no native blood. Like maybe the woman he married cuckolded Ames. Could be why he did her in—if'n he did."

"Pappy, honestly! Shirl took off. Uh, that cop show you like is on in ten minutes."

The old man surprised them by locating a pad and pencil. He handed both to Jo Beth before he left, saying, "Draw me a picture to hang on the fridge."

Mick demonstrated his computer program for Marlee. They discussed flight plans and talked for an hour while shuffling papers.

"I'll dig into this filing mess first thing tomorrow," she promised. "It's pretty straightforward. Same system Mom set up, except for the computer. I have a laptop. Maybe you could build a better tracking system while you recover."

"I swore you wouldn't have to fly. You *sure* you want me to set up this surgery?"

"Do it before I have second thoughts. Besides, seeing the planes and all…well, what flyer ever voluntarily grounds him or herself?"

Mick grinned cheekily and dusted his knuckles over her chin.

THE NEXT DAY he did phone Dr. Chapman. "It's all set," he told Marlee. "I'll watch you fly touch-and-goes in the Arrow this weekend. Monday you can take me to Kalispell for pre-op tests. By Wednesday I'll be the proud owner of a space-age hip socket."

"I'll write up a note to attach to my will. I'm sure the hospital has a notary."

"Sounds good. By the way, I'm taking Pappy with me today."

That gave Marlee a chance to begin establishing a routine for Jo Beth. All in all, the girl only threw one small tantrum, insisting she wanted Rose.

Marlee didn't hate Cole's mom. But with her worry over him and the fact that Marlee was gone so often, Rose had usurped her role as mother. The first time she'd come home on rotation, and Jo Beth refused to have anything to do with her, hurt more than Marlee had ever let on. Each trip, the gap widened. Still, after Cole died it'd been a shock when Rose sought legal custody of her granddaughter.

The remainder of the week passed in a blur. Marlee spent four hours a day bringing order to the office. The rest of her time she divided between getting reacquainted with Jo Beth, flying and leafing through her mom's old cookbooks to plan out nutritious meals.

She'd forgotten totally about the customer Wylie Ames until she picked up the phone on Saturday and heard him say, "You're still visiting Mick, huh? It's Ranger Ames. Tell Mick Don Morrison will have my stuff by noon on Wednesday. I'd like them brought out Thursday."

"Okay." Marlee jotted herself a note, but when she began to say she'd be the one delivering his order, she discovered Ames had hung up. Muttering about his rude phone manner, she slammed down her phone, as well.

She and Mick spent Sunday discussing his regular customers and their expectations. He talked about landing strips. "Most are primitive, sis. Only a couple of 'em have lights, so I usually try to always arrange morning deliveries. The smoke jumpers' camp has an asphalt landing strip. Wylie wired lights on either side of his strip, at the far end. If he knows I'm coming in late he'll fire them up with his generator."

"I'll make sure I only fly days, Mick. I'm glad Ranger Ames's parts don't have to go out until Thursday. That way, I can visit you in the hospital after your surgery, and collect his order in Kalispell."

"Call him Wylie. Don't want him to get the notion you're uppity."

Marlee dragged a hand through her thick hair. "Mick—about all the stuff Pappy said about him… I plan on taking Jo Beth along. Is he…is it safe?"

Mick merely laughed. "As a rule, I time my deliveries to eat lunch with Wylie. Dean, his son, is a great kid. I take him books on wild animals. He's always healing a bird, a raccoon, a deer or squirrels. I have a couple of books waiting for him."

She gestured dismissively. "I don't plan to socialize, Mick, only offload his order."

Over the next week, Marlee had so much on her

mind that Wylie Ames took a backseat until it came time to pick up his order in Kalispell. Even then, her mood was much improved because Mick's surgery had gone well. She left him flirting outrageously with an attractive nurse, and went to refuel the Piper Arrow. She was glad the plane handled like a dream.

Thursday was a beauty for flying with thready white clouds in the distance. Below, stretched the orchards Mick had told her about, and the vineyards, laid out like quilt blocks. Jo Beth was excited about getting to fly, and Marlee, who'd worried how her daughter would do, finally relaxed.

Having decided to make the ranger station her first drop, Marlee spotted the landmarks Mick had provided. It wasn't long before a short runway came into view. She circled once to get the layout and to test the wind. As she started down, Jo Beth pointed. "Mama, there's a boy waving." Jo Beth waved back. That was when Marlee noticed a man standing at the end of the runway. She throttled back, unable to take her eyes off the looming stranger who, by his dark presence, embodied every one of Pappy's innuendos and warnings.

It flashed through Marlee's mind that from a distance the raven-haired, broad-shouldered, narrow-hipped man reminded her of Cole before he'd taken ill and his fine body wasted away. Suddenly her hands shook and the plane dipped. She quickly regained control, but landed with an irritating little hop. A beginner's mistake that unnerved her as she powered down. Ripping off her headset, Marlee leaped from the cockpit and shook out her hair, only to discover, as she watched the taciturn Wylie Ames, that he was watching her, too.

She rounded the nose of the Piper to assist Jo Beth, and for some reason disliked the fact that Ames was too far away for her to see the color of his eyes. Ace-of-spades-black would be her guess—to go with the scowl he wore.

A shiver of apprehension wound up her backbone seconds before she decided not to let Pappy's rumors affect her and purposely stiffened her spine.

...NOT THE END...

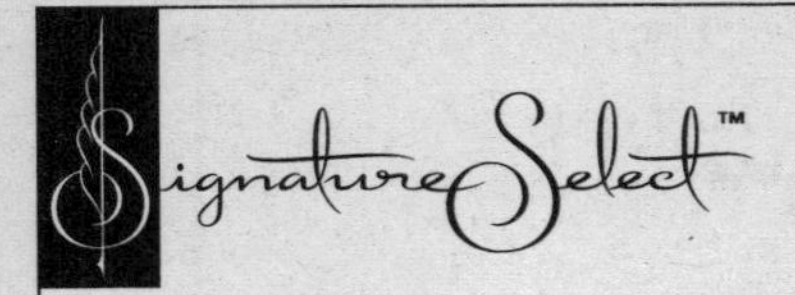

When a gift becomes a curse...

ANGEL EYES

A gripping new page-turner by national bestselling author

Myrna Mackenzie

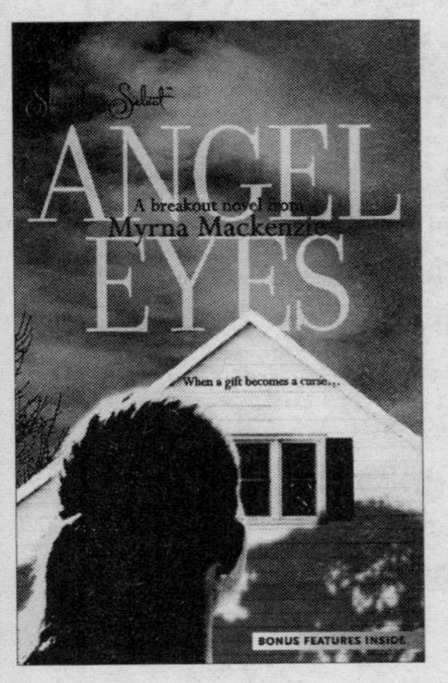

Her special clairvoyant ability has led to painful betrayal for Sarah Tucker, leading her far from home in search of peace and normalcy. But an emergency brings her back, throwing her headlong into her past—and into the passionate but wary arms of police officer Luke Packard.

Coming in May.

www.eHarlequin.com

SSAE

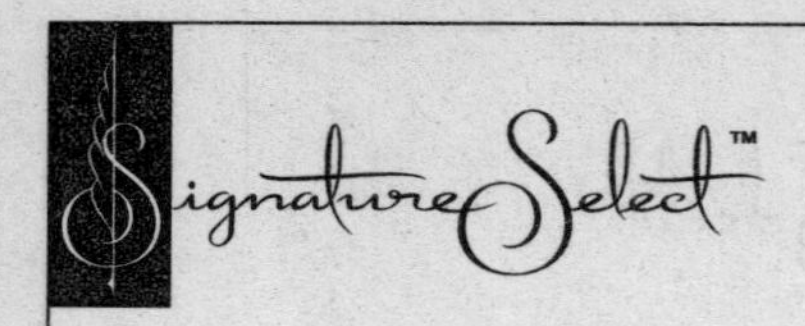

Take a trip to the sensual French Quarter with two favorite stories in

NEW ORLEANS NIGHTS

USA TODAY bestselling author

Julie Elizabeth Leto

The protector becomes the pursuer in two editorially connected tales about finding forbidden love with the bodyguard amidst murder and mystery in New Orleans.

"Julie Elizabeth Leto always delivers sizzling, snappy, edgy stories!"—*New York Times* bestselling author Carly Phillips

May 2006

www.eHarlequin.com

SMNON

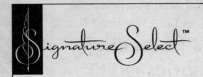